DIABLO®

THE SIN WAR

DIABLO®

THE SIN WAR

BOOK THREE
THE VEILED PROPHET

RICHARD A. KNAAK

POCKET **STAR** BOOKS
New York   London   Toronto   Sydney

Pocket Star Books
A Division of Simon & Schuster
1230 Avenue of the Americas
New York, NY 10021

This book is a work of fiction. Names, characters, places, and incidents either are products of the author's imagination or are used fictitiously. Any resemblance to actual events or locales or persons, living or dead, is entirely coincidental.

First Pocket Star Books paperback edition October 2007

POCKET STAR BOOKS and colophon are registered trademarks of Simon & Schuster, Inc.

For information about special discounts for bulk purchases, please contact Simon & Schuster Special Sales at 1-800-456-6798 or business@simonandschuster.com

Cover art by Glenn Rane

Manufactured in the United States of America

10 9 8 7 6 5 4

ISBN-13: 978-0-7434-7124-4
ISBN-10:   0-7434-7124-5

For all my readers serving in the
Armed Forces—the true heroes.

PROLOGUE

. . . And with the destruction of the main Temple of the Triune and the vanishing of its master, Uldyssian, son of Diomedes, and his edyrem then spread across the land, purging the last major traces of that sect. The flames of justice and vengeance burned bright together to devour much of what remained of the Cult of the Three.

But there still stood the Cathedral of Light, and in the vacuum left wherever the Triune had once preached, there came the missionaries of the Prophet. Never did they confront the edyrem, but ever were they there afterward to help rebuild and give relief.

Focused on his growing powers and certain that the Cathedral could not stand against the righteousness of his cause, Uldyssian blinded himself to what he considered such menial efforts. Having fought zealots and demons, he did not understand the subtle works of the angel, Inarius, who was known to the masses as the handsome, youthful leader of the sect. Even the dragon Trag'Oul and Inarius's own estranged son, the nephalem, Rathma, were ignorant of the angel's aid to their struggle against the Triune.

But if that was their sin, then so was it also Inarius's, for he failed to realize that others had taken notice of the struggle for the soul of the world called Sanctuary . . . others who might desire to take for themselves the prize, or choose instead to destroy everything.

And no one, not even the veiled Prophet or Uldyssian himself yet understood just what the son of Diomedes was gradually becoming. . . .

From the Books of Kalan
Twelfth Tome, First Leaf

ONE

The man in the middle of the pentagram shrieked as Zorun Tzin deftly used his magic to peel away another area of skin. The patch, a tidy three inches by three, methodically rolled back without hesitation. It left in its wake a bleeding gap that revealed the muscle and sinew underneath. Streaks of blood flowed from the gap down the naked figure's body to add to that already decorating the floor.

The gaunt, bearded mage was not at all bothered by the splatters on the stones. They would be gathered later for other uses having nothing to do with the dark-skinned Kehjani's current interest. The Council of Clans had managed to cease their feuds long enough to implore him to discover what he could about the fanatics pouring across the land, fanatics with powers unbelievable.

That these—edyrem, they called themselves—had brought down the mighty Temple of the Triune was not the point. The mage clans were more than happy to be rid of the powerful sect, which had been the first to wrest influence away from the spellcasters. Indeed, that had been in great part the cause of the first feuds, as clans had struggled to seize from one another what stature remained.

No, what disturbed the clans so much that they had been able to agree to something at last was the simple fact that the edyrem were nothing more than untrained peasants for the most part. They were farmers, laborers, and the like, and yet their leader promised them abilities that the mages had painstakingly toiled for most of their lifetimes. Not only that, but the use so far of those powers revealed a recklessness that endangered so very much. It was clear that the edyrem were a hazard and had to be contained.

And who better than the mage clans to do that? Under their strict guidance, these mysterious powers could be properly explored and exploited.

"I say again," Zorun rasped. "You saw the outsiders bring down an entire temple with only their bare hands! What words did they chant? What gestures did they make?"

"D-don't know!" bellowed the prisoner. "I—I swear!" The man was bald and still fit, despite the mage's interrogation. He had once been a temple guard, one of the few who had escaped the fanatics' grasp. It had taken Zorun some weeks of scrying to locate even this individual, so deep underground had any survivors of the Triune gone into hiding. "I swear it is s-so! They did—did n-nothing like that!"

With a gesture, the Kehjani had the square of skin finish peeling. A new shriek of agony escaped the captive. The orange-sashed mage waited impatiently for the cry to die down before speaking again. "You cannot expect me to believe that they just willed something to happen. Magic does not work that way. It takes concentration, gestures, and long practice."

From the prisoner, he received only gasps. Frowning, Zorun Tzin slowly paced around the pentagram. The octagonal chamber in which he had spent the last day interrogating the former guard was meticulously clean and neat. Each vial, each parchment, each artifact was set properly on the correct shelf. Zorun believed that neatness and order were paramount to success in the arts. Unlike some mages, he did not let clutter overwhelm him, nor did he allow dust and vermin to render his sanctum piggish.

Even when it came to himself, the Kehjani sought to be immaculate. His brown, wide-shouldered tunic and flowing pants were freshly cleaned. He kept his beard trimmed to a proper shape and length. Even his thinning gray hair was artfully oiled back.

The manner in which he ran his own life perhaps gave indication of why Zorun pursued the secrets of the fanatics as he did. They were a slovenly, disorderly factor, and their spellcasting appeared to be based on whim and emotion. In truth, when he had been approached by the council for this task, Zorun had already been delving into the situation in secret. Of course, he had not informed them of that; otherwise, they might not have granted him the list of demands he had given or promised even more should he succeed.

No, there was no *should*. Zorun did not fail.

"You saw the Ascenian leader, this Uldyssian ul-Diomed, he is called. Is this true?"

"Y-yes! Yes!" screamed the guard, sounding almost grateful to be able to respond to any question. "Saw him! Pale! H-he is—w-was a farmer, they say!"

"A digger in the dirt," the spellcaster muttered disdainfully. "Little more than a beast."

The figure above the pentagram let out a gurgle that might have been agreement.

"It is said that he brought down the temple himself. Did you see that?"

"N-no!"

The response caused Zorun to grow more exasperated. "You are wasting my time, then."

He gestured, and the bleeding figure suddenly gasped. A choking sound escaped the stricken guard. He tried to reach for his throat, which had now swollen monstrously around the apple. Yet, even had the Kehjani's captive been allowed to move his arms—which, of course, he was not— he would have been able to do nothing to stop Zorun's work.

With one last garbled cry, the guard slumped. Zorun Tzin finally let the body drop to the floor, where it sprawled, quite ungainly, over the pattern.

"Terul!"

At his summoning, a hulking Kehjani with too small a head came shambling into the chamber. He wore nothing but a simple tunic. The face much resembled one of the small primates considered sacred by many lowlanders, although Zorun saw as little divinity in them as he did in his servant. Terul was excellent at obeying direct orders without question, the reason the spellcaster had first picked him out of the slums.

Terul grunted, the closest he ever came to speaking. His too-small head dipped down to acknowledge his master.

"The body." Zorun had to say no more. The servant understood exactly what he desired. Terul hefted the dead guard as if the latter weighed as little as air, utterly ignoring the blood that stained his skin in the process. The giant had been trained by his master always to clean up afterward.

Terul shuffled out with the corpse. There were many passages in the sewers coursing underneath Kehjan the city. All eventually emptied into the river beyond the walls. From there, the wild lands beyond—also called Kehjan by the ancients—would deal with the refuse.

Glancing at the pool of blood and the trail following in Terul's wake, Zorun muttered an incantation and drew the proper symbols. He watched with immense satisfaction as the crimson liquid smoothly and cleanly began rolling toward the pentagram, leaving not a trace behind. How many on the council itself could perform such a feat? It had taken Zorun ten years to perfect that spell. . . .

He grimaced. No doubt, this Uldyssian ul-Diomed could do the same without more than a glance.

This must not be . . . or, if it must, then it shall be I who am able to do it, not some fool of a peasant!

Zorun seized a cloak and departed from his sanctum. There were those he needed to visit to gather the necessary items for his work. That would require some tricky bargaining that he had no desire for those who had hired him to know about. A mage's secrets were more valuable than simple coins or jewels. They were worth lives.

And if Zorun's plans fell into place as they should, one of those lives would be that of the Ascenian, Uldyssian.

"You must speak to your brother," Rathma encouraged, his generally toneless voice now hinting at concern. "He is growing reckless as his power further manifests itself."

"What can I tell him that is new?" Mendeln asked with a shrug. They were both contrast and similarity, the pair. Rathma was taller than most people and with perfect features that might have been chiseled by a master sculptor. His skin was far paler than that of any other living person, and that was made more noticeable by the cowled and hooded black cloak and robes he wore.

By comparison, Mendeln ul-Diomed, was average in height and more plain of feature. He had been a farmer's son, albeit not so good a farmer himself. His broad nose made him feel ugly in contrast to the one with whom he spoke. His dark hair seemed lighter against the pure black of Rathma's.

Yet in their manner, in their speech, and in their clothing, they were more like brothers than he and Uldyssian. Mendeln wore a cloak and garments similar to Rathma's, and his flesh, while bearing some pink tint, was still far paler than normal—especially for an Ascenian, who should, like his brother and Serenthia, be baked nearly as dark as the lowlanders.

It was not so surprising, though, that Mendeln should be very like Rathma. The latter had chosen the younger son of Diomedes to be his pupil, the first mortal to learn the path walked by one who was son of both an angel and a demon.

"He thinks he is being very practical," Mendeln went on. "Hints of the Triune's stirring again forced him once and for all to stamp out their kind. That makes sense to him, as it does to many of the others. Even I understand the logic."

Rathma's cloak swirled around him, despite there being no wind. Mendeln often wondered if the garment were alive, but he never asked.

"But he thus remains blind to my father," the tall figure reminded him. Rathma was an Ancient, one of the first generation born to the world known to a select few as Sanctuary. Like him, all of that generation had been the progeny of refugees from the High Heavens and the Burning Hells, who had forsaken the eternal conflict and bound together to seek a new existence.

They had found that existence, for a time, in a place of their own making, masked from the sight of the two great powers. Yet, in finding common cause, the refugees also had begun their downfall. Familiarity brought with it the intermingling and, with that, Rathma's generation—the first humans.

In the beginning, the new children had seemed harmless enough, but when they had started to manifest powers—powers unlike those of their parents and with unlimited potential—the angel Inarius, leader of the group, had declared them abominations. Only barely had he been convinced by a few of his fellows not to act instantly. He and the other refugees finally had agreed to retire to their separate sanctums carefully to consider the fate of their children.

But among them was one who had already made her decision. Inarius's own lover, the demon Lilith, secretly stalked the other demons and angels, slaughtering them one by one. In her madness and ambition, she saw herself as the savior of the children and also, thus, the only one with the right to mold their destiny.

A destiny that saw her as mistress over *all*.

However, she had dearly underestimated Inarius. Discovering her treachery, he cast her out of Sanctuary. Then, using the gigantic crystal called the Worldstone—which had been created to keep Sanctuary hidden—he had altered the artifact so that it caused the innate powers of the children to decline until they became so dormant as never to have existed.

Some of Rathma's generation, called the nephalem, had

protested . . . and they had been crushed. The rest had scattered, Rathma himself forced to hide beyond the mortal plane. Over the centuries, most of his kind had vanished, and the generations that followed grew up in ignorance of the birthright that had been stolen from them.

But no more . . .

Mendeln turned from Rathma as he considered the other's words. The two of them stood deep within the jungles of Kehjan, well away from where Uldyssian's vast following camped. The scent of smoke that wafted by did not come from the huge encampment but rather from Urjhani, a town about half a day to the south. There, Uldyssian had tracked down some of the last priests to a minor temple, which he had afterward burned to the ground.

"My brother is painfully aware of the angel," Mendeln finally responded. "Just as he will always be painfully reminded of Lilith."

The demoness, despite Inarius's confidence, had managed to return from exile. The angel, distracted by the incursion of the Burning Hells into his world, did not notice her slow, subtle manipulation of the Worldstone. That manipulation had reversed his intentions, awakening the potential within the many humans now inhabiting Sanctuary. Lilith had chosen Uldyssian for her pawn, stirring through violence and lust his latent powers.

In the end, however, she had failed to turn him to her cause. Uldyssian had fought her in the main temple, and although her body had not been recovered from the rubble that was all that remained of the towering edifice, everyone, including Rathma, was certain that she was at last dead. Unfortunately for Uldyssian, who had once loved her as the woman Lylia, the demoness would never truly be gone.

"And for that, I can but apologize to him. I knew my mother's evil, just as I knew my father's sanctimony . . . and for generations, I did nothing but cower."

Rathma had hardly cowered, but Mendeln said nothing

to assuage his mentor. Still . . . "I shall bring up the Cathedral's missionaries to him again. You said earlier that there are already a number of them en route to Urjhani, and we left that place only the other day. That would have to mean that they were dispatched from the Grand Cathedral itself even before we reached the town."

"Which is not the first time, either, Mendeln. My father almost appears to know Uldyssian's path even before he does."

"I will make mention of that also." But still Mendeln did not depart. He suddenly surveyed the jungle, as if expecting some beast to leap out at them.

"I am not hiding him," remarked Rathma with a rare show of frustration. "I am not pretending my ignorance of your friend Achilios's location. Both Trag'Oul and I have searched, but of the hunter there is no trace."

"But you were the one who raised him from the dead!"

"I? I only influenced the situation. You are the one who brought Achilios back, Mendeln. Your gift and your link to the realm of afterdeath are what enabled him to return."

Rather than begin an old argument over, Mendeln left the shadowy figure behind. Rathma did not call after him, and the human, aware of his mentor's ways, knew that the Ancient had already melted into the shadows.

Neither of them had uttered what both suspected concerning Achilios's disappearance. The one time in the past when they had discussed the possibility, Mendeln had nearly lost all heart. What point was there in trying to change the world, if the world was soon to be no more?

It was all too obvious to Uldyssian's brother what had happened to the hunter. Rathma had detected no demonic traces in the vicinity of Achilios's last known location. The absolute absence of any such trace could mean only two things. One was that Inarius had seized Achilios for some plot against them, a dire notion indeed. Yet, as terrible as that might be—especially to Serenthia—there was a second scenario that made the first welcome by comparison.

What if *another* angel had stolen away the hunter?

They all knew what that meant. The Burning Hells were already aware of Sanctuary and had been so for centuries. They had let it survive because of their interest in the potential of using humans as a turning point in the eternal war. The Temple of the Triune had been created by the demon lords—the Prime Evils—in order to bring Mendeln's race into the fold. Had not Inarius taken personal umbrage at their act—seeing Sanctuary and all in it as his—humanity might even now be marching into battle against the angels.

But now, if the High Heavens did know of the world, they were sure either to fight to possess it or simply to destroy it so that it could not be of use to the demons. That thousands of lives would perish was not of interest to either side.

It is essential that we find Achilios, Mendeln determined as he reached the edge of the encampment. *For all our sakes, it is essential!*

His thoughts were violently interrupted by an invisible force against which he collided. As he rubbed his nose, two figures appeared—one with the swarthy skin of a lowlander, the other as pale as any Ascenian tended to look next to one of the locals. Mendeln recognized the second as one of the dwindling number of Parthans, Uldyssian's first converts. There were perhaps a little more than a hundred of them left, where once there had been many times that number. Being among the earliest of his brother's followers, the Parthans had, unfortunately, faced monstrous dangers before having the chance to truly begin to come into their powers.

"Ah! Forgive us, Master Mendeln!" blurted the Parthan. "We couldn't know it were you!"

The other edyrem nodded nervously in agreement. Whether from the lowland jungles or the highland forests, nearly all of Uldyssian's flock treated Mendeln with a combination of veneration and fear. The fear came from Mendeln's calling, which dealt much with the dead. The veneration . . . well, he was wise enough to understand that it originated simply from the fact that he was their leader's sibling.

Oddly, a small handful had begun to come to him for learning, but Mendeln did not set any store by their interest. They were just morbidly fascinated by certain aspects . . . at least, that was what he told himself.

"You need not apologize," he told the pair. "I left without giving word. You did as you were commanded."

They opened the way for Mendeln, watching with some visible relief as Mendeln passed. He pretended not to notice.

And, as if by passing the guards, the younger son of Diomedes had entered a new realm, suddenly the area around him was filled with magic. Colored spheres of energy dotted the vast camp, as if arranged for some festival. Yet none of them was secured by string, but rather floated above those who had cast them. There were still fires, but mainly for cooking, not for illumination.

But the spheres were not all. As Mendeln strode through the throngs, a continual array of magical displays caught his gaze. One swarthy lowlander had created a glowing stream of energy that entwined around itself like a serpent. Another edyrem levitated a number of small stones, then proceeded to have them move around as if in the hands of an invisible juggler. A fair-haired Parthan woman created a spear from empty air, which she threw with perfect accuracy at a distant tree. The spear hung embedded for a moment, then dissipated as she forged a new one.

These were but a few examples. The many spells cast by the edyrem varied in power and skill, but that the seemingly insignificant faces around him—faces drawn from all castes and occupations—were those of people mastering what had once been available only to a select few was both astounding and troubling to Mendeln. Common folk such as himself were supposed to live out their lives toiling in the field. They were not supposed to become powerful sorcerers.

And that was what troubled him, even as he watched one inventive youth create for his smaller siblings—yes, Uldyssian's "army" even included children—bright butterflies that flew in a dozen different directions. In some ways, many of those who followed his brother were naïve about the potential they wielded. At best, they saw it as a tool, like a hoe, not as something that could possibly either turn on them or brutally maim one of their own.

Perhaps I am being too harsh, Mendeln considered. *They have fought for what they believe in and have been forced to slay those who would make them their slaves and puppets.*

Yet his misgivings did not go away. Despite everything, Mendeln felt magic was something that needed to be studied carefully and used with the utmost consideration. One had to grow into its use and learn to respect its dangers.

Then, ahead, there arose a soft, comforting blue glow. Mendeln hesitated but finally stepped toward it. He had no reason to fear the source. After all, it was only Uldyssian.

Even amidst so much magic, one could feel his brother's presence. A large group of edyrem sat or stood in a circle around the area Uldyssian had chosen for his bed. Mendeln could not see his brother, but he could sense exactly where Uldyssian was. Without hesitation, the younger sibling strode into the crowd, which immediately took notice of his presence and began to open a path for him.

And barely had Mendeln made it halfway when at last he caught sight of Uldyssian.

The sandy-haired figure had the strong build and looks of a country farmer, which, of course, Uldyssian had been. Quite good at it, too. Broad-shouldered and square-jawed, with a short, trimmed beard, the elder sibling was handsome in a rough-hewn way, and that helped him appeal to others. He did not look in the least like one of the haughty priests or fiery prophets with whom most of his followers were familiar. He was one of them, the common folk. He had prospered, and he had suffered, his greatest loss that of all his family save Mendeln years before to plague. At that time, Uldyssian had turned from one missionary to the next, seeking salvation for his loved ones and receiving nothing but empty words and suggestions of donations. That tragedy had given him a fierce hatred for sects such as the Triune and the Cathedral even before both had gone hunting for him.

Uldyssian sat atop a log, talking earnestly to all. Mendeln did not have to listen to know that Uldyssian was speaking words of encouragement to his flock, explaining what walking his path meant. His words all had great merit, but too often, Mendeln's brother did not follow them himself. Of late, Uldyssian had been letting his incredible abilities take command of him, not the other way around.

Urjhani was the latest example of that. Uldyssian had intended to capture the priests, not slay them. There were questions about their true masters, the demon lords, that he had wanted to ask. Yet, when one had struck at the edyrem in a desperate attempt to stave off the inevitable—an attempt that had been easily deflected—Uldyssian had angrily hit back.

What had once been the priests had been strewn for yards, each having *exploded* from the inside. Uldyssian had shrugged off the situation as if he had intended this end from the start.

"They were Triune" was the reasoning with which he cut off any other protest from Mendeln. That said, Uldyssian had ordered the final temple burned down so that no memory would remain of the sect.

Now, the same man who had so casually torn apart those living souls and burned their temple dismissed his followers with a genial nod. The glow muted but remained strong enough to be noticed.

Only one figure stayed behind: Serenthia, daughter of the merchant Cyrus, who had been one of the first slain by Uldyssian's powers. That had not been his fault, naturally, Lilith having manipulated the situation to bring about such terrible results. Serenthia was a beautiful woman, with long black tresses and bright blue eyes. Like Uldyssian's her once-pale skin was bronzed. In contrast to the brothers, she wore the loose-fitting, flowing clothing of the lowland regions. The spear in her right hand was a constant companion, and if anything marred her beauty, at least in Mendeln's opinion, it was the dread determination in her expression.

"Mendeln." Uldyssian rose and greeted his brother as if the latter had been gone for days. "Where have you been?"

"Beyond the boundaries."

"Ah." Some of the older sibling's pleasure faded. "Who was it this time? The dragon or *her* spawn?"

By "her," he meant Lilith. "Rathma, yes. He warns of his father—"

The aura abruptly blazed bright, causing some nearby to start. However, all eyes quickly turned away again. "As he does every time! Does he think I keep no watch for that one? Rathma could serve us better by standing at our side rather than running off into the dark after he whispers another fearful warning."

The glow continued to increase in intensity. Mendeln felt his own anger stirring but kept it in check. "You know he risks as much as any of us, Uldyssian . . . and you need not hate him for being Lilith's progeny. He regrets that more than you can ever imagine."

The blue muted again. Uldyssian exhaled. "You—you're right. Forgive me. The past few days've been long ones, haven't they, Mendeln?"

"To me, the days seem to grow longer and longer with each breath I take."

"I miss the farm."

"As do I, Uldyssian. As do even I."

Serenthia finally broke her silence. Gaze narrowed at Mendeln, she muttered, "And any word of Achilios?"

"You know I would speak if I knew even the slightest hint."

She thrust the bottom end of the spear into the ground. A brief scattering of red energy marked where the spear struck. Of all Uldyssian's acolytes, Serenthia was the most powerful. Some of that strength, unfortunately, was fueled by her concern for the hunter, and the longer he remained missing, the more careless she became. It was becoming not an uncommon trait among the edyrem, and as the only relative outsider, Mendeln appeared alone in noticing it.

"Achilios will find a way to return to you," Uldyssian interjected. "He will, Serry."

But she looked uncertain. "If he could've, he would be standing with us now!"

"You wait and see." Uldyssian put a hand on her shoulder, which, long ago, would have made the merchant's daughter turn red. She had adored him most of her childhood, only discovering her love for Achilios just before the demon Lucion had slain their brave friend.

Turning back to Mendeln, Uldyssian added, "And, as I said, I keep wary about the angel, but what can he do against us that the Triune didn't? Rathma's hidden so long it's hard for him to think that—"

There was a shout from the edge of the encampment and a host of angry voices that did not belong to the edyrem.

Uldyssian stared into the sky. He frowned, looking more frustrated than surprised.

"We've guests," he told Mendeln and Serenthia. "Many uninvited guests . . ."

"Triune?" she asked, almost eagerly. Serenthia hefted the spear, looking as if she intended to throw it now.

"I don't know, but who else can it be?" Uldyssian headed toward the direction of the cry. "Well, whoever they are, they'll receive the same greeting we always give the Temple."

Cyrus's daughter smiled, a look that reminded Mendeln just briefly of the expression often on her countenance when she had been possessed by Lilith. She raced eagerly after Uldyssian, the two quickly leaving Mendeln well behind.

He did not move, although it was not because he shirked battle. Rather, as the sounds of struggle rose, Mendeln wondered at this desperate surprise attack. It hardly sounded like the Triune, assuming that they could muster any size force now. Yet the only other choice in his mind was Inarius. Mendeln, though, could not conceive of something so overt, so simple, from Inarius, whom Rathma had often described as one who worked behind the obvious, manipulating events as he desired—

Mendeln swore, suddenly rushing to join the others. Whatever this attack appeared on the surface to be, it would have another, far more dread reason behind it—one that it might already be too late to stop.

TWO

Uldyssian was not in the least bit anxious as he rushed to the edge of camp. He and his followers had been attacked in such a treacherous manner before. Lilith had managed to mask the Triune's Peace Warders and the even-more-nefarious morlu through spellwork until the enemy had been nearly as close. Yet that had still not enabled her to defeat the edyrem.

Indeed, aware of their present surroundings, Uldyssian had set into motion enough security that should such a trick be repeated, the encampment would remain secure. Now that precaution was paying off.

Sure enough, a line of edyrem stood facing the jungle, out of which poured not the disciplined, silver-garbed Inquisitors of the Cathedral, but rather a horde of ragtag figures not unlike his own army. They were armed with not only swords but work axes, pitchforks, and a host of other tools turned into weaponry. They shouted and screamed and drove toward the waiting edyrem with what he sensed was strong anger.

"These are neither the Triune nor the Cathedral. These are merely people!" Serenthia declared needlessly. She readied her spear. "That can't be! This must be illusion designed to make us uncertain."

Her suggestion had merit, for illusion seemed as true as breathing to both powerful sects. Uldyssian shoved aside his uncertainty and thrust forward his left hand.

The area before him exploded with pure sound, the force of it barreling through the attackers' ranks as if they were nothing. Men—and women, Uldyssian saw—tumbled through the air, crashing against trees or vanishing into the black jungle. They shrieked as they died, sending a sudden chill through him that, however, did not prevent Uldyssian from striking again.

Next to him, Serenthia aimed and threw. The spear utterly impaled one man and went through him to slay another. As both fell, the bloody spear came flying back to her.

The rest of the edyrem did not leave the battle to the two of them. Another attacker burst into flames. He collided with two others, igniting them. The three, in turn, created chaos among their fellows, as the rest desperately sought to evade even the slightest touch.

Elsewhere, spheres of light lifted men into the air, then dropped them onto their comrades. Tendrils of energy encircled throats, tightening enough to strangle.

Some of the edyrem's defenses looked mundane, such as the use of bows, but even here, their powers came into play. The arrows, guided by the bowmen's will, struck their targets' hearts perfectly.

The attackers also had their archers, but it startled Uldyssian that they waited so long to use them. There was a whistling sound high in the air, and then the first bolts finally began arcing down toward the edyrem. The skills of the enemy bowmen were questionable, but with so many defenders, they no doubt did not fear too many misses.

Without even a gesture, Uldyssian seized control of the arrows. They turned sharply, heading toward the jungle.

One after another, the bolts struck those converging on the encampment. A line of six men dropped simultaneously, each pierced through the throat.

The ambush was swiftly turning into a debacle, as hardly any of the edyrem had suffered even a scratch. The shields that Uldyssian had trained his guards to create were impenetrable to mortal weapons, something that he was astounded the attackers would not have taken into account. More and more, they seemed exactly as they appeared: simple peasants, farmers, and the like. They were the type who should have been eager to join the edyrem's ranks, not slaughter them.

Yet still they came, their ferocity now touched with desperation. Most were dark-skinned, like the Torajians and many of their cousins, but among them were also the first few light-skinned lowlanders he had seen, so light-skinned, in fact, that they could have passed for Ascenians such as himself. Those were said to be from an area that included the northern part of the capital, but other than Lilith's false identity of Lylia, Uldyssian had seen none in all his time down in the jungle realms.

Still, their similarity to him did not save them from suffering as their darker comrades did. Uldyssian rewarded their base ambush with death a hundred times over. The bodies began piling up in a manner both grotesque and shameful, and yet he had no notion how to put an end to the struggle. The attackers refused to cease coming, and his people, well certain of their victory, had no inclination to end what was becoming pure butchery.

From behind him came words muttered in a tongue Uldyssian did not in the least understand. A faint glimmer arose at his back.

One of the dead attackers leapt to his feet like a marionette whose strings had just been pulled taut. At first, the macabre figure appeared ready to attack the edyrem, but then he whirled about, facing instead his former allies.

A second corpse and then a third did the same. Several others joined them.

The first took a step toward the enemy, and the sight of the dead walking was at last enough to put an end to the assault on the encampment. First one, then several, then *all* the attackers turned and fled in panic. They ran with no rhyme or reason, their only intent to escape what they thought was a rising army of ghouls.

A few of Uldyssian's followers sent balls of flame or flying tree trunks at the stragglers, but the enormity of what had just happened finally began sinking in. The area surrounding the encampment lay littered with bodies, not one of them edyrem. Triumphant cheers arose from the defenders.

Uldyssian turned to Mendeln, the one who had been murmuring in the strange tongue. His brother looked as deathly as the risen corpses, and clutched in his hands was the unsettling dagger that looked as if it had been carved from ivory . . . or bone. Mendeln held the dagger point down. The blade was the cause of the sinister illumination.

The younger brother turned the blade upward, then muttered a single word.

There was a heavy thud from the direction of the jungle. Uldyssian glanced over his shoulder to see the animated dead dropping in horrific heaps among the other bodies. Some of the edyrem instinctively made signs from either the Triune or the Cathedral, old habits dying hard even in the face of the sinister truth concerning both sects.

"I had to attempt something," Mendeln stated bluntly. "This was becoming tragic and demeaning."

"They attacked us. Ambushed us, if you recall." Still, Uldyssian could not fault his brother for wanting to stop the massacre, even if it was of the enemy. "They got what they deserved."

"Perhaps . . ."

Uldyssian knew that tone and found himself frustrated by it more and more. "They may look like us, but make no mistake, Mendeln. If they're not Triune, then they're somehow Inarius's minions."

"A pity we can't question any of them," remarked Serenthia, prodding one body. "The edyrem are getting very good, Uldyssian. There's not a living one among these."

"There wasn't supposed to be." Now Uldyssian's own tone startled him, if only for its coldness. "But yes, it would've been good to have someone who could tell us how this came to be. They had the power to mask themselves; that means demons or angels. But they fought like farmers and craftsmen . . ." He suddenly saw Mendeln's point. "That makes no sense. They should've known that they'd be torn to pieces by us. Word's spread by now of what we did in Toraja and the other cities where the Triune was. . . ."

"If I may?"

That it was his brother who seemed ready to offer a suggestion concerning the truth behind this attack disturbed Uldyssian more than he revealed. "What?"

Mendeln kept his voice low, for the rest of the edyrem still stood waiting for commands. "Allow me a moment among the—defeated—to choose. Then have the others begin removing the bodies for burning or burial."

"Choose?" Serenthia's face paled. "What do you mean, choose? Choose for what?"

"Why, questioning, of course."

Uldyssian kept his own expression unperturbed as he quickly commanded his followers to begin dealing with the dead. In a whisper to his brother, he added, "Go right now. Pick two . . . only two. I'll help you bring them to where we won't be disturbed."

"They might not be the ones with the knowledge. It would be best if I could survey a few more—"

"*Two*, Mendeln! Two. Just tell the others not to touch the pair. No more."

The black-clad figure let out a momentary sigh. "It will be done as you say. I'd best go now, then, while the majority of the dead still lay available."

Serenthia waited until Mendeln was out of earshot before finally saying, "I love him as a friend and almost a brother, Uldyssian, but I worry about him. This is not right, this constant dwelling in spells touching upon the dead."

"I'm not happy about it, either, but nothing he's done has ever been evil. He's saved many of us, including myself."

"And he brought Achilios back to me, if only for a few short moments. . . ." Her eyes moistened.

"I'm keeping watch over Mendeln, make no mistake. If he—or that damned Rathma—do anything I feel crosses the line, I won't let it stand, Serry. I won't. Not even for my own sibling."

He meant it, too, even more than she would realize. If Mendeln's studies brought him to the point where he did something ghastly—at the moment, Uldyssian dared not think just what that might be—then the elder son of Diomedes would have to see to it that the younger was stopped.

Permanently, if necessary. Uldyssian would have no choice.

There was no possible way to keep Mendeln's intentions completely secret, but Uldyssian and Serenthia did what they could to occupy the edyrem's attention while his brother located the two corpses he desired. The moment Mendeln found them, Uldyssian helped him remove the bodies from the sight of the rest. Serenthia remained behind in order to keep any of the others from wandering over to where the two worked.

"This will definitely do," the younger brother finally decided. They had first carried the bodies out of the encampment, then, one at a time, brought them to where Mendeln believed he could best work. They stood in a slight clearing, perhaps ten minutes away but still too close for Uldyssian's tastes. A stream flowed nearby, and thick, bushy trees draped over them. The dense jungle hid them well from the sight of the edyrem, although some of the more sensitive would likely notice the unsettling energies Mendeln summoned. That, unfortunately, could not be helped, as his brother had already informed him that any notion of shielding their work from the rest would interfere with his questioning.

Mendeln solemnly adjusted the bodies so that they lay side-by-side. They had their right hands on their hearts and their left on their foreheads.

"Why so?" Uldyssian found himself asking.

"Rathma and Trag'Oul taught me that the soul touches both the mind and the heart. I seek to call the souls of these two, and this strengthens that call. It is not necessary for what I seek to do, but it should help simplify matters . . . as I know you wish me to finish as quickly as possible."

"That would be preferable."

Nodding, Mendeln again brought forth the ivory blade. Uldyssian could feel its wrongness, as if it were not entirely of this world. He was repelled by it yet knew the good it had done for him and his people. Mendeln had sent to their deaths—again—morlu after morlu during the final great battle against the Triune's warriors. So many lives had been saved because of that . . .

And yet Uldyssian all but recoiled in the dagger's presence. It dealt in death and that which lay beyond death, the latter a thing into which no human should ever delve.

With the blade pointed down, Mendeln leaned over the chest of the first body. In life, it had been a middle-aged man who very likely had been a farmer, just as Uldyssian had. Balding, with a slight paunch but strong shoulders and arms, he looked as if he had merely fallen asleep.

Mendeln brought the tip of the blade directly over the heart. Uldyssian caught his breath, but his brother only began drawing runes over the chest, runes that flared to life in a blaze of white light before settling down to a dull silver. Mendeln drew five more in all.

When that was done, the black-clad figure repeated the process over the forehead, but with different runes. From there, Mendeln slipped to the second body, that of a woman perhaps only two decades old. She was thin, pinch-faced, but still too young in Uldyssian's mind to have been caught up in all of this. Was she truly what she seemed, he wondered? If so, the implications bothered him more than ever.

"Please take a step back, Uldyssian." When the older brother had done that, Mendeln took up a stance at the feet of the two corpses. Now he held the blade up. Words in the mysterious language he had magically learned through Rathma began spilling out, raising Uldyssian's hackles.

Small flashes of magical energy erupted above the two bodies. Still chanting, Mendeln knelt. As he did, he stretched far enough to touch the hand that had been set over the male's heart with the blade's tip.

Uldyssian started as the dagger drew a faint line of blood. He had no longer expected blood. Before he could say anything, though, Mendeln repeated the deed on the woman's hand. Oddly, the glowing dagger looked unstained when Mendeln pulled back.

His brother uttered something else, then waited. The wait was not a long one. A mist suddenly formed over the bodies, one that could not be at all natural. Tendrils grew from it, several darting down to each of the bleeding hands.

The blood just starting to pool over the hands dwindled as if rapidly drying up—or being absorbed.

"Mendeln—"

Muttering again, his brother waved him to silence. More and more of the half-congealed blood dissipated, until nothing remained but the open cuts.

And as the last of the crimson liquid vanished, the mist began to form into a shape—no, *two* shapes.

One vaguely male, the other possibly female.

The two men stood silent, Uldyssian relying on Mendeln for direction. The misty forms coalesced little more, which seemed to frustrate his brother.

"It should have done better," Mendeln reproved himself. "They should have become more distinct, more semblances of their former selves!"

"Can they answer us?" Uldyssian interjected, wanting this to end. "Isn't that the only point?"

"It is the most relevant point." Having conceded this much, Mendeln shook his head at his success, then pointed the dagger at the male shadow. "By what name were you known?"

At first, there was only the hiss of the wind, but then that hiss became words.

Hadeen . . . Hadeen . . .

Satisfied by this result, Mendeln continued. "From what place did you hail?"

T-Toraja . . . Toraja . . .

"Toraja?" Uldyssian frowned. "All the way from there?"

"It is some distance, I agree." To the spirit, the younger brother asked, "What was your calling? Were you a disciple of the Triune?"

There was a hesitation, as if Mendeln's questions had proven complicated for the shade. Then: *I tilled the land and grew wheat upon it . . . my father did, and my grandfather did, and my—*

"Enough! Answer now about the Triune! Were you a disciple?"

No . . .

"He must be lying, Mendeln; otherwise, why would he have come so far with such dark intentions?"

Shrugging, Mendeln asked of the spirit, "Why did you come with the others to attack us, if not to serve the Triune?"

Again came hesitation . . . then: *To save the land . . . to save all Kehjan . . .*

His answer sounded absurd to Uldyssian. "He wanted to save all Kehjan . . . from *us? We're* the ones trying to save everyone!"

"Patience, patience." Despite his response to his sibling, Mendeln, too, obviously did not understand the shade's reply. Mendeln scratched his chin, then turned to the female shape. "You. What name did you bear?"

Vidrisi . . .

"And did you come to save Kehjan from those in the encampment?"

The answer was as immediate as it was damning. *Yes . . .*

Before Uldyssian could interject again, Mendeln asked Vidrisi's specter, "What urged you to this course? What made you join with all these others?"

We knew . . . we knew that we had to—

"No! What I ask . . . what I ask is . . . who was first to suggest it?"

The shade did not answer. In fact, both spirits lost much of what little definition they had. Mendeln quickly began muttering more unintelligible words.

"What is it?" Uldyssian demanded. "What's wrong?"

"Not now!" His brother drew several symbols in the air, focusing most of them at the female shade. Her shape defined again, this time more distinct than before.

But Hadeen's spirit faded back into simple mist, which then dissipated.

"I have lost the one," Mendeln admitted angrily. "But she is still bound to the spell." He all but growled to the specter, "Who instigated this march to battle? Who first set you on this course?"

There was no answer at first, but neither did Vidrisi's shadow vanish. Mendeln drew more runes and muttered more words.

At last: *I recall . . . I recall the missionary . . . he said it was so tragic . . . what the fanatics had done . . . how many innocents were slaughtered—*

"Innocents?" blurted Uldyssian. "The Triune?"

So many innocents . . . caught up between the evils of the fanatics and the treacheries of the Triune. . . . I remember the missionary mourning . . . and wishing something could be done. . . .

"Enough," commanded Mendeln to the specter. The shade stilled but did not depart.

The brothers gazed at each other, the answer now known to both.

"Rathma did warn that his father would move behind events, turning them to his favor," the younger one reminded.

Uldyssian glared at Mendeln, although he was not angry at all at his sibling for bringing that up again. Instead, he was furious at himself for underestimating just how cunning and how thorough Inarius could be.

"The angel's turning everyone against us, isn't he, Mendeln? Wherever we've fought, his 'missionaries' have arrived afterward, tending to the wounded, feeding the hungry, and filling their heads with images of *our* evil!"

"Although we have tried, our hands are not completely clean. Inarius has no doubt magnified those regretful moments until they are all the survivors see."

Uldyssian let loose with an oath. There was no denying what Mendeln said. Uldyssian had thought that he had at least left Toraja and the other locations with an understanding of the truth concerning the Triune and the Cathedral. He had not expected those who had remained behind to think of him and his followers with love, but certainly there would be respect of some sort.

But human nature, he realized, ever veered on the side of suspicion, suspicion the Prophet's servants had fed well.

A great burning swelled within him. It erupted so fast and so furiously that it overwhelmed Uldyssian's good sense. He saw how foolish he had been to think that Inarius would let *him* guide events. Why would the angel grant a mortal foe that? With one cunning move, Inarius had already nearly won the battle. To be able to arouse ordinary folk to such determined anger that they would be willing to march through harsh jungle in order to fight what they knew would be powerful foes was a strength that dismayed Uldyssian.

The burning grew more intense. Uldyssian could not hold it back any longer.

He stared at the corpses.

Mendeln leapt out of his way just in time. Fire exploded around the bodies, reducing them to cinder in mere seconds. The flames rose high, eating at the nearest trees. The area quickly became an inferno, fueled by Uldyssian's frustration.

The woman's shade dissipated with a mournful wail. Someone seized Uldyssian's sleeve, but it took him a moment to register both his brother and the fact that Mendeln was shouting in his ear.

"You must stop it, Uldyssian! Stop it before you set the entire jungle ablaze!"

But he did not want to stop it, for the more the flames engulfed his surroundings, the better he felt. With some contempt, he shook Mendeln off.

Then something harsh struck his chest, and a new agony overwhelmed him. Uldyssian gazed down and saw that there was an arrow buried deep. His mind fleetingly noted that it was not just any arrow but one of a make familiar to him.

It was also an arrow encrusted with dirt.

Uldyssian toppled.

The assassin leapt through the thick jungle underbrush with a grace worthy of the swiftest predators. Even before he had fired, he had been on the move. It was not as if he sought to keep his anonymity. They would know him well enough, if only because of the arrow and the dirt upon it.

Achilios ran. Not because he wanted to but because it was demanded of him. He had fired, as he had been commanded, but that was not the end of it. Not in the least.

There was still Serenthia. . . .

With his smooth, hawklike features, he had been considered a handsome man back in the days when that was something that seemed to matter. Blond and wiry as a good hunter needed to be, with the swiftness to match, Achilios had been desired by many a young woman around the village of Seram. He, though, only had eyes for one. Back then, it had seemed to him such a tragic thing that Serenthia had wanted not him but rather Uldyssian.

Death had changed much of his perspective.

He paused to listen, one moon-white hand planted against the nearest tree to give him support. When no sound of pursuit arose, Achilios fell to human habit and rubbed his chin in thought. That caused him to gaze with eyes that saw no difference between day and night at the particles of dirt that covered the skin on the back of his hand.

In a sudden fury, he dropped his bow and rubbed at the dirt. Even though he felt it brush off, the hand grew no cleaner, just like the one with which he rubbed. Achilios did not have to see his face to know that it was the same. His entire body, even his green and brown hunter's garb, was grimy, almost as if he had freshly dug himself out of his grave. No matter how much he cleaned himself, there were always more particles, more bits of ground.

And now, worse, it was not only his flesh that he sought to clean but his conscience, too.

He had just shot his dearest friend, and although it had not been his intention to do it, that made it no less terrible a sin. Another had commanded, but Achilios had not found the wherewithal to refuse. He had bided his time, taken his aim, and, despite his mind screaming for him not to fire or to miss, Achilios had obeyed his master.

Retrieving his bow, the archer glanced back again. Whether the illumination he saw was from the fire Uldyssian had created in his rage or was simply from the encampment did not matter. If he could still see either, then he was too close. He had to continue his flight.

But where am I running to? Where?

He had only one answer to that, an answer he dreaded even to consider. Achilios was to run until there was no chance of being discovered. No farther. It had been commanded that he remain near but not too near. After all, Serenthia was next. Next . . .

Stricken by that horrifying thought, the hunter tried to let out a cry, but no sound came. Of course, that had nothing to do whatsoever with the gaping, crusted hole where his throat had once been. The magic that had animated him had given him voice, too, but that voice had been stolen, at least for this moment, by the one who now had utter mastery over him.

Thus, with no other choice left to him, Achilios continued to run. His pace would have exhausted to death the most powerful buck or horse, but, needing not to breathe, it was easy for him to keep up the grueling trek. Achilios dodged trees, slipped through narrow passages, and leapt over fallen trunks with an ease he had not had even in life.

And yet he could not feel even the slightest breeze. Even that small relief was forbidden him.

Then, without warning, the hunter stopped. It was not by his choice, and the abruptness of it nearly made Achilios lose his footing. He knew, though, what the extreme halt meant. He was now at the end of his invisible tether. All Achilios had to do to verify that was to look back and see that the glow was gone from view.

One thing that death had not forbidden him was a good, strong epithet. Now that he was far away and thus free to be vocal again, Achilios swore vehemently. The sound would not carry to anyone back near Uldyssian—or likely be heard by anything at all but a few animals—but it was one of the few things that made him feel *almost* alive.

But barely had he gotten the words out before a brilliant light of an unnatural blue appeared before him. Achilios swore again. He tried to notch an arrow, knowing all the while that the shaft would do no good.

A figure appeared in the midst of the light, a figure with wings that were tendrils of energy and who wore a silver-blue breastplate. The rest remained indistinct.

"I've done . . . your . . . your foul deed . . ." the hunter rasped. "Let me die now. . . ."

COME . . . commanded the ethereal form, gesturing with one gauntleted hand.

"I did your damned work!" Achilios insisted. He held up the bow and the notched arrow. "I used these to slay my best friend—my brother in all but blood." The archer laughed harshly. "*Blood* . . . now he's all in blood . . ."

But the winged figure did not show any sympathy. Achilios's despair finally drove him to aim and fire. The arrow soared exactly where he desired it, just above the breastplate where the throat would be.

But as had happened the last time he had attempted to slay his persecutor, the shaft flew completely *through* without pause. Achilios cursed yet once more; this very fiend had once enchanted his arrows so as to enable them to slay a huge, tentacled demon called the Thonos. They also had remained enchanted so that they would pierce *any* protective spell Uldyssian might have worn.

And so Achilios had prayed that perhaps they might also still work against the winged figure.

As if nothing had happened, the armored spirit repeated his command. *COME . . . WE ARE FAR FROM DONE YET.*

To Achilios, that could mean only one thing. "Not her, too! Not Serenthia—"

Against his will, his mouth suddenly clamped shut. The hunter's legs started forward of their own accord. In the same manner, Achilios's arms dropped. The bow dangled in his one hand, utterly useless.

Unable to do anything but obey, the undead archer followed the angel deeper into the jungle.

THREE

"Uldyssian!"

Mendeln seized his brother just before the latter could strike the ground. Panic such as Uldyssian's brother had not experienced since his parents dying filled him. He watched the blood pour from the wound, which, if it had not hit the heart, certainly had come close enough.

Uldyssian's body shook violently, and his eyes gaped up at the dark jungle canopy. He looked as if he wanted to say something, but what it was Mendeln had no idea.

Through the younger sibling's mind went all that Rathma had taught him, but nothing seemed right for the moment. There had been a spell that had enabled Mendeln to reattach the arm that one of the Triune's servants had severed, but that would certainly not do. Uldyssian and the others believed that Mendeln had healed himself after he had put the limb back on. Yet no one knew that the limb was not alive but *animated*. It was as dead as Achilios, moving only because of his magic.

It would not have even been possible for him to do *that* if he had not reattached the limb within the first hour of its loss. Any longer, and Mendeln could have done nothing. No, not even that spell, which on the surface had looked like healing, could avail him now.

And he did not want to resurrect Uldyssian as he had Achilios.

His thoughts went to Serenthia, whose skills were nearly as great as Uldyssian's. She might be able to save his brother.

Where is she? Mendeln suddenly wondered. Surely she,

of all people, had sensed what had happened? Why was there not a crowd of edyrem already swarming the pair?

Uldyssian coughed up blood, and then his body jerked even more violently.

The arrow burst into flames, the cinders spilling over Uldyssian's blood-soaked shirt. From the wound poured out a peculiar, thick liquid, which Mendeln at last recognized as what remained of the arrowhead.

And as the last of it poured out, the wound shrank and shrank . . . then finally sealed.

Uldyssian coughed again, but this time, it sounded only as if he cleared his throat. His eyes opened.

Mendeln gaped. "Uldyssian! This cannot be! You were—you were—"

"Where—" The elder son of Diomedes tried again. "Where is—is he?"

"Who?"

"Achil—Achilios . . ."

Only then did the arrow's origins register with Mendeln. Still holding Uldyssian tight, he stared out into the jungle, searching. Of course, he saw nothing, but these days, that meant little.

He suddenly considered the terrible accusation Uldyssian had just made. "Surely not! This was a trick, some ploy of Inarius's or possibly even the Triune. Achilios would never—"

With some effort, Uldyssian stood on his own. Mendeln marveled at his recuperative powers.

"The arrow belonged to Achilios, Mendeln. I know that. It's obvious to me, and it should be obvious to you. He fired it. It was intended to kill me swiftly."

Still hoping to deny that their friend would ever have any part, even involuntarily, in Uldyssian's murder, Mendeln pointed out, "If it had been him, there would be no doubt of your death. From a hundred paces in the thickest woods, Achilios could slay any creature with a shot directly to the heart. This one was close, yes, but—"

"Achilios meant to slay me," his brother insisted. However, Uldyssian's expression softened. "But you're right. He couldn't have missed unless he prayed to."

The conflagration that Uldyssian had started now rose high. That this, too, had not brought the other edyrem running perplexed Mendeln, until he watched his brother douse the fire with a simple wave of his hand. All that remained as memory were some scorched trees.

"It was you, then," he murmured to Uldyssian. "You are the reason no one, not even Serenthia, has come to our aid!"

Uldyssian grimly checked his chest where the arrow had struck. His right hand flared a faint gold as it passed over not only the area but wherever his blood had spilled. Mendeln shook his head in amazement as he watched.

In mere seconds, the stains vanished, and even the rip in his tunic repaired itself.

"In the beginning, I did it to keep anyone from joining us while you summoned the dead. I didn't want anyone else witnessing that, Mendeln. They've already seen enough to fear you."

Mendeln did not entirely believe that Uldyssian's reason was purely the protection of his brother, but he kept silent on it. "And when you were shot?"

"I assumed it would've vanished . . . unless that which turned Achilios into an assassin chose not to let it."

"Inarius?"

With a harsh, humorless chuckle, Uldyssian turned back to camp. "You don't believe that any more than I do, do you, Mendeln? Not like him at all. Something as *powerful* as he, maybe . . ."

His words only served to leave Mendeln cold. "You know that if it is such, we are lost."

But his brother, already walking, casually replied, "One angel, two, or a hundred. I'll bring them all down. All of them."

And as Mendeln stared at his sibling's receding back, he knew that Uldyssian meant it.

• • •

Serenthia stood waiting for them at the perimeter, the former Parthan brigand, Jonas, at her side. As Uldyssian
neared them, Saron—a dour Torajian who, with Jonas,
acted as Uldyssian's de facto officers—joined the other two.

"Did something happen out there?" Serenthia immediately demanded. "It felt as if—"

"We finished with Mendeln's work, that was all. It took
more than we expected."

"And were there answers?" she pressed.

Glancing past the trio, Uldyssian replied, "The Cathedral
was behind this. Inarius is placating the people and spreading vile rumors about what we do. He's trying to turn
Sanctuary against us."

Jonas frowned. Saron remained dour, his mood having
never truly lightened since the death of his cousin at the
hands of the Triune. They had been closer than brothers,
perhaps even closer than Uldyssian and Mendeln.

"We should march on the great Cathedral itself, master,"
he stated.

With a nod, Serenthia added, "That's not without merit.
Strike at the heart before it gets any worse. We can't do as
we did with the Triune, cutting away at it methodically.
Inarius isn't permitting us that chance."

Absently rubbing his chest where the arrow had penetrated, Uldyssian considered their view. Mendeln, who had
finally joined him, made a noncommittal noise.

"No," Uldyssian finally decided. "Not yet. We've one
more place we've got to go before we march on Inarius. Just
one more."

"Where's that to be, Master Uldyssian?" asked Jonas.

"The capital . . . we're going to the city of Kehjan to see
the leaders of the mage clans."

News of his decision spread fast among the edyrem, and
a sense of excitement filled the encampment. Many
among Uldyssian's flock had never been to the capital.

Discussions broke out everywhere about what Kehjan the city was like. Those few who had been there did their best to describe it, but from what Uldyssian heard, they all had differing memories.

He let their excitement go unchecked, despite some concern on the part of both Mendeln and Serenthia. They were rightly wary about confronting the mage clans, who had, as far as anyone could tell, avoided interfering in the struggle.

Uldyssian was also wary but at the same time confident. He had it in his mind that the mages, obviously no puppets of the Cathedral of Light, would be interested in a possible alliance. If not that, then certainly they would do their best to lessen the sect's influence over the masses.

It was worth the gamble to Uldyssian and, since the capital was somewhat on their path toward Inarius's sanctum, not so troublesome a detour in his mind.

His makeshift army left at first light, pushing through the dense vegetation with little effort. When a river had to be forded, what was easier than using magic to bring together tree trunks to create a bridge or, as some of the more skilled did, simply propel oneself over and land on the other side? When the terrain grew treacherous, how much simpler was it to have small groups of edyrem stand together and literally rip a path through?

At no time did Uldyssian discourage such displays of power among his people. The more confident, the more comfortable they were with their powers, the better chance they would have of surviving in battle, much less winning.

Mendeln, naturally, did not look at all pleased, but he kept his counsel to himself, which satisfied his brother. The edyrem made great progress the first day and the next. They had quite a distance still to go, but Uldyssian calculated that the rate at which they trekked would not give even Inarius's missionaries much time to raise others further against their cause.

Still, he pushed the edyrem's pace just a little more . . . and a little more . . . and a little more . . .

Just before dark on the fourth day, they came upon another river. The edyrem began crossing. Uldyssian was at his most cautious and set several sentries in place.

Yet it seemed that his concern was unwarranted. They were not attacked, and no one was caught by the river. When the last of his followers had made it over, Uldyssian ordered them on, while he stood and surveyed the area of the river with more than just his eyes.

And still there was nothing.

It made no sense to use the last few minutes of dim light to take them farther from such an obvious source of water. With reluctance, Uldyssian called a halt. He set up the usual perimeter and then, recalling the attack, placed additional sentries a bit deeper into the jungle. All of his guards remained in contact with one another.

Even with that done, he still summoned Saron for one more precaution. "I want you to find four others and begin a continuous patrol of the camp itself. Reach out with your minds. You need to be aware of any sensation that seems at all out of the ordinary."

"Yes, Master Uldyssian. I understand completely." The Torajian bowed and immediately went off to locate the ones he needed. Uldyssian vowed to himself to have Jonas and another band take over after a couple of hours. He wanted *all* his sentinels to be fresh of mind.

But as the night lengthened, Uldyssian began to wonder if he had just had a case of nerves. The nearer they got to the capital, the more his task there began to weigh upon him. It was very possible that confronting the mage clans might even get them at least to side temporarily with Inarius. Better the enemy they thought they understood, rather than Uldyssian's unknown and unpredictable powers.

That they would find themselves in a far worse situation if the edyrem were beaten would be something he would have to impress upon them.

But all that had to wait until they reached their destination. Uldyssian finally gave in to his exhaustion, his last thoughts concerning his overzealous precautions. It had only been his nerves—

A bright white light suddenly erupted in his face, blinding him. Uldyssian let out a shout, but his voice was so muted that even he could bearly hear it. He reached out with his thoughts to Serenthia and the others—but could not find them.

There existed only the light . . . only the light and then, gradually, a wondrous figure from whom it was clear the blazing illumination originated. Far taller than any human, he strode confidently toward Uldyssian, his breastplate gleaming and the tendrils of pure force that were his wings flaring a rainbow of fierce colors.

And as he neared the son of Diomedes, he transformed into the leader of the Cathedral of Light, the Prophet.

"Uldyssian ul-Diomed," came the musical voice. The youth stood just about the former farmer's height but seemed somehow still to be able to gaze down upon him from well above. His luminous silver-blue eyes penetrated to Uldyssian's very soul, making the human feel as if he could hide nothing. "My errant child . . ."

Uldyssian belatedly leapt to his feet. He stared into the Prophet's beautiful, perfect face—unmarred by scar, wart, or even the slightest beard—which was framed by glistening, golden locks that fell far past his shoulders. "I'm no acolyte of yours, Inarius, and certainly not your child!"

"No . . ." the beatific figure agreed with a glorious smile full of perfect teeth. "But you are the child of the child of the child several times over who was begat by my even more errant son, he who now calls himself Rathma."

Uldyssian had been told of a blood link between himself and the angel, but if there was one, it was as far removed from him as if he were related to the animals that he had raised. If Inarius thought to spark some familial bond, then the angel was sorely deluded.

"I do not seek to call family to family," the Prophet remarked with unsettling accuracy, "but I do come to you with power to grant you absolution even now. You need not continue on this path of sin after sin, my son. I can still forgive you."

His statements might have been considered mere audacity by Uldyssian if not for the jarring fact that not only was it still impossible to reach out to the others, but even the encampment could not be found. Uldyssian was completely surrounded by the light emanating from his adversary. Even when he took a step back, nothing changed. The ground itself was enshrouded by the celestial illumination.

"You see," continued Inarius, spreading his hands in a fatherly fashion, "there is no more reason to continue the bloodshed. The outcome is inevitable. Besides, it is not ultimately your fault. You were led astray by *her,* she who shall not be named, and your only mistakes were due to your own inherent deficiencies. You are mortal; you are weak. I mean that not as insult; all humans are weak. It is why they must be led toward the light."

It was not the words as much as something in the Prophet's tone, his manner, his very being, that made Uldyssian want to believe. He had felt much the same when confronted by the demon Lucion in his guise as leader of the Triune. Inarius, though, was a thousand times more compelling. Uldyssian had a desire to fall to his knees and beg for forgiveness—

For what? he suddenly wondered, his anger burning away his awe at the angelic figure. *I asked for none of this!*

"Fury is a demon's lover, my good Uldyssian. To give in to it is to abandon thought and heart."

"Spare me all that! What have you done with them? Where are the others?"

The Prophet nodded approvingly. "Concern . . . now, there is a goodly aspect. You would do well to be concerned about those who mistakenly follow you down this path, for what you decide may condemn them, too."

Serry! Mendeln! Jonas! Saron! Uldyssian located no trace of any of them.

He lunged for Inarius, at the same time summoning his power. Yet the Prophet was no longer where Uldyssian expected him. Instead, the angel stood just to the side. He watched dispassionately as the human fell forward.

"Fury leads only to more shame and disaster, Uldyssian ul-Diomed. It leaves you not only lying in the dirt but forever covered over by it."

Shoving himself up again, Uldyssian glared at the holy figure. He expected flames to rise around the angel and, if they did not harm him, at least wipe the smugness from the unblemished countenance.

But nothing happened.

"You see what chance you have, my good child. There will only be death and damnation for you and those dearest to you, unless you seek forgiveness. Follow the path of sin as you do, and you convict everyone. Is that what you wish? Do you have such conceit?"

Uldyssian spat. "If I've conceit, it can't compare to yours, Inarius. You don't own us any more than Lucion or Lilith did. This is not your world; it's ours! Ours!"

The Prophet's smile vanished. "I forged this world from raw forces taken from the place of Creation! I sculpted the lands and filled the seas. All exists because of me; all remains at my whim . . . including you, my child."

Before Uldyssian could respond, voices suddenly rose around him. At first, he took them for Serenthia and some of the edyrem, but then something about them jarred memories long buried . . . especially one female voice.

My poor Uldyssian! So confused, so angry! Let me comfort you. . . .

He choked back tears. His eyes instinctively sought out the one who spoke.

From the opposite direction, there came a child's giggle. Uldyssian whirled.

His mother . . . his little sister . . .

A shadow passed by the edge of his vision. What little he glimpsed of it was a burly man about his size. There briefly came a second shape, this one also male, but shorter, younger.

"You sacrificed so much to save them, my child, and though their bodies failed, they gained salvation. They fear for you, however, for you cannot join them if you refuse to accept my light. You will forever be parted—"

Tears spilled down Uldyssian's face. In his mind, he saw his family as they perished slowly, agonizingly. Although he had rejected the various missionaries and their empty words, Uldyssian still had hoped inside that his mother, his father, and his other siblings had at least found peace in whatever realm existed beyond death.

And that made him wonder at what Inarius revealed to him. With all the angel's power, why had he not offered to bring Uldyssian's family back to life? Not a semblance, as Mendeln had done with Achilios, but actually make them alive again?

Was it because he could not? If so, then the angel was not so all-powerful as he pretended.

Which made his summoning these shades—these false shades, very likely—even more abominable to the human. Inarius had dredged up the emotions that Uldyssian had prayed never to feel again. The hollowness, the despair, the bitterness . . .

Uldyssian roared at the Prophet, using those terrible emotions to intensify his powers. He let his family's loss overwhelm him and, in doing so, strip away any hesitations he had about unleashing all his might at Inarius.

The blinding light dimmed slightly . . . but that was all. The sanctimonious face still gazed down upon him. Despite no visible sign that he had done *anything*, Uldyssian felt so drained that all he could do was drop to his knees.

"You have chosen to sin," the Prophet commented slowly and without emotion. "I cannot help you but by putting an end to your misguided existence, my child."

With that, Inarius simply vanished.

As he did, the light winked out so abruptly that Uldyssian

felt as if he had been plunged into utter darkness. His thoughts were not for himself, though, but for the loved ones he had briefly thought were with him once again.

"Mother . . ." he rasped. "Father . . ."

Suddenly, his head jarred up from where it had been resting. Uldyssian discovered that he once again lay in the midst of the encampment, surrounded by sleeping edyrem. A slight breeze coursed through the area, and in the distance, the night creatures of the jungle chattered with one another.

Uldyssian shook. *It can't have been a dream! It can't have been . . .*

His fingers scraped the ground as he pushed himself to a sitting position. Every muscle in his body ached as if he had actually fought against the angel. Yet if that had been the case, surely all would not be so quiet. The encampment should have been in chaos.

It was only a nightmare, Uldyssian insisted. *Only a nightmare . . . nothing to fear . . .*

But then he happened to glance at the ground where his hand had lain . . . and where now dirt lay scorched for more than a yard beyond him.

How convenient, Zorun Tzin thought as he finished his divining. The seven-sided pattern he had scraped in the ground still glowed faintly from residual energies. Letting the crystal he had used for his effort continue to dangle from its gold chain over the center of the pattern, the mage looked ahead into the jungle.

How convenient that he comes to meet me, this Uldyssian ul-Diomed.

Straightening, the Kehjani kicked away the pattern, briefly sending traces of magical residue up along with the flying dirt. He glanced over his shoulders at those with him. In addition to Terul, who wielded both axe and torch, there were half a dozen guards in the loose red garments and golden breastplates of the mage clans' master council. The guards had been foisted upon him by his "employers" and were more likely there to keep watch on the spellcaster rather than assist with his mission. Thus was the way of the council even now. Not enough trust even in the one they had commissioned for this.

Zorun chuckled under his breath. They were right to be so wary.

The underbrush ahead suddenly shifted as if something large approached. The mage thrust the crystal into a pouch on his belt, then readied an incantation. Terul let out a grunt and moved forward to protect his master. The guards readied their weapons but remained where they were.

A figure burst from the darkness into the area, a man perhaps near the end of the third decade of his life. He looked to have once been strong and lithe and radiated a presence that indicated a high caste. However, black spots—almost burns—covered whatever could be seen of his flesh, including his face, and he looked as if he had taken neither food nor drink in days. There were still hints of a handsome face, and the eyes were penetrating, but in a manner that Zorun thought bordered on madness.

Madness . . . or some sort of plague.

"Stand where you are," he commanded. One hand began gesturing. "You will come no closer."

The eyes stared past the mage. A sickly grin spread over the stranger's countenance. Only then did Zorun and the rest see that his gums had turned black and his teeth were crumbling.

"You'll . . . do better . . ." he rasped.

Zorun started to chant, and the figure fell over.

Some of the guards started forward, but the spellcaster waved them back. It was not out of any concern for them but for himself. If there *was* any plague involved, he did not want any of those with him carrying it.

There was a quick and safe way to discover the truth. Reaching into another pouch, Zorun removed a small box he had kept with him since the last plague that had touched the capital. He took from it a powder that had once been bone ground from a victim of such disease. The body had first been safely burned to remove contamination, but the bone would still remember the disease. If there was anything similar to it on this body, the powder would fly from his palm and cover the stranger.

Muttering the spell, the mage poured just enough powder into his hand. The yellowed dust trembled as if ready to fly . . . and then stilled.

There was no plague. Zorun was about to dismiss the body as unimportant, when the rags it was clad in finally caught his eye.

"Terul! Bring the torch closer to him!"

The brutish servant obeyed. Zorun let Terul stand closer than him, just in case.

They were indeed the robes of an acolyte of the Triune and, from what the mage could glean, of a priest of some importance.

Deciding that it was safe to risk it, Zorun ordered, "Turn him over."

Setting down his axe, the servant used one huge hand to shove the dead man by the shoulder.

The priest suddenly gripped Terul by the wrist. The eyes opened—

With an uncharacteristic sound of dismay, Terul tugged his hand free. Both master and servant watched as the priest grew still again.

When the body remained unmoving, Zorun indicated that Terul should finish his task. Despite his earlier exclamation, the giant now did not hesitate. He shoved the priest onto his back.

Seen more clearly up close, the robes looked to be those of a follower of Dialon. Zorun had made a thorough study of the Triune—one had to know one's enemies—and noted markings still remaining that indicated that this man had once served in the prime temple itself.

"A pity you are dead," he murmured to the body. "What could you tell us about this Ascenian, I wonder?"

There was a chain around the neck, one that had not been visible before. Using a stick to lift it loose, Zorun saw that it held a medallion of office.

"I should know your name, it appears . . . let me see." The Kehjani had, through his varied sources, identified the senior priests of the sect and kept track of the changes and politics. He had been most intrigued by the High Priest of Mefis, one Malic, until word had reached him of that one's disappearance and supposed death. Zorun was no fool; there had been more to the Triune than it preached, a dark side that he had felt Malic best represented.

But this sorry fool was not Malic. Zorun ran through his remarkable memory and finally hit upon the name he sought.

"Your name was . . . was Durram. Yes, that was it. Durram." Next to him, Terul let out a grunt. Ignoring the sound, Zorun rose. "Yes, you would have been a fount of information to me . . . if you'd managed to live a bit longer, that is."

The mage used a sandaled foot to push the corpse among the thick vegetation. The priest's presence still interested him, in that Durram was far from where the main temple had been located and very enticingly near the current location of Uldyssian ul-Diomed. Zorun expected that given time, even Terul could fathom that there certainly had to be a connection. Durram appeared, against all sanity, to have been tracking the Ascenian on foot, despite an obviously debilitating condition.

"Admirable, if foolish," the mage declared to himself. "Better to have done something for his life first. Come, Terul! We are done here."

The giant, who had still been staring at the body, belatedly obeyed. He picked up his axe with one hand, hefting it over his shoulder. They and the guards mounted up, then headed farther into the jungle.

But not before Terul glanced back one last time at the body of the unfortunate Durram.

Glanced back . . . and ever so briefly smiled.

FOUR

It was a more somber Uldyssian who drove the edyrem hard that next day. He did not explain to anyone the reason for his change in emotion, and no one dared ask, not even Mendeln. That his brother likely suspected something dread, Uldyssian did not care. More than ever, what was important was to reach the capital and face the mage clans.

But now he wondered if even they were enough to aid in all arrayed against him. In Uldyssian's mind, Inarius had proven quite readily how little the human was compared with him. The angel made even Lilith's power seem inconsequential. Yet Uldyssian had no choice but to face his celestial foe eventually, face him and probably die quickly and shamefully.

The edyrem themselves that day faced nothing worse than a little rain. It was welcome at first, for it cooled the jungle some, but the moment the rain ceased, the humidity leapt. The Parthans were hard kept to maintain a reasonable pace after that, and even those from the jungle regions faltered sooner than he would have desired.

Yet when they made camp, they did so with the knowledge at last that the next day would enable them to see—at least from the treetops—the distant but distinct spires of Kehjan the city. That even gave Uldyssian something with which to cheer his thoughts a little.

He set down to sleep with the certainty that there would be a repeat of the previous night's horror, but only vague dreams haunted him. Uldyssian awoke in much better spirits, human nature enabling him to make less of the encounter with Inarius as time and distance grew. Still, he was determined to make his offer to the mages and other leaders as soon as they reached the city.

Near late morning, their trek was interrupted by a sight welcome to many of the edyrem. A much-traveled road divided the jungle, a road quickly verified by Saron and some of the others as leading directly to the main gates of Kehjan.

Uldyssian saw no reason he and his followers should not continue along the road. The edyrem fell into columns, he, Serenthia, and Mendeln at the head.

"Now we look like an invading army," the younger brother said with some distaste.

"We were given no choice."

"No, but I wish we had been."

Uldyssian shrugged, then squinted as someone came from the opposite direction. A small caravan. There were three wagons with rounded wooden roofs. Upon each were emblems on the side that Saron quickly identified.

"The merchant Fahin, Master Uldyssian. Some of his wagons, at least. He is one of the richest merchants in all the lowlands."

"I know that name," interjected Serenthia. "His people did business with my father. I even met Fahin once, when I was younger."

In addition to the wagons, a full score of mounted guards accompanied the merchant's wares. The evident captain caught sight of the immense throng marching toward his charge and quickly signaled the fighters to ride to the forefront. The wagons, meanwhile, began to try to turn about.

"He must be rich, indeed," commented Mendeln. "To find so many men willing to sacrifice themselves for his goods."

The riders did not charge but spread across the road. The wall they created was obvious; to reach the wagons would demand much death from those they likely considered brigands.

"Turn away!" the captain, a sharp-nosed young man

with a scar across his chin, shouted. "Turn away, or face our blades!"

"We're no thieves," returned Uldyssian, opening his hands in a gesture of friendship.

"That we know, Ascenian! Your crimes in Toraja and other places are well established. Our master is not yours to take, even if we die to make that so!"

"Fahin is in the wagons?" Serenthia put a hand on Uldyssian's arm. "If I could speak with him, we might have an ally before we reach the gates. It worked in Partha. . . ."

Her suggestion had merit, but to speak with the merchant, they first had to deal with the zealous captain and his men. Meeting the officer's condemning gaze, Uldyssian quietly said, "We want no bloodshed."

As he spoke, he spread his hands at each side. Among the mounted fighters, especially those in the center, horses began to stagger toward the outer edges of the road. The sight looked like some sort of macabre dance. Several of the guards let out curses and shouts as they attempted in vain to veer their mounts back into position.

The captain was the first among them to understand just what Uldyssian did. At the top of his lungs, he cried, "Attack! Attack that one!"

But although he and those nearest urged their steeds forward, the animals simply continued to stagger sideways. Despite the frustrated officer's best attempts, a large gap opened up in the road.

"Mendeln, you and the others wait here. Serenthia, let's go meet this Master Fahin."

The two strode past the guards, who could do nothing to reach them. The invisible barriers Uldyssian had created kept the mounted warriors trapped on opposing sides of the road.

The lead wagon had all but turned about, but the other two were still in progress. As he reached the first, with a gesture, he forced the driver to look his way.

"Which is Master Fahin's wagon?"

"The—the middle!"

Giving him a nod of thanks, Uldyssian led Serenthia to the wagon in question.

A guard next to the driver of the second vehicle tried to throw a spear at the pair but discovered too late that it now temporarily adhered to his hand. He fell over the driver. Both men might have tumbled to the ground, but Uldyssian kept them safe. It would be impossible to enlist the merchant's help if any of his people were injured or slain.

They came around to the back of the wagon, where a single door stood. It flew open at Uldyssian's desire.

A shouting guard dove toward the pair.

He managed no more than a foot out of the wagon before flying backward into it again. Uldyssian sent him to the opposite wall. The guard landed softly but found himself pinned.

From the left side of the interior, a heavyset figure wearing a jeweled nose ring leaned into view. His hair had once been rich black but now had gray streaks. He was lighter of skin than Saron yet still darker than either of the two before him.

"You have me," he proclaimed with dignity. Despite his girth and his extravagant clothing—there was enough actual gold decor on him to feed Uldyssian's village for a year—Fahin did not strike the son of Diomedes as so self-indulgent as to be oblivious to the needs of others. However, that still did not mean that he would see the truth. His next words, though, gave some hint of hope. "Bring no more harm to those who serve me. Let them go, and I am yours."

"No one has been harmed," Uldyssian returned. "I am Uldyssian ul-Diomed, and by my honor I swear to their safety. We came to speak, nothing more."

As the merchant's brow rose in obvious disbelief, Serenthia stepped forward. Leaning into the wagon, she said, "Master Fahin, do you remember my father, Cyrus of Seram? He dealt with you much in the past."

"Seram . . . Seram . . . I know the village, and the name Cyrus, too." The Kehjani closed his eyes in thought. "A virtuous man, I recall that. He had many children, a blessing, I hope." Opening his eyes, Fahin nodded. "Yes, I know Cyrus of Seram . . . and you are his daughter?"

"We met when I was young, Master Fahin." Serenthia hesitated. "I remember—I remember you had the most beautiful white pony with you. She had a silky, thick mane, and the only part not white on her entire body was a little streak just above her one eye that made it look like she was thinking something—"

"Sherah," Fahin murmured, a childlike grin spreading across his face. "Ah! I'd not thought of the little one for years!" He clapped his hands in cheerful memory of the pony. "And though you could have learned of her from someone else, I think, there is that which makes me believe you are who you say you are." Some of the pleasure left him. "But what that means now, I do not know. I have heard stories of an Ascenian leading an army of terror across the lands—"

"No one has anything to fear from us," Uldyssian interjected as he gently moved Serenthia aside. "No one unless they serve the evil that is the Triune or the Cathedral."

"Indeed? I could almost believe what you speak concerning the Triune, for rumors of secret rituals recently have reached the highest levels in the capital, but nothing but good is said about the Prophet, who even preaches peace with you despite Toraja and elsewhere."

"Preaches it while he twists the minds of others into trying to slay us. I can't prove what I say to you, Master Fahin, but I hope that you will give me the chance to plead my case . . . for the sake of all of us."

The stout merchant indicated his surroundings. "You see that you have a captive audience. I can do *nothing* but listen."

Uldyssian frowned. "That isn't what I want of you." An idea that he had not discussed with anyone else seemed his best hope now. "Hear me, Master Fahin. Would you listen if I stood alone before you and the leaders of Kehjan? Would they accept such an arrangement? I'll freely walk into Kehjan alone—" He cut off Serenthia, who started to protest. "And place myself under your guidance throughout it. Myself alone. Will they—will you—give me the chance to tell them the truth?"

The merchant leaned back. Uldyssian saw no subterfuge in the man's eyes, although he reminded himself that this man made his living dealing.

"Your—people—they would have to stay two days beyond the gates," Fahin declared. "Any closer with so many, the city would expect imminent attack." He pointed at Cyrus's daughter. "She could come with you, if you wish. That would be acceptable."

"It'll only be me."

"I won't let you go into the capital alone!" Serenthia blurted. "I'll go—"

He shook his head. "You need to keep the rest under control, Serry. None of the others can manage that. They certainly won't be comfortable around Mendeln."

"Then take him with you! You know that he'd gladly come!"

Uldyssian had already considered that. "The mages might find him far too unsettling. I won't risk him or anyone else. I'll be fine." Uldyssian eyed the merchant. "If Master Fahin says I'll be."

"If I take you into Kehjan, so it will be, Uldyssian." Fahin rose, moving very smoothly for one of his bulk. "Permit me to tell those with me that we will be returning home. Captain Aztuhl will need some placating, too."

A grateful Uldyssian bowed low. "Thank you. I apologize for disrupting your journey."

"The trip I was undertaking was for personal matters, not much business. Do you think me so destitute that I have but three wagons? I might have been more upset if I had been forced to have twenty or more turn around, not these few." Fahin waved off his assistance as he disembarked. Once down, the merchant glanced back inside. "Oh! My poor bodyguard?"

Uldyssian released his hold on the man. With a gasp, the guard slumped into a sitting position. He stared at Uldyssian as if the latter had two heads. That was likely to be one of the predominant expressions among the Kehjani, the son of Diomedes thought . . . that and, thanks to Inarius, hatred.

Captain Aztuhl proved to be an obstinate man, but in the end, he bowed to his employer's dictates. On the other side, Uldyssian faced many protests from his own followers. No one liked the notion of him entering the capital alone, but, like the merchant, he brooked no disagreement.

It was decided that Fahin would lead the way back to Kehjan, with Uldyssian riding beside his wagon. For the journey back, the merchant chose to sit next to his driver. He did not wish to appear afraid before his people, which Uldyssian could appreciate. However, Captain Aztuhl also remained near, ever ready should the Ascenian do anything he considered bordering on threat.

It was Master Fahin who indicated at last when they were approximately two days from their destination. Saron and others reluctantly verified this, not that Uldyssian had asked. In the short time that he had come to know the merchant, he had gained much respect for the man. Good fortune had finally smiled upon the son of Diomedes; with Fahin to introduce him to the ruling powers, there was hope that they might listen, not merely react.

"The fractious nature of the mage clans' council means that there is merit in meeting with Prince Ehmad. The young prince has sought to strengthen his position. He has gained backing from many of the guilds, and even the mages will pay attention to what he says," Fahin had explained early on.

"What about this feuding between the clans? How deadly has it been?"

"There was a time, my son, when not a day could pass without a body found in some terrible state. There are many deaths to this day whose cause no one outside the clans can decipher, so monstrous were the remains. That has lessened, but only in the sense of the survivors of a wild pack of hyenas still fighting over a morsel. They size one another up, awaiting their chance to take advantage of weaknesses, and at that point, there will be more blood."

Uldyssian had wondered if the spellcasters would be any use at all, so consumed with fighting among themselves. "Is there any hope in speaking with them, then?"

"If that is necessary for your desires, then yes. The council, even while its individual members seek to stab one another in the back, yet strives to make certain that nothing threatens what they have set up. They must abide the prince, for his lineage goes back far beyond their rule, but a danger to the magic they so worship, that would bring even the worst of rivals together for a time."

"But they allowed the Cathedral and the Triune to rise up and weaken their influence."

Fahin had conceded this point but then added, "Both arose with such swiftness that even I question how. The mages were caught unaware, and by the time they understood what was happening, there was nothing they could do." At that point, the merchant had leaned over from the wagon and nearly poked Uldyssian in the chest. "They have not made such a mistake for you."

"I've seen nothing of them."

"And that is what they wish. Be wary even as you offer them either truce or alliance, Uldyssian. Your back will always be open to them."

As much as he appreciated most of Master Fahin's advice, in this Uldyssian thought that the merchant underestimated him. After fighting demons and high priests, the mages were a danger he constantly considered and, thus, was prepared for. Only Inarius truly disturbed him.

Before he separated from them, Uldyssian gave the

edyrem a final speech he felt necessary to calm their worries. He also did it for the sake of the locals, for his followers now camped not that far from two small villages, and the path ahead was even more populated. They had met other wagons and travelers in the final day before reaching this point, some of whom had nervously passed by, while a few had fled back toward the city. Fahin had spoken cheerfully to all that he could, doing his best to reassure those who knew him that this was not some army . . . even if it was.

Mendeln bade him well after all else had stepped back, Uldyssian's brother whispering, "You know that not even Serenthia will be able to hold these people if they sense anything has gone awry. They will and *have* died for you. I would do no less, too."

"Have you spoken with Rathma? Has that one said anything in regard to this?"

Mendeln frowned. "I've not spoken with him since last we talked of it . . . and that makes me more anxious for you. Rathma would not be silent and absent without good reason."

Not having as much faith as his brother did in the Ancient, Uldyssian muttered, "I can't just do nothing because he's failed to show up. We have to move on constantly, Mendeln. This is our conflict now; his day is long past."

Mendeln only nodded, then clasped his elder sibling briefly on the shoulder.

Uldyssian and Fahin's caravan were soon far from the edyrem. By himself, Uldyssian seemed less of interest to those they encountered along the way than in previous circumstances. The reason for that became evident when two wagons heading away from the capital proved to be under the control of a merchant from none other than Tulisam, a larger town not all that far from his own beloved Seram. Uldyssian did not identify himself, for some of the comments the wagon master—a beefy, bald man named Larius—

made in passing had to do with the still-at-large murderer who had slain a pair of priests. Still, despite that moment, it was otherwise welcome to hear and see someone of a background similar to his own.

"There will be more such as you in the city," Fahin reminded him. "Kehjan is not like most of the other places you have been in the lowlands. All people, even those who have sailed from the other side of the sea, come eventually to the capital. It is possible that there even might be one who knows you . . ."

That briefly distracted Uldyssian, who imagined one of Serenthia's brothers perhaps spotting him. Unlike her, they might not be so forgiving when it came to their father's death. Uldyssian himself still mourned the man and wished that somehow circumstance—and Lilith—had not brought about that terrible day.

They passed not one but two armed patrols, both of which Master Fahin immediately summoned to him. Fahin explained the edyrem as pilgrims, with Uldyssian their head, and with his influence managed, at least for the moment, to keep the captains from riding out to investigate the throngs.

"Once we speak with Prince Ehmad," the merchant said after the first, "I am sure that he will send out those who will keep order and prevent any misunderstanding."

Fahin preferred his own wagon to local inns, his explanation having to do with not wishing to share with past sleepers whatever they had left in their beds. His decision suited Uldyssian, who distrusted the inns for other reasons, just fine.

Having committed himself to this endeavor, the merchant embraced it utterly. He had kept abreast of matters throughout Uldyssian's struggle against the Triune, for Fahin had business in every major settlement and several smaller ones besides.

"I will not lie to you that this matter with the temple did not affect me," he revealed to Uldyssian. "And that is why I also seek this talk between you and the city. I would have peace and prosperity, as any good man would want."

"And as any good merchant would, too?"

Fahin's eyes twinkled. "Just so."

It was a warm, windless night. His host offered his own wagon to Uldyssian, but, not liking to be boxed in, the latter politely refused. Instead, he chose an area near the horses, relying not just on his own powers but on their acute senses to warn him of any approach. Fahin looked a little askance at such a location, but Uldyssian, who had grown up with animals, found their nearness and scents comforting and familiar.

Sleep did not come quickly despite that, for Uldyssian found that he felt odd with Mendeln, Serenthia, and the other edyrem physically so far away. The only times he had been separated from them had been when someone or another, such as Lilith, had dragged him off. Distance also made the link between him and the rest more tenuous, but that could not be helped.

Captain Aztuhl came by, the officer eyeing him with continued distrust. "It would be best if you remained nearer to the wagons, Ascenian."

"I'm well enough here."

"As you will, then." The captain gave him one last glare, then strode off.

Uldyssian paid the man's lack of manners no mind. He expected to see a lot more of it in the capital, but it would be nothing he could not handle.

Still sleep would not come. Uldyssian impatiently began studying the trees above, hoping somehow that would lull him. Many had vines and others long, snakelike branches. He already knew that there were no predators hiding in the foliage, and even had there been any, Uldyssian would have not been overly concerned.

The trees all but created a canopy over this part of the road. Some of the branches hung so low that they nearly grazed the tops of the wagons.

He gradually began to calm. The rest of Master Fahin's party had settled down, only the sentries on duty moving about. There were two low fires for safety. The branches above the wagons rustled. Uldyssian at last shut his eyes—

Then he wondered why the branches would move when there was no wind.

Uldyssian leapt up. "Captain—"

The branches from every nearby tree came rushing down, seizing wagons, horses, and men. One guard screamed as he was tossed into the dark jungle. The branches dropped a horse on a wagon not yet plucked up, crushing in the roof.

Captain Aztuhl chopped his way free of the groping branches, then seized a log from one of the fires. He fended off his first few attackers, but more and more thrust toward him.

Glaring at the trees that were the source of the captain's predicament, Uldyssian used his powers to rip the branches off. The trees to which they had been attached shuddered, then stilled. A rain of broken limbs fell upon Aztuhl, but they were only an annoyance.

Uldyssian looked up at the nearest wagon, which he knew was Fahin's. The son of Diomedes clenched a fist at the branches there, then drew the fist down.

The trees shook with obvious effort as they fought his control. Whatever had unleashed this chaos on the party wielded tremendous magic. Still, for some reason, Uldyssian did not think it the work of Inarius. It was not his manner. Despite the skill involved, there was a certain clumsiness.

But clumsy or not, the attack had already proven a deadly one. Someone had clearly been watching and waiting, and somehow they had managed to avoid detection by him.

Fahin's wagon finally came to rest again. Uldyssian frowned, and as he did, the branches began peeling away from the wagon. They blackened as if burned, then shriveled until there was nothing left but stubs.

Yet even with so many limbs destroyed by him, there were still far too many. Uldyssian heard another guard scream. Of the last of the three wagons, there was no sign. Horses not seized ran in panic.

"Beware!" Captain Aztuhl leapt out of nowhere, colliding with a distracted Uldyssian.

The missing wagon came crashing down a short distance from the duo. As he struggled free of the captain, Uldyssian estimated that the wagon would have missed him even if Aztuhl had not come to his rescue. Still, he was grateful for the man's concern. It *had* been a close thing.

"You must help me get my father out of the wagon!" Aztuhl gasped. "Please!"

"Your father?" The only wagon left was Master Fahin's. "Do you mean—"

"I was not born of his wife," the captain hastily explained. "But he took me into his house after her death and acknowledged me as his."

He needed to say no more. Uldyssian and Aztuhl headed toward the wagon, where someone was already attempting to kick open the damaged door. As the door went flying open, the rotund form of the merchant emerged.

"Father!" called the captain. "Look out—"

Aztuhl's warning cut off with a gagging sound. Uldyssian quickly turned, but the captain, clutching at the vines around his throat, was already vanishing into the foliage.

"Aztuhl!" Fahin shouted mournfully.

But there was nothing even Uldyssian could do. He reached out toward where he had last seen the man, but although scores of branches descended at his will, none of them held Aztuhl.

Uldyssian seized the merchant. "There's nothing that can be done for him! I'm sorry!"

"It is—it is—" The teary-eyed merchant could say no more.

As he tried to maneuver Fahin away from the attacking trees, it finally occurred to Uldyssian that his focus had been all wrong. He had been reacting to the spell when he should have been seeking out its caster. There had been so much distraction that Uldyssian had not had the opportunity to think beyond the moment, but that would change now.

With Fahin in tow, Uldyssian did a sweeping search of the vicinity with his mind. At first glance, there was nothing, but he had become accustomed to the tricks used by his foes to mask themselves from notice. Uldyssian began seeking those areas where the absence of his unseen enemy was *too* great.

There! The area in question was so utterly calm that it could only be where the spellcaster hid. Uldyssian focused his will on the spot, seeking to rip away the other's protection and then strike him down.

"Uldyssian! There is—"

Something heavy struck the son of Diomedes on the back of the head. Uldyssian's thoughts swam. He stumbled past Fahin, unable to believe that an attack as simple as someone sneaking up behind him had succeeded.

"You foul wretch!" The watery image of the merchant drawing from his belt a jeweled but quite serviceable dagger passed before Uldyssian's eyes. Fearful for his friend, he made a feeble grab for Fahin but easily missed. Fahin vanished behind him.

Uldyssian tried to turn in that direction, but his reflexes were oddly slow. He had not merely been hit, he realized; some spell also overtook him.

In desperation, he tried to burn away whatever had control of him. His head cleared a little. Uldyssian heard struggling.

Master Fahin let out a howl. There was a chuckle; then a heavy body dropped next to Uldyssian.

Powerful hands grabbed the son of Diomedes by the collar. Uldyssian squinted, trying to strike, but something pressed against his chest, making it impossible to concentrate. His body felt numb all over.

A grotesque visage all but pressed into his own face. The head was much too small for the body, but there was that in the eyes that spoke to Uldyssian of an intelligence equal to, if not greater than, his own.

"A step closer," grunted the behemoth with an evil grin. The words were almost mangled by his huge mouth. "A step closer . . ."

He thrust a palm against Uldyssian's forehead.

FÍVE

Zorun Tzin grinned with almost childlike pleasure at his success. He had hoped to use this particular spell—one carefully plotted out over a period of months for another purpose—to cause enough commotion to distract the Ascenian, but never in his wildest dreams had the mage expected such success. Truly, his power was greater than even he had ever assumed.

The deaths did not in the least bother Zorun. He knew exactly who had been in the wagons and that there would be some repercussions, but no one would trace the killing of Master Fahin to him. They were more likely to set the blame at the feet of Uldyssian ul-Diomed, something that Zorun would encourage. The rumors of the Ascenian's might and violent nature were, after all, widely known.

It would also make the mage's capturing of the renegade all that more impressive . . . if he bothered even to tell the council. Thoughts had been circulating in his head, thoughts involving the gaining of much, much power.

Power enough so that all other mages would bow to him.

As far as Zorun could sense, no witnesses had survived. All proceeded as planned. He had kept a furtive, and necessarily distant eye on Uldyssian for several days, and the encounter with the merchant had proven just what the bearded spellcaster desired. The Ascenian had willingly separated himself from his herd and set things in motion just exactly as Zorun required them.

Just to be on the safe side, though, the mage ordered the

guards, "Go out and make certain that there are no survivors. Quickly, now."

They obeyed with some reluctance, clearly not comfortable with all he had done. Zorun watched them hurry out toward the ruined wagons. Again unbidden came the thoughts of what he could do with the power the Ascenian supposedly wielded. Of course, that made the guards a situation he would have to rectify.

The underbrush to his left shook as a hulking form dragged its burden toward him. Zorun had no difficulty recognizing Terul's too-small head.

"Ah! You have him! Splendid, Terul!"

The servant grunted, then brought the body closer. Daring at last to summon light, Zorun studied the Ascenian up close. "Not much to look at. A farmer, as they said. Hmmph! Still, more valuable than gold, eh, Terul?"

But the giant was gazing past his master. A deep frown spread over Terul's ugly countenance, and his thick brow wrinkled in apparent thought.

"Maybe not good, they come back," he suddenly declared in one of the most complete sentences that Zorun had ever heard him speak.

Terul's blunt comment reinforced the mage's own earlier concerns. He eyed the distant forms of the guards as they searched among the wreckage for any life. The mage came to a decision. "Yes. I wonder if I can continue the spell. . . ."

He bent down to the pattern he had earlier drawn in the soft ground. Part of it had been marred by his foot, but Zorun easily remedied that. He had drained himself with his earlier effort, yet somehow he felt that he still had enough for one last task.

Raising his staff over the pattern, Zorun Tzin gestured. He had designed this spell to be one where chanting was not necessary, for any noise might attract the attention of the target, or, in this case, targets.

The runes along his staff glowed slightly. A moment

later, illumination began to emanate from those in the pattern as well.

From the vicinity of the wagons came the rustling of leaves and branches. The shadowed figures of the guards gave no indication that they noticed anything amiss.

Zorun whispered a single word. "Jata."

As they had done before, the trees that still had branches and vines bent down. They reached with deadly accuracy for the six soldiers.

The first had no chance to scream. The vines wrapped around his mouth and throat and branches bore him into the foliage. A comrade nearby turned—

Branches seized him. He managed a cry for help, which warned the others. One guard made a leap for him, but the second man was already rising above the ground.

Their leader pointed in Zorun's direction. The four remaining fighters started toward him, their intentions obvious. However, two managed only a step before they were taken, and another barely more than that. They chopped at the insidious vegetation, but even with their sharp weapons, they could not make enough headway.

The officer was the last to disappear. He swore an oath at Zorun that colored even the mage's ears. Then the vines that encircled his neck tightened so much that he choked to death.

The trees dragged the remains above and out of sight. They would be deposited some distance from the area, where animals would remove any trace of them. Naturally, Zorun would also blame their deaths and disappearances on Uldyssian. As with the others, the Ascenian would be unavailable to protest his innocence.

Satisfied, the mage lowered his staff and kicked dirt over the pattern. He suddenly weaved uncertainly, his exertions too much even for him.

Fortunately, Terul was there to catch him. With the giant's assistance, Zorun mounted his horse. The servant then retrieved the still body of Uldyssian ul-Diomed.

Taking a sip of wine from a sack, Zorun Tzin nodded. The night's work had indeed gone well. He had bagged his quarry much more easily than even he had imagined. The mage swore not to be so humble about his own greatness in the future.

Zorun also finally swore not to tell the mage council that he had succeeded. He would just explain to them that Uldyssian had been waiting for him, that the Ascenian had, in his madness, slaughtered both those in the merchant's caravan and the council's noble guards. It would mean looking like a failure in the council's eyes—something that they would enjoy—but Zorun would know the truth, and that was all that mattered. After all, why should he turn over such a prize to them, who would only squabble over it? Better that Uldyssian ul-Diomed would be in the hands of one who best knew how to make use of his supposed gifts.

Zorun steered his mount around. "Come, Terul," he commanded, leaving to the servant, who had also mounted up, the task of guiding both his horse and the one bearing the Ascenian back to the city. There would be no difficulty entering Kehjan unnoticed, not even by the council. He was Zorun Tzin, after all.

"The soldiers' horses," rumbled Terul abruptly.

"Hmm?" The mage once again had to marvel at his servant's awareness. Yes, surprisingly, Terul was correct again; something had to be done with the extra horses. The council might wonder how all six animals had survived unscathed when their riders had not.

Of course, that was a situation more easily remedied than all previous. Zorun reached into a pouch and removed a small tube. He placed one end to his lips and blew.

The horse before him jerked, then collapsed in a heap. Two others fell just as easily. By the time anyone came across them, the potion in their bodies would have rotted away a good part of their carcasses. They would look as if Uldyssian ul-Diomed had cruelly slaughtered them along with the rest. Such a touch would only strengthen Zorun's story, which he was already formulating for the fools on the council.

"That should do very well, eh, Terul? The mage council will appreciate that I salvaged what little I could, don't you think?"

Terul grunted agreement.

Weary but feeling quite pleased with himself, Zorun Tzin rode on. Behind him, Terul tugged on the reins of Uldyssian's horse and, with a last grin at the unmoving figure, followed the mage.

In a place that was not a place, what seemed glittering stars swirled over an immense, black emptiness. Had there been someone to see those stars, he would have noticed in each a gleaming, mirrorlike scale.

And in each of those glittering scales, he would have seen a moment of his life. From the very beginning on into adulthood . . . and perhaps even the very end. Indeed, the lives of all who had ever been born on Sanctuary could be found among these scales.

The scales of what some might call—if they saw them arranged just so—a dragon but which was so much more than that.

His name was Trag'Oul, and he had existed since this world had been molded by the refugee angels and demons. The essence of creation that they had stolen to forge Sanctuary had included what was him. He had grown as the world had grown, and his fate was tied to Sanctuary as much as was that of the humans now populating it.

Because of that and because he knew the threat to Sanctuary of both the High Heavens and the Burning Hells, he had, with some hesitation, taken on a pupil, the very son of Inarius. He had called him Rathma after the Ancient had rejected his birth name, Linarian. Trag'Oul had found him quite the willing student and had imparted to him wisdom even the angels and demons lacked. And all the while Rathma learned, the two had, over the centuries, strived to keep Sanctuary from completely tipping to one side or the other of what Trag'Oul called the Balance. The Balance represented the equilibrium of the world. A descent into utter evil meant terrible destruction; a turn to the complete absence of evil meant stagnation and decay. The middle, where good and evil coexisted but neither had the great advantage, was, in their minds, the best and only choice.

But most of all, maintaining that Balance meant keeping the High Heavens from discovering the existence of the world, as the Burning Hells already had. The demons were kept in check not only by Inarius's efforts but by the dragon's as well. If the angels entered the fray, though . . .

Rathma, I would speak with you, Trag'Oul said to the darkness.

The cloaked figure suddenly stood below the shifting stars. "I am here."

We must prepare for the unthinkable.

"Must we? I am not so certain just yet."

For one of the rare times in his existence, the dragon was caught off-guard. *And why do you think such a thing?*

Rathma's cloak fluttered around him as if it were an extension of his thoughts. "If the High Heavens know about Sanctuary, why have they not swooped in en masse? There seems no point in delaying that."

They are studying Inarius and the Burning Hells, evaluating their positions.

"Sensible . . . but not if you include the hunter, Achilios, in the situation. He tried to slay Uldyssian, you know."

Which makes it more likely that it is your father who controls him. I fail to see your point. The stars reshaped themselves, becoming again a constellation resembling the long, serpentine creature of myth.

"It was not my father. I know that now with all certainty. I know where he is and what he has been doing. It was not he."

Then we are back to the belief that the High Heavens is aware of Sanctuary.

Rathma's brow rose. "Or but one of its august host."

But one? The stars realigned themselves as Trag'Oul digested this. *But one? Who, though, would come in secret, rather than immediately reveal Inarius's betrayal to the Angiris Council? There is none.*

"There is one. There is he who was closest to my father, as close as blood, despite neither having any. Yea, I might call him uncle, Trag, for as the angels count them, he and Inarius are considered brothers."

You cannot mean Tyrael.

There was a moment of silence, as if both expected that speaking this angel's name would cause him to appear. After a time, though, Rathma finally spoke, in a voice that, for humans, at least, could have barely been heard.

"Yes. Tyrael. I believe that the Angel of Justice has come on his own to judge his brother's crimes . . . and, in the process, Sanctuary."

Uldyssian awoke. At least, that was the best he could describe his change in condition. In truth, he felt somewhere midway between that and unconsciousness. His head swam in a manner that disconcerted him, making it impossible to focus.

But despite that disorientation, Uldyssian felt certain of one thing.

Inarius surely had him.

He could imagine no one else who could so easily trap him . . . and that made the figure who stepped before him all the more odd. He was dark of skin, with a long beard well kept. His eyes, though, were what garnered the most attention, for they pierced the fog of Uldyssian's mind as nothing else was able to do.

"You hear me, Uldyssian ul-Diomed? You hear me? I've kept you unconscious for the entire trip back, so you should be coherent enough now to respond."

Uldyssian tried to answer, but his tongue felt too huge, and his jaw seemed not to work. He managed a nod, which satisfied the robed figure.

"Good! Understand, then, that I am your captor. I, the great Zorun Tzin!"

He said this as if Uldyssian should know him and appeared slightly put off by the prisoner's lack of recognition. Zorun Tzin sniffed disdainfully, then went on. "They all feared you, but you proved quite simple to take, truly. I sometimes still wonder if it was even worth all I did, all I betrayed . . ."

Once again, Uldyssian tried to speak, with the same results.

"You shall be talking soon enough, rest assured, my friend! There is much I would learn about you before I decide just what should be done."

A huge figure lumbered past behind the spellcaster's back. For some reason, the brutish form seized Uldyssian's attention more than his captor.

Zorun glanced back. "Terul! Bring me that small black chest on the third shelf. Now!"

Zorun's servant stalked off to obey, but not before meeting Uldyssian's gaze. The captive felt the urge to say something but knew the futility.

"Does Terul upset you with his appearance?" the mage asked, misreading Uldyssian's reaction. "There are far worse things in the world. He's the least of your concerns, Ascenian . . . and I am your greatest."

He raised a staff that Uldyssian only now saw and muttered something. Various runes of the staff flared.

A scream echoed in Uldyssian's ears, but it took him a moment to realize that it was his own. Pain suddenly ravaged his body, as if every inch of his skin were slowly peeled away.

"It is only sensation now," explained the robed figure, "but soon it will be reality. I give you this demonstration to encourage you to be forthcoming with whatever answers I desire. Do you understand?"

"Y-yes!" That he could speak now in no manner pleased Uldyssian. All that mattered was the pain. His head still swam, enabling him to pay attention only to Zorun Tzin, nothing else. He still did not even know his surroundings, other than the bit of stone floor beneath the spellcaster's sandaled feet.

With a sweeping gesture of the staff, Zorun caused the pain to ease. From his left, the giant, Terul, returned with the box his master had demanded earlier. The servant did not give him the container but rather held it before Zorun.

The mage opened the box with the lid toward Uldyssian. Zorun eagerly peered within, then removed something. Clutching the tiny object in his free hand, the bearded Kehjani indicated that Terul should shut the box.

"Replace it on the proper shelf," he commanded the giant. As Terul departed, Zorun held up his hand for Uldyssian to see what lay in the palm.

Uldyssian tried to gasp, but it appeared that his captor had again sealed his mouth. He knew what lay in the spellcaster's hand, knew it far better than Zorun likely did.

It was a small piece of the same type of crystal as that of which the Worldstone was composed.

Whether it was actually from the monstrous artifact itself, Uldyssian could not say. He only knew that he had never seen such crystal anywhere else. If it were actually a piece, the son of Diomedes could only assume that Lilith, one of the Ancients, or some demon or angel had stolen it away from the caverns. Perhaps it had been part of one of the floating crystals constantly shattering around the main stone, or perhaps it had been stolen at the time of the Worldstone's creation. He could not say.

Indeed, all that mattered was that it was here, in the hands of Zorun Tzin.

"You sense the power inherent in this? Interesting. Perhaps you are more as the council said, after all. You like my little stone? It cost a dozen lives for me to obtain it, and in the decade before I became aware of it, apparently it cost twice that! All master mages or their agents. It is incredibly ancient, that much I know . . . and very useful for my spell-work, as you shall see."

He squatted down. Uldyssian's eyes followed, and for the first time he noticed the edge of some pattern written in chalk. It was likely the very pattern that held him in check. Zorun placed the crimson stone on one particular symbol, which flared as the crystal touched it.

"You would do best to be very cooperative," Zorun said as he straightened. "The stone will amplify the effects of everything I desire, including your pain."

The mage raised his staff. Again, the runes glowed.

Uldyssian screamed. Now it felt as if he were being turned inside out. He saw no change, but his attempts to deny the pain went for nothing.

As abruptly as the agony had begun, it ceased. Uldyssian would have let his head slump over if that choice had been allowed him.

The Kehjani chuckled. "What you experienced, Ascenian, can actually be done to you. I can turn your insides into your outsides. The stone is powerful enough to enable me to do that. I know, for I have tested it in that regard." He let that fact sink deep into Uldyssian's muddled mind. "An easy thing it would be, in fact—"

At that moment, Terul rushed into view. Zorun was not at all pleased by this interruption, but he listened as the giant tried to relate some imminent news.

"Upstairs . . ." the servant grunted. "Robes . . ."

The mage's expression radiated understanding. "Members of the council? Is that what you mean?"

Terul's tiny head bobbed up and down.

Zorun stroked his immaculate beard. "They cannot be here about the guards, as they've accepted the explanations for their deaths. Did they say anything to you at all about the reason for their visit?"

In reply, Terul could only shrug.

"Imbecile! Dolt! I shall have to deal with this immedi-

ately!" With a snort of frustration, Zorun waved the hulking figure aside. However, before departing, the spellcaster
paused to say to Uldyssian, "This will give you a moment
to put to order all information you will relate to me,
Ascenian. I suggest you have it all ready for when I return.
The questioning will begin in earnest then."

The mage vanished from sight. Terul remained behind,
the servant watching the direction in which his master had
gone.

Then an odd change came over Terul. The giant's expression twisted into something more *knowing*. His eyes once
again radiated the extreme intelligence that Uldyssian
thought he had briefly witnessed before.

Terul bent down and seized the crimson stone. A look of
avarice spread across his grotesque features. Up close,
Uldyssian noticed something else, a pair of odd lesions,
almost burns, near the left ear. They looked very recent.

"Mephisto smiles upon me," the servant rumbled as he
gazed up at the prisoner. His manner of speaking was now
more polished and in contradiction to the mind that such a
small head suggested.

Evidently, there came some sound that Uldyssian could
not hear, for Terul paused to glance to the side. Then, apparently satisfied that it meant nothing, the giant returned his
attention to Uldyssian. His eyes stared deeply into the captive's, and more than ever, Uldyssian was convinced that
Terul was far more than Zorun Tzin assumed him to be.

And possibly a deadlier threat to the son of Diomedes
than the mage was.

"Even this body, with all its brute strength, will burn out
much too soon," Terul informed him. "I thought it would
last a great deal longer, but perhaps the lack of a proper
brain has something to do with it. It would be interesting to
find out more concerning that. Later, of course."

Uldyssian had no idea what the giant was talking about,
only that it was hinting of a direction that he did not like in
the least. He tried to focus on his powers, but Zorun's pat-

tern kept his mind foggy where that was concerned. The spell enabled him to listen to whoever was in front of him but allowed little more than that.

"Poor Durram," Terul went on. "He provided me with more than I dared hope, but I knew that I wasn't going to make it to you, regardless of how quickly I raced through the jungle. I thought to cut you off near the capital—I knew you must go to the capital—but in pushing the priest's body so hard, I only burned it out more swiftly."

Terul's face continued to contort as he spoke in the unsettling, highly educated tone, and in the midst of those contortions, Uldyssian briefly felt as if he recognized something. Unfortunately, the spell on his own thoughts caused it to be a fleeting recollection.

The giant must have misread something in Uldyssian's face. "Fear not for that fool's imminent return. His arrogance, which I fueled by stirring all his spells to greater accomplishment, has left him open to more transgressions revealed than he imagines." Terul cocked his head. "And lest you suppose my chatter all this while idle, you might notice that the pattern below you has been slowly adjusted for my needs."

Even as he said it, Uldyssian felt powerful energies shifting around him. They constricted his will even more and amplified the effects on his mind to such a point that had an army poured into the chamber, Uldyssian doubted very much that he would have even noticed.

Indeed, there was for him only Terul. Nothing else existed for Uldyssian save the sinister servant . . . who spoke to the prisoner as if they had known each other for far longer than a few moments.

And somehow Uldyssian was certain that they had. He fought anew against the pattern's spells, struggling by physical, magical, and mental means to do something, *anything*.

One of Terul's overly shaggy brows rose. His dark eyes glittered enviously. "Such strength . . . the bitch chose well when she chose you, I will give her that much."

His words sent Uldyssian's tension to new heights. Terul could only be speaking of Lilith. Yet how could he know of the she-demon?

Uldyssian managed to recall what the giant had said earlier, that he had used a priest called Durram to reach this point . . . used his body. That meant that this was not actually Terul, not even a living being, then, but some malign *spirit* possessing the giant.

No, not possessing. That inferred that somewhere deep within, the servant yet remained. From what Uldyssian could see, this creature had engulfed Terul's spirit. Nothing, absolutely nothing, of the giant existed.

And now the malevolent shade intended to do the same with the son of Diomedes.

At that moment, the giant's eyes widened in pleasure. "Ah! All ready!" He gave Uldyssian a monstrous grin. "With the stone and the reset pattern, I will not have to worry about burning you out. I shall be whole at last! And your body will be the one with which I will raise a new sect, one where I and I alone am supreme Primus! Mephisto will reward me well, perhaps make me master of all men."

His tone again reminded Uldyssian of someone. It was at the edge of his memory . . .

"And wearing your body will be much more comfortable than wearing simply the skin of someone, say, like Master Ethon of Partha?"

His captive managed to gape. It all made terrible sense.

Terul laughed as recognition at last came to the prisoner. "Yes, I wanted you to know me well before I engulfed you, Uldyssian ul-Diomed."

Uldyssian would have shaken his head in disbelief and horror if that had been at all possible. The resurrection of either Lilith or her brother would have been only slightly more monstrous in his eyes.

Terul was possessed by the spirit of the High Priest of Mefis . . . Malic.

SIX

Serenthia felt the uneasiness strike her with all the suddenness of a lightning bolt. Something had gone wrong with Uldyssian's plan. She was certain of it.

Yet the fact that she had not been very pleased with his idea in the first place gave her pause. She had no right to supersede his commands based merely on her suspicions, no right at all. It was only a feeling, nothing more . . .

But, then again, she was an edyrem, and such feelings had a way of presaging actual disaster.

She sought out Mendeln, certain that he, of all people, would be able to look over her concerns with a proper analytical train of thought. He was where she could generally find him, at the remotest part of the encampment, speaking to three edyrem—a male Parthan and two lowlanders, one of them female—about something called the Balance and how death was merely a step to another level. On the one hand, Serenthia liked the thought of her father and mother still existing and even possibly watching over her. She also thanked whatever power Mendeln had drawn upon to bring Achilios back to her, albeit not quite as she would have preferred.

But there were other aspects concerning his newfound path that continued to unnerve her, especially his delving into matters concerning corpses and graves. There was also Mendeln's passing comment that he was never alone even when he was alone. From what Serenthia gathered, ghosts of the most recent dead were drawn to him, not an appetizing aspect to her.

He looked up at Serenthia before she had the opportunity to call out. He solemnly dismissed his equally solemn pupils. They silently ushered past her, and as they did, she noticed that they had taken to wearing black clothing such as Uldyssian's brother wore.

"They come to ask me questions," Mendeln said to her. "I but merely try to answer them . . . but that is not why you come, I know."

"Uldyssian—"

He cut her off, his expression darkening. "Uldyssian has been taken."

Cyrus's daughter was startled. "Did you feel something, too? How do you know? What exactly do you mean?"

"Calm yourself. Here is what I know. The caravan was attacked by foul magic. All were slain but him. He was the one sought by the spellcaster."

The news was even more terrible than she could have imagined. "When did you find all of this out?" Serenthia repeated. "I only just felt danger now!"

With a shrug, Mendeln replied, "Master Fahin told me."

The chill that she sometimes got around the younger brother returned. "Master—Master Fahin, too?"

"All . . . all save Uldyssian."

"And he? Is it the mage clans who have him?"

He drew himself up, a sign that he was not comfortable with what he knew. "One of them, at least. There were also men who perished who nominally served the spellcaster."

This brought some slight pleasure to Serenthia. "So, not all the scoundrels escaped retribution."

"They, too, were slaughtered by Uldyssian's captor."

"But that makes no sense!"

Mendeln shook his head. "Unfortunately, it does make sense, which is why I was just about to dismiss the others, anyway, and seek you out."

She tried to think. Something had to be done and done quickly. "Do you know where Uldyssian was taken?"

"He is in the city. The mage is an individual of some high

ability who calls himself Zorun Tzin. That is all I was able to find out. The spirits know nothing more, for they came immediately to me."

"Why?"

"Why what?"

"Why do they keep coming to you?" Serenthia asked with mounting frustration.

"Because it is so," Mendeln returned with another shrug.

Serenthia surrendered. All that actually mattered now was rescuing Uldyssian . . . if it was not already too late. "He's been taken to the capital, you say."

"Yes, likely to the abode of this Zorun Tzin, whose location even the shades of the guards do not know."

She had expected that. Serenthia also knew that they could not very well go and request that the mage clans return their leader. Somehow the merchant's daughter felt certain that Uldyssian would "vanish" to somewhere even more impossible to find.

"We have to go to the city," Serenthia determined. "That much I know."

"Yes, but may I point out that if we depart, the others are surely going to follow?" Mendeln gestured toward the rest of the encampment. "Even now, I suspect some of them, such as Saron, are beginning to feel the same uneasiness you did."

"Good! We'll tell them what you told me, and then we'll all march on Kehjan. Make the mage clans or whoever else is in charge find him, or else. All Uldyssian wanted to do was speak with them, and this is how they treat him!"

"They will see such numbers as a threat to the capital, Serenthia. They will see it as an attack."

She was undeterred. "It may very well be one if they don't return him to us safe and sound! Is that so wrong? Would you do less for him?"

Uldyssian's brother let out a great sigh. "No, though I wish the options presented to us were different. We will do as you suggest."

"Good!" Serenthia turned from him. "In that case, we'd better waste no time in alerting the rest."

She left Mendeln in her wake, at the same time shouting out Saron's and Jonas's names. Mendeln watched her for a moment and then, with a shake of his head, reluctantly followed.

"This will not be good," he muttered under his breath. "This will not be good. . . ."

It was *Malic* . . . the same Malic who had callously and horrifically had the lord of Partha and his young son stripped of their flesh so that he and one of his morlu could use the skins for trappings in order to fool Uldyssian. Malic, who served the order of Mefis—in reality, the demon Mephisto. Malic, who had been the right hand of Lucion, the terrifying master of the Triune.

And though Malic had suffered some justice when he had inadvertently attacked Lilith in her guise as Lylia—and thus perished as Ethon and his son had—the high priest had returned as a spirit bound to a bit of bone procured by Mendeln. At the time, Mendeln had utilized it to help them against Lilith, for she was the one thing that Malic hated more than Uldyssian. The spirit had done his task as commanded, guiding Uldyssian through the dangers of the main temple.

However, there had come a point in one corridor when Malic's specter had commanded Uldyssian to throw the bone fragment. Accepting that there had to be a good reason, he had obeyed. A moment later, the piece had struck hard the forehead of a priest—Durram his name.

Circumstance and Lilith had forced Uldyssian to abandon any attempt to retrieve the bone fragment, and he had assumed it and Malic's dread shade lost in the collapse of the temple. Now Uldyssian saw that he had been very, tragically, wrong.

And that mistake was going to mean oblivion for him, and his body and powers serving a man who was pure evil.

"We—or, rather, *I*—will be long gone from here by the time that fool Zorun can dare return. It was easy to sow holes in a story so full of holes already. I have manipulated his thoughts all along since taking this giant's body, building on his own vanity. That he would imagine his paltry power the reason for capturing you so easily! He was only able to do it because I, who know you so very well, my old friend, provided the true effort. I knew the chinks in your armor and played upon them." The face of Terul lit up in amusement. "And it all went so well that even I was astounded!"

Uldyssian listened. It was the only thing he could do, and it was his only tool. Malic insisted that time was on his side, but the more his prisoner appeared to pay attention, the more the high priest went on and on, like Zorun Tzin, so very proud of himself.

It was a danger of wielding such powerful skills, Uldyssian knew. He himself had already fallen prey to his ego more than once, and perhaps the fatal journey with the unfortunate Master Fahin was a grim reminder of that. Again, Uldyssian had believed himself infallible, untouchable. *He* had everything planned perfectly . . . or so he had thought. It now seemed so audacious, so ridiculous, to have assumed that he could just walk into the capital of the eastern half of the world and demand the right to speak with its leaders without fear of treachery or repercussions.

"Yes, I shall be able to make use of your body much, much better." Terul—no, *Malic*—clutched the fragment tight as he stepped toward Uldyssian. The giant's grin grew exceedingly sinister. "Now, is there anything you might like to confess, my son, before I grant you absolute oblivion?"

Uldyssian struggled to clear his head but feared it was too late. Malic's alterations of the mage's spell had done nothing so far to weaken its hold on him. True, that had been a desperate hope at best, but it had also been Uldyssian's *only* hope.

"Nothing? Well, we shall begin, then." Malic touched the

piece of crystal to Uldyssian's chest. The high priest quietly started to chant—

And at that moment, a warmth spread from the stone into Uldyssian. At first, he thought it part of the priest's spell, but then the haze that prevented him from concentrating began to clear. His strength returned. . . .

But the change in him did not go unnoticed. Malic's brow furrowed. "What are—?"

The spirit got no farther. Just as he had while in the jungle with Mendeln, Uldyssian let raw emotion take hold. There was no time to do otherwise.

A furious orange glow erupted from his chest where the fragment touched.

The giant let out a howl as the fiery force burned away his skin, his sinew, and all beneath. The grotesque face became more so as the ravaging energies tore away Malic's lips and eyelids. Then the eyes melted to empty sockets, and the jaw fell slack.

Uldyssian's tormentor fell back in an ungainly heap.

At the same time, the spell holding the son of Diomedes prisoner finally dissipated. Unfortunately, that meant that Uldyssian, worn and beaten by not only his effort but Zorun Tzin's tortures, dropped hard to the floor. He was unprepared to protect himself, and the simple fall left him battered and, more important, stunned.

What at last stirred him were what seemed to be voices, or maybe just one that echoed over and over in his head. Uldyssian rolled onto his side and was greeted by the stomach-wrenching sight of the scorched corpse. The crisp fingers of one hand twitched, and for a moment, Uldyssian thought Malic yet survived, but then the body fell motionless again.

Not certain if he would be able to repeat what he had done should Zorun Tzin or someone else now came upon him, Uldyssian now had only one desire: to be as far away as he could from the mage's sanctum. Away . . .

And so he vanished.

• • •

Zorun could not understand not only why three of the most
senior mages serving the council's enforcement arm had
taken it upon themselves to come to his abode but why they
had questioned absolutely everything he said as if they already knew he spoke lies. He sensed no truth spell and
knew that, as gifted as they were, this trio— even tall,
spindly Nurzani—did not have the power to cast one that
he, Zorun Tzin, could not in a moment ferret out.

The three stood before him like reapers, each wearing the
orange and brown voluminous cloaks with the narrow,
high-peaked hoods of the enforcement order. Kethuus
could barely be seen within his hood, his skin nearly as
black as shadow. Only his wily eyes were really visible.
Amolia, who traced her bloodline to the Ascenian colonists
whose descendants now filled much of the northern part of
the capital, was in comparison like a ghost. Her skin was as
pale as ivory, and Zorun knew that a full day in the sun
would not make it different.

"The Merchants Guild is insisting on a full investigation
into Master Fahin's death," Amolia had smoothly been saying. "And we, naturally, concur."

Zorun had expected that; some of his counterparts made
good use of the merchants' trade routes and ties to gather
items that they needed for their private work. Fahin's
death, while not affecting Zorun, had likely badly set back
the spellwork of several of the council.

Still, he had given them answers that should have completely satisfied everyone when first he had informed his
employers of his "failure" and Uldyssian's "bloodthirsti-
ness." It had been quite simple to think of just what to say
at the time, as he had afterward told Terul.

So why now did even Zorun have trouble with his own
story?

"I will be happy to provide the facts again, when a hearing should convene," he replied, knowing that he could say
nothing less. By the time a hearing was put together, the

loose threads that had begun appearing in his story as if by magic would be dealt with.

"Consider it to be convening now, Zorun Tzin," Kethuus murmured.

Emaciated Nurzani—whose powers for good reasons Zorun most respected—raised a bony hand. A yellow aura briefly coalesced around Zorun's front doorway. In a deep and startling baritone, the skeletal mage boomed, "By vote of the council, the mage clans give us right to begin a formal inquest into your actions, second son of Liov Tzin."

That any of them would invoke the name of his famous father was not a good sign. It was a sign that Nurzani did not worry about offending Zorun by pointing out that he was neither his sire nor his sire's firstborn.

Caught off-guard, Zorun thought feverishly about what to say next, at the same time wishing that something would distract the trio from this inquest.

And that was when the building shook. Rare vials and other arcane objects that sat in places of honor in his public room—as Kehjani called the elegant chambers that guests to their homes were initially ushered into—came crashing down. Zorun did not need to see the faces of the others to know that they felt the rush of untamed and powerful energies radiating through the floor and walls. Even an utterly untalented street vendor would have sensed them.

But he, unlike Zorun, would have run as far away as he could from the source . . . not turned and raced *toward* it.

Yet Zorun had no choice. Something unfathomable had happened below, and his only hope of salvaging anything was to discover the truth before the others could.

"Z-Zorun Tzin!" Amolia called as she sought to keep her balance. "You are not—not given permission to leave!"

Ignoring her, the bearded mage leapt through an inner doorway, then sealed it magically behind him. That would buy him a few minutes at best, but a few minutes meant all the difference. As he descended the stone steps leading to his true sanctum, Zorun sought in vain a logical reason for the unknown disaster. Terul would have touched nothing. Terul had been beaten enough to know never to touch anything his master did not order him to touch. Yet the spellcaster had to assume that something had gone dreadfully wrong with the pattern that kept the Ascenian at bay and that somehow his manservant had to be at least partially responsible. Otherwise, that meant that the Ascenian had destroyed all the holding spells by himself.

Perhaps the stories he had heard had actually *underplayed* Uldyssian ul-Diomed's might? Zorun could not believe that. Still, what other answer could there be?

He burst through the wooden door at the base of the steps, the staff ready for whatever protective spell he needed. Yet within there was no immediate threat, but instead absolute ruin.

The walls of the chamber were blackened, as if a terrible fire had rushed through the room. All the treasures, tools, and other arcane items that Zorun had gathered over his long life had been reduced to ash or melted globs.

But most important, the pattern had been eradicated, and of his captive there was no sign.

Zorun swore. Without Uldyssian, he had nothing with which to bargain with the others. His head was now on the block, a turn of events that he could have never foreseen. He was Zorun Tzin, after all! One against one, there were few his equal.

But against three who represented the power of the mage council . . .

Already he could sense their approach. They had gotten through the first doorway but would find an invisible barrier halfway down the steps. That gave Zorun a few more moments . . . but to do just what?

He thought of the crystal fragment, but a survey of the pattern did not reveal it. Naturally, Uldyssian had seen its value and taken it.

Then he cast his bitter gaze down upon the sorry sight of his servant. Zorun almost spat at the corpse, again blaming

Terul for certainly playing *some* part in the mage's downfall . . . but then he noticed the fingers of one hand seek to open.

The giant was still alive, if barely, and in his hand, he kept a feeble hold on the crystal.

As impressed with his own good fortune as he was with Terul's refusal to die, Zorun Tzin closed on the hapless figure. The crystal would balance matters out. How exactly that would happen had not yet occurred to the spellcaster, but it was a straw he was happy to grasp.

Not at all fearing a burnt man's touch, Zorun sought to pluck the fragment free.

As his fingers wrapped around the fragment . . . Terul's ruined ones wrapped around both. Tightly.

Zorun Tzin groaned. The world around him felt as if on fire. Something burst through that fire, a monstrous black shape that lived on pure hatred—hatred for one man, the spellcaster belatedly sensed.

The Ascenian, Uldyssian.

And then that which had been the great Zorun Tzin was engulfed.

The three mages burst into the lower chamber, ready to mete out punishment on the obviously guilty member of their calling . . . only to find nothing but destruction. The entire underground room had been ravaged by fearsome magical energies, the evidence of its intensity displayed graphically by the corpse of what they knew to be Zorun's halfwitted servant.

But of the culprit, of Zorun Tzin himself, there was no sign.

Amolia all but floated about the chamber, inspecting shelves and corners with practiced eyes. Nurzani bent to examine the fragments that were all that remained of a pattern recently drawn. Kethuus went to investigate the body and the object next to it, the missing mage's rune-enchanted staff.

"There is nothing of value left on the shelves, and they themselves do not hide a secret path out of here," Amolia declared after completing a circle. "The corners and the shadows likewise hide no avenue of escape that my arts can unveil."

From the pattern, Nurzani boomed, "This was originally designed not only to hold something powerful but also to disrupt its ability to concentrate. But someone has altered the design in a manner not of the mage clans' teachings."

"So Zorun attempted something unusual?"

"These few lines here are not from our ways. They remind me . . . of the Triune."

Amolia glided closer. She peered down at what Nurzani indicated. "We suspected that Zorun had taken one or two survivors for questioning . . ." What happened to members of the Triune was of little concern to the mage clans, so long as their fates did not reflect publicly on the spellcasters. "Perhaps one of them escaped."

"Zorun Tzin, whatever we think him, could certainly handle a priest of the Temple," the gaunt mage replied with a snort.

"Indeed. Kethuus, you are oddly silent."

The shadowy figure remained bent by the corpse. "This was Terul, of course, but there's something odd about him. It feels as if he was slain *days* ago, not mere moments."

"The halfwit answered the door; he hardly looked dead then."

Kethuus grinned mirthlessly. "Perhaps his little brain hadn't yet registered that fact."

The other two joined him. Amolia prodded the body with her sandaled foot. Part of Terul's rib cage caved in.

"He suffered far more than the rest of this place. He was the focus of the attack."

"The giant would be the least of any prisoner's problems," the dark mage responded. Then, shrugging, he added, "But I concur that he was the focus."

Nurzani emitted a disgruntled sound that brought him

to the attention of the pair. "And has no one else considered the even more significant clue before our eyes?"

Amolia's gaze narrowed. "What is that?"

He pointed near the corpse. "Zorun Tzin has left his staff. That staff is a prize to any mage, yet Zorun Tzin has abandoned it. Why?"

Neither other spellcaster could give him an answer . . . and that bothered all three so very much.

Oris fretted like a mother as she strode past the elegantly carved twin doors for the hundredth time that day. They remained sealed even from the very guards standing just outside them. The Prophet had not been out of his personal chambers in days, something the gray-haired priestess could find no reference to in all the journals kept by herself and her predecessors. He had *never* gone into such seclusion, and thus she feared the worst.

"You do yourself and him no favor worrying so, dear Oris," the voice of Gamuel called. The other senior priest strode down the shining marble corridor like a warrior, which he had been until the Prophet had shown him the light. Gamuel was a little younger than Oris and had not held his post quite so long, but he was every bit as devoted as she. "He likely has good reason for what he does, and if he deems us worthy of sharing in that knowledge when he emerges—and he will emerge, Oris—then you'll see how silly it was to fret."

"You would think that he might wish us to know how he is so that we can assuage any concerns of the flock," she returned. Oris did nothing to hide her love—her *physical* love—for her master. She had been a beautiful woman when she had first come to the Cathedral, and traces of that beauty remained in her oval face even now. However, the Prophet had only seen her as he had all the rest: as one of his children.

Still, Oris had never told even Gamuel a suspicion that she had about their leader, that his heart had once belonged to another female, one who had been unworthy of him. Oris was certain that this was one of the reasons he had not chosen her when she was young. Now that she resembled more his grandmother, there were a thousand other bitter reasons.

But still she loved him, and like wife, mother, and grandmother combined, she tried to take on whatever she imagined his troubles as her own burden.

Gamuel politely took her by the arm so as not to embarrass her before the guards. "As for the flock, some matters have come up that must be discussed immediately."

The distraction worked. Oris became the veteran that she was. "The peasants' army? Has it regrouped?"

"Somewhat, but, as you know, they were just a necessary sacrifice to awaken the people to the fanatics' true nature."

Both paused to make a momentary prayer to those who had perished futilely attacking Uldyssian ul-Diomed's followers. The Prophet had explained that the dead would have an honored place in the teachings of the Cathedral.

Finishing her prayer, Oris asked, "Then what is it?"

"We knew that the Ascenian intended to go speak with the mage clans, the guilds, and probably even the prince, but something happened, and he disappeared, leaving many dead in his wake."

The priestess nodded gravely. "I had thought it the Prophet—"

"And it may be. He'll tell us if and when he chooses. That's not important now. What's important is that the Ascenian's people now know he's missing, and his rabble's only two days from the gates of the capital even as we speak!"

Oris paused in mid-step. She stared into the broad-shouldered man's face, seeing that he was not exaggerating. That made her immediately look back at the sculpted doors. "He *must* know of that! He wouldn't let them march on the city without doing something about it. He must come out now and tell us what to do next!"

They stood there, even Gamuel—caught up by her declaration—expecting the Prophet to fling open the doors and stride out to ease their troubled minds with some great plan.

But the entrance remained sealed.

SEVEN

Uldyssian had no notion where he stumbled or even how he had gotten there in the first place. He only knew that he had to keep going. His explosive effort against Malic, with what he had already suffered at the hands of Zorun Tzin, had left him like one of Mendeln's walking dead.

He was not even certain where he was anymore. Vaguely, Uldyssian noted others on the streets through which he wended. Mostly dark of skin, not light like home. Toraja? Hashir? No . . . those were in the past. Where was this? Kehjan? Yes, that was it. The capital.

The capital. Who was it he had needed to see here? Not mages. Uldyssian dared not put himself in the hands of mages. At the moment, they were to him as treacherous a lot as the Triune or the Cathedral.

Who else, then? There had been someone. Master Fahin. He had mentioned someone. Who—

A prince. Uldyssian recalled a prince. Amrin? No. Emrad? *Ehmad.*

"Ehmad," he gasped. "I need Ehmad. The prince . . ."

He weaved past shops and places where raw foodstuffs were sold, occasionally blundering into someone. Most of the Kehjani tried to pretend he did not exist, although a couple muttered something in a vile tone as Uldyssian brushed past.

To one who merely glanced at the ragged figure as he traversed the capital's high-walled, narrow avenues, Uldyssian appeared to be wandering aimlessly. He staggered into one area, then another. Yet even though he himself did not realize it, he headed exactly where he needed to.

The two white horses reared when the stranger stepped out of the shadows before them. Trained not only for the task of pulling a chariot but also to defend the ones riding it, they sent their hooves crashing down at Uldyssian.

But somehow, not one hit. As the son of Diomedes registered the animals' presence, the horses grew oddly quiet. They stepped back, then waited.

The charioteer, who had been shouting at the beasts, grunted in approval of himself, in the mistaken belief that it had been his efforts that had enabled him to regain control. Behind the soldier, standing with one hand on the rim of the golden chariot, a young, handsome figure in equally resplendent breastplate and metal kilt peered at the cause of the near collision. Rich, dark brown eyes focused on the Ascenian in the path.

Less interested, the charioteer raised his whip to ward off what he no doubt thought a beggar or madman. However, his master grabbed his wrist.

"Prince . . . Prince Ehmad . . ." Uldyssian uttered, weaving to and fro at the same time.

"Yes, that is who I am." The voice was strong and full of the confidence of youth.

"Master Fahin . . . he said to find you . . ." Mentally, Uldyssian began to feel more himself, but physically he was exhausted.

"Master Fahin." The prince's expression grew calculating. "Sehkar. Help him onto the chariot."

"My lord," growled the charioteer. "It was ill advised enough to take this ride without escort, but to bring this—whatever he may be—so near your person—"

"Do as I command, Sehkar."

With much grumbling, the driver handed the reins to his master, then leapt out to deal with Uldyssian. The son of Diomedes eyed the man warily but then glanced again at the prince. Ehmad gave him a polite nod that somehow put him at ease.

"Come, you!" Sehkar commanded, grabbing for Uldyssian's arm. Around them, a crowd had begun forming.

The soldier's arrogant attitude drew Uldyssian's sudden ire. He glared at the man, instinctively summoning his power.

At that moment, Prince Ehmad called out, "Treat him with respect, Sehkar!"

The charioteer relaxed his hold. Uldyssian fought down his anger and, with it, the potentially explosive repercussions.

With Sehkar guiding, the pair joined Ehmad. The prince himself assisted Uldyssian up.

"Thank you," Uldyssian managed wearily.

Ehmad inspected him. "You are no beggar. Your bruises, they seem the eager work of someone. You mention Master Fahin. You knew him?"

It suddenly felt as if the entire world sat upon Uldyssian's shoulders. "I was there when he . . . when he died."

"You—" The noble gave him a tight-lipped smile. "It seems good fortune smiles upon me today to have run across you so accidentally."

"It wasn't good fortune. I wanted to find you."

Prince Ehmad looked around them. "Indeed! I think it best we talk more at my palace. Take us there, Sehkar."

"Gladly, and with haste," muttered the charioteer. He cracked the whip and, as the horses started running, tugged hard on the reins in order to make them turn.

The crowds pushed back as the prince's chariot shifted around. Prince Ehmad waved to the people, who cheered him. Uldyssian could see that their enthusiasm was real. They truly liked the young man.

He wondered how they would feel if they knew who their prince had in the chariot with him.

Sehkar cracked the whip again, then gave out a yell. The horses picked up the pace. The chariot and its riders swiftly left the crowd behind.

But not before Uldyssian caught an ever so brief glimpse of a familiar face among them, a face he had not expected to see.

The brooding face of Zorun Tzin.

HE ...

   HE ...

Inarius had sat in utter darkness in the chambers that he used as the Prophet, sat in the silken chair staring beyond the walls. Staring at a place he had ceased calling home centuries ago.

HE ... THAT VERMIN THAT SHE SEDUCED ...

He did not wear the guise of the Prophet now, but more or less had resumed his true form. Inarius had no fear of discovery; an army of his acolytes could not have breached the doors, and no one with even the hearing of a bat could have noted a sound within.

ULDYSSIAN . . . SPAWN OF A FOOL NAMED DIOMEDES ... HE DARED DO IT. ...

Inarius had not moved since his return from invading the mortal's dream, but now he leapt up, wings spread in glorious fury and arms outstretched in righteous anger at this latest sin.

HE ... ULDYSSIAN ... HE DARED BRING ME PAIN!

It should not have been possible, but it had happened. During his intrusion into the human's dreams, Inarius had easily manipulated the mortal's mind, letting him believe that his powers were no more. He had done it to give Uldyssian the chance to beg for forgiveness, beg for the chance to be one of the angel's flock again.

But instead of seeing sense, the sinner had dared *strike* him! Indeed, although Uldyssian imagined that his attack had failed miserably, it had, in truth, seared through Inarius, disrupting for the slightest of moments his very resonance.

For just that brief moment, the angel had been, by mortal standards, *dead*.

And while Inarius was not mortal, he had experienced the emptiness of a universe without him, and that had shaken his very foundation. Not even in the battles against the Burning Hells had he come so close to such a fate. Oh, he had felt pain before, especially during battles against the demons, but this had been something far different—and the work of a mere human, yet!

Uldyssian ul-Diomed had to be punished for his grave sin. His life had to be crushed, his very existence cursed by all, then, finally, all knowledge of his abilities erased from the memories of the rest of the mortals. It was the least he should suffer for all he had done.

And with him had to go the edyrem. Inarius had considered one method or another of bringing the rest back into the flock once Uldyssian was pacified, but they were tainted with the same filthy traits as Linarian, worse even. Whatever alteration on the Worldstone Lilith had done had created a thing more foul than their son.

Indeed, Uldyssian himself had also altered the Worldstone, and in a manner impossible. Inarius hesitated as he recalled that. One reason he had wanted to turn the mortal to his cause was that he wanted to make Uldyssian reverse the change in the artifact's crystalline structure. He needed the fool to do it, because every attempt by the angel, who was not only bound to the artifact but drew upon it for his tremendous might, had gone for nothing.

NO . . . HE MUST DIE. . . . THERE MUST BE ANOTHER WAY TO HEAL THE STONE. . . . EVEN IF I MUST START WITH ONLY IT AND NOTHING ELSE IN ALL OF SANCTUARY . . .

A thousand methods by which to punish the human properly for his transgressions coursed through Inarius's mind, but each had a fault. They all required the angel to confront Uldyssian directly. He saw no reason for that. Uldyssian was beneath him, not even as worthy as a worm crawling in the ground. There was no need for Inarius to debase himself by such close contact again, no need. It had nothing to do with the unexpected pain; it was merely unworthy of the angel.

But . . . if it was a task unworthy of him . . .

Inarius stared at the sealed doorway, then suddenly gestured.

The doors flung open.

GAMUEL, I WOULD SPEAK WITH YOU, MY CHERISHED SERVANT. . . .

The powerfully built priest dropped the scroll from which he had been reading and quickly abandoned his private quarters. He had been doing his best to monitor matters concerning the capital since his conversation with Oris, feeling that the Prophet would expect it of him.

To his further astonishment, he arrived to find the doorway wide open. The guards saluted him sharply as he neared, their spirits revived by their master's "awakening."

"Gamuel!" Oris came charging from another corridor. "I was just alerted by a guard. When did—"

"I can't speak now. The Prophet has summoned me!"

She looked disconcerted. "Summoned *you*? What about me? I heard nothing from him!"

"I only know that he summoned me, and the summons was urgent," Gamuel responded with as much patience as he could muster. "Really, Oris, I must go to him!"

The female priest did not argue that point, but neither did she slow. Clearly, it was her intention to join the audience, and Gamuel would not stop her. The Prophet would bid her to leave if he did not wish her there.

Gamuel reached the entrance. Oris followed at his heels and then halted as if striking an invisible wall. She tried to step forward but instead moved *back*.

The male priest eyed her sympathetically as he continued on. The Prophet had made his will known. This audience was for Gamuel only.

The doors shut on Oris's disbelieving face. Gamuel forced her from his thoughts. He doubted that she had offended the Prophet in some manner; the master merely had some thought that he believed Gamuel could better discuss alone with him.

What it was, the priest could not fathom.

The golden-haired youth awaited him not on the long, elegant couch where he often rested but in the very center of the chamber. The Prophet stood not in repose but in what Gamuel would have taken for—had it been any other person—pensiveness. The Prophet's hands were clasped behind his back, and his eyes watched with impatience the priest's swift steps.

Gamuel went down on one knee before him. Bowing his head low, he muttered, "Forgive my sloth, great Prophet! I sought to be as the wind but fell short. . . ."

"We all have our failings, my child," the glorious figure declared. "And so when we fall to them, we do seek to quickly make amends, do we not?"

"In whatever manner I can, I shall! I swear!"

The Prophet touched him lightly on the shoulder, causing Gamuel to look up. "You are a man of many skills, Gamuel. You are one who has also lived so many aspects of life, however short human life is."

"I've gone down . . . several paths," the priest agreed. He did not like to talk about his past endeavors, especially those related to his years as a soldier and, on occasion, mercenary.

"And if some paths led you astray from the light, they did also teach you much that helped make you who you are today."

The master's words touched Gamuel, who still retained some guilt for events in his past. Each day, he tried to live as the Prophet preached, using the Prophet's own life as his example.

"Rise, my child."

The priest obeyed.

The Prophet proudly looked him over. "Good Gamuel, you were once well skilled in the arts of war, especially."

"A sorry time for me. I try to forget—"

His answer brought a reproving glance from his master. As Gamuel let his head drop, the Prophet quietly remarked, "Lies ill become you. You still practice moves in your private quarters, then pray for my forgiveness. You are yet every bit the warrior that you were when first I found you."

"I . . . am . . . sorry!"

"Why? The Cathedral has its Inquisitors. Are they so different?"

Trying to look dignified, the broad-shouldered priest returned, "Master, you know what I did as a . . . a fighter. My sins are as great as those of all the Inquisitor guards and officers put together!"

"And yet you stand at my hand, do you not?"

"A miracle of which I feel unworthy."

The Prophet granted him the glory of a smile. "Would you seek to feel more worthy? Would you wish to prove yourself as none other can to me?"

Gamuel now understood why he alone had been summoned. The Prophet had a special task for him! The priest's eyes brightened. He was honored beyond belief. "I would give my life and soul, if it must be!"

"As you should, my child, and as you might. This is no easy affair. I must trust that nothing will deter you from seeing it through."

"I swear, nothing will! Nothing! Just tell me what I must do!"

Steepling his fingers, the Prophet calmly said, "I grant you the glory of personally removing from life the sinner Uldyssian ul-Diomed."

Despite the bluntness with which the words were said, it took Gamuel several seconds to understand them. Then, as realization struck him, he put on an expression of fanatic determination. "I shall bring his head to you!"

"His death shall be enough. You have the skills, both

with the spells I have taught you and, more important, the training of your life."

Beaming, Gamuel stood straight. "Consider it done, master!" Then a brief hesitation came over him. "Forgive this one question . . . but for so long, Oris and I urged something to this effect, and you forbade it—"

The eternal youth nodded. "And now I do not."

It was enough of an answer for one so devoted as the priest. He bent low again, kissing the Prophet's hand.

"It shall be done, master."

And because he kept his head low, Gamuel did not see the hardening of the young face. "Yes, I shall make certain of it, Gamuel. I shall . . ."

Mendeln assisted Serenthia in leading the edyrem as they marched on the city, but he knew that if it came to it, hers would be the orders they would follow. That suited him, for he felt uncomfortable leading armies.

They met with no resistance the first day. The villages that lay in their path emptied of people before they neared. Mendeln was glad about that, for it meant less chance that innocents would suffer. However, he knew that would soon change, for there was no chance that the capital itself might be abandoned. There, some would try their best to slaughter the edyrem.

However, it turned out that they did not have to wait until the capital for their first confrontation. The mounted patrol the edyrem encountered numbered a good hundred men and, to Mendeln's eyes, had likely been created by combining two or three smaller patrols. The men were grim of aspect and obviously well aware that they were tremendously outnumbered, but they held their ground.

In a scene reminiscent of the encounter with Master Fahin's guards, the chosen captain demanded that they turn away.

"We mean no harm," Serenthia responded, her tone hinting that she found the officer's order absurd under the circumstances. "You'd best move aside."

The Kehjani patrol did no such thing. The captain tried one more time. "You are ordered by the august authority granted to me by the grand capital to either disperse or surrender yourself to my control!"

In the front ranks, Jonas and some of the other edyrem laughed defiantly at the officer's demand. Serenthia herself wore a smirk.

Mendeln grew worried. Taking the forefront, he said, "There is no need for concern, captain. If I could—"

A soldier went flying off his horse. Some of the edyrem laughed as he landed hard.

The captain wasted no time in drawing his weapon. "Arrest them!"

And as quickly as that, pandemonium broke out. The mounted guards charged. Edyrem rushed up to meet them. Mendeln looked to Serenthia for assistance in curbing the violence, but she was at the head of those going into battle.

No! This should not happen! This destroys any hope of peacefully rescuing Uldyssian! But only Mendeln seemed to see that. The edyrem had given in to their emotions yet again. Like Uldyssian in the jungle that night, they let their powers control them more than they controlled their powers.

The Kehjani soldiers paid the price for that. A hundred armed men on horseback were nothing to thousands of edyrem. Mendeln did not have to see the struggle to know that the riders were being torn to ribbons without so much as landing a glancing blow against the invaders.

In desperation, he forced his way toward Serenthia. Only she could make the others listen, but first he had to make *her* do the same.

Only because of the edyrem's almost-inherent unease of him did Mendeln manage to reach her quickly. He seized Serenthia by the arm and tried to pull her back.

Her fury startled him. "Mendeln, you fool! Let me go! Now!"

"Serenthia! Look what is becoming of you—of all of you!" Even as he spoke, a soldier let out a horrific shriek.

Mendeln saw the head and an arm go flying through the air. "This is the work of beasts, not men!"

"They brought this on themselves! They—"

Mendeln had been surrounded by ghosts so consistently that he paid their presence little mind save when he required an answer to something. Rarely did they speak without being spoken to.

Yet now there came from more than one a sense of impending threat that made the black-robed figure not only ignore his friend's demand to be released but instead pull her harder toward him.

The arrow did not hit her, as clearly had been intended. Instead, the angle sent it soaring into his shoulder with such velocity that Mendeln was thrown to the ground.

That alone brought Serenthia to her senses. She grabbed for him even as he fell, resulting in her dropping with him. Around them, the edyrem continued forward unchecked.

"Mendeln! Mendeln!" The merchant's daughter used her body to protect his from the crush.

While he did not have his brother's remarkable recuperative powers, Mendeln did have other resources upon which to call. He used the techniques that Rathma had taught him for reducing pain, managing to bring the searing agony to a dull, insistent throb. "I—I will be fine, Serenthia . . ."

"I'll make the soldier who shot you pay, I promise."

He clutched her forearm tight. "Serenthia . . . do not blind yourself. The bolt was not meant for me."

"No, but it hit you because you tried to save me!" Her eyes burned with fury.

"Listen! I said not to blind yourself. I want you to gaze at the arrow, which should not have come so close to you in the first place save for one obvious reason."

She finally looked—truly looked—and her mouth went slack. Serenthia shook her head.

Like Mendeln, she easily recognized an arrow crafted by Achilios.

"He would not—he would not try to slay me—or even you!"

"He would." Uldyssian's brother seized the shaft. Summoning all he knew from Rathma and the dragon, he worked to free the arrow. "He already tried with Uldyssian."

As he freed the shaft, Serenthia quickly put her hand to the wound. It healed so quickly that even Mendeln, who knew how powerful she was, gasped in surprise.

Around them, the flow had slowed. There were few sounds of violence. It was already too late for the soldiers, and Mendeln mourned that terrible mistake. How could they peacefully approach the leaders of Kehjan now?

But that was a point of contention for later. Serenthia knelt over him, unable to believe this latest vile betrayal by her love. "He would never! Not Uldyssian!"

"He did. That night when my brother and I took the two bodies beyond the encampment—" Mendeln grimaced at the memory of what had nearly happened. "It was a miracle that Uldyssian survived."

"What do you mean?"

"You know Achilios's marksmanship. He would have hit your heart with ease. I was fortunate enough not to be the target and so only received this—simple wound."

"And Uldyssian?"

"Any nearer the heart, and he would have been instantly slain. Somehow, though, Achilios just missed. He never *just* misses . . . unless he wishes to."

This brightened Serenthia's mood. "You see? He would've done the same for me!"

"Let us be grateful that we did not have to see whether that was true or not. And it does not excuse him for trying, does it?"

"But he saved our lives against that giant demon! Why would he then try to slay us?"

"Not him . . . another. An angel, I believe, who is *not* Inarius."

She shook her head in disbelief. "Not possible. There is no such being!"

"More than possible, I am afraid, especially to Rathma and Trag'Oul, who have been suspiciously absent. What they know, I would like to also."

"Does this—does this other angel work with Inarius?"

Mendeln finally felt well enough to rise, which he did with her assistance. He eyed the arrow as he straightened. "I doubt that he does, at least directly. He is an enigma that we have little time to solve, especially now that we are at war with Kehjan."

Serenthia glanced around, for the first time noticing the subdued atmosphere. She knew as well as he what that meant in terms of the lives of a hundred men. "It couldn't be helped, Mendeln! It couldn't!"

"There is so much that 'couldn't be helped,'" he retorted almost bitterly. "So much. What are the edyrem—what are you and Uldyssian—becoming, Serenthia? I saw his powers consume his mind, just as I saw them do the same to you and the rest here. As you grow more comfortable in them, they grow more dominating of you."

"Ridiculous!" Her tone suddenly bordered on anger— anger at him. "Maybe you're just a little envious, Mendeln!"

He had seen that same look just before the edyrem had rushed the soldiers. Mendeln quickly diverted Serenthia back to the other subject. "You know that Achilios would not wish to slay you, that this arrow—" He held the feathered end before her eyes. The anger at him faded, replaced by sorrow at the archer's continued absence. "—was intended for you by another. Another angel, I am certain of that."

"But Achilios missed!" the dark-haired woman said proudly. "He missed both of us despite that!"

"Indeed . . . and what do you suppose that angel will think of that, Serenthia?" Mendeln tried not to imagine the hunter at this very moment. "What do you suppose he will demand of Achilios for that failure?"

The color drained from her face.

• • •

Achilios was caught between relief and concern. Mendeln's unexpected reaction had saved the archer from possibly succeeding despite every iota of his will striving for the opposite. When he had discovered that Uldyssian had survived, Achilios could only assume that it had been his own powerful determination that had made the difference. That had been his one hope when finally commanded to fire at Serenthia.

He was glad that Mendeln had made it unnecessary for him to find out if he had been right.

Once again, Achilios had fled even before the shaft neared its target. He was now deep in the jungle, although the path had been a more meandering one than last time. The edyrem were moving into more and more populated areas, which meant individual settlements in unexpected places. Neither he nor his tormentor desired him to be seen.

And even as he thought of the angel, Achilios felt his limbs slow. He came to a stumbling halt in a densely overgrown area that allowed so little light that he almost felt as if night had fallen again.

His body no longer obeyed him. Achilios wondered if he was to fall unconscious again, as had happened in the past. For one who was dead, unconsciousness was an unsettling thing. Achilios had been afraid of waking up buried or being burned.

When more than a minute passed and he still stood there, the archer finally lost his temper. He knew that it was ill advised to rail against the being but did not care. Achilios had already been forced to try to kill the two people dearest to him. What more monstrous thing could the angel expect?

Monstrous . . . angel, The irony of such thoughts all tied together was not lost on Achilios.

At that moment, the familiar glow erupted at his side. Despite its brightness, no one but Achilios was near enough to notice it.

"All . . . right! I did your damned work again . . . but someone outsmarted you! I saw it as I was fleeing, and I know bloody well that . . . that you did, too!"

THE BROTHER OF ULDYSSIAN DID NOT SAVE HER.

"What?" The words sent a sudden panic through the undead hunter. "No! I saw the shaft . . . the shaft miss her! She's alive! She's got to be—"

The ethereal warrior formed in the light. Somehow the blazing energy that radiated where his eyes were supposed to be seemed to hint at pity for Achilios. *YOU MISUNDER-STAND. SHE LIVES, BUT IT WAS NOT HE WHO SAVED THE FEMALE. THAT WAS YOU, ARCHER, JUST AS BEFORE.*

He could not have given the blond hunter a better answer. Achilios grinned wide—an image that would have frightened any mortal seeing him—then gestured defiantly at the winged figure. "I did it? I beat you then! Kill them . . . kill them both . . . you commanded . . . but I didn't."

He said this expecting—nay, *hoping*—that the angel would grow so incensed that he would destroy Achilios on the spot. Then there would be no possibility of the archer being forced to try over.

But no celestial fire burned him to cinder. Instead, the heavenly light around the winged being dulled. The tower-ing figure cocked his head.

NO. YOU DID NOT, . . . AND THAT MAY CHANGE EVERYTHING.

EIGHT

The palace consisted of four rounded buildings surrounding a fifth one several times their size. Small, decorative points topped each. The main entrance was a wide, columned affair that could only be reached by a lengthy series of wide stone steps.

Six columns flanked each side of the brass doorway. Every column had been carved to resemble some animal respected by the ancient Kehjani builders, including the great cats of the jungle and the massive, prehensile-snouted creatures the lowlanders used for heavy burdens.

He was ushered inside by the prince, who seemed far less in awe of himself than his followers were. Uldyssian marveled at such a lack of ego from one who clearly had the hearts of many in the capital.

Perhaps he was not the first to show some indication of this, for as they walked down a corridor filled with brilliantly painted images of human and jungle life, Ehmad cheerfully informed his guest, "I have no true standing in Kehjan, you know. The mage clans and guilds such as the merchants rule outright here. If they wished, one of them could just come in here and have my head!"

Uldyssian doubted that it would be as simple as that. Ehmad's rivals would then probably have an insurrection on their hands that even the mage clans could not suppress. If Master Fahin was an example, there were even those among the guilds and clans themselves who willingly supported the young noble.

A black-haired girl in a low-cut blouse and billowing, gauzy leg coverings raced barefoot to greet Prince Ehmad. In her delicate hands, she held a small, decorated tray with a silver goblet atop it.

Ehmad gave her a smile that made her giggle. However, instead of drinking from the goblet, he proffered it to Uldyssian. "You look like you could use this better, my friend!"

Unable to argue, Uldyssian gratefully accepted the drink, which proved to be one of the sweet wines that he had heard were favored in the capital. Parched, he swallowed it in only three gulps.

Retrieving the goblet from Uldyssian, the prince gave it to his servant. "Kaylei, bring us tea and some fruit at the Balcony of the Chadaka King."

"Yes, my prince." Kaylei bent low, then retreated from their sight.

There were few guards around and none near Ehmad himself. The prince walked with Uldyssian as if they were old friends, not two strangers who had met but a short time ago. The son of Diomedes finally decided that the young noble was either very reckless or very daring . . . or both.

And then Ehmad surprised him further by casually commenting, "You are not at all what I expected, Uldyssian ul-Diomed."

Suddenly, all the courtesy and friendliness struck Uldyssian as nothing more than false front. He leapt back from the prince. The few sentries reacted immediately, charging toward the duo with spears ready.

"No!" shouted Ehmad at the men. "To your places."

It said something for his command of them that the guards obeyed without hesitation. Ehmad's dark eyes studied Uldyssian.

"I will have my little jests, won't I? They will get me killed, my mother used to say. Judging by your expression and the fact that your hands now glow the color of molten iron, I suspect that I came closer than I first imagined."

Uldyssian looked down at his hands and saw that the prince had not exaggerated. His hands were now a burning orange and radiating a similar heat.

"I'm sorry," he told Ehmad, mentally willing the hands to return to normal.

But they did not.

Unaware of the truth, Prince Ehmad took Uldyssian's continued display as distrust. "I knew who you were the moment I saw you. Master Fahin saw to that."

"Master Fahin?" As he listened, Uldyssian concentrated harder. The glow emanating from his hands cooled, then finally disappeared. The heat dwindled away a breath or two after.

"You did not know? Master Fahin, he sent a pair of messenger birds on the night he agreed to bring you to the city. He wished me to know in advance of your coming." The handsome youth looked sad. "He was a strong supporter and a stronger friend. . . ."

Uldyssian looked down at himself. "You knew who I was even though I resembled a beggar?"

"I had but to look into your eyes. Master Fahin was right about them." What that meant, Ehmad did not say. Instead, he gestured to a corridor on the right. "Come, let us go to the Balcony of the Chadaka King."

Their destination was indeed a huge balcony overlooking a good portion of the northern part of the city. It also had, as Uldyssian had expected, images of chadaka, the large tailed primates he knew lived in the nearby jungle. Although they were not the only primates worshipped in Kehjan, the chadaka were considered the cleverest, and in the lowlands, he had come across many myths of their king, whose antics taught valuable lessons about pride and rule.

The floor itself, a mosaic masterpiece using hexagonal pieces, had an array of chadaka kings scampering about. The rails were also carved to resemble chadaka kings trying, sometimes unsuccessfully, to sit in contemplative repose. There were chairs—brass ones with padded seats—near the edge, for which Uldyssian was grateful. He had managed a second wind once discovering that he had found Prince Ehmad, but that wind was failing him now. He all but fell into the nearest chair.

"Forgive me," declared the prince. "I should have given you a place to sleep."

"I don't dare right now."

"Ah, but all men must sleep. Even you, I imagine."

"Not now . . ." Still, the chair felt more and more comfortable.

With a shrug, Ehmad sat not in the other chair but rather on the stone rail. His expression grew more serious. "What happened to Master Fahin?"

That question stirred Uldyssian back to waking. Summoning his wits, he told Prince Ehmad everything he could recall. The prince's eyes widened as he heard about the magical attack, then narrowed at the death of the well-liked merchant.

"I have . . . sources . . . who say that you are responsible, my Ascenian friend. Sources who heard this among the mages."

"I would've never killed Fahin or any of the rest. That work was done by one of their own, Zorun Tzin."

The name did not appear to surprise Prince Ehmad. "Zorun Tzin is known well to me. He is a jackal among men. For too long, the bickering mage clans used him for that which they dared not soil their own hands with." The Kehjani studied Uldyssian closer. "He is very formidable."

But speaking of the spellcaster reminded the son of Diomedes of something—or, rather, *someone*—more sinister. "There're things more formidable than Zorun Tzin."

"Yes, you, for instance, as you escaped his sanctum so readily." At that moment, the serving girl returned with the tea and fruit her master had requested. She set both trays on a tiny marble and iron table next to Uldyssian's chair. "Please. Eat and drink at your convenience."

Uldyssian did not argue, digging into the fruit and even risking some of the tea. Despite the heat of the region, he expected the tea to be hot. However, Uldyssian found it not only cool but sweet with the scent of some nectar.

"Taiyan tea," his host explained. "It will help rejuvenate you."

As he poured a second cup, Uldyssian said, "What of Zorun Tzin?"

"From all you describe, it sounds as if the mage clans will have to deal with the beast that they themselves loosed upon you. Master Fahin had friends and alliances with many of them. Zorun Tzin will be outcast even from his own blood. You need not concern yourself with him."

But Uldyssian still recalled the fleeting glimpse. Tzin had followed him through the streets, and the look Uldyssian had read in the mage's eyes had indicated a hatred for the son of Diomedes that was nearly as deep as that of—

He jerked straight. The cup of tea slipped from his grip. The delicate container shattered on the floor, spilling tea.

"No . . ."

Prince Ehmad leaned close in concern. "You are ill?"

Uldyssian rose. "Prince, I must speak with the mage clans immediately!"

"And I have begun to send out entreaties to them and the top guilds, my friend. I did so the moment after I'd read Fahin's messages. It will take a little time—"

But the prince's guest was only half listening. How could he have not seen it before? Uldyssian berated himself for a fool despite the fact that his powers were only now enabling him to recover from the horrors of the mage's sanctum. Yes, he had seen the figure of Zorun Tzin in the streets. . . .

But the eyes had been those of Malic.

"You don't understand, prince!" Uldyssian growled. "There's a new concern for the mages that they need to know about before he's got a chance to take over one of them!"

"I must admit, I am at a loss. I have no idea what you are talking about—"

"Neither do we," came a cultured female voice, "but we are certainly willing to listen . . . for the moment."

Both men turned to see a trio of figures who could not have simply walked onto the balcony behind them. Uldyssian took up a defensive stance. He knew what these had to be.

However, Prince Ehmad boldly—or possibly fool-hardily—stepped between his guest and the mages. "Nurzani," he said to a spindly figure that looked like something Mendeln might have summoned from the ground. "My greetings, Kethuus," the noble then declared to one who seemed more shadow than man. At last, to the woman who had first spoken, Ehmad finished, "And ever, ever a pleasure, my beautiful Amolia . . ."

Unlike most females Uldyssian had thus far seen, Amolia did not react to Ehmad other than to nod slightly. However, as she pulled back the odd, high-peaked hood, Uldyssian nearly let out a gasp, for Amolia was close enough in appearance to Lilith's guise of Lylia as to be her sister. Clearly, she came from the stock that the demoness had used for her disguise.

She noted his staring, and the flaring of her eyes warned him against any impudent action.

"You are Uldyssian ul-Diomed."

"I am," he replied, not relaxing in the least. He stepped around his host. After Fahin, Uldyssian did not want Ehmad also paying a price for his friendship.

But all the woman did was say, "The prince has introduced us." Her two companions left their own hoods up. "You spoke of the traitor and murderer Zorun Tzin."

Uldyssian measured each of them but could not decide just who was the most dangerous. "I did. I need to warn the mage clans—"

"You warn us, you warn them. You wish to speak to them, you speak to us."

This was not how Uldyssian had intended it, but he had no choice. First, the spellcasters had to be warned of the danger in their own midst. That in itself might create an opening he could use to forge some sort of alliance against the Cathedral.

"First, have you found Zorun Tzin?" he asked.

"It should be obvious that we have not."

"I mean, when was the last time anyone saw him?"

"We saw him last." Amolia glanced at her two companions, then continued, "Just before he fled to his underground chambers. Something must have happened—and we assume it concerned you."

"It did, but not as you think. Tzin had a servant, too, the giant."

"Terul. We saw what was left of him. Your work?"

Uldyssian dared not deny it. "But not for the reason you think. That thing was no longer Terul. I don't know for how long that was true, but I suspect he'd already possessed the giant when Zorun Tzin chose to slaughter Master Fahin's personal caravan."

"You verify it was Zorun who slew all?" asked the one called Nurzani in an incredibly deep voice. "That is what was suspected."

"Yes, he did it . . . but there was another who enabled him to do so with such . . . completeness. It was he who possessed the servant. You know him by the name of Malic."

Amolia frowned. "As in the high priest of the Order of Mefis? Malic, who is, by our best reckoning, dead?"

The son of Diomedes reluctantly nodded. "Dead . . . but deadly still."

He explained to them what had happened to Malic and how the priest had been brought back. Uldyssian described his shock when Terul had admitted to being the spirit of the priest come back for vengeance and then his desperate battle to escape the vile specter. He left out only the stone, not certain if it was something that he wished to bring to the attention of the mages.

"And how does this pertain to Zorun Tzin?" the shadow called Kethuus demanded. "You said that you killed the giant."

"I thought I did . . . but I think Malic still survived in the body long enough. I saw Zorun Tzin in the streets just after the prince found me . . . only now I think the eyes weren't his."

Nurzani leaned toward Amolia. "Recall the mage's staff lying abandoned as if of no consequence. A priest would not require such."

"Malic's accomplishments were known well to the mage clans," Kethuus interjected, "but to move on from host to host after death, that sounds too incredible!"

Amolia glared at Uldyssian. "It was not the high priest's skills that enabled him first to cheat his doom, but the questionable acts of two brothers . . . but yes, I think Malic capable of perverting it further still."

"But the bodies don't last," pointed out Uldyssian. "How long Tzin's might, I don't know."

"Zorun Tzin was a spellcaster of exceptional skill and questionable judgment," the female member of the trio stated. "But his physical worthiness would certainly not make him my first choice should I be in such a state as you claim Malic is in."

"I'm making no claim! I'm speaking the truth! If your people find Zorun Tzin, they've got to make certain that they don't touch him." Uldyssian remembered something else. "And watch for black lesions. I think they worsen as the body burns out. . . ."

He expected the three mages to act immediately, but instead, Amolia looked to her two companions. The trio stood in silence, simply eyeing one another.

Then, without a warning, Kethuus vanished.

"Word has gone out concerning your suspicions of Zorun Tzin," Amolia announced. "Now we turn to the question of what to do about you, Uldyssian ul-Diomed." Her gaze narrowed dangerously. "What, indeed . . ."

And suddenly, an emerald sphere materialized around him.

• • •

This body was not going to last for very long. Malic knew that the moment he had taken it, but his choices had been very limited at the time. He had managed to linger in the corpse of the giant for far longer than even he had thought possible. Mephisto had surely been smiling on him when the fool spellcaster had reached for the crystal.

That piece remained in his hand, although for what reason, Malic did not yet know. He was not certain that he would have time to use it to amplify his transfer to another host. For that matter, who was to say that his next victim would be one worthy of keeping permanently?

Only Uldyssian thus far matched the criteria.

He kept to the shadows, using what he knew of his own spells to hide him from the inner sight of the mages. It was more difficult to cast properly in this body, for its former occupant had been of a calling using other forces. Given time, Malic supposed that he could have adjusted, but time was not on his side.

He had to find Uldyssian. No other body would suffice.

Malic passed a barrel whose top was covered in moisture. On a dread hunch, the high priest peered as best he could into the water. The image was distorted but still clear enough to reveal a dark spot near his left ear.

"So soon . . ." he muttered in Zorun Tzin's voice. Malic had barely even worn this body! It had taken two days for the lesions to start on the giant, and Durram's young form had lasted *weeks* before the first had grown evident.

"Time grows shorter with each one," the specter realized. "I must have you soon, Uldyssian."

But first he had to find his quarry and escape a city full of mages who thought him a renegade from their ranks. For that, Malic would need another body already, one that would hold for a time. It would do him little good to switch to a host that would fail him almost immediately.

Then a sudden suspicion made him crouch further into the shadows. A moment later, a cloaked figure stepped into the alley in which he had gone. The figure carried with him a staff, marking him immediately as one of Tzin's fellow mages.

As if to make matters worse, another mage appeared at the opposite end. He, too, wielded a staff. Both men slowly wended their way toward each other, with Malic in the midst.

But hidden in the dark, the undead priest was not concerned. He had seen the trappings of each man and knew exactly what to do. After all, he was still a servant of Mephisto, was he not?

As the pair closed, Malic drew the proper symbols in the air, then thrust a finger at the mage on his left.

At that very moment, his target saw him. Raising the staff to shoulder level, the spellcaster growled, "Stand there, Zorun Tzin! You are my prisoner!"

Unperturbed, Malic pointed at the second of his pursuers.

That mage also raised his staff. "You presume too much, dog of Harakas! He is mine!"

"Sarandesh pig! Like all your clan, you seek to steal instead of earn your prize!"

They confronted each other as if Malic did not exist. The Harakasian mage thrust one end of his staff at his Sarandeshi counterpart. The latter countered the attack. The two magical staffs clattered together with a flash of unleashed energies.

"Crawl back into your mud hole, Sarandeshi!"

"I'll wipe such words from your ugly face, Harakasian!"

The Sarandeshi rubbed a glowing rune on his staff. A red aura began to form over his adversary.

The other spellcaster immediately touched one of his own runes. A golden glow formed around the red, devouring it.

The two let out guttural cries and went at each other, using both physical and magical means. They fought like two frenzied cats, nothing existing for them but their mutual hatred.

And as they fought, Malic calmly slipped past them. The power of his master, the Lord of Hate, had once again been proven supreme. His two would-be captors would either slay each other or have to be forced apart by any other mages who found them. Either way, the distraction would serve Malic well.

But he needed to do more. As he slipped from one alley to the next, the spirit considered carefully. The Triune was in ruins; there would be no help from there. His lord Lucion was also no more, a victim of Uldyssian. . . .

From Zorun Tzin's lips erupted a curse at his own stupidity. He was in *Kehjan*. The capital. He was *not* alone.

The city was the culmination of generation upon generation of building, often over the sites of older structures. The current populace had little, if any, notion about parts of their home's past. Malic, however, knew much.

The entrance he sought was completely hidden from those who trod upon it. That had been done for aesthetic reasons in part, but also for reasons of safety. The depths below were dark and dangerous and, in places, populated by things undreamed. The underside of Kehjan's history could be found there in the form of stolen and lost treasures and the bodies of the dead.

It was simple for Malic to locate the hidden lever in the decorative column on the corner of the next alley. The lever, barely an inch long, creaked with age as it finally moved.

Next to the column, a portion of the street dropped open. Malic leapt down into the hole. Then, when the stone did not move back into place as it was supposed to, he struggled to close the hole again. Zorun Tzin's body made the task more difficult, the mage obviously not as concerned with physical superiority as the high priest had been.

Once Malic had finally sealed the hole again, he climbed down a cracked and ancient set of stone steps into a blackened chamber in which the rush of water could be heard. The small globe of light Malic summoned revealed dark, turbulent waters pouring through a canal as wide as the streets above. The depths of the canal could not be made out, but he knew that a man could disappear below with ease.

Aware that the hunt continued above, Malic scurried along the edge of the canal deeper and deeper into the maze of tunnels. The system ran underneath all of Kehjan but rarely was visited by those above, unless some terrible blockage occurred and water levels rose to threaten the streets. The mage clans would also be loath at first to search for him down here, for different and more deadly reasons.

And it was for one of those reasons that the spirit had ventured into this hellish place.

Rats, serpents, and other vermin fled from the unaccustomed light. Some of the creatures lacked any eyes, generations of breeding in darkness making such features useless.

Something bobbed in the water not far from Malic. He paused to inspect its familiar shape.

The body had been down here for some weeks. Much of the flesh had been nibbled away, but enough remained to keep part of the corpse intact. It had been a man of middle age and, from the looks of his garments, fairly prosperous. A robbery victim, no doubt. There were few who would venture down here, but bandits were among that lot.

In fact, ahead he heard a pair of voices in argument. They spoke with the accents of the low caste, and their argument appeared to concern the division of spoils, in this case a ring and a jeweled broach.

"The ring I'll take," declared one. "I cut it off his finger, so's it's mine!"

"Never so! The broach, it'll be harder to sell! You take it. You said he'd have gold! If'n I can't have gold, I deserve the ring."

Around the corner, an old brass lamp on the ledge illuminated a pair of scruffy figures in beggar's rags. They paused in mid-argument when Malic, his glow light dismissed, appeared.

"Who's this?" growled the one who had cut off the finger of their absent victim. He was short and wiry and, other than some missing teeth and a few scars, looked in relatively good shape.

His partner, on the other hand, while taller and fuller, clearly suffered the first stages of some disease that would eventually eat away his flesh.

"I want his sandals," snarled the second, indicating Malic.

The high priest did nothing until they were nearly upon him. Then, with one hand, he slammed his stiff fingers into the throat of the larger bandit, while with the other, he seized the wiry one by the chest.

The taller thief fell back against the mossy wall, clutching his ruined windpipe. His partner stood frozen, caught by Malic's magic.

The spirit reached into a pouch and removed the bit of crystal. He thrust it into one open hand of the thief, then closed the fingers. Malic then thrust his will into the man before him—

And suddenly, he stared out of different eyes at the slack-faced figure of Zorun Tzin.

The mage slumped into his arms. Malic let Zorun fall from him into the dark water. The dull splash echoed through the ancient tunnels.

Next to him, the second bandit struggled to breathe. He stared at what he thought was his partner and reached out a hand for help.

Malic pressed him against the wall with a strength inhuman. He pulled from his new host's waist a dagger.

"Not fit for me," the spirit whispered to the choking, frightened man, "but fit enough for what I seek."

He brought the dagger up and, as the bandit squirmed, cut a simple, shallow pattern over the chest. Streaks of blood dripped down.

When that was accomplished, Malic placed the blade in his teeth, then reversed his grip so that he could now set the fragment directly in the center of his design.

The other bandit grew more frantic. His struggles intensified, nearly causing Malic to lose the crystal. The spirit grew incensed. He forced his victim to look straight into his eyes.

Caught by those eyes, the thief froze. Malic began muttering under his breath.

A slight bubbling sound caught his attention. He kept his gaze on the bloody pattern but spoke faster.

The bubbling suddenly intensified. It was now not far from him. Out of the corner of his new eye, Malic glanced toward where Zorun Tzin's corpse floated.

The body bobbed up and down—then, with a swooshing sound, it vanished beneath the surface.

Malic went back to his chanting. The tunnel had suddenly grown quite cold. In the dim lamplight, both his breath and that of the hapless bandit could be seen.

Something erupted from the black waters, rising well above Malic's back.

Without the least sign of concern, the spirit turned around. Behind him loomed a bone-white thing that resembled some of the jellyfish of the inner sea. Yet this apparition was several times his size, and in the center of the translucent mass, two pale, bulbous orbs fixed on the puny human figures.

A forest of leafy tentacles hung under the fiend, each one arrayed with serrated edges. Fragments of meat and other grisly objects hung from many of the appendages, but they were not nearly so horrific a sight as within the boneless mound that was the creature's body. In there, already dissolving, was the carcass that had once been Zorun Tzin.

In addition to droplets of water, other things fell from the monstrous creature, inedible bits of the mage's clothing.

Malic faced the beast. "You understand the hidden tongue, demon! You answered it."

A thick bubbling sound escaped the fiend.

"My master is Mephisto, brother to your master . . . Diablo. . . ."

Again, the demon bubbled. By this point, there was hardly anything left of the dead mage save a few bone fragments, including the skull.

"By the pact of the Three, you must bow to my power. You must obey my will! Understand?"

Some of the leafy appendages moved. Malic recognized this as an affirmative response. He smiled.

"You must have a better sacrifice, though. That is also agreed upon by the pact. A living sacrifice, not that sorry appetizer you just swallowed."

The hundreds of appendages shook more vehemently.

"He is yours," Malic said, stepping aside.

The demon's limbs sought the remaining thief. Malic waited until the first had seized the man, then released his hold.

Suddenly granted the ability to move, the cutthroat screamed and tried to pull himself free. He might as well have been a fly caught in a web, though. His struggles only served to tangle him more, and the serrated edges of the demon's appendages cut into his flesh with ease.

Malic watched with patience as the beast's victim was drawn up shrieking into the gelatinous cavity. Within, a thick liquid swept over the unfortunate thief. Despite his damaged throat, his screams continued for several seconds. Then, even as his skin started to slough away, he finally stilled.

As the demon began the process of digesting its latest meal, Malic spoke to it again.

"Now you are truly bound. Your magic is mine. First, you will give me the power to keep this body longer than the last." He did not have to explain what he meant by that, for the demon saw him for what he truly was. "That will buy me time."

The creature waved its appendages, signaling acknowledgment.

With a smile worthy of his old self, Malic went on. "Then we shall begin the process of finding again one Uldyssian ul-Diomed."

ΠÍΠΕ

Furious at the mages' duplicity, the son of Diomedes glared. Struck by his will, the emerald sphere shattered easily. Uldyssian stepped out of its wreckage to confront the two remaining mages.

Amolia's eyes widened perceptively. Kethuus grunted in what sounded like admiration.

"Is this all there is in Kehjan?" the son of Diomedes angrily demanded. "Deception and betrayal?"

Kethuus gestured. What seemed like frost settled over Uldyssian's shoulders, then turned into something harder than rock.

But even that was not enough. His fury mounting, Uldyssian shrugged.

Amplified by his power, the shrug easily sent the frost flying.

"Stop this!" ordered Prince Ehmad to all of them. "Stop this now!"

To Uldyssian's surprise, the mages stilled.

The prince stepped around until once more he stood between the two parties. He glared at the mages especially.

"The palace has been dictated to be neutral ground, my dear Amolia," the young noble said pointedly. "No mage shall cast upon another mage. You've violated seven wards by attacking him."

"He is not of the mage clans," the blond enchantress replied. "The covenant does not cover him."

"Are you certain?"

Amolia glanced back at Kethuus, who cocked his head.

The pair did not respond further to the prince, but neither did they follow up on their attacks.

Ehmad turned to Uldyssian. "Please forgive what happened, Master Uldyssian. It was an error of judgment."

Uldyssian did not see it that way, but for Prince Ehmad's sake, he nodded.

To the female spellcaster, the prince continued, "He wishes to speak to the mage council and the leading guilds. Is that not so, Uldyssian?"

"Yes."

"Amolia, would it not make for simpler conversation and likely more coherent answers if Uldyssian stood before both of his own free will?"

From the woman, Ehmad received only a curt nod.

"I would recommend that you arrange it, at least with the mage clans. I know whom to speak with concerning the guilds. Uldyssian can talk to both at the same time, so no one's feelings are hurt."

Kethuus let out a slight snicker at this last comment, a snicker that vanished quickly the moment Amolia glared at him.

Pretending not to have noticed the incident, Prince Ehmad went on, "And as Master Fahin did before me, I place myself as Uldyssian's sponsor in this, with all the protections my name gives."

"Are you sure that will be enough?" the woman muttered.

"I think that's all there is to say," the prince concluded, folding his arms.

Kethuus stiffened. Even though she did not face him, Amolia appeared to sense the change.

"They thought they had him," the shadowy mage announced, his eyes staring off. "But the rat slipped through the trap!"

"They found him that quickly?" asked Uldyssian, impressed despite mention of the escape.

"No renegade mage can hide from the clans in this city," Amolia explained with some arrogance. "All spellcasters have agreed to leave a small piece of their essence that is hidden away until such an occasion occurs. It did so now with Zorun Tzin as it has with others in the past."

"That sounds very risky to all mages, especially if one of the council decides he wants Kehjan for himself."

"It requires three-fourths of the council to open the way to where what we gave is secreted. There is no chance for catastrophe or betrayal."

Uldyssian was not about to argue, but he felt that the spellcasters trusted in themselves too much, especially considering the feuds that had been going on. Worse, now that he had nearly been caught while in Tzin's body, Malic would surely seek another, and very likely that one would *not* be one of Amolia's ilk.

"We will see what the council desires," she finally agreed. "But do not be surprised if they reject hearing a farmer speak to them about what they should and should not do with their training and skills."

"That isn't what I plan," Uldyssian snarled.

Neither Amolia nor Kethuus replied to that. Instead, the pair stood side-by-side . . . and then vanished.

With their departure, Prince Ehmad let out an exhalation of relief. "Thank goodness! I feared that if you and they continued fighting, this entire balcony might go."

"I'm sorry for my part."

Uldyssian's host waved off his apologies. "Conclude this matter with the clans and the guilds without more chaos and bloodshed. That is all I ask of you, Ascenian."

The son of Diomedes nodded. "And that's all I want."

But as night fell, there came neither word concerning Zorun Tzin nor any gathering before the mage clans. Prince Ehmad assured Uldyssian that the latter simply had to do with the usual bickering between the spellcasters about how best to arrange matters.

"They will argue this point or that point and eventually come to the same conclusion that they would have if they had not argued at all. It is the same with the guilds, of whom I am also awaiting word still."

The hunt for Uldyssian's former captor continued to result in nothing. Since the one sighting early on, Tzin—or Malic, rather—had utterly vanished. To Uldyssian, that meant that the high priest probably had already taken another host. He could now be *anyone*.

Explaining this to the prince was simple enough; knowing what to do about it was another thing. Ehmad assured him that he would pass this on to Amolia and the others, but to Uldyssian, that was not enough. Malic would come for him again, of that he was certain . . . and that meant that anyone in the fiendish spirit's path might become a victim.

Ehmad refused Uldyssian's suggestion that the son of Diomedes should find shelter elsewhere. "First, unless this dread shade knew that you had left here, he would still attempt to infiltrate the palace. Second, if you leave the palace, the mage clans may use that as an excuse to say that you are no longer under my protection. They are opportunistic like that, Master Uldyssian."

"You make me wonder if it's worth dealing with them at all. You make me wonder if there's any room for trusting them."

"Oh, there is. When they swear to an oath, they will keep it. You must just be certain of the wording."

Ehmad left Uldyssian with that less-than-encouraging thought. The prince had provided him with a sumptuous room the likes of which the former farmer had not experienced even as the guest of Ethon of Partha. The plush, rounded bed—much softer than he was used to—had a high, richly woven canopy upon which the beautiful aspects of the jungle had been set. Various animals and flora were intertwined in images that proved restful, not jarring, as Uldyssian first thought. Two golden lances, crossed at their centers, occupied each corner.

The entire motif of the room was typical of what, as a simple villager, Uldyssian would have found garish. The brilliant reds, oranges, and golds were a sharp contrast to the forest colors that one found in a farmer's abode. Uldyssian's people had never had much opportunity to adorn their homes so; they were too busy trying to earn a living from the soil.

On his right, there were two large filigreed windows facing the northern end of the city. A gauzy curtain likely made of silk subdued most of the light from without. Uldyssian had quickly learned that the capital never completely slept; there was always something going on. He marveled that people could go about their lives, especially considering the monumental and deadly events of which he was not only a part but a major cause.

His thoughts returned to Mendeln, Serenthia, and the others. For some reason, as the day had progressed, Uldyssian had grown more and more concerned about them. It was as if something was wrong, but what that was, he could not say. He was afraid of actually reaching out to them, for fear that if all was as he had left it, they would suddenly grow more disturbed themselves over his safety. Uldyssian did not want the edyrem acting hastily. Anything that eliminated his chances of garnering the mage clans' and the guilds' support against the Cathedral meant calamity.

But a sense of uneasiness continued to grow within him. After some debate, Uldyssian decided to try to reach out to Serenthia alone. He would do his best to reassure her quickly that all was well. There was no need to worry her about Malic's return, at least for now.

But as he started to call to her, one of the lights outside grew more distracting. No matter which direction Uldyssian turned, it seemed that either the light or its reflection caught his eye.

The solution to his problem was simple enough. Rising, Uldyssian sought a thicker set of curtains flanking each window. He started to draw one across—and then halted. Uldyssian stared at the distant light, trying to identify where it came from. It was far, far away, well beyond where he would have expected it. It almost seemed beyond the city walls, but what so distant from the palace would still be so bright?

Then what sounded like a low growl made him jump. Uldyssian glanced behind but saw nothing. He stood there, poised to defend himself, and finally decided that he had imagined things.

Exhaustion seized him. Abandoning any interest in the light, Serenthia, everything, the son of Diomedes stumbled to the bed. He threw himself on it, then rolled onto his back. Desiring nothing more than sleep, Uldyssian stared up at the comforting patterns in the canopy.

Serenthia and the edyrem came to mind again. Feeling guilty, Uldyssian struggled back to consciousness and tried again to focus on her. Staring up at the canopy, he imagined the jungle there as the same one where she and his brother could be found.

As his focus increased, the imagery above him was defined, becoming almost real. He could hear the jungle sounds and imagined some of the animals actually being there at that very moment. Uldyssian heard their cries. He saw himself in the jungle, not far from his followers.

Somewhere along the way, his eyes closed—and then snapped open as a thick, feline growl erupted.

Uldyssian was surrounded by jungle, but not that through which he had so long trekked. Instead, he was in the midst of a strange, brightly colored jungle. The trees had an odd uniformity, especially the leaves. There was no discernible source of illumination, but he could see as if it were daytime.

And what he saw next was a huge, shimmering cat leaping at him.

Uldyssian gestured, but his powers seemed muted. He managed to shove the cat to the side but did not send it flying away as he had hoped.

Another growl arose from his left. Uldyssian barely had time to throw himself to the side as a second cat lunged.

Both predators immediately turned back. Uldyssian tried to summon a ball of fire, but nothing happened. He was forced to push back through the odd vegetation in order to avoid the sharp claws and teeth.

But barely had he moved into the brush when a massive, armored beast with two long horns on its snout nearly ran him down from behind. Momentum sent it barreling along toward the cats, which leapt out of its way.

And as the larger beast slowed, Uldyssian stared at it. That it shimmered like the cats did not surprise him as much as that it was *exactly* the same strange coloring. Both it and the cats were gold with a dotted orange line on the edges and uniform red, leaf-shaped marks along the sides of their torsos.

But his inspection was put to an abrupt end as the first of the cats jumped at him again. Unable to avoid it this time, Uldyssian braced himself for the collision.

The cat proved oddly light when it struck, but still the pair went tumbling back. The teeth snapped within inches of his face. Uldyssian, who had grown up around so many different animals, discovered something else disconcerting then.

The cat did not breathe. There was not the slightest exhalation, nor was there even any of the stench that he would have expected from an animal, especially a predator.

Claws tore at his chest. Uldyssian let out a gasp of pain. Something poured forth from his wounds, odd ribbons that looked like cloth parodies of blood.

And then the son of Diomedes recognized where he was, even as he managed to throw the cat to the side. His fears were verified when he glanced up and around and saw only the same odd leaves and trees. There was no sky. One did not exist here.

He was in the tapestry.

How that had happened, Uldyssian had no time to wonder, for the second cat and the horned beast were upon him. Aware of the unnatural lightness of his inhuman foes, he kicked hard at the fanged feline, then jumped over the armored beast.

A shadow dropped upon him. Talons raked his cheek. A raptor with similar markings to the other creatures flew past. It was nearly as large as the cats. As it circled to attack a second time, Uldyssian nearly tripped into the jaws of one of the sinister river reptiles he and his friends had first encountered when entering the jungle lands. A mouth filled with teeth sought his leg, and although the human suspected the creature of not having a true gullet, he had no intention of finding out otherwise. Uldyssian managed to roll just out of reach of the snapping jaws.

More animal cries filled his ears. From all over, the beasts in the tapestry were converging upon him. In addition to those he already faced, Uldyssian saw long, wicked serpents, savage primates as huge as men, and antelopes with spiraling horns.

He also saw something else. His only hope. He ran as quickly as he could, struggling past a hissing serpent and kicking at another of the reptiles.

There! They stood just as he recalled them. Lengthy golden spears. Uldyssian had barely seized one before another raptor dove down at him. He rewarded the creature for its efforts with a thrust of the spear that skewered the avian in descent. The bird let out a squawk, then died.

Shaking the carcass free, Uldyssian spun around to face the next nearest animal. The cat about to attack suddenly pulled back, spitting. The armored beast behind it did not slow, though. Undaunted by the spear, it tried to trample the human.

But Uldyssian used the spear to help him vault onto the creature. As it raised its head toward him, he plunged the weapon into its unprotected head.

Snorting, the behemoth dropped like a rock. But in doing so, it ripped the spear from Uldyssian's grip.

He had no choice but to throw himself toward the other, which still hung at an angle where he had left it.

A thick hand grabbed his arm just before the son of Diomedes could reach his goal. A hirsute countenance that was a parody of a man's filled his view.

The giant primate wrapped his huge limbs around Uldyssian and squeezed. He gasped as the air was crushed out of him.

This is not real! Uldyssian insisted. *I'm not trapped in the tapestry!*

Yet how could he be certain that he was not? Everything around him indicated that he was.

But whether or not that was the case, Uldyssian was positive that his powers should have remained his. There was no conceivable reason they should be of so little use.

He tried to think of something simple but effective. As earlier, fire was the first thing that came to him. Yet the last time, he had failed to create so much as a spark.

What other choice did he have, though? Uldyssian concentrated harder than ever. Fire. He wanted fire. . . .

And suddenly, the nearby jungle burst into flames.

It was not a fire like Uldyssian would have expected. Its flames did not blacken the trees and undergrowth—it burned *holes* in them the way it might fabrics.

The creatures attacking him reacted as animals would by fleeing in panic. However, those caught in the immediate conflagration perished in the same odd manner as the jungle itself. Holes burned into them, and perhaps the most disquieting thing about that was that the animals continued to run until they had no more legs or body. Only then were they truly "dead."

Although serving to frighten off Uldyssian's bestial foes, the flames created a new threat. They were rapidly eating away at the surreal jungle, leaving little avenue for him to escape . . . if escape was at all possible.

Uldyssian did not give up hope, though. Satisfied that his powers were indeed his own once more, he focused on his room. Somehow he was certain that he was still in the room, that this jungle was all illusion. If there was a threat, it lay there, not here. The only threat here was the fire, and that was his creation, his to control.

And as he thought this, the flames held back. At the same time, the tapestry jungle lost substance and receded. Although pleased by his successs, Uldyssian focused harder, certain that he was in danger in the true world.

Without warning, Uldyssian found himself standing at the window, one hand still on the curtain that he had been moving to block the piercing light. He realized that his eyes gazed without blinking directly into that light.

He also knew that he was not alone in the chamber.

Uldyssian threw himself to the side as a shadow coalesced into a man as tall as him and more powerfully built. Of the face, he could make out nothing, for although the figure moved past the illumination, shadow remained over his features.

Then Uldyssian saw the two curved knives, each almost a foot long. They glinted quite well in the light from outside, and their use was obvious. Uldyssian's mysterious attacker slashed over and over, each blade taking its turn.

Raising a fist, Uldyssian imagined a ball of energy. It materialized, then flew without hesitation at his adversary.

A moment later, it scattered in all directions, becoming a rain of sparkling lights that evaporated without any effect.

His failure received a harsh laugh from the assassin. He thrust down with one knife. Uldyssian, startled by the protections surrounding the other, failed to stop the blade.

The knife's edge cut through his garment, then drew a horrific red line down his torso. Uldyssian grunted. He managed to stagger out of reach, but when he sought to heal the wound, it resisted.

"Heretic!" rumbled the shadowed figure. "Your demon-spawned magic is nothing to his glorious power!"

Those words were more than enough to tell Uldyssian just who guided this astounding attack. Inarius had planned well.

Uldyssian knew that he could use his abilities to bring down the palace without harming himself, but he could scarcely protect anyone else, including Prince Ehmad. He had no doubt that Inarius had concluded that same thing; the angel had tied his rival's hands. His assassin was well protected, and the Prophet had already proven to Uldyssian that his power far outshone the mortal's.

Or did it? As the assassin sought to corner the son of Diomedes, Uldyssian wondered why, then, had Inarius sent this servant rather than return himself? Did he consider Uldyssian so beneath him that he need not bother with the human personally? That seemed doubtful, for what shielded the faceless man surely had to be the angel. Inarius was staying far away from the struggle yet guiding it.

Why? Why not simply crush Uldyssian to a pulp?

Was it . . . could it be because the angel could not so easily do that?

His back collided with a wall. While he had been considering the possibilities, his well-trained foe had managed finally to steer him to where he wanted him.

The blades came from both directions, each arcing in such a manner as to make it impossible to keep an eye on both. Uldyssian thrust out an arm to block the one he thought more deadly—and the assassin plunged the second into his stomach.

He let out a moan as the knife sank deep. A triumphant chuckle escaped the shadowed man.

"Blessed Prophet!" the figure gloated. "The heretic is dead!"

His attacker spoke true. Uldyssian felt the unmistakable cold spreading through him. He had sorely underestimated the angel.

But despite the bitter certainty of his death, Uldyssian fought back the horrific cold, fought against it . . . and *won*. It receded from his body into his hands, where it stayed. Life rushed through Uldyssian once more, but he continued to hunch over, letting the assassin think that his target was about to collapse.

The shadowed man leaned close, the knives held ready for what would merely be excessive butchery on his part. With the blow he had struck, there was no reason to attack again. Yet still the assassin looked eager to bury the blades in his victim. He raised them high—

Uldyssian took the coldness of death, Inarius's gift to him, and, planting both hands against the chest of the startled slayer, sent that eternal chill into his foe.

The assassin let out a garbled cry as his victim's death instead flowed through him. The knives dropped from his hands, clattering onto the floor. He clutched his torso exactly where he had stabbed Uldyssian.

The son of Diomedes felt the last of the cold leave his fingertips. He pulled away from the shadowed man. Letting one of his hands graze his wound, Uldyssian discovered that it had finally healed.

Weaving, the assassin stumbled against the curtain. He turned toward the light.

"Great Prophet, G-Gamuel has f-failed you! F-forgive me, please!"

It occurred to Uldyssian only then that there might be something about Inarius that he could learn from this special servant. He reached for the one who called himself Gamuel, but at that moment, the same light again caught his eye.

This time, though, it blinded Uldyssian so much that he faltered. His gaze turned from Gamuel and the window.

There was a sudden, harsh wind. The curtain shifted, and the light no longer blinded him. He reached again for the assassin—

No one was there.

Rushing to the window, Uldyssian looked out. His eyes immediately went to the area below his room. However, there was no hint whatsoever that the zealous Gamuel had chosen to finish his fading life by flinging himself to his death. The guards down at the palace steps stood at attention as if nothing had disturbed them for hours.

Uldyssian's legs wavered. He returned to the bed, where he thoroughly inspected the canopy. As he suspected, it was not in the least burned. There was, in fact, nothing in the room at all to indicate that there had even been an attack, much less that Uldyssian had slain the would-be assassin. Part of the carpet surrounding the bed had been kicked up, and there was the cut in his garment, but neither was sufficient proof of what had just happened.

But though there was not even a scar on his body to attest to events, he knew he had not imagined the struggle. He just could not prove it to the mage clans. He could not prove it even to Prince Ehmad, who might have actually believed his story.

His attention returned to the window. The light that had so harried him earlier was still there, albeit much dimmer. He now knew exactly what it was and where it was located. Uldyssian's room did face north, after all.

North . . . the direction to the Cathedral of Light.

The body lay before the Prophet just as it had come to him through his spell. Gamuel had died before he could even utter an apology to his master's face. Oddly, the mercenary-turned-priest-turned-assassin had not been killed. What he had suffered was actually not only far more complex than that but something that even Inarius could not recall ever seeing in all his centuries.

Gamuel had not suffered his own death . . . but rather Uldyssian's.

Impossible as it seemed even to an angel, Uldyssian, who should have died from the wound he had taken, had instead passed that death on to his killer. He had thrust his *dying* into Gamuel, who, unable to do anything else, had been forced to accept it.

Inarius frowned. The reason for his frown had as much to do with the cause of Gamuel's doom as the servant's inadequacy. Lilith's pawn had done the unthinkable. That meant that Inarius would have to alter his entire strategy. The danger he had always believed the nephalem—or edyrem, as these called themselves—to be had come to pass.

THEN . . . IF I MUST RAZE SANCTUARY TO PUT AN END TO THIS ABOMINATION . . . SO BE IT.

In an unaccustomed display of anger, the angel waved his hand at the body.

Gamuel's corpse turned as white as marble, then crumbled to ash that blew away despite there being no wind.

Inarius turned from the spot, his failed assassin already forgotten.

SO BE IT, he repeated coldly. *SO BE IT.*

Ten

They would reach the walls of Kehjan come the next day, and yet neither Serenthia nor the other edyrem could sense, much less contact, Uldyssian. Mendeln, who shared a different sort of link with his brother, thought that he could vaguely note Uldyssian's presence in the city, but that was the extent of it.

He had a theory on that troublesome point, and it focused on the mage clans. They considered the capital their domain, and the closer Mendeln got to it, the more he felt the saturation of magical energies that had built up over generations. There were spells upon spells, and many of them had likely been designed not only to shield the work of the mages from one another but also to keep the prying eyes of the Cathedral and the Triune from learning too much. How successful the spellcasters had been in doing that last was debatable, but they were certainly causing consternation among the edyrem. Many feared that their leader was either captured or dead, and neither he nor Serenthia could prove otherwise.

More and more, it appeared likely that Uldyssian's army would attack the capital if they reached the gates without learning anything contrary about his fate.

Mendeln did not even want to imagine the bloodshed should that happen. Caught between the edyrem and the mages, the innocents would surely die by the hundreds.

But there was nothing he could do to prevent it.

The nearby villages had again emptied out in advance of their coming. The shells that had once been homes seemed more eerie to Mendeln than a graveyard, for they were supposed to be inhabited with life. This was all wrong. . . .

There were soldiers farther ahead, most of them hiding in preparation for the assault that they thought would come tomorrow. As many as Mendeln sensed there were ahead, they were not nearly enough even to *slow* the edyrem. What magic he could sense among the city's protectors was minimal.

Serenthia sought to maintain order over the edyrem, but even with the aid of Saron and Jonas, it was becoming more and more difficult. Aware that his own presence would be more detrimental than helpful, Mendeln had finally slipped away from the throngs and entered the nearest village. He knew that he should not have separated from the others, but it was always easier for him to think in solitude. It was not as if he were alone, either, for there were always a few shades trailing him, in this case random deaths from the vicinity of the capital. He had already questioned them and learned nothing of value. They were all simple people who had worked hard just to stay alive for as long as they had.

Undisturbed by the night, Mendeln wandered from one empty house to another. He did little more than peer through the occasional window. It was not that he was interested in the lives the locals had led, but he missed his own past.

That made him smirk at himself. There had been many times in Seram when Mendeln had dreamed of becoming more than a farmer, many times when he had wished to travel to the exotic places on the maps and charts Master Cyrus had often let him peruse.

His boot kicked up something. It rolled a few yards from him. Mildly curious, Mendeln retrieved it. A girl's doll. It had dark hair and was dyed a deep brown, no doubt so that it would resemble its owner. He thought of his youngest sister, dead these many years from plague. There had been times since Mendeln had learned his skills that he wondered if it was possible to summon her spirit. Each time the notion had occurred to him, though, revulsion had immediately followed. She was dead. His parents were dead. He wished them to remain at peace.

He did not wish them to know what he and Uldyssian had become.

Mendeln put the doll back where he had found it, in the hopes that, should violence somehow be avoided, the child who had lost the toy would someday be reunited with it. However, as he straightened, Mendeln sensed that he was not alone. He glanced among the empty homes . . . and saw Achilios, notched bow in his hands, stare back at him.

Uldyssian's brother reacted instinctively. The ivory dagger came out with a swiftness that apparently caught even the undead hunter unaware. Mendeln muttered some of the words Rathma had taught him.

Achilios leapt into the shadows just before a series of toothy missiles struck where he had been standing. Mendeln cursed, then barreled his way into the nearest house. He sent the ghosts flanking him out into the village to locate Achilios's position.

But as they left, the archer saved him part of that trouble.

"I mean . . . no . . . harm . . . Mendeln," rasped Achilios from what seemed the other side of the wall against which Uldyssian's brother leaned. "Come out . . . and we'll . . . talk."

Inverting the dagger, Mendeln whispered another spell.

Before he could complete it, something shot just past his ear. It struck a wooden beam in another wall with a resounding *thunk*.

The arrow had come through a window only a few feet from Mendeln. Uldyssian's brother dropped to the dirt floor, then moved toward the back of the building. As he did, he began a different spell.

The front wall—including the window through which Achilios had fired—exploded outward.

From beyond the explosion came a growl and a curse. At the same time, Mendeln burst through the back door and out into the nearby jungle. Two ghosts, a young man stricken with pox and an older woman who had perished of a weak heart, needlessly informed him that Achilios had not been brought down by the explosion.

As he caught his breath, Mendeln cursed his own hesitation. There were spells he knew that were far more effective in permanently dealing with something like his former friend. Yet the black-robed figure could not bring himself to speak them. This was *Achilios*, after all, and even though the archer hunted him with the obvious intention of slaying Uldyssian's brother, Mendeln held out some vague hope of freeing the undead.

A noble thought . . . and one that was certain to get the younger son of Diomedes killed.

Another ghost, a comely noblewoman who had taken poison rather than continue her arranged marriage to a much older and somewhat violent man, materialized just in time to point out the direction from which Achilios was coming. Mendeln tumbled into the thick underbrush behind the wooden house, and although he did not hear the hunter's pursuit, he knew that his former friend was not far behind.

Indeed, not a breath later came the familiar gasping voice. "Mendeln . . . I come to . . . talk . . . there is no . . . no need for this! Let us both step out—"

In response, Mendeln drew a pattern in the air, then directed it toward Achilios's voice.

"By the . . . stars!" grated the archer from where he hid. At the same time, there was a rumbling sound, as if a small quake had begun.

Although unable to see the results of his spell, Uldyssian's brother could imagine them. The ground around the undead Achilios should have risen up, seeking to engulf him and thus return him to the grave. It was a spell that Mendeln himself had created based on something Trag'Oul had shown him. Mendeln was sickened by the notion of doing such a thing to his old friend, but he dared not give Achilios the opportunity to fire a second time.

As the churning of dirt continued, Mendeln ran toward the distant encampment. He did not like taking the chance of drawing Achilios back to Serenthia, but the hunter was less likely to try that attack again . . . or so he hoped. In truth, Mendeln was at a loss for exactly the best option. He only knew that he had to keep moving.

That point was made particularly well a moment later, as a second bolt cut past his arm. Not only did it sink into the trunk of a nearby tree, but when Mendeln felt his arm, he discovered that the arrow had ripped open the fabric. Another half inch, and the head would have been buried in his arm.

That made him think of Serenthia again and what might happen should Achilios decide that he had to try to slay her once more. That the archer had escaped so readily Mendeln's last spell spoke of the powerful force behind him.

Against an angel, Mendeln very much doubted his chances, but he decided that he was willing to take the risk rather than put the merchant's daughter in more danger. Gritting his teeth, the son of Diomedes veered off into the thicker areas of the jungle. The wild might be Achilios's domain, but the dark was Mendeln's.

He went several yards farther away from both the village and the encampment, then pressed himself against a wide tree. Clutching the dagger against his breast, he started molding a spell to his specifications. Despite his care for Achilios, Mendeln forced himself to see the hunter as what he was: a walking corpse. There were spells that could animate such; Mendeln had used them against Inarius's innocent dupes. To stop animating those, he had merely ceased his incantation. For a thing like Achilios, though, Uldyssian's brother hoped that by actually *reversing* the animation spell, he would send the archer back to the afterdeath.

In theory, it should work. In reality . . .

He sensed rather than heard Achilios approach. Mendeln was struck by the utter silence with which his friend moved. Even as good as he had been in life, surely then Achilios had made some slight noise, especially the intake of breath.

Mendeln finished assembling his spell. He would have one chance, and one chance only, to use it. It would require him stepping out to face the hunter, but Mendeln was willing to chance that. This had to end. Achilios had twice missed slaying his targets, but it was doubtful that he would keep missing. His master would not permit that.

For Serenthia and Uldyssian—assuming that his brother still lived—to survive, Achilios had to die . . . again.

I raised you from the ground, and to the ground I will send you again . . . and may you forgive me for both!

There was something to his right. He noticed only now that none of the ghosts was nearby to help warn him. Achilios's master wanted no failure this time.

A shadow broke from the darkness.

Mendeln stepped away from the tree, thrusting the downturned dagger toward that shadow. In its pale light, he saw Achilios's grit-covered face. The archer's expression was passive . . . lifeless.

And much to Mendeln's dismay, Achilios had just finished firing at him.

Mendeln knew he was dead. This close, even a fair archer could not fail to hit him directly in the heart. Despite that, the black-clad figure tried to call out what he could of his spell. It was for his brother's and Serenthia's sake, for it was already too late for him.

The bolt cut past his throat, scarring the neck and continuing on. Mendeln faltered in mid-word as he grasped at the stinging but shallow wound.

Behind him, the arrow hit the tree he had just abandoned.

Achilios lowered his bow. "You should be . . . slain . . . you know that."

His declaration caused Mendeln to hesitate. What the hunter said was true. Uldyssian's insistence that Achilios had meant to miss came back to the younger brother. Mendeln had wanted to believe then, but the near killing of Serenthia, with its more questionable intentions, had made him think twice. And when Achilios had come for *him*, then surely it meant that there would be no third reprieve.

Yet there had been, and Achilios himself was able to point that out.

"I find it hard to believe," he dared at last reply, "that you would spend so much time not quite slaying your targets."

This earned him a dry chuckle from the undead figure. "It was by sheer will . . . and not a little . . . luck the first time. Even more so . . . with . . . with her." If the blond archer could have shed a tear when speaking of Serenthia, he surely would have now. "And you . . . you only required three . . . three shots because you're . . . so damned *obstinate*, Mendeln."

"What do you mean?" It was proving harder and harder for Mendeln to bring himself to start over his dark spell. If not for the raspy voice, the hints of dirt that he could see on the face, and the knowledge that under the collar that covered Achilios's throat was a gaping hole, the son of Diomedes would have felt as if he and the archer were just having one of the many talks they had had as youths.

"I came . . . to talk. You made that . . . very difficult. I finally fired . . . fired the one shot . . . to show you that if I wanted . . . to kill you . . . I could. You didn't pay it . . . any . . . mind at all."

"There were circumstances, as you might recall. The last two times you appeared, you tried to put arrows into Uldyssian and her. I remained unconvinced that anything had changed."

The archer shook his head, unveiling part of his gaping throat wound in the process. "And so . . . I fired a second . . . a second time . . . to prove again . . . that . . . I could've killed you . . . or at least wounded . . . wounded you . . . if I'd wanted to."

Mendeln lowered the dagger. "Not yet convincing enough, I would have to say."

"No . . . apparently not." Achilios's expression suddenly tightened. "You . . . you tried to . . . to *bury* me . . . Mendeln. There was . . . was a moment then . . . that I wanted to . . . kill you."

The dagger came back up. "And now?"

"It was . . . it was only . . . for a moment . . . and I still . . . I still wouldn't have . . . done it."

There was something so believable in his voice that Mendeln finally put away the dagger. "Did you escape? Is that why you are back now?"

"No . . . I didn't . . . escape. He . . . he changed his . . . mind."

"What do you mean?"

"I was . . . I was to kill you all . . . especially Uldyssian and . . . and Serenthia . . . because of what . . . what you were becoming."

This was already obvious to Mendeln. "And so?"

"Now . . . now he wishes . . . wishes otherwise."

"Wishes otherwise? I am not certain that fills me with trust! And who is *he*, exactly, Achilios? Other than an *angel*, I mean!"

"Someone who might be . . . our only hope . . . against Inarius," the undead archer replied. His gaze suddenly shifted past Mendeln, who felt the hair on his neck rise. "The only hope."

IF IT IS STILL POSSIBLE . . . came a voice that sounded too much like that of Inarius. *FOR IT SEEMS THAT ONE OF THE THREE HAS NOW ENTERED THIS WORLD.*

Spinning around, Mendeln faced the angel. It was not Inarius, of that he was somehow certain. There was so much that reminded him exactly of Rathma's father, yet he knew somehow that this was not him.

But more important was what the celestial being had just said. "One of the Three?" Uldyssian's brother blurted. His mind raced. The only "Three" that he could think of were the patron spirits of the Triune, spirits who were, in fact, actually— "No!" Mendeln vehemently shook his head. "You cannot mean—"

The faceless figure gave an almost imperceptible nod. *YES, ONE OF THE DEMON LORDS HAS COME TO SANCTUARY.*

This was not how it was supposed to be. From time immemorial, all had proceeded as Inarius intended. Whenever some slight trouble had reared its head, the angel had attended to it with a draconian efficiency that would have left even his brethren reeling. He had learned from that one foolish error, learned from falling prey to his lover's false words. Since that distasteful event, Inarius had never let anything go beyond his immediate control.

Until now.

The angel, still in the guise of the Prophet, stalked his sanctum as his emotions grew unchecked. Uncertainties that he had not experienced in centuries seized hold of him.

Oris had come in search of her counterpart, who she did not know was no longer even dust on the floor. Inarius had granted her no more than a minute with him but had paid her words little attention during that period. His blunt comment that Gamuel was to be forgotten left her pale, but he did not care. Human concerns were trivial compared with his own.

The night had grown old by this point, and although he was eternal, the passing of the last few hours only served to make the Prophet more anxious. In the past, there had never been a situation that had required more than a few moments' consideration on his part. Now his mind could not function, save to repeat over and over his recent failures.

THERE HAS BEEN A MISTAKE! he insisted to himself. *THERE HAS BEEN A MISTAKE! A FAULT NOT MINE!*

The mortal Uldyssian had dealt with the Triune, just as Inarius had wanted. The next step should have been the simple downfall of the angel's pawn. Inarius's agents had turned so many people against the edyrem that in the end, the abominations would surely fall.

But Uldyssian himself could not be stopped . . . and he was coming for Inarius . . . coming for him . . .

Glancing up at the glorious panorama that sought, in a feeble manner, to describe the perfection of the High Heavens, the angel started. He could have sworn that one of the figures had moved. Inarius stepped back, studying the painted form.

No, it could not have moved. It had only been his own imagination—

The face of the Prophet twisted in fury. His fears melted away at the same time, melted away with little difficulty, for they were not exactly his own.

"I know you now," he declared to the empty chamber in his human voice. "Your little games will not work on me, demon! You forget with whom you deal!"

I deal with a traitor, a liar, and a murderer, said a voice that, despite Inarius's claim, sent a slight chill through him. *It's almost like dealing with one of my brothers.*

"Insolent as ever." Inarius sought out the darkest shadow and faced it. "So very insolent."

The shadow moved. Within it, a figure vaguely coalesced.

Inarius showed no sign of anxiety when that figure became another winged warrior he knew so well. "You are not Tyrael, and I am not afraid of him."

Are you not? Then why do I resemble him?

"Because you are a fool, demon."

This brought a chuckle. Then, as the other "angel" moved forward, he shifted form again. Now he was a human, but not just any. He was Uldyssian ul-Diomed.

The Prophet bared his teeth. "Again, you are a fool. You have some reason for approaching me. Do so without the theatrics!"

The shadow in the corner suddenly spread forth, all but enveloping the false Uldyssian. As it did, his form distorted. The demon grew less distinct and certainly far less human. He became as much imagination as substance, and as he did, Inarius again felt unsettled, though he dared not show it.

The shadows now encompassed most of the chamber in the direction where the dark being stood. The angel was aware that beyond his sanctum, his followers were suddenly experiencing fears that they did not even know they had. The guards at his doors would be trembling, and there was even a good chance that some had fled their positions. More than a few of his priests would likely be on their knees already, praying that the darkness touching their souls would soon leave them.

They did not know how fortunate they were, for the demon who visited Inarius could have done much worse. It was only that he, like the angel, dared not fully reveal himself.

There were those even the Lord of Terror feared.

The thing in the shadows towered over Inarius. At times, the demon had a shape that was reminiscent of a twisted mix of man and animal. Yet it was the face that most stirred the fears within, for it kept shifting. Inarius saw a skull with horns. Out of the eyes and jaws oozed blood. That horrific countenance became a melting head whose flesh was being constantly devoured by black flies and great worms. A more reptilian face then appeared, feminine and much like that of another demon Inarius had known.

But even Lilith's visage vanished a moment later, to be replaced again by that of the other angel. As the Prophet frowned, the demon laughed and changed again. Now empty shadow greeted Inarius, and for inexplicable reasons, this disturbed him more than any of his visitor's other forms.

Is this better, oh Prophet?

Ignoring the mockery, Inarius quietly replied, "When previously we faced each other, Lord Diablo, it was agreed that it would be the last time."

There are always more last times, Inarius. Although not so many as there used to be.

"And is that the reason for your coming?"

The demon's shape continually shifted in small ways, as if Diablo had no true form of his own. Each alteration, no matter how small, touched some chord with Inarius, although he ever kept his emotions masked. Diablo fed off the slightest fear.

My reason for coming is simple. His name is Uldyssian.

"Ah, of course. You and your brothers spent so much effort creating the Triune! I did warn you that it would fall."

Through no effort of yours.

Now it was the angel's turn to mock. "Are you so certain? You would do better to take a closer look."

He sensed the demon's fury and felt a wave of fear seek to take hold of him. Aware now, though, that it was Diablo's effort, Inarius shielded himself against the dark lord's power. The effort proved quite a strain, but Inarius succeeded.

Yet had both he and Diablo been human, their hesitation during the moment that followed might have been seen as two exhausted adversaries needing to draw a breath and recover.

Inarius was aware how powerful the demon lord was and knew that part of his own success came from Diablo's need to shield himself from other eyes. That, at last, revealed to the angel just why he had been visited so suddenly.

"So . . . that is it," the Prophet murmured, more confident now. "You are afraid of losing everything. The Lord of Terror is afraid."

I fear nothing! the emptiness that Diablo currently used as his face retorted. *No more than you, that is!*

"All goes as I desire—"

Taloned paws scraping across the immaculate marble, the demon moved closer, the vast shadow swelling with him in the process. Somehow, even lacking eyes, he managed to stare into Inarius's mind. *I tasted your fear, angel.*

There would have been nothing for me to devour if what you say is true. This mortal, this Uldyssian, he has become more than any of us would imagine. He risks all that either of us desires of Sanctuary!

Inarius could not prevent a frown. "Two different desires, I might point out."

But with one overriding link. Diablo leaned close. There was a hint of that other angel's countenance before the emptiness returned. *Neither of the destinies we fight for will happen if this mortal continues along his path.*

The Prophet turned away from his unwanted guest, but not because of fear of Diablo. Rather, he saw too well the demon lord's point and could not help but consider it.

As often as Inarius had threatened to wipe clean Sanctuary and begin anew, in truth, he did not wish to go to such an extreme. He had molded the world to his liking for far too long. He had grown too . . . *comfortable.*

The demons, of course, sought Sanctuary and, especially, its humans, for another, more base reason. They saw in humans the warriors that they needed to tilt the struggle in their favor.

And as Diablo had said, if Uldyssian managed to keep raising his people beyond what even Inarius had imagined their limits, then very soon neither he nor the demons would have say over man.

THAT CAN NEVER BE! Inarius thought angrily. He turned back to the demon, who had stayed silent during his considerations. "You are offering an alliance."

The Lord of Terror laughed harshly. *You make it sound as if such a thing were unthinkable, angel! I recall that you have made pacts with my kind more than once.*

Inarius could certainly not argue with him there. As in those other times, though, he intended that the advantage would be his. He had learned from his one mistake, learned from Lilith.

And against the cunning of Lilith, even Diablo paled. A pact could be manipulated. Diablo would certainly try it.

With practiced ease, the Prophet went to his favorite couch and settled there, as if the figure before him were a supplicant, not a master demon. He sensed Diablo's anger at this insult but knew that the Lord of Terror needed his resources, his Cathedral of Light, for whatever he planned.

Still, Inarius was curious about what Diablo had to offer this alliance. "I will listen."

Clearly restraining his powers, the monstrous being explained, *Through a minion of mine, I have learned of one who would be eager to help us. Indeed, he is near and already eager for Uldyssian's blood . . . or body, that is.*

"Body?"

Yes . . . and for it as his reward, he will be the key to eliminating the threat this mortal makes.

"Of what use is another demon?"

Diablo grunted at what apparently was Inarius's ignorance. *He is not demon, though his mind is worthy of one. He is a man . . . or, rather, was. Alone, he will fail, but with both of us to guide him, he cannot but succeed.*

"A mortal against another mortal?" It made an ironic sense to Inarius, and if a mortal was Diablo's pawn, he would be that much easier for the angel to manipulate later. "And who is this man who no longer is?"

You knew him well . . . so very . . . when he was the high priest of Mefis.

Mefis. Mephisto. Yes, Inarius knew very well of whom the demon lord spoke. "Malic?" The Prophet allowed a slight smile to grace his mortal countenance. "Malic."

Yes. Diablo allowed a face of his own—a less disturbing one, of course—to shift into focus . . . and with the angel shared another smile.

ELEVEN

Mendeln was hiding something, that much Rathma sensed. As he materialized among the marching edyrem—startling not a few—he felt a part of his pupil's mind hidden from him.

Immediately, he reached out to Trag'Oul to inform the dragon of this.

I know it already, the creature replied. *And whatever method with which he shields it is immune to even my inquiries.*

But that's not possible! Rathma knew of no manner by which the mortal, even as gifted as he was, could achieve such a feat.

No, it is not, agreed the dragon. *For him.*

Rathma also noted that Mendeln was doing his best to ignore him. This infuriated the Ancient more than he could believe.

"Mendeln ul-Diomed, we need to talk."

Uldyssian's brother glanced back. "We are nearly at the gates of Kehjan. It'll have to wait. I am trying to figure out how to avoid a war."

"Any blood spilt between the edyrem and the mage clans is insignificant against the true danger."

"Not if some of that blood belongs to Uldyssian!" Mendeln snapped with unusual vehemence.

His reaction only convinced the son of Inarius that there was indeed more going on than Mendeln wished to tell him. Rathma had a terrible idea what that might be.

"We will talk, son of Diomedes—and now."

His student paused. The other edyrem wisely moved on as the two black-clad figures stared at each other.

"Talk? At your convenience, as usual," the mortal blurted. "When I need to talk, you are elsewhere! When I need answers, you only provide puzzles!"

There was something terribly amiss. Rathma surreptitiously reached out with his powers. He searched the jungle very carefully, thinking in terms of his father's cunning.

And there he finally saw what he believed Mendeln was hiding.

Achilios shadowed the edyrem horde.

His expression not changing, Rathma murmured, "I see. Forgive me for not understanding the problem."

Mendeln reached out to him. "No! It's not—"

But Rathma had already vanished, to reappear in the jungle behind the stalking hunter.

"I am sorry to do this, Achilios," he declared.

Almost too late, the Ancient recalled that this was not a being bound by living limits. Before he had even finished speaking, the archer had spun around and readied an arrow.

It flew past Rathma's ear, distracting him more than anything else. That was apparently all that Achilios desired, for instead of attacking, he immediately leapt into the underbrush.

But if the hunter thought that sufficient to keep Rathma from him, he was sorely mistaken. Now better prepared for what he faced, the Ancient vanished.

The look on the archer's deathly countenance when the son of Inarius materialized right before him might have been humorous under other circumstances. Achilios gaped, then grabbed for a good-sized knife at his waist.

NO.

The voice stopped both dead in their tracks. Rathma was struck far harder than Achilios, who had likely heard that voice often in the past days. Rathma whirled around, seeking the speaker and growing anxious that he could not even sense the slightest trace.

Eyes blazing, he turned back to the archer. Achilios said nothing, but his expression told Rathma all that he needed to know.

"It is him," the Ancient breathed. "It *is* him."

But before more could be said, there came shouts from the direction of Mendeln and the edyrem. Rathma looked that way.

The sky ahead had suddenly turned an unsettling green.

He looked again to Achilios, whose expression had not changed. Rathma hesitated for a moment, then vanished from the spot.

The son of Inarius reappeared near Mendeln—and beheld a sight that without doubt had no natural origin.

The green filling the sky was that of a brightly colored insect—to be precise, the mantis. Never in all his long life had Rathma ever witnessed so many mantises, especially together. Mantises were solitary creatures, but these swarmed in numbers that dwarfed even the greatest gatherings of locust. From the direction of the capital, they came, and Rathma did not have to have the wisdom of generations to know that there was no coincidence. The only question remained was just who was responsible. The mage clans, perhaps, or his father.

Or perhaps Achilios's new master.

But that hardly mattered now. The swarm was nearly upon the edyrem, and as the mantises descended, they seemed to swell in size. From a few inches, they grew to more than a foot and kept growing.

While initially stunned, Uldyssian's followers did not continue to stand and wait. Serenthia gave a shout and threw her spear into the swarm. As the weapon flew, a fiery aura burst into being around it, one that swept over any nearby insect the spear passed. Engulfed by the flames, more than a dozen of the creatures immediately perished.

And as this happened, those with her attacked in a variety of manners designed for maximum carnage. Balls of energy, buffers of pure sound, whatever could slaughter the mantises by the scores struck the gargantuan swarm.

But Rathma noticed quickly that despite the hundreds of huge bodies already littering the area, the mantises' numbers did not appear to diminish. If anything, the swarm seemed to grow.

He wasted no time in calling to one who might better understand. *Trag, do you see all this?*

The dragon's reply was immediate. *I sensed its beginnings and quickly sought what was going on.*

This is not the work of the mage clans, is it? Rathma asked, even as he prepared to join the conflict.

No . . . this was brought together by a power far greater than they.

Trag'Oul did not have to elaborate. Rathma understood exactly what he meant.

He searched the area for Mendeln and was not surprised at all to discover Uldyssian's brother among the missing. The Ancient could scarcely believe that Mendeln would betray the rest, but no other explanation made sense.

Something else occurred to him. He reached back to where he had last sensed Achilios and found him also gone.

This is a diversion . . . this is all a diversion.

To verify that, Rathma surveyed the tableau. The edyrem attacked and attacked, and the mantises kept coming and coming. There could not be so many of the insects in all of Sanctuary, yet they were without end. The creatures landed among Uldyssian's followers, biting and scraping them, but thus far, he saw not one serious injury, not even among the younger and older. The swarm also never flowed any faster than the humans could handle them. Just enough to keep them harassed and unable to advance.

Unable to reach Kehjan.

Rathma did not have to ask why. He knew that if Mendeln had not already somehow transported himself into the capital, then he was well on his way.

The question was, what did the angel he now appeared to serve desire of the younger brother?

There was only one way to discover the reason. With a last glimpse of the struggle, Rathma went to Kehjan.

Uldyssian reached out to Serenthia and Mendeln and again confronted a vague barrier. A part of him chided the son of Diomedes for not immediately heading back to them, but another kept reminding Uldyssian of what could be gained for not only the edyrem but all humanity if he succeeded here.

And it appeared that his hopes were not without reason, for Prince Ehmad came to him late in the day and said, "We don't have much time. The mage council has agreed to meet with you, but it must take place just after the sun has gone down. No later."

"Why the sudden urgency?"

"I am a mere prince," his host said with a mock shrug, "and understand little of the ways of spellcasters."

Uldyssian suspected that Ehmad knew far more than he indicated but left it at that. He trusted in the prince. "And the guilds?"

"They will be there also. I should tell you, Ascenian, that such a swift gathering of both sides together says much concerning their interest in you."

Uldyssian's head suddenly pounded, but even as he reached a hand up, the pounding went away. Prince Ehmad looked concerned. "My friend, are you ill?"

"No . . . I'm fine." Still, there had been something familiar about the sensation, as if it originated with someone else and not him, someone he knew well, too. Mendeln? Serenthia? Was one of them seeking to contact him?

Before he could pursue the thought, Uldyssian suddenly sensed another presence.

The mage Kethuus materialized before them. "Zorun Tzin is dead."

At first, Uldyssian was not certain whether the shadowy

man referred to his captor or Malic in his guise as Zorun.
Kethuus quickly corrected himself.

"Zorun Tzin was traced to an area below the city. There
was some hint of his magic, but it faded in one particular
location. That can only mean that he's truly no more."

"And Malic? What about Malic?"

"This spirit of which you speak cannot be sensed in any
way. It's been suggested that when Zorun's body perished,
so, too, did this Malic."

Uldyssian could scarcely believe that. "There must be
some way to be certain!"

"All manners of detection that the mage council's established have been used. They verified Zorun's death at the
location and found no trace of any such creature as you
describe the high priest." Kethuus grinned, his white teeth
a great contrast to his almost-invisible face. "Perhaps you
can do better."

It was not a suggestion but rather a challenge. Uldyssian,
aware more than anyone of what a threat Malic was, could
not refuse it. "Will you take me to where you last traced
Zorun Tzin? Are you allowed to do that?"

"Of course."

"It is but three hours until the sun sets," Prince Ehmad
reminded him. "I would recommend not being delayed."

"Have no fear. I'll see that the Ascenian gets back in
time and in one piece." Kethuus sneered. "He'll find the
council and the guilds far more trouble than this Malic,
believe you me."

"This must be done," Uldyssian told his host. "Believe
me. I failed to make certain that he was truly dead the last
time. Whatever harm Malic causes in his hunt for me I feel
in great part responsible for."

"May the ancestors watch over you, then," Ehmad
replied with a bow.

Kethuus sneered again, obviously not as strong in his
belief in such things as the noble. "Shall we be gone, or do
you wish to natter on for a while longer?"

Although well impressed by Kethuus's abilities, Uldyssian cared little for the mage himself. He seemed typical of the arrogance that the son of Diomedes expected of his kind, which did not bode well for the upcoming gathering.

The sooner they were back, the better Uldyssian would like it. "Take me there."

Touching his chest, Kethuus obeyed.

The transition was nigh instantaneous. The two stood in an alley in the midst of the capital. Tall but obviously neglected buildings crowded around them.

"I thought that we'd appear in the tunnels," he said to his companion.

Kethuus lowered his hand. For the first time, Uldyssian noticed the medallion the other wore. Runes etched around the blue stone in the center faded from illuminated gold to dull brass even as he watched. This was the equivalent to Zorun Tzin's staff, Uldyssian realized.

"One doesn't go blindly belowground," Kethuus explained in a tone that mocked Uldyssian for not knowing that. "The tunnels are the oldest places in all Kehjan. Some say they were built for a previous city raised before men ever existed."

"And who would've built it?"

The hooded mage stamped his boot on a small pattern carved into the path. To Uldyssian's astonishment, part of the rock slid away, revealing a hole down which rusted metal rungs could be seen on one wall. "Some say angels and demons."

Kethuus did not elaborate, instead dropping down into the hole and climbing out of sight. The son of Diomedes quickly followed suit.

As he descended below the alley, the stone slid back into place above him. Uldyssian tried unsuccessfully to shake off the notion that he had entered a trap.

At the bottom, Kethuus created a small, illuminating globe. Uldyssian did not imitate him, preferring for the moment to let the spellcaster assume that his powers were greater than the outsider's. It had become abundantly clear that, at least where Kethuus and his two comrades were concerned, Uldyssian's power was suspect. That despite Amolia's earlier attempt to seize him.

Shrugging off the prejudices of his possible allies, he waited with growing impatience while Kethuus led him along the ledge of the vast water system. Uldyssian had expected to descend only a short distance from their destination, but Kethuus turned from one confusing passage to another.

And only then did Uldyssian wonder if it was actually the mage he followed.

Unseen by the figure in front of him, his hand balled up into a fist that glowed a faint crimson. Uldyssian could not believe that he had not considered such a trick by Malic. The dread spirit was cunning enough to take one of the very hunters after him and use that body to bring his ultimate prey to where the high priest could deal with him. Malic would know that his foe would insist on trying to track him, which meant that the high priest would be certain to lay some sort of trap.

But now alerted, Uldyssian had every intention of turning the tables on Malic. If he was correct, then Kethuus was already dead, and so there was no fear in harming him.

"Is it much farther?" he asked, seeking to keep his adversary unaware of his discovery.

"Not far. Have no fear. . . ."

The continually mocking tone only further encouraged Uldyssian that he was correct in his assumption. Certain of his triumph, Malic could not even hold back his disdain.

The only thing that held Uldyssian back from attacking was curiosity about just what Malic planned when they reached wherever it was they were going. Uldyssian suspected that perhaps the high priest had located some surviving acolytes of the Triune to assist him. If so, it would behoove the son of Diomedes to see that none of them left the tunnels alive.

They journeyed on in silence, the only other noises the churning of the water and their own breath. Just when Uldyssian decided that he would wait out Malic's little game no longer, the figure ahead paused.

"Here. The entrance we descended was the nearest physical way to reach this spot. Don't worry, though, Ascenian; we'll get you back in time to meet the council."

"I don't doubt that at all," Uldyssian replied, keeping his hand hidden.

The hooded spellcaster leaned down near the water's edge. He pointed at an area just to his left. "That's where all trace of Zorun Tzin ends. His body is not in the water. We would've detected that. It simply ceased to be."

"The safer for covering Malic's tracks, wouldn't you say, Kethuus?"

The mage looked up. "Or simply where this supposed ghost ended when the body was no longer able to sustain him. You said yourself that the bodies didn't last long."

"But long enough to find him another." Uldyssian pretended interest in the findings as he maneuvered closer to his companion. He wanted to make certain that Malic would not escape him this time. It put him at risk as well, but to Uldyssian it was more than worth it.

"We've found nothing to the contrary. All trace of Zorun Tzin stops here, as I said!"

"But we're not looking for him," Uldyssian reminded. "We're looking for Malic, high priest of Mefis."

Kethuus rose. In the glow of his sphere, his dark face looked monstrous. "If such a creature as you say he was exists, we would've found something! You were tortured, Ascenian, and Zorun Tzin would've been a master of that. What you thought happened was, in the opinion of more than just myself, your imagination."

"Was it just that . . . Malic?"

The mage's expression contorted as he registered just what the other had called him. "You can't seriously believe that I am—"

Uldyssian raised his fist . . . and the water before the two men erupted. Both were drenched by a foul-smelling wave. Uldyssian lost his balance and fell into the channel. Kethuus tumbled into the wall, and only a last-minute grasp by the mage kept him from joining the son of Diomedes.

Sinking below the surface, Uldyssian fought to breathe. Something that was not a fish moved past him in the murky water. He blindly struck out at it, the water boiling as he unleashed what he had planned to use on Kethuus.

The mage was not Malic. Uldyssian cursed himself for falling prey to such a notion. Malic would hardly have let himself be so endangered, and certainly he would not have wanted to risk the body he had so avidly sought.

Something akin to a serpent wrapped around his leg. Pulling against it, Uldyssian felt several sharp edges cut into his flesh. He almost cried out, only at the last moment able to prevent himself from doing so and thus filling his lungs with water.

As it was, he already ached for air. Uldyssian tried to reach the surface, but whatever held his leg kept him just inches from salvation.

In desperation, he reached up, snatching at the air his lips sought. If he could only bring it to him . . .

And as his cupped hand came back underwater, it brought with it a huge bubble that radiated a faint golden aura. Uldyssian dragged the bubble to his mouth and inhaled. His lungs filled. He brought to his mouth another and another, all the while kicking to keep the unseen threat from pulling him down farther.

From above, there came a glow reminiscent of the sphere Kethuus had summoned. A moment later, that very globe shot down through the water, heading past Uldyssian. It soared deeper, descending, he realized, toward whatever held him.

As it struck, Uldyssian caught sight of the demon.

He knew it could be nothing else. Nothing born of Sanctuary could have so grotesque a form. It had a multitude of leafy yet sharp tentacles and a bulbous body that reminded Uldyssian of a bubble. Odd things floated within. He had the horrific feeling that he was to join them inside.

Again, Uldyssian felt his lungs aching. As Kethuus's glow light faded away, the son of Diomedes used the last of the light to aim at the demon.

But the creature immediately released him, vanishing into the dark muck. Uldyssian had to forgo his attack; he needed air and needed it fast.

The instant his head broke the surface, Uldyssian inhaled. The air tasted so sweet to him that for a moment he thought of nothing else.

And that was when the demon attacked again.

There were tentacles everywhere, even around his throat. One wrapped around his mouth. He was pulled under.

From somewhere came Kethuus's shout, then the water filled Uldyssian's ears. He was pulled into the darkness.

However, the air that he had managed to gulp enabled him to think better. Uldyssian focused on the demon's many appendages.

Despite the surrounding water, the son of Diomedes made them *burn*.

A manic bubbling sound erupted from below him, so loud that Uldyssian thought he would go deaf. The demon withdrew its fire-engulfed limbs from him and began in vain to try to shake the flames off.

Uldyssian glanced down as he headed toward the surface. In the light of the unnatural fire he had created, the demon looked even more horrific. There were tentacles everywhere, half of them burning. The flames created an aura about the creature that would have been even more terrifying if not for the fact that it was actually harming the demon, not a part of it.

Uldyssian's head broke the surface again. He blinked clear his gaze, then focused on a dim illumination ahead.

Kethuus, another glow ball near his head, crouched low

as Uldyssian swam toward him. He reached out a hand, which, after a moment's hesitation, Uldyssian accepted.

"By the seven!" the shadowy man blurted. "I have seen things that would turn a man's skin whiter than yours, Ascenian, but never anything so . . . so . . ." Unable to come up with an appropriate word, Kethuus let his exclamation fade away.

Climbing onto the ledge, Uldyssian spat out some of the rank liquid and gasped. "It was a demon . . . a demon that Malic surely summoned!"

"I know not whether to believe you on that last point, but certainly it adds to your claim!" The hooded spellcaster grunted. "And you destroyed it with fire that not even water could lessen! You are truly what the stories claimed you to be!"

While Uldyssian was not unpleased to hear respect at last in his companion's tone, he was more concerned with discovering just where Malic had gone.

The water bubbled again. Kethuus, staring past Uldyssian, raised a hand and began chanting.

Uldyssian spun around. The soaked ledge nearly caused him to slip back into the water, but he managed to keep his hold.

A fiery storm rained down upon the two men. The demon had ripped free its burning tentacles and now threw them.

Uldyssian clapped his hands together. An explosion of air tossed the tentacles away from him and Kethuus.

Yet as he succeeded there, the demon itself surged toward Uldyssian. From the bulbous body, a much-shorter appendage shot forth.

"I have it!" the mage called. He sliced at the air, and an arc of energy severed the tip of the short tentacle.

The limb fell, but the tip continued on. Uldyssian gestured at it, and it exploded in their faces.

Kethuus screamed. At first, Uldyssian did also, but then the pain abruptly vanished. In fact, his entire body grew numb. His legs collapsed. As he fell against the wall, he saw that Kethuus, too, had lost all control of his body. The mage slumped nearby.

The now-familiar bubbling sound grew louder and louder. A stench that had nothing to do with the water filled Uldyssian's nostrils. The monstrous shape of the demon loomed over him.

A pair of tentacles wrapped around Uldyssian's torso, lifting him up like a rag doll. The demon drew its victim close.

Uldyssian's mind began to fog. Worse, he had no one but himself to blame for this catastrophe. He had walked into Malic's trap fully confident in his ability to outwit the spirit and had only succeeded in proving himself a great fool.

One thing kept him puzzled. Why would Malic wish him dead if he needed his body? The high priest had been determined to make Uldyssian his new host. Had he found someone better?

The demon raised him higher, then began moving away from the ledge. It appeared to have no interest in Kethuus, which boded even more ill for Uldyssian. That made him wonder if the creature intended to bring him to Malic. That would explain some things.

But no sooner had Uldyssian thought that than the demon lowered him to just below its odd body, then pulled him underneath. There, for the first time, the son of Diomedes saw what he assumed was the creature's mouth. The oval hole unsealed, and although within the demon there seemed some odd liquid, none of it spilled out.

This close, with the mage's second glow ball still burning, Uldyssian could see at last what some of the objects within were. Small bits of metal, things like buttons and belt hooks.

He now knew why the searchers had found no trace of Zorun Tzin's body.

His head was nearly at the mouth. Uldyssian could only imagine the terrible digestion process that would take place once he was within.

He fought back the fog. It finally receded, if only slightly. Uldyssian felt his powers returning. He had no time to think about what to do; as in such moments in the past, Uldyssian relied strictly on raw emotion to fuel his efforts. He stared into the demon's body.

The thick liquid within bubbled. The demon let out a squeal as the bubbling intensified. A brownish tint began to form all over the bulbous body.

The creature flung Uldyssian high in the air, battering him against the ceiling. Even through the remaining numbness, Uldyssian felt the tremendous shock from the collision. Yet he refused to falter in his own attack.

Squealing louder, the monstrous creature again threw his prey at the ceiling. Uldyssian used the new pain to fuel his emotion-driven assault.

The demon's body turned a dark brown. Inside, the sinister liquid began to vaporize. The bulbous body swelled.

The demon exploded.

In its death throes, it tossed Uldyssian up one last time. Caught unaware, Uldyssian hit his skull against the stone. The world spun around.

He struck the water, small bits of the demon spilling over him in the process. Uldyssian tried to orient himself, but his body would not function.

He sank beneath the water.

TWELVE

Rathma.

There was no reply to the dragon's call. There had been no reply to the dozen before it. It was as if a veil had been thrown over part of Sanctuary, a veil that covered nearly all of the land of Kehjan and was, without a doubt, centered on its same-named capital.

But by Inarius alone, such a thing was not possible.

By Inarius alone.

And from everything that Trag'Oul could sense, this veil was not the work of two angels. No, there was a combination of powers involved here that Sanctuary had not experienced since its birth.

Angel and demon working together.

The glittering stars shifted about as Trag'Oul anxiously considered this. Angel and demon working together . . . and with but one possible reason.

There is no choice! he insisted. *There is no choice! I must act! I must go to the mortal plane.*

He began to draw forth the cosmic energies that would open the way for him. Only once before had Trag'Oul entered Sanctuary, and that had been just after the slaughter of the refugees by Lilith and Inarius's subsequent reactions. At that time, the dragon had materialized for just a few seconds, long enough to lay the groundwork for Rathma's discovery of him. He had chosen the son of Inarius well before that, seeing in him the spark that might help save the world should the angel decide it must be destroyed.

But now Trag'Oul would need to spend far longer than a few seconds. There would be no hiding himself from either the angel or the master demon with whom he worked.

And in revealing himself, Trag'Oul knew that he also risked ensuring the destruction of that which he had so long protected.

There is no choice, he told himself again. *No choice!*

The gateway was nearly complete, and then the voices struck him from all directions.

You cannot! You cannot! You cannot!

At the same time, the gateway disintegrated despite his best efforts to keep it from doing so.

Filled with an unaccustomed anger, he confronted the voices. *This is my burden! This is my duty! You have no say in this, none of you!*

There was a moment of silence, and then, together, they responded, *But we do . . . this goes beyond Sanctuary now. Beyond all of us who stand sentinel.*

The dragon grew wary. *How so? How can that be?*

As ever, they answered as one, and, as before, their words struck him as nothing else could. *Because the war is coming to Sanctuary, and if you interfere with what the Balance demands, it and* all *existence may be forfeit.*

They left him, then, all the others who stood guard as he did over their separate worlds, left him with the knowledge that it was his Sanctuary whose imminent fate might decide theirs. They left Trag'Oul with the understanding that all his years of aiding the Worldstone in shielding Sanctuary from the outside had come to naught.

It was not merely one angel who had discovered Inarius's creation. The High Heavens themselves now knew of the world.

The eternal war was coming to Sanctuary . . . and he had just been forbidden to do anything about it.

• • •

Amolia appeared before Prince Ehmad, her dark expression matching her mood. "The council is not pleased. Uldyssian ul-Diomed does his cause no favor by slighting them like this!"

The prince sat in his personal chambers, sipping quietly from a flagon. There was but one candle lit, on the small table where he now set his drink.

"It was wrong to trust in him," Ehmad remarked with a frown. "I only just found out from a spy of my own that he's gone and made a pact with the Prophet to bring down the mage clans and the guilds and share all the land between his followers and the Cathedral."

The blond woman looked not entirely surprised. "I thought him a base villain. You have proof of this?"

"I do, but I must present it to the council." He rose. "It would be best if you took me there immediately, since they are already assembled."

"There's been no discussion of you appearing before them. If you have something to relay, give it to me, and I'll tell them myself."

"That would not serve. I must face them. It is the only way."

Amolia shook her head. Her hand toyed with a medallion identical to that worn by Kethuus and others who served the mage council as they did. "Your daring is renowned, Prince Ehmad, as is your growing presumptuousness. You have no true authority; the love of the people means nothing in the end. If you were to cease to be, they would forget you in a day. The council has no need to grant you an audience. Whatever you wish to pass on, you can pass on through me."

Ehmad thrust a hand into his pocket. "As you say. That might be for the best, after all. They certainly would not expect it."

"Expect what?"

The prince reached out with his other hand. Amolia moved to brush it aside, but instead Ehmad gripped her wrist tight.

"Expect me to strike from in their midst," he answered, smiling in a dark manner, "as one of their own."

"You're not—" was as far as the mage got.

Prince Ehmad's body crumpled. The other hand slipped out of the pocket . . . and from its grasp rolled a tiny crimson crystal.

The female spellcaster smiled exactly as the prince had a moment before. She reached down and retrieved the precious fragment, slipping it into a pouch on her belt. A gilded mirror caught her attention. She walked over to it, examining herself.

"Yes . . . you will do for the time. Long enough, anyway."

"It would be wise to cease unnecessary admiration for yourself, my son," came a musical male voice.

The mage turned to find the beatific figure of the Prophet standing over the body of the prince. A scowl crossed Amolia's features. "It pays to adjust my thinking before moving on. The better to play the part."

"There is only one part with which to concern yourself. That is the ultimate elimination of Uldyssian ul-Diomed. Nothing else matters," the Prophet insisted imperiously. "And certainly not your vile tastes . . . Malic."

The spirit sneered at the angel, despite the fact that the latter could likely send him permanently back to the grave. "Vile, am I? But I serve the cause of the Cathedral and its glorious master."

"And that is the only reason you are still permitted to walk this plane. You have had a holy task set upon you; do not waste what little chance of redemption you have by making it otherwise."

But Malic laughed regardless. "A so holy task! Such blood and slaughter are worthy of any of the orders of the Triune! You would have made as good a Primus as my lord Lucion!"

The youthful figure stretched forth an open hand toward the spirit, and suddenly Malic felt himself wrenched from the latest body he had stolen. The mage's form weaved back and forth as he desperately sought to maintain a tie to it. Despite his efforts, the high priest was pulled forward.

Inarius closed his hand, then let it casually fall to his side. Malic's spirit was flung back into Amolia's body. The specter teetered from the strain of what had just happened.

"You will know your place, sinner," the Prophet remarked. "You will be grateful that you are deemed worthy to serve me."

"And . . . and another," rasped Malic in Amolia's voice. "The Lord Diablo."

The angel paid his slight defiance no mind. Instead, Inarius gazed down at the prince. "This was a good man, and I weep for his necessary sacrifice, just as I do for the guard you used to reach him and even the brigand whose shape you wore to reach the guard. I weep for all my children who must pass from Sanctuary in order to save it. Their loss will be remembered fondly by me always."

And with that, he waved his hand over Ehmad's corpse. As had happened to Gamuel, the prince became dust that blew away to nothing.

Malic watched silently, his breathing still heavy. He did not need to ask for the Prophet to deal with the other two bodies mentioned, for the high priest had his own methods of disposing of unwanted evidence.

That made him consider what he would have to do after this latest shell had served its usefulness. He wanted an end to this; he wanted the body that would serve him best . . . serve him forever.

"I still claim his corpse when this is done," Malic reminded his tormentor. "That was the offering by you and the Lord of Terror. Do this thing as you say, and I become Uldyssian ul-Diomed. That was promised!"

"You will receive your reward for services rendered, yes. I do not lie."

The Prophet might not lie—and Malic was not so certain about that point—but there were many variations of his truth. Malic could not see the angel stomaching his continued existence; Inarius surely intended the specter's time in his desired body to be short.

But the high priest had notions of his own. Whatever agreement the angel and Lord Diablo had, Malic would see that it would benefit him, not mean his end.

"The council and the guilds are waiting," Inarius stated, his form beginning to lose definition. One ethereal hand drew a series of flaming runes in the air. "Touching this pattern on the medallion will enable you to utilize its ability to transport you to them."

Malic had already known that, but he bowed his head regardless. He had shown enough defiance; now it was time for contrition.

"Do not fail in this" were the angel's last words before he vanished.

"I have no intention," the specter murmured to the empty air. "Not, at least, where my plans are concerned."

Now fully recovered from Inarius's painful lesson, Malic glanced again at the mirror, then touched the medallion. The runes glowed.

"Soon . . ." he whispered, imagining Uldyssian's face before him. "Soon . . ."

The swarm had finally retreated. It had not been vanquished, however. The sky had still been filled with the vicious insects, but just when the edyrem had been about to fail, the mantises had at last risen back into the sky and fled in the direction from which they had come.

The edyrem could do nothing but slump to the ground in exhaustion. Had the mage clans or the city sent out a force to attack them, there would have been some question of how many of Uldyssian's followers would have survived.

Serenthia was as exhausted as any of the others, but she forced herself to continue walking around the encampment, appearing as a symbol of confidence for the rest. In truth, her spirits were low, and not merely because of the bizarre attack. Now Mendeln was missing. The merchant's daughter had little doubt that the swarming had something to do with that.

They're all gone, Serenthia thought as she kept a false smile on her lips. Saron wearily saluted her, then went back to trying to organize some of the others. Of Jonas, there was no sign, but she felt certain that he was in the midst of a similar task. Serenthia was grateful for both men's loyalty and assistance, but they were not Uldyssian, Mendeln, or . . . or even Achilios. She was alone, and there was a fear that it would remain that way.

So close to the capital, the illumination caused by so many torches and oil lamps could be seen over the treetops. Out of necessity, Serenthia posted guards, all the while hoping that there would be no need of them.

When she felt that she had shown herself enough, Serenthia retired to a secluded area near the rear of the encampment. She ate a small meal that one of the edyrem offered her—they never let her cook for herself—then settled down and prayed for a decent night's slumber and the good news of Uldyssian and his brother.

But a comfortable sleep was not to be hers. The dreams came quickly, and all of them had to do with losing Achilios again. If she did not relive his death, then she stood at the opposite end of a great gulf, stretching her hands out in vain to him as he receded farther and farther away. In every dream, the raven-tressed woman cried, and as she slept, actual tears slid down her face.

Serenthia . . .

Her eyes immediately opened, but whether or not she was still asleep, she could not say. It was not possible that she had heard *his* voice. Achilios's voice.

But then it came again. *Serenthia . . .*

Rising, the merchant's daughter peered into the nearby jungle.

A pale figure half hidden by the underbrush stared back at her. Serenthia almost shouted his name, so thrilled was she. Then, suddenly more wary, she surveyed those nearby. The nearest sentry was far away, and the other edyrem were asleep. Only she had heard the archer's voice.

If it *was* actually him.

Suddenly cold with anger that someone might be using his image to lure her, Serenthia seized her spear. She reached out with her power, seeking any hint of another presence, but barely even finding that of the hunter.

There was only one way to settle whether or not this was actually Achilios. Aware that her heart was leading more than her head, Serenthia slipped out of the encampment.

As she neared him, the pale figure retreated deeper into the jungle. Serenthia readied her spear, more wary than ever. She continued to survey the region but still sensed no one but herself and what might be the man she loved.

When they were just out of sight of any possible onlookers, Achilios paused. Serenthia did the same.

"Is it you? Is it you, Achilios?"

He nodded once. "Yes . . . Serenthia."

She was still not convinced, although her heart ached to be. "Why now? Why at this point when you fled the other times?"

The archer brushed some loose dirt from his cheek. His effort proved futile. "At first . . . it was so that . . . that I would keep you . . . keep you from seeing me . . . as I am."

"Oh, Achilios! You know that I don't care about—"

He cut her off with a slashing gesture. "I'm *dead*, Serenthia! Dead!"

She would not accept that even such a state meant the end of what had been between them. "With all that I've seen, with all that I've fought, death doesn't scare me, Achilios."

"So it would . . . would seem." A rueful smile stretched across his face. "Why did you . . . have to fall . . . to fall in love with me . . . at last?"

It was more than she could take. Still clutching the spear, Serenthia rushed to Achilios. She wrapped her arms around him and held tight. He did not resist, but neither did he imitate her actions.

When it was clear that he would merely stand there, Serenthia finally looked up into his face and happened to see up close the dark, congealed gap where once his throat had been.

It made her gasp and back up, but not for the reasons the archer thought. As Achilios turned bitterly from her, Serenthia realized just how it had appeared to him.

"No! Please! It wasn't out of fear or disgust! Achilios!" Ignoring how loud her voice was growing, Serenthia cupped his chin in her free hand and made him look into her eyes. "I was angry! Angry for what happened to you!"

He shook his head. "You're . . . you're truly . . . amazing."

"I love you, that's all." Her eyes narrowed. "You said 'at first' that it had to do with not wanting me to see you as you are! What was the reason after that?"

Achilios pushed back from her. He gritted his teeth, as if seeking to keep in the answer. "For the same . . . for the same reason . . . that I tried to kill . . . to kill both you and . . . and Uldyssian! For the same . . . for the same reason . . . I'm finally with you . . . at last . . ." The undead hunter looked to his right. "Because of him . . ."

A brilliant light blossomed from there, one that made Serenthia immediately tighten her grip on her spear. In the midst of that light, she saw the tall figure emerge. Vast wings composed of tendrils of energy rose up behind him.

"Inarius!" Shoving Achilios back, she raised the weapon.

"No, Serenthia . . ." The archer grabbed her wrist. "Not Inarius . . ."

"Not—" She had no idea how that was possible to know, never having seen him. All Serenthia had to go by was Rathma's and Mendeln's descriptions, which certainly fit the celestial figure before her. True, there were minor details that she thought should have been different, but this was an angel! How many angels were there on Sanctuary, after all?

Belatedly, she recalled that there might be another, but her mind wanted to refuse that. They could not fight two angels.

"He comes . . . in peace."

That stirred her anger anew. "Peace? Isn't this the one who made you shoot at Mendeln and me?"

THAT WAS BEFORE.

The voice resounded in both her head and her heart. Serenthia's pulse raced.

THAT WAS BEFORE, the angel repeated, the light around him—light surely visible to all in the camp—pulsating with each word. *WHEN IT WAS NOT CLEAR TO ME THE COURSE NEEDED.*

"What does he mean by that?"

"He will . . . tell you . . . just be . . . patient."

THE EDYREM MUST BE READY, the angel answered unhelpfully. He did not exactly walk toward them but rather seemed to be closer, then closer yet, then even closer than that.

There was no face, but more something that seemed a visor made of light. The angel was impossibly tall and so bright that Serenthia had to squint a little. She was also surprised that no one had yet come running to see what was going on.

IT IS NOT MEANT FOR THE OTHERS TO SEE US TOGETHER, AND SO THEY DO NOT.

Which meant that, no matter what happened here, the other edyrem would not know the truth. That revived her wariness of the angel.

"Please, Serenthia . . . please listen . . . to him. I know . . . I know that's much to . . . to ask . . . believe me."

It was only because she was certain that Achilios spoke for himself and not because of some spell of the angel's that the merchant's daughter relaxed her grip—a little. "All right. I'll listen."

"Mendeln knows, too," Achilios continued, sounding a bit more human. A bit more . . . alive. "He knows . . . and that is why . . . why he was sent . . . ahead."

"To the city? By himself?"

"Mendeln is . . . never alone . . . and he of all of . . . us . . . can best find Uldyssian . . . if there's . . . if there's hope."

Serenthia dared gesture at the angel. "And what does this have to do with him? Why is he now trying to help us?"

It was not Achilios but the winged figure who answered that question. *BECAUSE INARIUS HAS DONE—AGAIN—THE UNTHINKABLE. HE HAS MADE A PACT WITH ONE OF THE THREE . . . MADE A WILLING PACT. THAT, TOO, DEMANDED MY COURSE CHANGE.*

"One of the Three? Is he referring to the Triune, Achilios?"

"To the . . . the truth of the . . . Triune." The archer grimaced. "You know . . . you know that demons . . . demons created it. You know that . . . the spirits of Mefis, Dialon . . . and Bala . . . are not what they . . . are made to be."

"No, of course not! They're each master demons, supposedly the rulers of—" She stopped short as the enormity of what he was trying to tell her finally became clear. "Surely not!" Her eyes wide, she looked to the angel. "One of the . . . one of the Three? Here?"

The angel dipped his head ever so slightly. *AND PERHAPS THE WORST OF THE THREE . . . HE WHO IS THE ESSENCE OF TERROR . . . THE LORD DIABLO.*

And as he said the name, Serenthia not only felt a chill throughout her body but sensed that the angel, too, fought back some anxiety. That such a mighty being as the one before her would be unsettled by merely speaking of this master demon gave indication of just how terrible this news was.

Trying to make sense of it, she blurted, "But if this demon is so powerful, how can Inarius risk any pact with him? It's sure to lead to his downfall."

AND IT WILL . . . ALTHOUGH HE DOES HAVE GREAT REASON TO FEEL THAT, IN THE END, IT SHALL BE

*LORD DIABLO . . . NAY . . . ALL OF US . . . WHO KNEEL
BEFORE HIM . . .*

"How is that possible? Was Inarius always so powerful
among angels?"

There was a hesitation, as if the figure had to consider
carefully what to say. *POWERFUL, BUT NO MORE SO
THAN ANY ON THE ANGIRIS COUNCIL. . . . IT IS HERE . . .
IN THIS WORLD THAT HE HELPED MAKE . . . WHERE
INARIUS WIELDS POWER THAT MAKES THE LORD
DEMON SEEK ALLIANCE . . . IT IS HERE WHERE HE HAS
SUCCEEDED IN DISTORTING THE WORLDSTONE FOR
HIS OWN GAIN, HIS OWN POWER.*

The Worldstone. She knew of it from Uldyssian, knew
that it was a phenomenal artifact, a massive crystal, that not
only preserved Sanctuary's presence from the outside but
had been manipulated by Inarius once to dampen the latent
powers of humans. Lilith had managed to alter its magic
slightly, just enough to encourage the rebirth of the
nephalem—or, as they were called now, the edyrem.

*SOMEHOW HE WAS ABLE TO ALTER THE WORLD-
STONE'S FOCUS—PERHAPS WITH THE UNKNOWING
HELP OF HIS FELLOW RENEGADES—THEN BIND HIM-
SELF UTTERLY TO IT AND THUS ENSURED THAT NONE
WHO HAD ASSISTED HIM IN ITS THEFT WOULD BE AS
POWERFUL. . . . IN TRUTH, IT IS ONLY HIS CONCERN
FOR DISCOVERY BY THE ANGIRIS COUNCIL THAT PRE-
VENTS HIM FROM DRAWING UPON ITS POWER EVEN
MORE.*

His words made Serenthia's hopes plummet. "Then all
this time, Uldyssian never had a chance against him? All
this time, the Prophet—Inarius—has been toying with us?
It's all been for nothing?"

"No! Not nothing," Achilios interjected, at the same time
seizing her by the shoulders. "Uldyssian is the only one . . .
the only one who might be . . . be able to actually *defeat*
Inarius here!"

"But how is that possible? How?"

"Don't . . . don't you recall what . . . Uldyssian did, Serenthia? Don't you . . . remember . . . what he said . . . happened? At the . . . the Worldstone?"

The Worldstone. Despite the growing turmoil of her thoughts, the raven-haired woman quickly focused on what Achilios had said. Uldyssian had seen this Worldstone. He had been brought to it by Inarius's son, Rathma. Even Uldyssian's cursory description of it had left her marveling that such a thing could have been created, much less exist at all.

And then Serenthia recalled what Achilios had been trying to point out.

Uldyssian himself had *altered* the Worldstone in its very makeup. Altered it in a manner that apparently even Inarius could not unmake.

Inarius could *not* unmake it.

"Uldyssian is . . . the one hope against Inarius," Achilios acknowledged. "Even he . . ." The archer pointed at the angel. "Even he can't alter what Uldyssian did."

That knowledge stirred her as nothing else could. "Then we need to move on Kehjan as quickly as possible! If we awaken the others now, we can be there in just a few hours. Despite what you say, I'm certain that Mendeln can't do this by himself. We need to be there, need to march to the gates and tear them down if we must! We've got to find Uldyssian!"

The angel—who had yet to give any name—suddenly stood on her other side, causing Serenthia to gasp. *IF YOU WOULD DO SO, THEN YOU WOULD FALL DIRECTLY INTO THE TRAP ALREADY SET INTO MOTION . . . A TRAP THAT EVEN I CANNOT UNDO AT THIS POINT.*

"What? What is it? Is it about Uldyssian?"

IT IS ALL ABOUT YOUR FRIEND. For the first time, the angel appeared weary. *AND THE LIVES LOST THAT WILL NOW BE BLAMED ON HIM AND THE EDYREM.* He raised a gauntleted hand to her forehead, without permission touching the palm to her skin. *BEHOLD WHAT IS HAPPENING . . . WHAT WILL HAPPEN . . .*

There was something about this angel that still caused Serenthia concern, but she had no choice but to obey as what felt like her soul was ripped free of her body. Suddenly, she raced along the landscape toward the capital. It reminded her in some ways of the search that she and Uldyssian had made using their powers. That allowed her to regain some of her composure.

Over the massive walls, her view flew, over the walls and into the vast city. Images of buildings raced past, and even people briefly appeared.

Then . . . and then, somewhere deep in the middle of the city, her gaze dove directly into a heavily walled gray building. She passed through stone as if it did not exist and entered first a small, torchlit chamber and then, almost instantly, a much larger, more elaborate one.

And there Serenthia beheld horror that convinced her of the angel's every intention.

THIRTEEN

The mage council consisted of one chosen member from each of the dominant clans, which numbered seven. There were lesser members from the next seven smaller but still powerful ones below those, but they had no vote. They could recommend or bring up articles for debate, though. This gave them some influence and, thus, less inclination to protest the rulings by the senior members. In this manner, the mage council kept order among themselves, even when many clans were involved in bitter and deadly feuds with one another.

There was an additional factor that served to keep the council above the infighting. The enforcement arm had been created to make certain that no mage, whatever his position, escaped punishment for breaking the covenants set in place by the council. It drew to its ranks spellcasters willing literally to give a part of their essence to the council and thus no longer belong to a clan. Such mages were chosen carefully using many criteria, including trust in their determination to see their orders through to the end regardless of the obstacles.

And so, when Amolia appeared in their midst, she was acknowledged by the council and other attending mages as befit her position. The visiting masters of the guilds also eyed her respectfully; to them, the enforcers were the most trusted—if that word could be used for any of those present—of spellcasters.

The current leader of the council—the bearer of the title changed with each new moon in order to maintain fairness—stared down from the high platform where he and his counterparts sat and, in a voice cracked with age, demanded, "Where is this Uldyssian ul-Diomed? You were supposed to return with him!"

"He won't be coming," the figure before him replied. "I am here in his place with a message."

A combination of surprise and disdain crossed more than one wrinkled face among the mages. Several merchants, most of them far more corpulent than the council, also appeared disproving of the announcement.

A well-coiffured figure with an elaborate emerald-encrusted nose ring declared, "We agreed, in great part due to the request of Prince Ehmad and the memory of our own lamented Fahin, to come to this gathering. If the mages have played some trick in cooperation with this Ascenian—"

"The Ascenian has made no advance pact with the council and would be turned away if he dared so," returned the council leader. "We would not think of such a disrespectful action against our brothers in the guilds. . . ."

Several of the guild masters smiled knowingly. As powerful as the spellcasters were, they depended too much on the guilds' wares.

Throughout this exchange, Amolia—Malic—remained quiet. Only when all eyes turned back to him for explanation did he continue, as planned. "Master Uldyssian is not coming, but, as I said, I am to be his messenger."

"'Master' Uldyssian?" The council leader grunted. "You have no masters but us, Amolia. . . ."

Bowing low, Malic put a smile on his stolen face. "No longer! Master Uldyssian has shown me the truth. I exist to follow his path and remove from it all he has deemed heretical."

"What does she mean by that babbling?" demanded a guild master. Several of those beside him rumbled their approval of this question.

Malic turned slowly to face the man. "It means that he

has given me the honor of taking the first step toward liberating the people of Kehjan from the mages and the guilds!"

There were shocked protests from all around at this damning statement. On both sides, members of the gathering rose in anger.

Malic suddenly felt the might of the two who had sent him on this mission fill him. He suddenly knew how puny the powers of any of those in attendance were compared with Inarius or the Lord Diablo . . . or even him now.

"Amolia!" grated the council leader. "Your very words condemn you. Such foolishness! You know too well the hold upon all of your order. It shall be used now to mete out proper punishment for your declared betrayal, after which the Ascenian—Uldyssian ul-Diomed—shall be declared enemy of Kehjan and marked for death by all."

Roars of approval rose from both spellcasters and guilds. Malic was unconcerned about the threat of punishment to Amolia. As she no longer existed, what essence they had of her was useless.

Besides, it was time for him to follow his commands.

"But it's not I who is to be condemned," he retorted, his smile widening. "Master Uldyssian had already condemned all of you!"

Malic did not even have to gesture. All he had to do was stare around him and let the will of the angel and the demon be done.

The tiny, glittering blades formed in the air around him, then shot forth like hungry flies in every direction. They spun with a swiftness that caused each to emit a faint buzzing sound, a sound multiplied by the thousands.

The guild masters certainly had no chance. Some wore protective talismans bought from greedy mages, but none of those so much as slowed the slaughter. The twirling blades cut through thick garments, then flayed flesh. Men screamed and tried to hide, but there was nowhere for them to go, for before unleashing the blades, Malic had sealed the exits.

The mages fared little better than the guildsmen. Most were too caught by surprise to cast any protective spell. A few managed to ward off the initial blades, but the power of Inarius and Diablo far outstripped even the most powerful of those assembled here. What success any mage initially had proved fleeting.

And so they were slaughtered. The gleaming silver blades—shaped like arced slivers—fulfilled their monstrous purpose. Blood splattered the chamber everywhere, so much that it pooled in many spots on the floor. The screams died down, becoming sobs from here and there . . . and then silence.

There was little left recognizable. Not an inch of skin remained on any of the victims. Aware that the Kehjan methods of torture preferred flaying, the angel and the demon had visited upon the gathering what they felt was quite an appropriate fate.

With the smile still playing over his host's face, Malic, untouched by either blade or blood, calmly made his way around the chamber. He paused here and there to inspect a body, but, not finding what he was looking for, he quickly moved on.

At last, the dread spirit located his prize—or two, to be exact. One was a mage, a part of the council, in fact. His life was passing swiftly, but Malic put a hand to his gory torso just where the heart—partially visible—was beating its last.

He felt the will of Inarius flow through. The flayed man let out a gasp. The heart beat a little faster. Of necessity, the pain had also been slightly lessened. They wanted this one alive . . . temporarily.

Malic performed the same ritual for a guild master whose left leg had been all but amputated by the blades. Gobbets of the rotund man's flesh lay spread around him like some macabre blanket. He, too, received the angel's gift.

There were witnesses now. They would survive just long enough to relate their tales, then pass on. The same spell that had kept them from death would also guarantee that they would recall enough but not too much. Their stories would be very similar but from their differing perspectives. The angel and the demon had made certain that there would be no questions from those who discovered them about just what had happened and who was responsible.

Uldyssian, of course.

Already there came banging on the doors. The guards and the mages with them likely did not understand why nothing they did opened the locks or removed the protective spells.

Malic sensed one or two more fleeting lives but knew that those poor fools would not be able to answer any questions. His mission here was done. Under normal circumstances, the medallion he had used to enter would now have required the work of one of those on the council to allow him to leave again. However, the powers he currently served made that unnecessary.

Malic grinned at the carnage, bowed . . . and disappeared.

He should be dead, drowned in the water.

But he was not, a fact made stranger by the discovery, when at last he was able to open his eyes, that he was *still* at the bottom of the underground canal.

To his credit, Uldyssian kept from panicking, despite this unnerving revelation. He could vaguely make out movement above him, most of it refuse flowing on. Without moving so much as a finger, the son of Diomedes cautiously sought to find the cause of his salvation—if that was what it was.

At first, Uldyssian thought it the work of the demon, but that made no sense at all. It had been intent on devouring him, that much had been obvious. Therefore, why preserve his life?

What else, then? Or rather, *who*? Kethuus? Again, Uldyssian knew that he followed a false lead. He had been conscious long enough to see the mage fall. Kethuus was either dead or immobile. There had been no help from him.

Then . . . who?

Something moved against the current. It was little more than a dark shadow, but it immediately made Uldyssian think of the demon again. He tensed, watching it as best he could.

It hovered at the corner of his eye, never quite coalescing into something that he could recognize. There were glimpses—mere glimpses—of what he *believed* were long, plantlike appendages and maybe the bulbous body, but never could Uldyssian be absolutely certain. Nonetheless, his heart pounded faster, and had he been on the surface, the son of Diomedes would have broken out in an anxious sweat.

Then there came a voice in his head, one that sent chills through him. *I've saved you, mortal . . . saved you from certain death.*

Who are you? Uldyssian thought back. *What are you?*

The shadow moved a bit more into his line of sight. Again, Uldyssian thought he caught glimpses of something that resembled the attacking demon, but now there were other images as well. For a moment, he could have sworn that it was Inarius himself who hovered so close, and the fear that the angel had at last trapped him sent his blood surging yet faster.

It is not he who has come to you here, the voice said with some hint of mockery for having been mistaken for the Prophet. *The angel would leave you to die, but I am not so heartless!*

Who are you? Uldyssian repeated, now wondering how he could have ever thought for even an instant that this shadow was his foe. Inarius did not touch his primal instincts so. *Who?*

The shadow shifted closer yet. Dread memories of Malic arose, then passed, only to be replaced by a beauteous yet even more unnerving face briefly crossing Uldyssian's thoughts.

Lilith.

He fought down these resurrected fears. Lilith was dead, and Malic would not have left him untouched. They had nothing to do with what was happening now.

The shadow receded slightly. It spoke again, its tone soothing, placating. *They cannot touch you, Uldyssian, not while you're under my protection. As for who I am, I've many names, and some you know. One of those is Dialon.*

Dialon! Uldyssian understood immediately both who and what had prevented him from drowning. Dialon, said to be the spirit of Determination by the Temple of the Triune. Dialon, who Ulydssian knew was actually of the same blood—if one could use that term for demons—as Lilith, for he was brother to her father, the terrible Mephisto.

Diablo, Lord of Terror, was the only thing that kept Uldyssian from drowning.

You need have no fear of me, Diablo said, no doubt sensing the human's unease. *All things are turned about on Sanctuary, where angels commit sin and demons must try to make amends. I saved you because we two are much alike, for we're all that stands between Inarius and this world's death.*

Despite his predicament, Uldyssian found himself caught up by the master demon's words. What Diablo said about Inarius was very true. The Prophet clearly saw sin as something others did, not himself. His actions were "necessary." That hundreds died because of the angel's ego did not matter in the least.

Yes . . . you see him correctly. Inarius is mad in a manner that sends fear through the High Heavens and the Burning Hells. Yet he cannot be touched, for he's tied to the very foundation of Sanctuary, the Worldstone! It's his power, his existence!

Uldyssian could find no fault in Diablo's statements, though he had not considered that both the High Heavens and the Burning Hells knew all that was going on. That sent a further chill through him. If both sides in the celestial conflict of which he had learned feared Inarius, then what did that mean for humanity's hopes?

The demon drew so close that Uldyssian could swear Diablo stared directly into his eyes. The son of Diomedes steeled himself. He had faced demons before.

There was a moment of silence, as if, for some reason, Diablo had to mull over his thoughts. Then . . . *But the angel is not so invulnerable as believed. You proved that . . . and you proved that you can reach into his very core and put fear into him.*

Me? But how?

You changed the Worldstone without even understanding it! You did what no other could and what the angel could not unmake. This gives us a chance if we are willing to strike quickly.

It had come to what Uldyssian had not believed possible. Diablo, Lord of Terror, was offering a pact. The demon wished to ally himself with a mortal against an angel.

It was so mad a notion that Uldyssian would have laughed if able to do so.

I am not Lucion, son of my brother, who preaches only hate. I am also not she who lived to twist all around her finger and then rip out their beating hearts. There is much I can offer in trust.

There was only one thing that Uldyssian wanted at the moment, and that was to reach the surface again. He found it suspicious that not once had Diablo offered to raise him out of the channel. Did the demon expect that Uldyssian would consider his offer while still trapped motionless yards underwater? If so, then truly Diablo and his ilk did not understand the thinking of mortals.

Return me to the ledge, he demanded. *Then we can continue talking.*

The shadow weaved about in the water. Uldyssian was very aware that he did not see the true form of the demon lord and was grateful for that favor.

In truth, you are safer here for the moment than anywhere else, mortal. Both the natural magic of water and my own power shield

*you from Inarius even now. Were I to bring you to the surface,
you would immediately risk discovery.*

Uldyssian did not care one bit about such a danger. Like
most humans, he had a healthy respect for water, especially
how easily it could fill one's lungs. *I want away from here!*

*The danger is too great, but perhaps there is a way. But for it to
succeed, you must open your mind to me, allow me in a very small
way to touch the power within you . . . just the slightest touch
should do it.*

As the shadow spoke, Uldyssian suddenly felt as if the
water pressed down a thousand times harder on him. He
grew claustrophobic, the sensation that he was about to be
crushed or drowned magnifying beyond belief. Uldyssian
started to agree to the demon's suggestion . . . but at the last
moment somehow held back. A part of him questioned
anew Diablo's reluctance to do anything until after the
human had opened himself up.

That same part also finally questioned whether the Lord
of Terror was actually even the one who had saved him.
Why would Diablo leave him like this? Uldyssian doubted
the reasons the demon had given. They sounded more like
a means to keep the human at this terrible disadvantage,
where he might be willing to sell himself entirely in order to
escape this predicament.

And that made Uldyssian finally realize just who had initially kept him from drowning after he had destroyed the
other demon. It had been none other than himself. Only
now did Uldyssian sense the truth of that, and he knew that
the reason it had earlier escaped him was Diablo's machinations. The demon lord had fed his innate terrors, making
the son of Diomedes unable to focus enough to understand.

And still Diablo tried. *I sense Inarius near! Hurry! If we
bind our strength together, we can bring him down!*

An urge to do as the shadow said arose within Uldyssian.
Only with extreme effort did he manage to hold back from
agreeing. Then, before anything else could deter his
thoughts, Uldyssian began concentrating on freeing himself.

A wave of anger struck him. The demon lord dropped all pretense. *You're mine! You have no hope against me, human! With but a whim, I shall rip off your arms and legs and slowly feed your bleeding torso to my ravenous pets who even now fill the waters!*

Scores of dark shapes swam through the water toward Uldyssian. He suspected that they were only illusion, for Diablo still likely sought his surrender but dared not take the chance. With all his will, Uldyssian sought to rise from the channel and release himself from the spell his subconscious surely had created.

The insidious school closed on him. Crimson saucer-shaped eyes stared hungrily. Mouths full of rows of sharp teeth opened to bite.

With a swooshing sound, Uldyssian shot upward. He broke the surface and continued several feet higher. Only when his head was mere inches from the ceiling did his momentum abruptly cease.

His arms, his hands . . . his entire body was his again. Uldyssian marveled that he floated above the water. As a youth, the former farmer had often imagined what it might be like to be a bird, but never had he expected actually to experience such flight himself.

From below came a wild roar. Out of the water burst the monstrous shadow, and as it rushed up at Uldyssian, it transformed a hundred times. Each incarnation was more horrific than the last, and nearly all the son of Diomedes could trace to his own innate terrors.

But despite his fear, Uldyssian stood his position. He also knew that he had to do more than that. He had to find some defense against Diablo. Only one thing occurred to him, one wild hope that seemed more likely to leave the Lord of Terror laughing in his face.

At his will, a fountain of water rushed up between him and the demon with more swiftness than Diablo could summon. That water even more quickly froze, its sides taking on a frosty but also mirrorlike finish.

And so Diablo looked upon *himself.*

Under any other circumstances, Uldyssian doubted that the demon would have been affected. Prepared for such a trick, the Lord of Terror would have adjusted. Here, though, Uldyssian's spell happened so quickly, and with so much instinct as opposed to preparation, that the demon could not have known what to expect.

Thus, Diablo inflicted upon himself that which he did unto others. The fears he had been thrusting upon the human altered to his *own*.

The shadowy figure let out a shriek that nearly made Uldyssian flee in mindless panic. Somehow, though, the son of Diomedes held. To do otherwise was to fail.

Diablo twisted and turned as his own insidious power wreaked havoc on him. He had only glanced for a moment, but the fears of the master of fear were evidently monstrous, indeed.

Still howling, Diablo rushed up into the ceiling—and through the very stone. His cry echoed throughout not only the underground passage but Uldyssian's soul.

It took the human a moment to realize that he was alone. Extreme exhaustion seized hold of Uldyssian. The frozen column of water collapsed, returning to the flow. Only with effort did he manage not to join it, instead using his will to push him to the ledge.

Once there, he leaned against the wall and caught his breath. Although Diablo was gone, and with him what little illumination there had been, Uldyssian saw well in the dark. First, the magical field that had kept him from drowning, and now this. Again, his powers had adjusted to his needs without him even consciously summoning them.

That made him recall what Mendeln had said, about his abilities controlling him more than he controlled them. For a second, Uldyssian seriously considered the repercussions that his brother had hinted at—and then laughed at himself for fearing such. He and his abilities were one; how could he possibly be a danger to himself or anyone else because of that?

His head finally began to clear a little. Recalling Kethuus, Uldyssian rushed over to the mage, who still lay unmoving.

Even before he touched the spellcaster's chest, Uldyssian sensed that Kethuus was still alive. In fact, the dark-skinned man was in the same state the son of Diomedes had been in when first captured by the aquatic demon.

Not certain exactly what he was doing but positive that he could succeed, Uldyssian held his hand a few inches above the mage's body and ran it along the length from the heart to the head. At the same time, he willed Kethuus to be released.

The mage gasped, then coughed several times. His eyes, which had been staring blankly, now focused.

"Ascenian . . ." he murmured. "Uldyssian . . . is it . . . is it dead?"

Only then did Uldyssian realize that Kethuus knew of nothing concerning what had happened past the moment of his capture. That struck Uldyssian odd, for he had been conscious all the while. Had his will been that much stronger than the other man's?

"It's dead. I boiled it alive, which was no more vicious than the fate it planned for us."

"Of that I have no doubt." He accepted Uldyssian's hand. The latter pulled him to his feet, where Kethuus wobbled uncertainly for a few moments before regaining his balance. Once that was accomplished, the mage immediately summoned a light. "Without any aid, I do not think I would've fared as well as you."

Uldyssian eyed the murky water. "Wanting to live can enable someone to perform miracles."

"Not like yours." All trace of haughtiness had vanished from Kethuus. "You are everything I heard and even more. You could have also left me to rot, and you did not do that."

The mage's change of heart encouraged Uldyssian greatly. If someone as hard-skinned as Kethuus could be made to see the truth, then there was true hope of persuading the mage clans to join with him against not only Inarius but apparently a demon lord as well.

The mage clans. Uldyssian grimaced. "Kethuus, how long have we been down here?"

His companion immediately saw the reason for his concern. "I fear many hours. But have no fear. I will speak for you, Uldyssian! I—"

Kethuus suddenly clutched at his chest. Uldyssian reached to help him, but the dark man shook him off.

"They are . . . using that part of me that I sacrificed to the council to find me! It is how they track enforcers who vanish, for our tasks on occasion are met with violence." He straightened. "They know now where I am. No doubt, when we did not appear, they questioned Prince Ehmad and discovered we were together."

"Odd that they couldn't find you before now."

His comment was rewarded with a white but grim smile. "The demon's spell must have shielded us from such."

They had no chance to say more, for around them there materialized not one but nearly a dozen hooded mages. Among the newcomers was the lone figure that Uldyssian would have recognized, the gaunt baritone, Nurzani.

"Kethuus," intoned the skeletal mage, his deep-sunken eyes darting between his comrade and Uldyssian. "Stand away quickly!"

"Nurzani! What—"

The new arrivals raised medallions and staffs in Uldyssian's direction. Kethuus held up a hand in protest, but Nurzani gestured impatiently, and the dark man suddenly vanished from Uldyssian's side. A moment later, he appeared behind the other mage.

"Now," Nurzani commanded.

But before they could do whatever it was they intended to a stunned Uldyssian, there came a rush of water that caught the attention of all. From out of it flew a flood of ivory-colored objects varying in size and shape. In less than the blink of an eye, they gathered between the circle of mages and their intended target.

A familiar and very welcome voice resounded through the tunnels. "Uldyssian! To me!"

Mendeln! There was no one whose appearance could have gladdened Uldyssian's heart more. Nevertheless, he hesitated a moment, as startled as the others by what his brother had clearly wrought.

A wall formed of *bone* not only prevented the mages from reaching Uldyssian but momentarily deflected whatever spells they were attempting. The bones themselves were of many origins, from obvious scraps dropped from the world above to those of the types of creatures that lived off the garbage—and one another. There were also human bones, far too many human bones, a grim reminder of not only the city's lengthy history but the violent aspects of it through-out the generations.

Mendeln had attempted something like this in the past, but not nearly on so grand a scale. The macabre wall shim-mered under the mages' onslaught, but it held.

Kethuus appeared to be shouting a protest to Nurzani, but the other spellcaster was clearly disinclined to listen to him. The skeletal figure reached into a pouch.

Frustration surged through Uldyssian, frustration quickly shifting to outrage. These mages now attacked him without giving any cause. He could only assume that they had planned betrayal all along.

His outrage stirred his power. He felt it strain to be unleashed and saw no reason why not.

A hand grabbed his shoulder. Teeth bared, he turned to find his brother.

"Stand away, Mendeln!" Uldyssian growled. "They've brought this on themselves."

"No," his sibling replied soberly. "They have very good reasons for hating you."

Mendeln's statement caught Uldyssian by surprise. He started to protest—but his brother, eyes narrowing, sud-denly looked behind him.

"No!" He thrust something into Uldyssian's palm, then

shouted a word that the elder son of Diomedes could not understand.

The tunnel was momentarily filled with searing light, and then whatever Mendeln had given his siblng emitted a glow of its own.

Uldyssian's surroundings altered. The tunnels and the burning light vanished. A calming darkness swept over him. He landed on something soft—moist ground. Around him, different sounds arose, the sounds of jungle life.

Still needing to orient himself, Uldyssian dropped to his knees. His breathing calmed and the rage that had engulfed him in the tunnels faded again.

As reason returned, he noticed a faint but comfortable coolness in his hand. There was also a dim glow that reminded him of starlight.

Peering down, Uldyssian discovered Mendeln's ivory dagger. Even as he eyed it, the faint glow ceased.

Thinking of his brother, Uldyssian twisted around to return the dagger to him . . . and only then discovered that Mendeln was not with him.

"He was more concerned with you and what you might do," declared a voice from the opposite direction.

Turning, Uldyssian faced Rathma. "I have to go back for him!"

"Nothing would please me more than to rescue him, especially as it was my lapse that allowed him to be manipulated into following you to Kehjan." The cloaked figure approached. "But if you return to the tunnels and confront the mages, there will be no hope whatsoever of healing what may already be beyond our abilities to mend."

As usual, Uldyssian understood very little of what the Ancient meant. He only knew that his brother was among enemies after seeking to rescue *him*. "I'm going back!"

Rathma shook his head. "Uldyssian, you are not aware of what has taken place these past few hours. The mage council and many of the leading guild masters—all gathered to meet with you—were brutally slaughtered."

The news struck Uldyssian like a rock. "Slaughtered? How?"

"By one of their own . . . who claims she did it in your name. They seek her, too, but more to the point, you are now declared a fiendish murderer whose followers must also be put down. The mage clans—nay, the entire capital—rise up to war upon the edyrem."

It was the nightmare that the son of Diomedes had feared early on but was certain that he could prevent from ever happening. He did not have to ask who was behind it. Inarius, naturally. Inarius—and for some reason, the demon lord Diablo likely had a part in the matter.

And then there was this female mage who, no doubt through the angel or the demon or both, had wielded such might as could brutally slay seasoned spellcasters. He suspected that it had been Amolia—but not truly her. She was not the type easily turned.

Malic had a new body and evidently a pact with those seeking Uldyssian's downfall.

Yet his concern for himself was minimal. Uldyssian held up Mendeln's dagger, intending to use it to help him return to his brother or even bring him back. However, the dagger looked different from any time he had seen it previously. It was pale in a more ominous manner, pale and lifeless.

The Ancient shook his head. "I feared as much. When I sensed you but not him, I feared the worst."

"Stop speaking in riddles, and help me do something!"

"But there is nothing you can do for Mendeln," Rathma said with utter calm. "Nothing you can do for him at all. Look at the blade. The link between him and it is cut." He bowed his head. "Your brother is lost to us."

FOURTEEN

Is this death? Mendeln asked himself. *Is this it?*

If it was, it was far less than he had imagined. Of course, imagination and truth did not always cross paths or even travel within the same world. Still, Mendeln would have thought that there was more—considering what he had witnessed while alive—than this utter emptiness. He could see nothing, could touch nothing, and did not even know if he had anything reminiscent of his old corporeal form.

His mind raced back to the events in the tunnel. Through the guidance of the other angel, he had not only entered the city swiftly and without notice by its guardians—physical or magical—but been then able to use his own blood tie and the skills Rathma and the dragon had taught him to find his brother. Unfortunately, retrieving Uldyssian had not been as simple a matter as he had hoped.

What had brought about the situation in which he had found himself when finally locating his brother, Mendeln knew better than most. The *ghosts* had come to him, of course, the ghosts of dead spellcasters and guild leaders. More than usual, these spirits had been eager to impart upon him the cause of their murder. Mendeln knew the details as well as if he had been there himself, and he knew without a doubt that the woman, Amolia, was not what she seemed. Indeed, when the ghosts had verified this, they had done so in the worst possible manner.

They had revealed to him that it was by *his* doing that all this calamity and bloodshed had happened. They had revealed this by telling him the story Uldyssian had claimed as truth.

The dread spirit of the high priest, Malic, had been responsible for all the heinous deaths.

Somehow, he had escaped the bone fragment to which he had been bound by Mendeln and now, like some terrible disease, spread from one victim to the next. Worse, if Mendeln's suspicions were correct, all the deaths caused by the specter's continued existence were merely incidental as he pursued the one body he truly coveted: Uldyssian's.

Filled with guilt by the horror he had unleashed upon others, only one thing had suddenly mattered to Mendeln. He had to get his brother out of the capital, where he was certain Malic still lurked. For a time, though, the search had gone nowhere. It had been as if Uldyssian did not exist at all, but in the end, Mendeln had finally managed to locate him. His mistake had been seeking above when his sibling had been below.

And sure enough, he had found Uldyssian, but in the midst of a group of vengeful hunters who would not be willing to listen to reason. There had been no hesitation on Mendeln's part. The spell creating the wall of bone had been driven by his fear for his brother, and the results had astounded him as much as they had the mages and likely even his brother.

But then, when Uldyssian had not only refused to leave but appeared ready to strike back—and become the very evil the Kehjani thought him to be—Mendeln saw no recourse. He had abandoned the other spell and instead cast one that he hoped would take his brother from harm. That had meant sacrificing the dagger, but he had not cared.

The spell had worked. Uldyssian had vanished.

And the mages had attacked him as they had intended to attack Uldyssian.

That was the last Mendeln remembered, save for a brief spark of incredible pain. The next instant, he had discovered himself in this *limbo*, for lack of a better word.

If he was dead, then at least he had done what he had most desired. Uldyssian was outside the city and surely safe. That was all that mattered—

His heart jumped as a voice from nowhere and everywhere called, *AWAKEN, MENDELN UL-DIOMED! AWAKEN! THOUGH FOR YOUR SINS, DEATH WOULD BE THE LEAST OF THE PUNISHMENTS YOU DESERVE, YOU HAVE BEEN SAVED.*

The emptiness through which Mendeln had been floating gave way to a glorious chamber of gleaming marble. Uldyssian's brother found himself lying on a soft, elaborate couch. Above him, a vast panorama detailing an idyllic realm populated by beautiful winged figures covered the entire ceiling.

The words, if not the voice itself, had already warned Mendeln just who had him. His wondrous surroundings informed him where that being had taken him.

He leapt to his feet, reaching for the dagger that was no longer there, and found himself standing before a towering figure with wings composed of tendrils of energy who was not the angel in the jungle.

The celestial warrior then rippled as if seen through water and became a being equally anathema to Mendeln: the Prophet.

"Mendeln ul-Diomed," sang the master of the Cathedral of Light. "Once I spoke to your brother, seeking his redemption from his great downfall. He chose the path of sin rather than a return to the light. I pray for your soul's sake that you do not repeat his error."

Mendeln did not know when this supposed conversation with Uldyssian had taken place, but he could imagine that his sibling had remained defiant. He wondered why Inarius would think him different.

The Prophet gestured, and next to Mendeln materialized a figure that seemed half golden sunlight, half wind. It was neither male nor female and had no legs, but rather what seemed a stream of tendrils akin to those of the angel.

With hands that consisted of only three digits, the being held a glittering tray upon which appeared a goblet made of pure diamond. In the goblet was golden nectar.

"You would do well to refresh yourself, my child, after such a traumatic encounter."

Without hesitation, Mendeln took the goblet from the ethereal servant. The moment he held the cup, the being dissipated. Uldyssian's brother took a sip; *nectar* poorly described the astounding liquid.

He did not fear that something in the drink would make him more susceptible to Inarius's suggestions. The angel did not need so mortal a trick. There was certainly something else to come.

"You would be dead now, you know," the Prophet said with a solemn expression. "They were determined to slay your brother, and when you stole that chance from them, they turned their magic upon you, my child." He steepled his fingers. "You would be dead now . . . if not for me."

Despite the fact that this was an angel, Mendeln was not sure how much he should believe. He suspected that Inarius could easily manipulate any facts to serve his desires. Still, Mendeln wisely bowed his head and replied, "I thank you for that."

The Prophet nodded approvingly at his attitude. "Your brother would do well to learn from your manners. Such sinful arrogance will only destroy him. I know that you would not wish that."

They were coming closer to whatever it was Inarius wanted of him. Mendeln chose to play along, especially since he saw no other choice at the moment.

"You have seen into death, Mendeln ul-Diomed, in ways no other mortal has. You have begun this unique journey in great part due to the influence of my errant offspring. It is something that he should have never done."

There were times, too, when Mendeln had thought the very same thing, yet he could not have turned back. The path upon which he had been led was now as much a part of him as breathing.

"But I do not think it the influence of him alone," continued the angel, his youthful aspect revealing at last a hint of an emotion Mendeln would hardly have expected.

Anxiety.

"No . . . my son is not the fount of knowledge from which you both draw. There is another, and you know who it is."

Mendeln tried to fight down his sudden fear. Inarius knew about Trag'Oul!

He suddenly worried that by thinking of the dragon, he had verified for Inarius the truth, but oddly, the angel gave no sign that he had sensed anything. In fact, Inarius continued to appear anxious.

The Prophet's first words came back to him, and Mendeln realized that his captor had not actually responded to the mortal's curiosity over whether he was dead or not but had merely started out their conversation in the most logical manner the situation warranted. Anyone in Mendeln's state would have wondered if he had been slain and Inarius had used that to press his point about how much the son of Diomedes owed him.

But not even his life was worth betraying the dragon, for Mendeln knew that Trag'Oul's efforts to protect Sanctuary far outweighed whatever contribution the human had made. Certain that Inarius would punish him severely for defying him, Mendeln nonetheless kept silent before the robed figure.

Yet, while there was some discernible anger, the Prophet did not strike him down. Mendeln observed with morbid fascination that Inarius more and more displayed human emotions. So long among men, the angel could not help picking up some of their ways, even if he himself perhaps did not acknowledge it.

There was now clearly tension in the angel's manner as he proclaimed, "Denial of the truth is also a sin, my child.

Do you wish to condemn yourself by not stating what we both know? Such foolishness!"

The last vestiges of uncertainty concerning whether or not Inarius could read his thoughts vanished. Mendeln could only assume that Trag'Oul had managed to create some mental shield that Inarius could not penetrate.

Mendeln swallowed the last of his drink as he tried not to think of what his captor might attempt in order to break that shield. Then he wondered why Inarius would even bother. After all, the Prophet already knew about the dragon.

However, Inarius continued to grow furious. With a single gesture, he sent Mendeln's goblet the way of the servant. With a scowl, he raised Mendeln himself up into the air until the human nearly floated among the winged figures in the vast mural.

"Repent for your past misdeeds, Mendeln ul-Diomed, and admit the truth we both know. *He* is here! *He* is the one who guides you from the shadows. Speak his name! It is *Tyrael*. Tyrael! Admit it now!"

Tyrael! The mage's assault had obviously left Mendeln momentarily disoriented for him to have forgotten the one who had truly instigated this particular quest. Because of the second angel, Mendeln had even willingly abandoned the edyrem, an act for which he felt little guilt. After all, it had been for his brother's sake.

Tyrael. Of course, the Prophet would be concerned about one of his own kind in his very midst.

Inarius's voice boomed like thunder, but it was not the only sound deafening the son of Diomedes. There was also, oddly enough, the flapping of many huge wings. In fact, the flapping grew to dominate all other sounds. The unseen wings made such noise that they drove Mendeln to tears.

Something tore at his arm. A hand, small but with sharp nails. A second ripped at his shoulder. There then came another and another . . .

And through his bleary eyes, Mendeln saw he was being attacked by the images from the huge mural. More than a dozen already assailed him, and others were in the process of tearing themselves free in order to join the first. They were literally as they looked in the painting, and when one turned to the side, Mendeln saw that it had *no* depth.

Mendeln tried to bat them away, but there were too many. They clawed at his face, tore at his breast. Despite their thinness, when he sought to punch through them, his fist met what felt like stone.

As they swarmed around him, they took up the Prophet's demand. *Speak his name! Tyrael! Speak it! Admit that he is the one!*

Even then, even when it seemed so easy just to agree with Inarius, Mendeln held back. Not being certain who all his enemies were did more to disorient Rathma's father than anything else Uldyssian's brother could imagine. Even if that meant torture and death, Mendeln at least could hope that he gave the others a better chance.

Without warning, the winged figures suddenly pulled back. Recovering, Mendeln watched as they returned to their positions in the mural. He expected Inarius to let him fall to the floor, but instead, the Prophet brought him down gently astride the couch.

"I am so very sorry, my child," Inarius said, his expression now piteous. "So very, very sorry that you wish to continue to sin as you do. I did what I could to try to persuade you to come back to the light, but, like your misbegotten brother, you would rather choose the darkness." The pity transformed into condemnation. "And so, into the darkness you shall be cast."

The vast marble chamber twisted around Mendeln as if turned fluid. The couch upon which Mendeln had landed became a vast, sucking hole. Uldyssian's brother let out a cry of dismay as he fought in vain to keep from being drawn into it.

"A pity . . ." was the last he heard the Prophet speak.

It seemed to Mendeln that he was to fall forever, but then, at last, he landed hard on what seemed stone. The collision knocked the air from his lungs and the sense from his head. Mendeln had no idea where he was.

And then a woman's voice from somewhere in the darkness stirred him to waking. "Who is it? Who's there? Tell me! Tell me!"

The first thing out of Mendeln's mouth was a low moan. That instigated movement from the direction of the new voice. A figure leaned over him, close but not touching.

"Who are you? How did you get here?"

Mendeln rolled over to face the shadowed woman. She wore a cloak of some sort, and what little he could see of her consisted of blond hair and what he suspected was a fairly attractive face. That, though, immediately put him in mind of Lilith, and he shoved himself away from the figure.

She, too, recoiled. "Who are you?" the woman demanded again. "Are you a mage?"

The voice did not sound at all like Lilith's, but Mendeln knew that a demon could change voices at will. Still, it finally registered on him that Lilith was dead, killed by his brother. This was someone else and, considering that Mendeln suspected that he was again in the capital, probably one of those Master Cyrus had said the false Lylia resembled.

He steadied himself. "No. I am no mage." There was no sense in trying to explain just *what* he was. "My name is Mendeln."

There was a brief intake of breath, then a momentary silence. The woman finally murmured, "Praise be! I feared it was one of those murderous mages. They're everywhere! They're hunting down anyone who's been helping a man called Uldyssian."

"Uldyssian!" Mendeln could scarcely believe his luck, especially considering that Inarius had been the one to cast him here.

That thought immediately made him cautious again. It was probable that the angel wanted Uldyssian's brother caught up in the mages' sweep, although how exactly that helped Inarius was another question.

"You sound as if you know him," the woman said, a hint of hope in her tone. She edged closer. "I heard that he had a brother named Mendeln. Are you he?"

"Yes." He wondered if the Prophet had erred when he had cast his prisoner here. This looked more to Mendeln's advantage. If the woman had had contact with Uldyssian, then there was perhaps a way by which he could use her link to his sibling to find him.

But that would involve explaining to her that despite not being a mage, he was still a spellcaster of sorts. The loss of his dagger would—

The dagger! Mendeln could not believe his addled thoughts. He had used the dagger to send his brother to safety. He did not even need the woman's aid! What a fool he had been. The dagger was bound to him; all he had to do was reach out to it and, thus, to Uldyssian.

"Listen to me," he said in his most reassuring tone. "Uldyssian is safe outside the city—"

"Outside? How can that be?"

Here he had to be careful. "You must trust me when I say that I am not part of the mage clans, but I do know a magic of sorts. I was able to send him to safety just before the mages would have attacked. There is a blade I use that was able to send him beyond the city walls."

"And this blade . . . you have it now?"

"No. It is with him." Mendeln began preparing himself for the effort. "It may be—I think—that I can reach Uldyssian through the blade and either have it bring us to him or perhaps have him do so. Yes, he might be able to cast such a spell also."

She stood next to him. "All that power. Amazing!"

"I cannot promise for certain that it will work," he was quick to add.

"But it must!"

Trying to calm his companion, Mendeln replied, "It has great hope of succeeding, I think." He hesitated. Then, to keep her from thinking of failure, he asked, "What is your name?"

"A-Amolia."

"I will not leave you here, have no fear of that."

She reached a hand toward him. "I know."

Mendeln shivered and, without at first realizing it, pulled his shoulder away from her oncoming fingers. He blinked, then stared at the shadowed woman.

"I *know* you!" he rasped, astounded and dismayed. "I know you!"

"Oh, yes, you do," she replied, closing on him. Only now was it apparent that the shadows somewhat obscuring her features were stronger than natural. This close, Mendeln, whose vision was better than that of a cat, should have been able to make her out perfectly, and yet only with effort could he see a bit more. Amolia did remind him of Lylia, as he had thought, but there was one significantly different feature that marred her otherwise attractive features.

Dark lesions covered her face.

No . . . not her face anymore. How he could sense the truth was something that perhaps Rathma could have explained. This was not a woman called Amolia . . . not anymore.

This was the spirit of the high priest Malic possessing her body.

How this nightmare had come to be was impossible for him to say, but now he knew why Inarius had cast him here. That the angel would make use of a fiend such as Malic did not entirely surprise him.

The false Amolia grabbed his shoulder. "How appropriate that you should be the one to finally give your brother to me."

Mendeln felt an emptiness press at him. It was almost as if he were being cast out of his body.

Not sure what else he could do, he muttered the first words he could think of in the ancient tongue.

Malic cried out as a white light erupted where his hand touched. As the specter pulled the appendage back, both could see that it was blackened as if burned—but by cold, not by heat.

"Impossible!" the high priest raged, his inhuman fury distorting the woman's face further. "Impossible!"

Recovering from his own surprise, Mendeln put on a confident front. "I summoned you from the dead, Malic! You cannot touch me, but I can send you back to whatever damned pit you belong."

The woman's face continued to contort, but now to a different emotion. To his further astonishment, Uldyssian's brother recognized that emotion: *fear.*

Malic was afraid, possibly for the first time from anyone other than his masters.

But fear alone was not enough, especially if this parasitic ghost desired to shed his current victim for Uldyssian. Mendeln thrust a hand out toward the demonic shade.

"No more!" he growled at Malic. "It is time you died again . . . this time forever!"

The words he needed came rushing from his lips.

With a garbled cry, Malic seized a medallion hanging from his host's neck. Too late did Mendeln understand just what the shade intended.

Malic vanished.

"No!" The younger son of Diomedes desperately finished his incantation—which, with no target, simply ceased to happen.

Where the high priest had vanished to, he could not say. Malic had acted in panic, and that meant it was possible that even the specter did not know where he had sent himself. Mendeln wished that Malic had by sheer bad fortune cast himself among the hunting mages, the only part of his story that had sounded believable. At this point, they likely would have known him for something vile.

But he could not rely on that. Mendeln had to make amends for the monster he had unleashed upon the world. He had to find Malic and finish him.

First, though, Mendeln had to find his brother. He had to know that Uldyssian was actually all right.

The plan he had intended before discovering Malic's presence was still sound. Mendeln refocused, seeking out the dagger with his mind. Surely, Uldyssian still had it with him. Mendeln prayed that it was so.

A heavy force bowled him to the floor. He sensed several figures begin to coalesce around him. Mendeln knew exactly who they were. The mages had no doubt noticed his magical confrontation with Malic and reacted accordingly. Now, instead of Uldyssian or the ghost, they would find themselves with a different prize.

Head pounding, Mendeln tried to finish his spell, but he could not.

Hands roughly seized him and then let go as shouts filled the shadowed chamber. A moon-silver light briefly enveloped everything.

Again, a pair of hands took hold, but this time more gently.

The silvery light momentarily blinded Mendeln, and then the sounds of the jungle prevailed.

"Be at ease," came Rathma's weary voice. "He is unharmed."

At first, Mendeln believed that the Ancient spoke to him, but then came a welcome second voice. "I could've gotten him myself, Rathma! I could've!"

Mendeln's vision cleared. He beheld Uldyssian, his brother, still clutching Mendeln's ivory dagger. The older sibling stared with wild eyes.

"The dagger was dead," Uldyssian muttered to Mendeln. "I thought you were dead . . . and then it flared to life again."

"I was a guest of the Prophet," the younger brother revealed. "Likely, that was why the dagger and I had no link." Mendeln saw no need to mention having suffered through a similar situation before finding Uldyssian in the tunnels.

Uldyssian cursed. "I knew it! I told you, Rathma. I told you I should've been the one to go."

"But if you had gone back," Inarius's son answered,

"there is little doubt that my father or his so-called ally would have been waiting."

"That's precisely—"

"Or worse," Mendeln interrupted, testing his balance. "Malic."

"Malic?" Uldyssian faltered. "You saw him?"

"*Her*, at least at the moment. A female mage named Amolia, I think it was."

Uldyssian nodded gravely. "I'd wondered what had caused the mage clans to turn on me without hearing me out."

Rathma shook his head at Mendeln, a hint of disappointment in his otherwise emotionless countenance. "What I revealed to you must always be wielded with caution. The variations on your teachings that you have accomplished are to be marveled at, but in the way one would marvel at the jaws of a great beast held from ripping you apart by a thin strand of hair binding it to a wall."

"I am brutally aware of my deficiencies," Mendeln muttered. "I—and only I—will deal with them and him."

His declaration did not go unchallenged. "No," Uldyssian interjected. "Malic's mine."

"You are susceptible to his touch; I am not, as I have discovered."

The argument might have gone further, but Rathma unexpectedly said, "The situation regarding the malevolent Malic just might be of no true concern, I fear. In fact, nothing that we have struggled against for so long or so hard might matter whatsoever."

He had the brothers' complete attention. Uldyssian it was who dared to ask the question to which neither wished to hear the answer. "Why? Why is Malic—or, more important, *Inarius*—no longer something to fear?"

"Because they, too, may be swept away like the most insignificant vermin by the cataclysm that even now hovers just on the horizon." Rathma shook his head. "The celestial warriors of the High Heavens are approaching Sanctuary.

They come to eliminate it and all upon it as abominations that should never have existed." A grim smile crossed his pale features. "They will make my father seem benevolent by comparison."

"We'll fight them just as we've been fighting him," Uldyssian immediately declared. "With or without the mage clans, we'll fight them."

"And very likely lose, unless we do the unthinkable."

"What's that?"

Rathma shivered. "Why, join forces with my father, naturally."

FIFTEEN

"Make a pact with Inarius?" Uldyssian could scarcely believe his ears, and from the look of his brother, neither could Mendeln. Uldyssian wondered if perhaps the centuries had finally caught up with the Ancient. His mind had surely gone. How else to explain such a mad suggestion?

"One might as well deal with Diablo, I know . . . and we may yet have to do that. I would willingly accept any other suggestion, but in the light of things, I see no other course."

"No!" Mendeln stepped between them. "There is another chance. Another angel. Tyrael."

"Is the very reason that the High Heavens now descend upon Sanctuary. Do not think that my father or the demons are alone in their mastery of manipulation. Tyrael—and it dismays me yet to hear you verify that it is he who is here— would see no contradiction in his role as a warrior of light by twisting his words and leading you and likely Achilios to believe him kindly and benevolent!" Rathma's cloak fluttered almost nervously, an effect more pronounced by the fact that there was no wind. "All he has desired during his time here is to create more chaos that will keep those interested in the world's survival at one another's throats, the easier for them to be judged by the High Heavens and erased from existence."

"Not possible!" Mendeln blurted. "I spoke with him. He was concerned over Inarius's madness and the fear that demons were gaining control over humanity. He—"

"The truth can hide many lies within it." The Ancient's shoulders slumped. "To Tyrael, we would be monsters, things that should have never existed. Therefore, we are not worthy of trust or truth. All that matters is our annihilation, so that we do not blemish creation. No . . . we must seek alliance with my father, and quickly."

Uldyssian could not believe that they would get anywhere with the Prophet. There had to be another way. "What about the dragon? Can't he do anything?"

"He has. He warned me of the High Heavens coming."

"And that's all? He'll do nothing else?"

Rathma glared. "I did not say he would remain idle. Even now, he attempts to blind them to Sanctuary's true location. And if that fails, he will try to bar their way with his power."

But judging by Rathma's tone, it sounded unlikely that Trag'Oul would succeed.

There was one other question that bothered Uldyssian, and that concerned Inarius himself. "Why does this other angel go through such subterfuge? Is your father so powerful?"

"By himself not, but he has tied his essence to the Worldstone and draws upon it like a leech. It has made him far, far stronger, such that even the Three will deal cautiously with him."

"Diablo!" Suddenly, what had happened to Uldyssian in the capital's water system could be seen in a different light. "He tried to trick me into allowing him into my mind—or my soul! I fought him off, though."

"The Lord of Terror was in Kehjan?" Inarius's son considered. "I have this terrible feeling that there is more going on there."

"Much more," agreed Mendeln. "For it was the Prophet who sent me to Malic!"

It was impossible not to draw the only logical conclusion. The master demon in the city. Inarius tied to Malic. The sinister creature in the tunnels. "They've a pact," Uldyssian muttered. "Those three had a pact." He shook his head in disbelief. "And it included the slaughter of most of those who actually rule Kehjan!"

"Ah, how Tyrael would laugh . . . if he laughs at all."
Rathma spat. "So, either by his manipulation or by the plots
of my father and the demon lord, all is falling into place for
the High Heavens. The greatest city on Sanctuary, the nexus
of power that might have stood, at least for a time, against an
army of angels, is in utter chaos. It is made more ironic in that
I am certain that neither Inarius nor Diablo sees the matter as
anything more than the chess game between themselves."

The thought was a sober one, for it now made it even
more unlikely that Inarius would hear reason.

Uldyssian started, realizing that he had suddenly
begun considering an alliance with the Prophet something
desirable.

"Will he speak with us?" he finally dared asked.

Apparently, he even surprised Rathma with his change
of heart, for the Ancient eyed him for a moment before
answering. "It may be that he will . . . though what that will
lead to could be not at all what we wish."

Meaning that Inarius was just as likely to try to kill them
as to listen.

"If there is to be any hope of approaching him, though,"
continued the angel's son, "it must be me who does it. The
bond between us is tenuous but better than the feud
between you and him."

It was not how Uldyssian would have preferred it, but he
saw the truth of Rathma's words. "How'll you do it?"

"I will simply go and speak with him . . . and now, in
fact."

And with that, Rathma vanished.

Startled, Uldyssian reached out a hand to the Ancient but
was too slow. "Damn him! There's more we needed to discuss!"

"Indeed," returned Mendeln. "What do we do about
Achilios? He serves this angel unwittingly or unwillingly,
but he serves him nevertheless."

There was no question in Uldyssian's mind what to do.
"We act in whatever way necessary to see to it that the

edyrem are all safe. That means we return to them immediately." He gestured for his brother to draw near, in the process returning the dagger. "And if that means we have to fight this Tyrael, then so be it."

Mendeln only nodded. Uldyssian thought of Serenthia and the others. He sensed their general presence not all that far from the siblings, yet it was all but impossible to specifically locate Cyrus's daughter.

And as Uldyssian concentrated, he worried what that might mean for her.

They vanished from their location and reappeared instantly among the edyrem. Startled shouts arose from those around them as the sons of Diomedes materialized. Wary of accidental attacks, Uldyssian shielded the pair—a good thing, since a moment later, a fireball sought to incinerate them.

"Stop!" cried Saron from somewhere. A moment later, the Torajian fell on one knee before Uldyssian. "You are back! We had feared the worst, Master Uldyssian!"

"I also, Saron." Uldyssian patted the shorter man on the shoulder, then quickly surveyed those around him. "Where's Serenthia?"

"I have not seen her in some hours. To be honest, Master Uldyssian, I was concerned, but she did once touch my mind and say that she was preparing the way for us."

"And what does that mean?"

The Torajian shrugged. "At the time, I assumed that she referred to our march on the capital. We—we sought to rescue you."

"For which I'm grateful." Uldyssian concentrated harder, but still he could not sense Serenthia.

However, he did note something else to the north, something that reminded him of Achilios.

Thoughts racing ahead, Uldyssian absently said, "Stay with them, Mendeln. Do what you can."

"Uldyssian! Do not—"

But it was already too late. Uldyssian left the edyrem,

materializing instead in the jungle to the north. His eyes adjusted to the dark surroundings . . . but not soon enough.

The invisible force struck him like a battering ram, sending Uldyssian flying. If not for the son of Diomedes taking the precaution of shielding himself even before he arrived, he would have been very dead. As it was, Uldyssian crashed through first one thick trunk, then another, completely shattering both. The third finally stopped his flight, but not without nearly cracking in two.

He was not even given time to recover. Two arrows struck him, and despite the fact that they should have been far less of a threat than the magic, one *penetrated* his protection. Fortunately, it was slowed enough that it left only a shallow wound . . . a wound directly over his heart.

He tore the arrow from him, then rolled to the side. Uldyssian knew that a trap had been set for him. It had been no mistake that he had sensed Achilios but not Serenthia. That had enabled her to strike before he could orient himself.

But why they were trying to kill him was not entirely clear. The angel who manipulated them played a game nearly as twisted as Inarius's. Achilios had managed to avoid successfully assassinating him earlier yet now seemed quite convinced that Uldyssian had to perish.

What was the point, though? Rathma had said that the hosts of the High Heavens were bearing down on Sanctuary. Why, then, did this Tyrael wish to bother with one particular human, no matter how powerful?

In asking that question, Uldyssian realized that he knew the answer.

But what mattered most was stopping this madness. He leapt to his feet. "Serenthia! Achilios! It's me! It's—"

Another tree bent over and sought to smother him in its thick foliage. As Uldyssian began ripping his way free, blue flames engulfed the branches.

The heat momentarily seared him. Sweating, Uldyssian waved a hand and sent a cold blast of air all around him.

The flames died instantly, the blackened branches and leaves a dread reminder of what had been intended for Uldyssian.

Despite his concern for both his friends, he was also fast becoming angry. Serenthia and Achilios had come much too close to actually harming him. They were not even giving him an opportunity to try to tell them the truth. What did they think of him that they wanted his death so badly?

Strengthening his shields, he took a step forward and tried once more to talk reason. "Serry! We need to speak. The angel with you is as deadly as Inarius. Perhaps deadlier. He wants to destroy the entire world—"

"Spare us your pretense, high priest!" came her voice. "We know what you are and what you've done. By Uldyssian's memory, we'll make you regret all the lives you've stolen, especially his!"

He cursed, understanding at last what—or, rather, *who*— they thought him to be.

Malic.

How the angel had managed that, Uldyssian did not know. Still, what mattered was that the son of Diomedes now knew just why the two were so adamant about killing him.

And there was no manner by which he could think to convince them that he was himself.

The spear caught him under the ribs. Distracted by Serenthia's revelation, Uldyssian had left himself open. His shields should have still held, but as he fell back, wounded, Uldyssian had no doubt that Tyrael had done something to assist the weapon in reaching its target. That also would have explained the arrow's luck earlier.

Pain coursed through him. His head pounded. He gripped the spear and burned it to ash. Panting, Uldyssian put a hand over the wound, healing it.

His frustration mounted. He could not just stand there, letting them take chance after chance to slay him. The overall situation was far more important than this fight.

Uldyssian had to put an end to things . . . even if it meant harming one or both of them in the process.

Or even doing something worse.

He straightened—and immediately, another arrow raced toward him. This time, though, Uldyssian had been expecting it. He threw his power first into reducing the bolt to ash, then striking where the archer had surely stood.

The trees and undergrowth for yards ahead flattened under the force of his spell. A scream arose, but it was feminine and came from another direction.

"No!" Serenthia shouted. She leapt out of the jungle, hands raised toward Uldyssian. The trees he had just flattened went soaring back at him.

He managed to deflect the first few, but while that was happening, Serenthia summoned a new spear and threw. Uldyssian managed to catch the spear just inches from him, then tossed it point first into the soil.

As it struck, a wall of dirt erupted. It rose several yards and immediately solidified.

Tree after tree slammed into the wall, but, strengthened by Uldyssian's power, the dirt barrier held. The makeshift missiles struck with what sounded like a thunderclap.

Before Serenthia could attempt anything else, Uldyssian slapped the air in her direction. It struck the merchant's daugher as if he had actually hit her himself. With a groan, she fell backward.

Taking a deep breath, the son of Diomedes looked around. Sensing no other threat, he rushed to Serenthia's side.

She lay sprawled amidst the ruined undergrowth, her head tilted to one side in a manner that at first made Uldyssian fear that he had injured her badly. However, a quick study revealed nothing threatening.

The merchant's daughter moaned. Her eyes opened, and she saw Uldyssian leaning over her.

An epithet worthy of a demon escaped her lips. She tried to move, tried to use her power, but Uldyssian had already prepared for that. Serenthia quickly found that she could do nothing.

"Please be calm, Serry," he murmured, deciding that calling her by her childhood name might serve to alleviate her suspicions. In truth, her expression did immediately grow confused, yet the wariness did not completely disappear. "It's me—it's Uldyssian, I swear!"

"No . . . he said . . . I *saw* the carnage in the capital. He showed us what happened . . . and that it was *Malic's* ghost seizing body after body . . . including yours!"

"The angel lied," he bluntly replied.

"But . . . no . . ." Her eyes shifted ever so slightly.

Uldyssian sensed the figure behind him but made no move. Instead, the former farmer muttered, "At this close range, you should be able to hit me dead on, Achilios."

"And if he even tries," remarked yet another voice, "I shall send him back to where he came from."

"Mendeln?" Serenthia gasped.

With the utmost care and casualness, Uldyssian looked behind him. As he had noted, the pale figure of the archer stood right behind him. A few leaves still clung to the undead's body. Achilios had another dirt-encrusted shaft ready to fire, but even as Uldyssian watched, his childhood friend lowered his bow.

Just barely visible behind Achilios, Mendeln held the ivory dagger point down. The mystical weapon glowed faintly like moonlight.

"Mendeln . . ." rasped the hunter. "You . . . you don't know . . . the truth . . . This is . . . is not Uldyssian! This is that . . . that creature . . . Malic!"

"No, this is my brother," Mendeln replied calmly. "I would know Malic if I saw him, no matter what the body. I've learned that."

"But—"

"The angel lied to both of you," Uldyssian interjected. "He used you for pawns." As he spoke, he released

Serenthia from her invisible bonds. She eyed the hand he offered her with suspicion but finally grasped it.

"I believe it's actually him, Achilios," Serenthia said. "I really do."

Her admission only seemed to anger the archer. "He nearly made . . . made me . . . do it again! I almost . . . killed you!"

Mendeln joined them. Keeping the glowing dagger by his side, he added, "I do not know if the angel wanted Uldyssian dead even now. I think that he is merely maximizing chaos wherever he can in preparation for the coming of the armed host."

Both Serenthia and Achilios looked at the brothers in total bewilderment.

"What armed host?" the hunter asked.

Uldyssian explained. His friends' expressions transformed swiftly to horror as understanding hit them hard.

"*All* of the world?" the dark-tressed woman exclaimed. "Nothing . . . no one left?"

"If Tyrael and the angels have their way. The other alternative seems to be enslavement by the demons . . . or by Inarius."

"This can't be happening. That means all we've done has been for nothing, Uldyssian!"

He shook his head. "No, Serry. I won't believe that. I plan on fighting until the end. This is our world, not Inarius's, the angels', or the demons'!"

"What of . . . of Rathma?" asked Achilios grimly. "Can he . . . can he persuade Inarius . . . to join with us? Is that . . . even possible?"

"Is that even desired?" Uldyssian retorted. He vehemently shook his head. "I think Rathma's doomed to failure, but he's got to try—and in the meantime, we need to prepare."

"For the angels' coming," Mendeln concluded.

But Uldyssian shook his head again. "No—no, I think first for Inarius, actually."

• • •

Rathma had never been inside the Cathedral of Light, but he had heard tales of it. It was everything those tales had said, but despite that, he was not in the least impressed. All the glory, all the grandeur, focused around the megalomania of his father, not good, as it pretended.

The guards lining the corridors did not see him walk among them, nor did even the senior priests. He had not sought to materialize directly in Inarius's sanctum, for his father would have taken that for a sign of disrespect. While Rathma did indeed have no respect for the angel, he felt that now was not the time to push that particular point.

The zealous guards stationed at the doorway to the Prophet's sanctum stared as blindly as the rest. The cowled figure strode right past them and, a moment later, *through* the doors themselves.

Rathma did not announce himself as he entered the vast, elegant chamber. Inarius knew full well that his offspring was there.

Indeed, a moment later, the voice Rathma so despised echoed through his head and heart. *MY WAYWARD SON . . . AND HAVE YOU COME TO BEG FORGIVENESS FOR YOUR SINS?*

The angel materialized in his full, grand glory just a few feet above Rathma. His wings were spread wide across the chamber, the full spectrum of their energies filling the marble room with an astounding array of colors. Despite himself, Rathma had to admire the beauty inherent in what his father was, if nothing else.

"You can spare us both that constant question, can you not, Father?"

BUT IF THAT IS NOT THE REASON, THEN WHAT? WHEN LAST WE SPOKE, YOU REJECTED FOREVER THE LINK BETWEEN US. THEREFORE, IF YOU DO NOT SEEK FORGIVENESS, I SEE NO REASON FOR ANY FURTHER AUDIENCE.

"There is a very good reason, and you know it!" the Ancient said, his vast cloak fluttering. He raised a fist toward the angel. "The whole of Sanctuary is in imminent threat of destruction. There is only one hope to save it—"

COMBINE MY MIGHT WITH THAT OF THE HERETIC ULDYSSIAN AND HIS RABBLE, NOT TO MENTION YOURS AND PERHAPS WHATEVER HANDFUL OF THE FIRSTBORN STILL HIDE UNDER THE ROCKS? Inarius's disdain was clear in his tone. *PERHAPS ADD EVEN THE BURNING HELLS TO OUR RANKS? OR MAYBE THE SO-CALLED MAGE CLANS?*

As he spoke, the angel glowed ever more brilliantly, so much so that Rathma had to shield his eyes. Rathma struggled against the ever-present urge to kneel before his father. Inarius gestured toward the images in the ceiling, his gauntleted hand twisting as if he sought to grasp each and every one of them.

IN THE HIGH HEAVENS, I WAS ONE AMONG MANY. AGAINST THEIR HOST, I WOULD NOT HAVE BEEN ABLE TO STAND. He looked down at his son once more. *BUT WE ARE IN MY WORLD NOW . . . MY WORLD! ITS LIFE . . . ITS DEATH . . . ARE AND HAVE ALWAYS BEEN MINE TO DECIDE, LINARIAN!*

This was turning into a conversation that Rathma and Inarius had had too often already during the ages. The Ancient had always suspected his progenitor of teetering on madness, but now he began to see that the angel was utterly insane.

Nonetheless, Rathma continued to try. "Father, you know that Tyrael has found Sanctuary—"

NO! The winged figure descended to just a few inches above the immaculate floor. *THE PLOY FAILED! THE TRUTH BECAME KNOWN TO ME! TYRAEL IS NOT HERE; TYRAEL WAS NEVER HERE. AND EVEN IF HE WAS, NOT A THOUSAND OF HIM OR ANY OTHER COULD STAND AGAINST ME, SO LONG AS I AM BOUND TO THE WORLDSTONE! NO, LINARIAN,*

*TYRAEL IS NOT HERE. YOUR TRICKS HAVE BEEN UN-
VEILED TO ME. YOU WORKED IN LEAGUE WITH ALL
THE REST. YOU ARE NO MORE TO BE TRUSTED THAN
THE LORD DIABLO, WHO THINKS TO BLIND ME TO HIS
TREACHERIES BY OFFERING HIS OWN "ALLIANCE."*

The words verified some of Rathma's suspicions and
fears concerning recent events. "Then . . . then the slaughter
of innocents in the capital is in great part your doing! You
have left the mage clans in confusion and anger and made
Sanctuary that much more unstable. You play into Tyrael's
hand, do you not see that?"

*ALL PLAYS INTO MY HANDS, YOU MEAN. THE CITY
IS TURNED AGAINST THE HERETIC, ULDYSSIAN, AS
ARE MORE AND MORE OF THE FLOCK THROUGHOUT
THE REALM.* A very *human* laugh escaped the celestial
being, a laugh filled with mad triumph. *THEN LORD DIA-
BLO OFFERS ME WHAT HE BELIEVES WILL IN THE END
GARNER HIM DOMINATION OF MY WORLD AND
MAKE THE HERETIC'S LEGIONS SOLDIERS FOR
DAMNATION. HE PROVIDES ME WITH THE PATH TO
THE VERY CHAOS I DESIRE UPON SANCTUARY, THE
BETTER TO SWEEP IT CLEAN AND REBUILD IT WITH
THE PERFECT ORDER IT WAS MEANT TO HAVE SINCE
THE BEGINNING.*

Rathma had earlier sensed Uldyssian's reluctance when
the Ancient had suggested seeking a pact with Inarius, and
although the angel's son had expected little, he saw that
even Uldyssian had underestimated just how impossible
success might be. Rathma's father lived in a world of his
own, but it was not even Sanctuary . . . it was a fantasy
within his own mind.

And because of Inarius's blind madness, everyone else
would suffer.

Rathma made one last, desperate stab. "Father, Tyrael is
not—"

He got no farther. Inarius gazed down upon him with
eyes that were not even remotely human but blazing

energy. At that moment, Rathma realized the gap between even himself and what his sire was. It was a jest of the cosmos that they were father and son; there was more of a physical bond between Rathma and a toadstool.

WHETHER NO TYRAEL OR A THOUSAND THOUSAND TYRAELS, THIS WORLD IS MINE, LINARIAN! MINE.

A sensation of extreme claustrophobia overwhelmed Rathma. His father swelled in size, rapidly growing into a giant.

No . . . the entire room matched the angel, which meant that it was the angel's *offspring* who was transforming. Without Rathma even being aware of it, Inarius had shrunken him down to the size of a rat—and then even smaller.

The winged figure alighted, then reached out to his son. A smoky sphere immediately formed around Rathma. The Ancient battered his cage with all the magic he could muster, but for naught. Alone against his father, he was nothing.

The tiny sphere flew up from the floor and onto Inarius's open palm. By the time it did that, it was no larger than a pea.

YOU ARE SO VERY MUCH LIKE YOUR MOTHER, Inarius said. *A SHAME, THAT.*

With that, he cast the sphere and Rathma into the void.

SIXTEEN

It was neither Inarius nor the other angels who struck first. That honor went to the city of Kehjan.

The sentries sensed their approach just before dawn the next day, but Uldyssian noted them several minutes before that. He did not immediately tell his followers, or even his friends, instead trying to think of what he could do to prevent so many innocent lives from being lost.

Unfortunately, little came to mind.

When word came from the sentries, all he could do was summon Mendeln and the others he trusted for command and quickly discuss whatever suggestions they might have to stopping the impending disaster. They had barely more to offer than he had and, with the exception of Mendeln, saw no reason to be so concerned over the fate of the Kehjanis.

"You tried to come in peace," Serenthia pointed out. "They never gave you the chance. If not for Malic's evil, there would've been some other reason to betray you. Look how they attacked you even in the palace of Prince Ehmad!"

"We will crush them easily," Saron piped up.

Jonas nodded agreement, adding, "Once they see they can't win, Master Uldyssian, they'll go running. That'll save a lot of their lives."

"But not enough," the son of Diomedes returned. "Not nearly enough . . ." He suddenly looked up. "How the angels and demons must be laughing right now." Uldyssian wondered especially about the one identified as Tyrael. This was surely what he desired. Keep all the abominations at one another's throats until his brethren swept down and cleansed the world of them.

And Inarius? Inarius would not be idle. Curiously, Uldyssian was most concerned about him—and the fact that Rathma had not returned. He glanced at Mendeln and saw something in his brother's eyes that indicated the same thoughts had crossed his mind as well.

One of the sentries touched his mind. Uldyssian shoved aside all thought about Inarius . . . at least for the moment.

"Get everyone ready. Make sure those who need to be protected are. At my signal, we move to meet them." He would not allow his foes to dictate this battle; come what may, Uldyssian would take responsibility for his part in what was to happen.

Saron and Jonas ran off to relay his orders to others. Serenthia started to follow but then faltered. She looked to Uldyssian.

He knew immediately what disturbed her. Achilios had left them during the night, but only to keep the edyrem— from whom he was shielded—from growing disturbed by his presence. However, the hunter had promised that he would be near when the conflict began.

"He's not far," Uldyssian reassured her. While the son of Diomedes was in great part responsible for keeping Achilios hidden from everyone else, he maintained a link with his friend that even Serenthia could not create. "He'll be at our side, so to speak."

She gave him a grateful nod and raced off.

Mendeln glanced at his brother. "This does not feel right, Uldyssian. In many ways, these people do not deserve what will happen."

"We can't do anything about it. It's out of our hands, Mendeln. We need to defend ourselves, not only for our sakes but for the world's."

"But if we slaughter hundreds for no good reason other than that they were blinded by Inarius and others, of what value will that world be?"

Uldyssian shrugged his question off. "That might not even matter."

He strode off before they could argue. Mendeln followed at his heels, silent. Uldyssian knew that despite his sibling's words, Mendeln would fight as best he could.

No one would be spared bloodying his hands. . . .

The sky thundered even though the clouds did not warrant it. Mendeln sensed that the mages were beginning what they thought their grand spellwork. The Kehjani were not stupid; they knew the stories of Uldyssian and the edyrem. They knew the tales of Toraja, Istani, and other places where Uldyssian had brought down the Triune. They also had the supposed betrayal in their own ranks, the blame falling on Mendeln's brother.

The spellcasters would want this over quickly, and the guilds and nobles would back them on this entirely. If this Prince Ehmad was also dead, as Uldyssian suspected, the last vestiges of hope for anything other than war were indeed gone. However the mages struck, it would be fearsome.

And if that failed, an army of thousands was ready to die in the mistaken belief that the edyrem were coming to raze their homes and slaughter their families.

The angels and demons had done their work oh so well.

Despite his understanding of all this, Mendeln summoned what knowledge and power he had gained in preparation for his own efforts against the Kehjani. He could ill afford to let his doubts keep him from standing beside his brother. No matter what the outcome, nothing was more important.

Now, in addition to the thunder, the trees shook as if caught in a violent wind that neither he nor the edyrem could feel. What Mendeln *could* detect, though, were the magical energies building up before Uldyssian's followers.

But the edyrem were not idle, either. Under the silent direction of their leader, they were combining their wills toward two goals. The first was shielding themselves against whatever it was that the mages intended to throw at them. The second, naturally, had to do with Uldyssian's intentions for striking back. Although he had no idea what his sibling intended, Mendeln shivered at the thought of Uldyssian's retribution. If he should lose control at some point, there was no telling what devastation he might cause.

Something was happening. Whatever it was the mage clans intended to unleash, it was coming. He readied the dagger.

Mendeln! came Trag'Oul's voice. It struck the human like thunder amplified a thousand times. Caught up in their own efforts, the edyrem—even Uldyssian—failed to notice his fall.

Mendeln! repeated the dragon. As he sought to recover, Uldyssian's brother noticed with shock that for the first time since he had been confronted by the creature, Trag'Oul's voice sounded *strained*.

Struggling to keep his head from exploding, Mendeln acknowledged the dragon. Immediately, he felt the celestial being seize upon that acknowledgment. *You must help me, quickly! I can barely keep hold! Come!*

Trag'Oul's words penetrated, especially the last one. Mendeln immediately sought to protest. *I cannot leave Uldyssian! I cannot—*

But his words were for naught.

The ground started to shake. It came as no surprise to Uldyssian, who knew what the mages intended. What was more devastating to any enemy force than an earthquake? Rifts began to open up around the edyrem. Trees toppled over. A wall of dirt arose in the south.

Linked to his followers, Uldyssian drew upon their power as much as his own. With but a glare at the rising ground, he forced it level again. With not even so much as that, he stilled first the trees, then the land beneath the edyrem's feet.

And with a single contemptuous gesture, the son of Diomedes caused the cracks to mend themselves so that they looked as if they had never even been.

Uldyssian appreciated the incredible forces that the mages had put into the creation of their great spell and appreciated more the consternation that likely was going on at that very moment. They had surely expected some injury and death among the edyrem, not this simple shrugging off of their might.

He allowed himself a smile, albeit one with little pleasure in it. Uldyssian hoped that the Kehjanis would realize their hopelessness and retreat, but he did not expect it. The masters of the city would either try something more desperate—and, thus, possibly actually more effective—or simply drive their army into the edyrem's waiting arms.

Either way, the blood was soon to flow.

Uldyssian found himself as impatient with the situation as he was disgusted by it. All that would ultimately happen here would be to waste time and strength against those who were not the true threat. He knew that Mendeln felt that way and understood his brother's earlier reluctance, but what could he really do? Simply put a stop to the oncoming collision between his people and the Kehjani?

The thought so distracted Uldyssian that it made him stumble and nearly lose his link to the others. As he quickly regained his attention, the son of Diomedes considered what he had just so casually asked himself.

Could he somehow keep this battle from happening? It was not as if that would put an end to the conflict. There were both Inarius and this angelic host that was—seemingly still fooled by whatever it was Trag'Oul was doing. Neither of them would be possible for Uldyssian to avoid, especially the Prophet, who had the most to lose or win.

Certain of their impending victory and ignorant of how little it might mean, the edyrem eagerly pressed forward. They were almost at the point of not even being able to be stopped by Uldyssian. He knew, therefore, that he had to do whatever he hoped to do as swiftly as possible.

For that, he needed coordination between those he could best trust. Uldyssian simultaneously reached out to Serenthia and his other trusted commanders, informing them in an instant of his hopes. He received the expected disbelief from many, including even the merchant's daughter.

You may only be opening us up to the mages, she was quick to point out. *This'll definitely put a strain on our own defenses.*

It can't be helped! he shot back. *And it will be done!*

No one argued further with him. The edyrem would live and die by his judgment, a painful understanding on Uldyssian's part. However, there was nothing he could do to change that.

Be my shield, he ordered the others. They willingly obeyed. That allowed Uldyssian to focus on letting his mind separate from his body. He shot forth, his view racing through toward the Kehjani defenders.

It did not take him long to locate the physical aspect of the capital's attack. The soldiers moved in a fine, orderly fashion, but Uldyssian could sense their wariness and even growing anxiety. They knew that something had been attempted by the spellcasters, something that had utterly failed. They also knew that the enemy they approached was responsible somehow for the slaughter of many of their leaders.

But still they came to defend their homes.

That did much to instill in Uldyssian a determination that he would change what was supposed to be. Inarius would not have his bloodbath . . . at least, not this one.

He flew beyond the marching ranks to where the officers rode, then far past them. Over the walls he dove, then deep into the city's heart. It was there at last that he found the true commanders of the Kehjani force, the mages.

There were twenty, and the colors of their robes indicated that they were of that many different clans. Most were old, but where their bodies were withered, they radiated magic such as Uldyssian had rarely seen.

Most formed a five-sided pattern in the midst of which they were now summoning up fantastic energies that set the stone chamber aglow like a sinister rainbow. A handful of others stood to the side in heated discussion, likely trying to decide just what to do next in the face of such a grand debacle.

Some of those in the second gathering stilled as he neared. They looked about uneasily, perhaps sensing his astral presence. Then an elderly figure with a beard nearly down to the floor snapped his fingers, demanding their return to their conversation.

Those in this chamber were the ones with whom Uldyssian first had to deal. These mages represented the backbone of any fight mustered by the Kehjani. Of course, he did not want to harm them any more than he wished to harm the soldiers; the spellcasters, too, reacted because of treachery.

But what *could* he do that would not demand their deaths? He had little time to think, for it was clear that the mages were nearly ready to strike again. This time, they would try to learn from their mistake. If there were only some way to simply cut them off from the battle.

It was so simple that Uldyssian could not believe he had not thought of it sooner. The only question was whether it was actually *possible*.

There was, of course, only one way to find out.

He withdrew from the building that housed the spellcasters' efforts, surveying as he went all that was taking place nearby. By the time Uldyssian situated himself where he thought best, he knew where all the mages involved were located. It almost made him laugh when he discovered that there were many more spread throughout the areas surrounding the initial groups and that those were involved in creating defenses for the citadel itself.

Uldyssian had crossed those defenses without even noticing them or apparently setting any off.

His confidence increased, Uldyssian called upon the others. He wanted to make this work the first time.

They need simply to be contained, he told them. *I will guide you.*

They fed him their power. He was slightly surprised by how much they gave and realized that it was far more than he even needed. The might of his followers grew by leaps and bounds.

But would it ultimately be enough when the true threat came to Sanctuary?

A swelling of magical energy brought him back to the situation at hand. Reprimanding himself for the distraction, the son of Diomedes stared at the mages' sanctum. Then, imagining his present form had a hand, he cupped it over the distant but foreboding building.

And under his hand, what seemed the upper half of an eggshell took shape over the structure. It grew to encompass all that he desired, then descended. As it did, the shell turned translucent, then invisible.

Uldyssian nodded in satisfaction. He sensed the spellcasters only now noticing that something was amiss. Their consternation rose as they tested what could not be seen but completely enveloped them. They would find that they could not leave by magical or physical means, nor could they make any contact whatsoever with those outside. To onlookers, the sanctum would appear empty, desolate.

More important, if Uldyssian had done as he hoped, the attack they had just been conjuring would be no more. He tested that hope, seeking any trace of the surge he had earlier noticed.

But there was nothing.

Uldyssian returned to his body. As he opened his eyes, he silently informed the others of his success. The soldiers of Kehjan had no magical support. They were truly like lambs to the slaughter, save that Uldyssian had no desire for that.

Just this once, he prayed. *Just this once, let there be no deaths.*

He reached to all the edrem now, asking of them what they could give. His reasons for this he made apparent, so that they would understand. There were no protests, just some surprise and a little regret. However, this was what Uldyssian wished, and so they would obey.

Again, he felt guilty that they trusted him so much.

Once more, Uldyssian sought out the Kehjani soldiers. It did not take long at all, for they were nearly within sight of his followers. He had little time to plan; it had to happen now.

It was a matter of wills, his—magnified by the contributions of each of the edrem—against theirs. The soldiers numbered more than his following, but they were merely men and had not been introduced to the gifts they carried within. Thus, there was no comparison at all between the two forces.

But still, Uldyssian would not know if he could succeed until he actually tried.

Sleep, he commanded the Kehjani.

What seemed a light, pure snow—snow in a land seething with heat—showered the oncoming army. Their perfect marching faltered as many looked up in bewilderment. Uldyssian sensed apprehension on the part of the officers, for they knew that this could be nothing good.

The first man to be touched by the gentle flakes yawned. He stopped marching, then dropped to his knees. By this time, several others in the ranks had joined him. An officer rushed up to a pair and raised his whip . . . then followed their example.

One by one, then by the dozens—then the hundreds— the army of Kehjan set down their weapons, fell quietly to their knees, and simply went to sleep. They did not lie down but just knelt there in row upon row, their arms dangling, their heads cocked to one side or another. Eyes closed and mouths slack, the soldiers rested peacefully.

Those mounted, including the commanders, had no time to flee from their comrades' fate. Riders merely went limp, slumping over in the saddle. Their horses did as they often were inclined to when sleeping; they lowered their heads and slept standing up.

An entire army still faced the edyrem, but it was one that would not awaken until Uldyssian commanded it.

From among his followers, there was at first silence. It was not that they were disappointed in the lack of any bloodshed but that most were not certain that if by shouting out, they would somehow shatter the spell. Once Uldyssian reassured them that this would not happen, the cries rose from everywhere. The edyrem cheered the incredible sight, an image made all the more arresting by the faint snow cover on helmets and shoulders.

Uldyssian ended the shower of sleep-inducing flakes. He smiled gratefully, thankful that his prayer had come to pass—and then wondered just to *whom* he had been praying. Not Inarius or the Three, certainly.

But that hardly mattered at the moment. What did was the welcome vision that he had made come to pass. There would be no horrific fight between his people and Kehjan. The situation was temporary, but it would last long enough, he hoped.

Long enough to deal with Inarius.

Mendeln cursed at the dragon and at matters in general. He swore with a passion he rarely displayed. It had much to do with once more being treated as if he had no say in what was happening. Each time someone desired to use him, he was snatched away from his brother's side and dropped wherever they pleased. That the same thing had happened to others did in no way assuage him. At the moment, Mendeln felt particularly picked on.

His fury was such that he did not even at first pay any mind to Trag'Oul's distress, clearly evident in the creature's voice.

Mendeln . . . Mendeln . . . can you feel him? I can barely . . . maintain a link.

"Return me to my brother! I am sick of this! How many times must I bow to you and Rathma? I am grateful for what I have learned, but this is not—"

Listen to me! demanded the dragon in a tone that cut off any further protest by the human. *Look about you! See where you are!*

Uldyssian's brother did just that—and only then registered that the blackness in which he floated was not the domain of Trag'Oul. This place radiated such emptiness that Mendeln suddenly clutched his arms tight around his body and wished fitfully for the relative cheer of the dragon's home.

Do not fall prey to it! If you do, not only Rathma but you, too, will be lost. Pay heed!

Trag'Oul's warning began to sink in. Trying to focus, Mendeln held the dagger to his face and focused on its reassuring light. Some of the fear began to recede.

"Where—where is this?" he finally managed to ask. "And did you say that Rathma is here somewhere?"

Here . . . and trapped possibly until the end of all. Sent to this accursed place by Inarius as a reward for seeking to do the right thing.

Mendeln had feared that the Ancient's visit to his father would prove to be a fool's errand, but even he could not imagine the angel so vicious as to condemn his offspring to this hellish abyss. "What is this place?"

Trag'Oul's voice sounded fainter, as if he were farther away now. *What could be called the remotest part of existence! A place so far from all else that to be trapped here is to be cursed forever.*

New chills ran through Mendeln as he heard this. He imagined floating here for all eternity, never to see or hear anything again.

The strain . . . the strain of reaching out all the way here is . . . is growing worse. Mendeln ul-Diomed, you must act as the link between myself . . . and Rathma . . . if we are to save him.

While Uldyssian's brother more or less understood what the dragon explained to him, a point that Trag'Oul had inadvertently mentioned made him very anxious. The dragon had just revealed that he was not even with Mendeln but rather had sent the human here alone. Trag'Oul kept a *link* with the son of Diomedes but no more.

And if that link—already strained, as the celestial being had informed him—broke, Mendeln's fears of being lost forever would come very true.

Concentrate! Trag'Oul demanded almost angrily. *Do not give in to the fear!*

Mendeln tried his best to focus. Trag'Oul was powerful. He would not let the human be lost. The dragon was very concerned about his pupils. Was he not doing his best also to rescue Rathma?

"Let this be done," the human said to the darkness. Then, in more of a mutter, "If it *can* be . . ."

It is up to you now . . . you know Rathma . . . you must seek his presence out . . . you must call him to you. I cannot do more than I have . . . there is so much else going on.

Despite his curiosity, Mendeln dared not ask to what other tasks the dragon referred. Instead, he turned his mind completely to seeking the Ancient, using the bond that Rathma and he had forged through their roles as mentor and student. He called out to Rathma and sought with the dagger to locate the lost soul.

It was difficult to measure time in this place. Mendeln felt as if he spent an entire lifetime seeking Rathma, seeking and finding nothing.

And then . . .

Mendeln.

It was faint . . . so very faint. Mendeln searched in every possible direction but again found nothing. He held the dagger everywhere, silently calling over and over again.

Mendeln.

There! He focused the dagger in the direction from which

he believed the call had come. It *sounded* like Rathma, but he still was not certain.

His name came once more, now a bit stronger. *Mendeln! Where—*

"I have him!" he all but roared to Trag'Oul.

Use your power to draw him near. Hurry! They suspect the ruse!

Who "they" were, Uldyssian's brother feared to know. He chose to ignore the comments, instead following the dragon's suggestions about Rathma.

Clutching the dagger with both hands, he threw all he had learned into summoning Rathma to him. The dagger flared bright, its light comforting in the emptiness.

Rathma, he called in his head. *Rathma . . .*

Then Mendeln felt something drawing near. He could see nothing but was certain that it was attracted by his spellwork. A faint presence that reminded him of the Ancient grew noticeable.

Something formed in the emptiness. A sphere. It was opaque, almost as if covered by frost. This surely had to be Rathma's magical prison.

But then Mendeln sensed something else. There was still that about the oncoming sphere that hinted of Rathma . . . but also something else.

Something sinister . . . and familiar.

Mendeln pointed the dagger directly at the sphere and altered his spellwork.

The frostlike coating burned away, and the maddened face of *Lilith* glared out at him.

"Mendeln!" Her expression immediately shifted, turning from bestial to beguiling. The rest of her transformed as well, turning more human. She resembled Lylia again, but also Serenthia and other women Mendeln had known and admired over the years. "Dear, sweet Mendeln . . . my savior . . ."

His heart pounded. Mendeln knew that it was as much because of her sorcery as her unearthly beauty, but he found it difficult to reject her presence. She was helpless now, entirely dependent upon his might. For him, Lilith would do anything, *be* anything. Whoever he desired. She was willing, Uldyssian's brother could see that in her wondrous eyes. They beckoned and promised. They called to him.

Lilith stretched forth her hand. Mendeln started to reach to her.

The dagger flared as if of its own doing. In its even more brilliant light, Mendeln saw her again as she truly was.

Disgust at his own weakness overtook him. "No . . . no more from you, harpy!"

He uttered words of power, and the sphere shot backward into the darkness. The demoness's shriek was terrible to hear, filled with both fury and despair. Lilith cursed his name even as she called for him.

And then Mendeln could hear the temptress no more.

The shock of confronting her—especially since she was *supposed* to be dead—shook Mendeln so much that he nearly demanded that Trag'Oul immediately return him to his world. However, just as he became determined to do this, he felt Rathma's faint presence again.

Mendeln hesitated but could not risk abandoning this one last hope. He repeated his earlier magic, using the dagger to draw whatever it was he had sensed.

A breath later, another sphere drifted close. Like the first, it was covered with the peculiar, frostlike coating. Keeping wary, Mendeln removed the latter as he had previously.

Before him floated a weary but grateful Rathma.

"I have him!" he shouted to Trag'Oul.

Yes . . . I know.

And suddenly, Mendeln felt himself propelled through the emptiness. As stunned as he was by the effect, he had the presence of mind to keep focused on Rathma.

Vertigo struck the younger son of Diomedes—and then he landed on something hard.

Above him, the glittering stars that were the dragon proved a welcome sight.

And a voice from his right proved even more welcome. Gasping for breath himself, Inarius's son said, "You have no idea, Mendeln . . . my gratitude . . . for that risk."

"It was Trag'Oul who was able to send me there," Uldyssian's brother pointed out as he turned to face the Ancient. "He who managed to find where you had been cast in the first place."

Rathma nodded. "And to him, too, I am grateful, but do not underestimate your part. The risk you took was monumental. You could have easily been lost there . . ." He shook his head. "To be alone in the void—forever—I could imagine no worse fate, not even death."

As Rathma talked, Mendeln watched him carefully, seeking any sign that he knew what had happened just before his rescue. Yet Lilith's offspring gave no sign that he had noticed the nearby presence of his murderous mother, who Mendeln had to assume had been drawn to his spell because of her physical ties to Rathma.

Lilith alive . . . but, as Rathma had pointed out, suffering a fate surely worse than death. It was also one she could not possibly escape. After all, it had only been because of Mendeln and the dragon that Rathma had had any chance.

He suddenly wondered why Trag'Oul had been silent all this time. Surely, their success was worthy of some celebration.

Even as Mendeln thought that, Rathma stood. The Ancient stared up at the constellation, his expression not at all pleasant.

"What is it, Trag?" Rathma demanded. "What's happening?"

There was a long, worrisome pause before the celestial answered. When he did, it was in a tone of weakness and defeat that shook Mendeln as even the dark emptiness had not.

The strain . . . was too . . . much . . . I could not maintain the . . . the ploy at the same time . . . we may have saved you . . . only to condemn you . . . with the rest of us . . . Rathma . . .

"What do you mean?" he asked, sounding every bit as concerned as Mendeln felt. "What ploy? What happened?"

Sanctuary is no . . . no longer shielded from their . . . sight! The Heavenly Host knows they were misled. Trag'Oul's grief at his failure was so very evident. *The winged warriors are closing in on our world.*

SEVENTEEN

IT IS GOOD.

Tyrael had surveyed the situation sweeping over this false world one last time and found it to his immense satisfaction. The creatures were all at one another's throats, and those who might cause the host some minor difficulty were in complete disarray. There was only one being in all this place that truly concerned him now, and that was the fallen one, Inarius.

The list of the renegade angel's crimes was lengthy, but foremost among them was the very creation of these *humans*. Tyrael understood their origins, and the wrongness of such a thing made him shiver. Angels and *demons*. He could not imagine why even Inarius had not seen fit to eradicate them early on.

But that would happen soon enough. Tyrael could sense the others fast approaching, and the only question he had was why it had taken them so long. There was more to this place—this *Sanctuary,* as he now knew it to be called by the renegade—than appearances suggested. There was some force, some vast reservoir of power, that Inarius had come upon that might be the reason. Tyrael was still investigating that. Likely it was what had caused the delay of the host. In the long run, it would not matter.

He returned to the subject of the angel/demon spawn. Abominations they not only were, but their unsettling potential—which he recognized as easily as the demons he smelled surely had—ultimately demanded their extinction. They offered the possibility of throwing the eternal war utterly on its head, which even he could not fully fathom. True, after he had first seen them, Tyrael had briefly contemplated suggesting their use as soldiers for the High Heavens, but immediately after, the thought of any demon-tainted strain beside him in battle made him completely reject such a notion. No, the humans—and all else here—had to be cleansed from existence.

The angel drifted among the clouds that overlooked both the city and Inarius's sanctum. He had focused much of his energy on shielding himself from the renegade's sight and magic so that he could more readily observe events as they played out. There was little else the angel felt he needed to do; now he was content to watch and wait. Soon the others would arrive, and they would see that he had acted accordingly, opening the way for the cleansing.

Soon, Inarius's blasphemous creation would be no more.

Malic bowed as low as the marble floor allowed. He had no choice. The face of the woman Amolia was covered in black lesions. Before he had come to this place, the specter had looked over the rest of his body and discovered the same held true for his limbs, his torso . . . every part. The body was nearly spent. He had little time remaining.

Finding a new host had proven harder than he could have imagined. Malic needed one that not only would hold him until he seized Uldyssian's but also had magical ability of its own.

The trouble was, the mage clans had proven quite adept after the slaughter of their council in alerting all their ilk to just who the assassin had been. At the time, Malic had assumed that he would already have Uldyssian's body, and so he had lost valuable opportunities. Then the mage clans' enforcers had begun hunting for him in groups that prevented him from picking off one of their number.

Thus it was that Malic had been grateful when Inarius had given him what seemed a gift—Uldyssian's accursed brother, Mendeln. As it had been Mendeln who had, through some arcane force, brought him back to existence, Malic had found the use of his body a priceless jest.

That incident had turned into the final debacle, though, and led him to this sorry state. He had been forced to make a new deal . . . and now grovel before one he hated almost as much as Uldyssian.

Inarius stood before him not as the angel but as the youthful Prophet. Malic no longer sneered at the image; he was now desperate for the first time in his life . . . and after-life. This had to go as planned.

The angel was clad in gleaming silver armor that hinted of his true status. In fact, a stylized winged warrior was the centerpiece of his breastplate. Over his golden hair, he wore a rimmed helmet with an arched metal crest that ran all the way back to the base. At the Prophet's side hung a scabbard containing a sword with a jeweled hilt.

Under other circumstances, Malic might have laughed mockingly at what he thought was such a gaudy vision. After all, the figure before him was so much more powerful than what his mortal flock saw. These trappings were nothing but stage dress so that Inarius could look that much more impressive when he destroyed the fanatical edyrem.

"I have given you more than one opportunity, Malic," Inarius said. "Opportunities that you have squandered!"

"Circumstance was against me," the high priest dared reply. "And, in one case, betrayal! The water demon was to have secured Uldyssian for me but chose to give in to his hunger instead."

"A matter that you would best take up with the Lord Diablo . . . if you can find him." Inarius allowed his human aspect to sneer at the absent demon. "He ended this farce of a pact quicker than I expected—which perhaps shows he has some wisdom, as I was about to turn it all against him, anyway."

"He tried to take the Ascenian for his own purposes," offered Malic. "Tried and failed."

"Not unlike yourself." The angel gazed down at the bent form. "Still, there is, perhaps, some use left in you. . . ."

Malic glanced up. "Whatever I must do, I will!"

"That you shall—and, if possible, for that I will yet grant you the heretic's body."

A heavy cough escaped the high priest. Malic was unable to prevent himself from suddenly throwing up on the pristine floor.

Inarius frowned. Under his baleful gaze, the disgusting spill vanished.

"F-forgive me," the specter managed.

"If you do as I command, I shall." The Prophet gestured, and Malic rose to his feet like a puppet. "But that shell will no longer suffice. You need a better one."

The entrance to Inarius's chamber opened. Out of the corner of his eye, Malic saw an older but quite athletic woman in the robes of a senior priest standing somewhat startled at the doors. Her hand was still formed into the fist she had intended to use to knock politely.

Immediately, the woman bowed her head. "Great one, you summoned me."

"That I did, Oris. Approach us."

For the first time, the woman saw Malic. Her brow furrowed as she strode toward the pair. Behind Oris, the doors sealed tight.

With a fatherly smile, the Prophet said, "My loyal Oris, you know there is no one closer to me than you."

The priestess's cheeks reddened. Malic realized that she loved her master not only as a believer but as a woman loved a man. "I live to serve you. . . ."

"So you do." Inarius held out his hands to her. Oris approached him. The angel gently took hold of her by the shoulders and leaned forward.

The kiss was short and little more than a grazing of the lips. To Malic, it was clear that the kiss meant nothing to Inarius. The woman, however, stood stunned and redder than ever.

"My dear, lovely Oris," the Prophet began anew. "Your devotion to me has been commendable."

"Proph—Prophet! I—" She looked entirely confused by his action.

"Please, Oris. I have need of you. I wish you to help this unfortunate wretch."

For the first time, she studied Malic closely. "What terrible disease is this that plagues her?"

"One you need not concern yourself about. What she needs most right now is your comforting hand."

"Certainly!" The priestess turned to Malic. "Come, my young one, let me help you."

The specter smiled. "Thank you."

Oris had no chance to scream. If the bodies were burning out faster than Malic desired, at least his possession of a new one was taking less and less time also.

He watched as the mage's limp body collapsed in a heap at his feet. Malic had to admit that Oris was a healthy and strong specimen. She would last longer than his previous host.

"There will be no more need of this," the Prophet murmured, gesturing toward Amolia's corpse.

Malic watched as the spellcaster's body turned to dust and blew away into nothing. He was grateful not to be in it any longer. At most, he had likely had a day left.

The angel nodded in satisfaction. "That shall suffice for the time necessary. All that remains now is for you to be clad appropriately." He casually flicked his hand toward Malic, adding, "Thus!"

The body of the female priest now also wore a breastplate and helmet. A mace with four jagged hooks on the crown hung on the left hip.

Eyeing the changes, Malic looked confused. "What's this for?"

Inarius eyed him as if the ghost were a fool. Malic immediately put on a humble expression.

This appeared to satisfy the angel. "It should be very

obvious to you, high priest," the Prophet replied. "What else can it be for?" He smiled just as he had before betraying his loyal servant. "We are going off to war."

"We're not entering Kehjan," Uldyssian informed the others. His eyes and power continued to search for Mendeln, but to no avail. "We leave the city alone."

"After all this?" blurted Serenthia. She pointed in the direction of the slumbering army. "We could walk in and take the capital without anyone stopping us!"

"That was never the reason. The reason always had to do with Inarius. Well, he's thrown down the gauntlet. He's inviting us to come to him, can't you feel that?"

They could not. Even now, as powerful as the edyrem in general had become, they could not feel the angel's touch. Uldyssian did not like that.

"What do we do, Master Uldyssian?" asked Jonas, the gaunt Parthan ever ready to obey.

"We're not far from the grasslands between the city and the Cathedral of Light. We turn in that direction."

Serenthia frowned. "And then what?"

"Then we fight for our lives . . . again."

Despite the abrupt change in their intended route, Uldyssian's followers argued little when told. Yet again, they trusted in their leader and what he planned. Uldyssian hid from everyone the fact that he had no true idea what to do save face the angel himself. In his mind, the rest of Inarius's followers were nothing. Inarius was the one who had to be defeated.

And even that might not be enough to save Sanctuary.

The edyrem wasted no time in moving on, their easy victory over the Kehjani army spurring their spirits. The grasslands, an open area in the midst of the all-consuming jungles, were believed to have been the reason the Cathedral had originally chosen a northerly location for its base of operations. It allowed for an easy path for pilgrims going to and from the shining edifice and the capital.

It now made for the perfect place for war.

As the edyrem marched, Uldyssian kept watch for any covert strikes by either Inarius or one of his minions. However, nothing happened. At first, he did not understand why the angel would let all of them travel unmolested, but as the journey progressed and still nothing happened, it slowly dawned on him just why that might be.

But it was not until Mendeln returned—with Rathma beside him—that Uldyssian was able to confirm his suspicion with Inarius's offspring. Guiding them and Serenthia slightly away from the others, he asked Rathma his opinion.

"Yes, that is exactly it," the cowled Ancient agreed. "You have come to know my father well. He is indeed preparing a spectacle that will show all those in Sanctuary that his is the ultimate power. He intends your defeat to be a glorious one!" Rathma shook his head, a rueful smile on his lips. "And that even if the world itself should exist no more than a few minutes past his victory. Such madness!"

"He might not even have the few minutes," Uldyssian pointed out. "The angels could arrive before that."

Rathma grew grimmer yet. "You have no idea how true you speak. They were distracted by Trag's ploy, but that is no more. They now know exactly where Sanctuary is. Time flows differently for them, but I would say that we have maybe a day or two before they fall upon us."

The others—even Mendeln, it appeared—looked aghast. Uldyssian could not help but gape. "As little as that? I thought maybe a week—"

"A week would be a blessing."

"Damn Inarius for not listening! There might've been some hope against the angels if he had."

Rathma said nothing. Uldyssian looked around at the others. His expression grew stubborn. "We don't tell anyone else! If we're all to die, better we die fighting! If somehow we defeat Inarius, then we can worry about anything else. No one else must know. Agreed?"

He received no dissension. They rejoined the edyrem and moved on.

Uldyssian had hoped to make it to the Cathedral that day, but his estimation of their pace proved too ambitious. They barely reached the edge of the grasslands just after dark. He knew that to go on was to play into Inarius's intentions yet could not help feeling that to stop would do the same.

"He will not attack this night," Rathma finally informed him. "My father wants the slaughter of the edyrem—and, especially, your downfall—completely visible to his followers. No, he will wait for daylight, foolish as that might seem to us."

"If only we could reach the Cathedral during the night and still have the strength to fight him . . ."

The Ancient glanced out at the night-enshrouded grasslands. "I cannot say exactly why, but I feel that if you would attempt that, you would regret it. There is something out there, something best left for the light of the sun."

Frowning, Uldyssian stared at the landscape ahead. Now that Rathma had mentioned it, he, too, noticed something unsettling about the visually tranquil grasses. The view was innocent enough; the tall brown and green grasses swayed gently in the breeze. A few creatures called out, most of them insects or the occasional night bird. There was nothing that in any manner hinted of threat.

Yet he felt that Rathma was right.

The edyrem made camp just within the jungle. Aware of how inviting the grasslands looked, Uldyssian was adamant in his decision that no one, not even the sentries, step a foot beyond the last of the trees.

But it turned out that there was one who did not obey. Once most of the edyrem were asleep, Uldyssian waited for Achilios to join them, yet as the minutes passed and the hunter did not appear, the son of Diomedes believed he knew just what had happened.

"He's out there, isn't he?" Uldyssian asked Rathma.

"You know him better than I."

"Can't you sense him?"

"No." The Ancient looked to Mendeln. "Can you?"

Uldyssian's brother held up his dagger, then pointed it toward the grasslands. The faint glow did not change. "I think . . . there is a hint . . . but I cannot be certain." As he lowered the blade, he added, "But it would be like him, wouldn't it, Uldyssian?"

Serenthia grew upset. "We've got to go after him! If there *is* something out there, it might—"

She refrained from using the word kill, as Achilios was already dead, but they shared her concern. Uldyssian put a foot into what he considered the true boundary between the jungle and the grasslands, then concentrated as hard as he could.

"He's out there. I can't place where, but he's definitely out there." A part of Uldyssian wanted to go chasing after his friend. "He's scouting for us."

Even Rathma showed some surprise at this. "Was that wise of him?"

"This is Achilios," Uldyssian returned. "He makes his own choices . . . and he's very capable."

Inarius's son nodded, then prudently left with Mendeln while Uldyssian dealt with Serenthia.

"This is ridiculous!" she blurted. "Uldyssian, he can't be allowed to risk himself like this! I know why he is. Because he thinks that since he's dead and I'm not, what we have can't go on."

"There's a good chance that we'll all be dead soon, Serry. I think Achilios is just doing what he can maybe to save the woman he loves. You can't fault him for that."

She suddenly beat her hands against his chest. "I fault him for leaving me over and over! I fault him for thinking that I don't love him enough—"

Her fists flared with unbridled energy. If not for his own inherent defenses, Uldyssian knew that he would have been badly injured. As it was, both of them were suddenly surrounded by a green fire that originated from him.

"Serry! Stop this now!"

The merchant's daughter shook uncontrollably, then started sobbing. The fire vanished from around her hands. As it did, Uldyssian retracted his own spell.

Or, at least, he tried to. The green flames resisted. The heat around both of them continued to increase. Sweat began pouring down Uldyssian's face, and he heard Serenthia gasping for breath.

Gritting his teeth, the son of Diomedes focused harder. He demanded that his power obey.

And it did. Just like that, the flames ceased. Yet the effort took more out of Uldyssian than he had expected.

Serenthia shifted in his arms, bringing his attention back to her. She looked up, her face drawn from her outburst.

"I'm . . . I'm sorry, Uldyssian. . . . I didn't mean to lose control of myself . . . but . . ."

"It's all right. I understand."

She wiped the moisture from around her eyes. "It's just that . . . I suddenly feared that I might not see him again this time."

Her fear was a reasonable one, but Uldyssian could not tell her that. "You'll see him again. I know Achilios. Nothing can keep him from you. You should know that by now."

"I hope . . . I hope he'll be all right out there," the dark-haired woman murmured as she stepped away from him. "I hope he will be."

Eyeing the grasslands, Serenthia quietly walked away. Uldyssian kept watch until he was certain that she was simply going to sleep, then turned his own attention back to the grasslands. Try as he might, he could not determine exactly where Achilios was.

"You'd better come back to her," Uldyssian whispered. "You'd better come back to her. . . ."

If only so that they could die *together* this time . . .

Serenthia looked as if she slept, but she did not. Regardless of what Uldyssian had said, she could not merely leave things be. Achilios had been reckless, true, but Serenthia would not abandon him because of that trait. After all, he had always been reckless, but also extremely loyal.

And so, while her body lay still, her mind went in search of the man she loved.

Serenthia soared over the grasslands, seeking any hint of Achilios's presence. She was aware that, being dead, he did not leave a trace as Uldyssian or she might, but the merchant's daughter was certain that her bond with the archer more than made up for that. She *would* find him.

The grasslands had a surreal calmness that should have set her mind at ease, but instead, Serenthia soon felt as if something watched her from behind. Yet when she reversed her view, it was to find nothing.

Finally shaking it off as nerves, Serenthia pushed herself faster and faster. Achilios could not be far.

Something to the east caught her attention. She veered toward there with ease. There was nothing visible, but then, the hunter would hardly be standing out in the open.

As she neared the area in question, Serenthia was finally able to tell that what she had thought might be Achilios was instead something else. Secure in the knowledge that she could neither be seen nor heard, Serenthia hovered over the spot, seeking the source of the strangeness she felt.

When that failed, she descended. Lower and lower she brought her view, until at last Serenthia stared into the very ground.

And then she saw the hole.

It was not truly physical but bordered between that and some plane of existence almost akin to that which she currently inhabited. The gap was wide enough to fit a man or something slightly larger, but the edges seemed in flux, as if prepared to close . . . or open farther.

Curious, Serenthia descended lower yet, directly through the center of the gap.

The moment she passed into it, her entire perspective shifted. Serenthia knew that she was no longer in Sanctuary, but where she was, it was impossible to say.

Something black and seemingly consisting entirely of huge, sharp teeth shot up at her.

Serenthia tried to retreat through the gap, only to discover that it was far, far above her mental form. How she had descended so deep, she did not know, but all that mattered now was to escape.

The thing closed on her, its many teeth gnashing. Up close, she saw that it had a circular mouth and two tiny, almost-blind eyes. Somehow, though, the fiendish beast clearly knew where Serenthia was despite her not being there physically.

Undulating like a snake, the creature pursued at a pace far greater than hers. Serenthia feared that it would catch up before she reached the gap, and if it did, there was no doubt in her mind that despite her lack of body, it would destroy her. It was possible that her powers would work against it, but for some reason, Serenthia suspected that it was better to run rather than fight.

But she was not going to make it. The gap was still too far away. Just below, the horrific mouth opened wide, filling her view. Serenthia smelled decay, and the fact that she could smell anything at all added to her fear that she was not safe from harm.

She wished she had her spear. With the weapon, she would have at least had the ghost of a chance. Serenthia's desire was so intense that she could almost feel the spear in her hand—

And suddenly, she realized that she held it.

It was not actually the spear, Serenthia saw, but rather a magical representation her mind had created. Nevertheless, it gave her hope. Readying it, she aimed for the center of the creature's cavernous maw, not hard to do, considering how wide the mouth was now.

It all but had her. The teeth gnashed eagerly. Serenthia

threw, knowing that her entire will had to go into this last desperate attempt.

The gleaming spear vanished deep into the beast. Serenthia then imagined the weapon burning with fire hot enough to melt rock and, therefore, the insides of this night-marish thing.

The wormlike beast let out a gargling sound. Its body glowed like hot coals.

It exploded.

Bits of the monster flew through Serenthia, who instinc-tively sought to protect herself. Ichor rained down, then dissipated.

Although she had destroyed her attacker, Serenthia's first thought was to flee. Yet she had barely started to with-draw, when it occurred to her that there had to be more going on here than a simple den for a monstrous beast. Studying her surroundings better, the raven-tressed woman reaffirmed her belief that she was no longer in Sanctuary. However much that disturbed her, it also came to her mind that *Achilios* also might have discovered this "passage" and investigated it. That might be why Serenthia had not been able to trace him thus far. If she left without making sure that he was not here . . .

Decision made, she flew down the passage. As she did, she could not help but glance more and more at what passed for its walls. Inspecting closely, Serenthia discov-ered that they were not even completely solid but actually like black pitch that constantly dripped.

Then, up ahead, there came a disconcerting light, a light as crimson as blood. Serenthia slowed, suddenly uncertain about going any farther.

Once again, it was Serenthia's deep love for Achilios that drove her on toward the monstrous light. Had she had any true flesh, it would have crawled from fear and disgust. Whatever lay ahead radiated an evil so strong that even Lilith paled by comparison.

It was all Serenthia could do to push herself to the end of the passage. Once there, she peered into the light, trying to focus on what lay within it.

And what she saw made the slaughter of the Kehjani merchants and mages insignificant by comparison. Her courage finally broke. Serenthia wanted nothing more than to return to the relative safety of her own body. With all the will she could muster, she strained to escape the magical passage and what lay at the other end.

There was a tingling sensation when Serenthia finally passed through the gap. But even when the grasslands once again filled her view, she did not slow. Serenthia did not look back once, fearing that in doing so, she would find creatures more monstrous than the worm giving chase.

She returned at last to her body.

Serenthia jolted up, her eyes already wide. She quickly spun around, certain that fiends loomed all about her. When she found nothing, the frantic woman immediately raced back to where she had left Uldyssian.

He was still there, still standing and watching the grasslands. At any other time, Serenthia would have been touched by his determination, for it was obvious that he continued to hope to find some trace of Achilios out there. However, what she had seen outweighed even her concern for the man she loved.

It was all Serenthia could do to keep from shouting as she neared Uldyssian. He turned as she arrived, his expression telling her that he sensed her tremendous anxiety.

"Serry!" The son of Diomedes took hold of her arm. "What is it? A bad dream about Achilios?"

Naturally, that would be his first thought when she came running so. Serenthia shook her head.

"No!" she gasped. Then, thinking better, Serenthia lowered her voice to a whisper. "No. Uldyssian . . . no dream. I—I went out there to look . . . to look for Achilios—"

"What?" It was clear to her that he was doing all that he could to keep from raising his own voice. Uldyssian understood exactly what Serenthia had done in order to search for the archer, and his fury was understandable. "You should've told me first! No! You shouldn't have tried anything at all! What would have happened if—"

"Uldyssian, hush! Listen to me! You need to hear what I found!"

"Why? Was Achilios . . . was he—"

"No . . . though I pray that he didn't run across it and fall victim to the guardian!" Serenthia gazed down, lost in that horrible thought. What if Achilios *had* discovered the magical gap and had entered? What if she had not noticed any trace of him, but he *had* been there, a prisoner, all the time?

"Serry! Serry!" Uldyssian forced her to focus on him again. "Come back! Now, tell me. Tell me what's shaken you."

"It's . . ." Taking a deep breath, she tried once more. "It's . . . horrifying!"

With that, the story came spilling out of her. The sensation that something was amiss, the discovery of the magical gap, her decision to investigate it, and what happened when she did.

Uldyssian was stunned . . . and even more furious than ever. "You should've turned right back!"

"Listen! There's more. So much more. Listen!" Serenthia described the beast guarding the way and how she had managed to destroy it. Uldyssian's brow rose at this, but he refrained from interrupting. "And then . . . and then I reached the end of the passage and saw them . . . *all* of them! An endless sea of them. So horrific. So terrifying!"

She became caught up in the nightmarish vision again. The grotesque, fiendish faces. The macabre, chilling forms. The incredible aura of evil . . .

"Serry!" Uldyssian shook her by the shoulders. "*What* did you see?"

The merchant's daughter steeled herself. In a low, steady voice, she managed. "I saw . . . I saw into what could only be what Rathma called the *Burning Hells,* Uldyssian! The passage in the grasslands leads out of our world and into wherever *they* must exist!"

He opened his mouth in what surely would have been a denial of her words, then shut it tight. Uldyssian nodded grimly. They had all dealt with demons long enough. A magical gateway to the infernal realms was no longer a stretch of the imagination.

Seeing that Uldyssian would not argue, Serenthia forced herself to tell him the worst yet. "They were there. They were there. Thousands and thousands of them! Maybe more. I don't know—their numbers looked endless."

"Who, Serry? Who?"

Her eyes grew wide as saucers as she continued to envision their ranks. "An army . . . an army of *demons*. And they can only be getting ready to march on Sanctuary!"

EİGHTEEП

Not for a moment had Achilios hesitated to go out and scout for his friends. His existence—if he could even call this miserable suffering through which he went that—was expendable. It was important for the others to survive . . . for Serenthia to survive.

With Uldyssian so distracted, it had been simple for the hunter to slip away from where he had been lurking. The tall grass hid him well, and the soft ground eliminated whatever unlikely sound his boots *might* make.

As ever, he kept an arrow ready. The quiver was filled with more. That was the only useful gift that the angel Tyrael had given him, a never-ending supply of sharp and, in some manner, magical arrows. Achilios wished that he could show his gratitude to the treacherous angel—to *both* angels who had used him—by managing to fire a few into whatever served as their hearts.

But, for now, he cared only that the bolts would prove of use against whatever might lurk out here.

And there was certainly *something* hidden in the grasslands. Inarius would have planned some trick by which to wear Uldyssian down before any true confrontation. At least, that was the impression Achilios had of the Prophet.

He was long gone from the encampment by this point, but thus far the only thing he had discovered was the disconcerting lack of any wildlife whatsoever. It was not just that Achilios had run across no rabbits, cats, or other large animals, but there were also no birds or, judging by the complete silence, even one insect. The creatures of the grasslands had found it prudent to flee, and that did not bode well.

There was also hardly anything that could even be called a breeze anymore. What had existed when Achilios had first set out had lessened more and more as he progressed, to the point where only his trained eyes could see the barely perceptible movement of the grass.

Achilios hesitated. For the first time, he noticed that some of the grass ahead was weaving contrary to others. No wind could cause that.

He raised the bow, suspicious that the odd movement meant that something moved low through the grass. Out here, it might be an animal as powerful as one of the jungle cats, but Achilios doubted it. Most animals *fled* his presence, acutely aware of the wrongness inherent in him.

But if it was not an animal, he could think of only one thing, a demon of some sort.

Standing as still as a rock, Achilios waited. The grass continued to weave in its odd fashion, but nothing emerged.

Finally growing impatient, the hunter took a step forward. Instantly, he noted some more agitated movement from the nearest plants. Again, Achilios paused, bow ready to fire.

And again, he was disappointed. Achilios had heard as a child an expression *the patience of the dead*, but he found it held no truth when it came to him. There were limits to even the hunter's will, and he had reached those limits long ago. Indeed, if anything, being dead had made him *more* impatient than he had been in life.

Still keeping the bow steady, Achilios finally trod forward. To his surprise, the spot where he expected something to be hiding revealed *nothing*. No animal. No demon. It was almost as if the grass moved of its own accord.

Frowning, the blond archer scratched a dirt-flaked cheek. His instincts—and possibly what passed for his edyrem abilities—were as strong as if he were still breathing, and they insisted that something was amiss. Yet whatever it was he could not discover.

That it was night bothered him less than it did Mendeln or Uldyssian. Even as a youth, Achilios had always had exceptional night vision. Undead, it had heightened. He surveyed the area meticulously, seeking some hint of the threat he felt certain surrounded him.

A small, dark form buried in the grass to his left caught his attention. Setting the bow next to him—but keeping his fingers close to it—Achilios used his free hand to tug at the object. The grass was thickly wound around it, so tangled, in fact, that he nearly tore apart what he was trying to retrieve.

Frustrated, Achilios pulled his hand from the bow and grabbed his knife. The grass proved stubborn to cut, but he finally did.

The mangled thing had once been a black bird. The body had nearly been crushed to a pulp, and some of the grass had wound so tightly around the body that the head and wings had nearly been severed.

Achilios judged its death to have been no more than a day. Had there been the usual flies about, the body would have been in worse shape. As it was, it unnerved him that nothing had thus far come to feed on the carrion. He turned the avian over, trying to decide just what had killed it. Other than the tightly wound grass blades, there was no evidence of anything that would have left injury.

He stiffened. Keeping his eyes fixed on the dead bird, he slowly lowered the corpse to the ground. At the same time, Achilios manuevered the hand with the knife toward the now-open palm. He slipped the blade into his other hand, then started to reach for the bow.

His fingers never reached it. His wrist was snagged, what suddenly bound it tightening enough to cut off the blood of a living man.

Achilios spun around, bringing the knife down. The sharp edge cut deep into *grass*.

His other hand came free, the grass blades wrapped around the wrist falling off and wriggling on the ground. The hunter grabbed for the bow—

The grass lunged at him from all sides. It snagged his arms like a hundred coiling serpents. Achilios managed to slash a few more blades, but then his bound hand could not reach the rest.

Suddenly, the grass underneath began churning around and around. The ground there grew soft, and to his horror, Achilios started to sink.

Not again! Not again! He remembered with dread the tentacles of the demon in the forest and how at one point he had been certain that the creature would drag him under. Instead, it had sought to tear him apart, but that fate—more welcome to him than the other, obvious choice—was not what was intended here.

And as he struggled to keep himself above the surface, the hunter knew that this was no lone occurrence. He had discovered part of the Prophet's strategy. The angel intended to strip all hope from Uldyssian by the time the two of them actually confronted each other. There were probably other such terrifying spots hidden all through the grasslands, perhaps even with different menaces.

Achilios's leg sank beneath the soft, turned-up soil. He fought to free himself not only for his own sake but for that of his friends.

For Serenthia . . .

But although the archer fought with a strength beyond mortal extremes, he could not stop his other leg from following the first, then the rest of his lower half. That left him all but facing into the dirt.

The empty hand went next. Achilios shifted his knife around, trying to cut his remaining wrist free. The sharp edge sliced through several grass blades, and at last Achilios could maneuver his hand better. He quickly slashed at what remained around his wrist.

The hand came free. With monumental effort, the hunter

ripped his forearm loose. Unfortunately, his other arm was completely under, and now fronds were seeking his throat. The dirt—the hungry dirt—was only inches from his face.

A desperate growl escaped Achilios. He turned the knife around and dug furiously at the base of the grass nearest his head. Achilios madly chopped at the ground, ripping away at whatever plants he could reach. He felt the pressure on his arm ease up. Like a wet dog, he shook the soil from his other shoulder.

With a grin only death could allow, Achilios raised himself slightly. That gave him even more room to adjust his reach. He immediately put the knife to work. More and more of his buried arm came free.

But then, from beneath the ground, from what surely were the few roots he had left after severing the grass blades, new shoots darted up. They grew to full maturity in less time than it took him to grasp the enormity of their rising.

And with an eager vigor, the new blades coiled around him in such numbers that it seemed Achilios wore a shirt of grass. They tightened their grip on his hand, and although he refused to release the knife, their work made it certain that it was as useless to him as all else.

Both arms were pulled under. The hunter's torso became buried up to his chest. Achilios shook his head frantically as he sought to keep it from coming closer to the ground.

Then, from beneath his face, a new patch of sinister blades blossomed to life. Achilios knew that he could do nothing to stop them and in his fury screamed his anger.

Grass thrust up into his mouth and nose. Other blades snared his head, hugging him like a lover as they forced his open mouth to kiss the dirt. Darkness closed over Achilios's face as he was dragged under. . . .

Seconds later, the only sign remaining of his presence was the abandoned bow. The grass that now filled the entire spot gently weaved back and forth.

Waiting . . .

•   •   •

Achilios had *not* returned, and there were demons in wait. Inarius surely had his own followers ready to attack and even if they did not, there was an army of angels coming to destroy everything.

Despite that dread reality, Uldyssian had no choice but to march the edyrem into the grasslands. He was now playing a game whose rules had been decided by some force beyond his ken. His only hope lay in doing the unexpected . . . but whatever that might be, he could not say.

The sun had risen, but what might have been something to lift his spirits quickly proved extremely troubling. Not only had the fiery orb seemed to rise sooner and faster than normally, but it also rose in the *wrong* direction. It now hung in the north, the same direction the edyrem had to march to meet their foe.

Somehow, Inarius had *moved* the sun.

Although no one made mention of it out loud, the astounding feat left the edyrem slow and disheartened as they journeyed. The question in everyone's head was obvious to Uldyssian: How could someone who could move the sun be defeated?

It was Rathma who offered him some ray of hope, however slight. He was the only one among them who looked upon the sight unimpressed.

"That is not the sun," he informed Uldyssian. "What you see is illusion. The sun is still where it was, but our perceptions see it in the north."

"Which means?"

Rathma almost sneered at the sun. "What my father did took much power, but in the end, it is only your imagination that makes it real. It does not make his true might any greater than it was before."

It was an unsatisfying answer in many ways, for Uldyssian still did not know the angel's limits. As far as he could see, if this was but an illusion of sorts, it was a *damned* impressive one.

And what was worse, it was constantly blinding.

Still, if it was an illusion, it occurred to him that there was something he could do to negate Inarius's trick, something Uldyssian had already done more than once in the past. True, the very first time, it had also been achieved through Lilith's manipulation of him, but now he was far past needing her foul power to augment his. It was certainly worth a try, at least.

Uldyssian concentrated on the sky, focusing on one of the tiny clouds scattered here and there. All he needed was the one.

A wind arose, the first cool breeze anyone had felt in weeks. Around him, the son of Diomedes sensed the others react. They knew that whatever was happening was his doing and took heart from it.

And with that to further stimulate his hopes, Uldyssian threw himself into the spell. The air shifted. The cloud expanded, becoming ten, a hundred, a thousand times its original size. It also thickened and, as it did, grew a deep gray.

Uldyssian not only called upon his own power, but he continued to press it and his will on his very surroundings. He had done this before, albeit not on such a grand scale. It concerned him to expend himself so much before facing Inarius, but the Prophet had left him no real choice, which he expected was just the way his rival wanted it.

But Uldyssian could not think about such things. He had to concern himself only with the moment at hand.

The cloud now absorbed all those others around it, then expanded farther. It crept purposely toward the north, eating away at the blue sky.

Then—at last—it reached where the sun stood defiant. Uldyssian's will almost faltered then, for surely he could not so simply defeat the angel's strategy. Yet the first edges of the massive gray cloud soon spread across where the sun shone.

As it did, the light grew less blinding. A hopeful murmur arose among Uldyssian's followers. His own pulse quickened as the sun went from fully dominant to partially seen, then to barely a sliver and, finally, a vaguely hinted-at shape that did just enough to keep the grasslands from being plunged into darkness.

Daring to breathe, Uldyssian glanced around.

The edyrem broke into a cheer.

He looked to Rathma, who bore a rare, if brief, smile. The Ancient bowed his head.

"You have just put uncertainty back into the heart of my father," the cowled figure complimented.

Mendeln grinned at his brother. Only Serenthia did not share the general outpouring of confidence, but the pain on her face lessened slightly.

It also immediately reminded Uldyssian that whatever he had just accomplished, he still faced a legion of terrible foes.

But he could not let the others see his concern. Maintaining a façade of triumph, Uldyssian led his people on. At the very least, they could now concentrate better on the path ahead— and he hoped that would give the edyrem some chance against whatever next struck at them.

The grass grew thicker the further into the region they marched. Uldyssian had warned everyone to keep on guard, and he was pleased with the attentiveness he felt throughout the band. The most promising of his followers had been placed at the front and outer perimeters, and as usual, those least able to defend themselves were in a position within the main body but toward the back. For once, Uldyssian had wanted to leave them behind, but no one could think of anywhere they would be safe. He could not be certain that the mage clans just might free themselves, then take revenge on what edyrem they could find. Never mind that the group would consist mainly of defenseless children and elders.

No, the edyrem were best off together, especially if they were all to perish. At least then there would be a fighting chance.

"There it is," Mendeln suddenly and quietly declared.

Uldyssian would not have had to ask what his brother meant, even if he had not seen it at the same time. The gargantuan edifice gleamed despite the thick cloud cover, gleamed as if made of diamond. Uldyssian could not make out any details save the sharply pointed spire towering over all else.

As far away as the edyrem still were from it, its appearance meant that there remained little time before Inarius would wait no longer. Uldyssian's followers were nearly midway between the Cathedral and the city, the perfect place for any monstrous tableau the renegade angel wished to create.

"Should we not also be able to see the Golden Path?" Uldyssian's brother added. "I would expect it to be very close by."

The Golden Path was the direct route between Kehjan and the Cathedral of Light, the way by which pilgrims trekked to the holy site and then back to the capital. The name was of spiritual reference and had nothing to do with its appearance, for the Path was merely a shaved-down area first cut by the Prophet's acolytes. It was now completely maintained by the sandaled or bare feet of the legions of daily suppliants, who came in such numbers that they trampled down any plant foolish enough to try to grow along the way.

But although it had surely only been a day or two since the last pilgrims had come this way, there was now, for as far as the eye could see—and farther for Uldyssian—nothing but more tall grass. The Golden Path was no more.

"My father," Rathma stated bluntly, not that everyone had not already guessed that.

Uldyssian raised a hand to signal the edyrem to halt. He would permit no one to proceed until he had thoroughly investigated the area ahead. This could also be a trick by the waiting demons, who he assumed had to be in league with Inarius. After all, they had as much at stake as the angel did in guaranteeing that Uldyssian fail.

Making certain that the sky remained cloaked in gray, Uldyssian looked inward. He let his gift reach ahead and then began the process of methodically searching. A part of him also hoped that he might yet find some sign of Achilios, although that was becoming more and more a dream.

All else faded from Uldyssian's attention as he made certain that the way ahead was safe. He would not let his people fall prey to Inarius's machinations. He would not let that happen—

The screams buffeted him from all sides, edyrem everywhere sending mental cries of fear. As he ripped himself from his search, Uldyssian felt Serenthia violently shaking him.

"Uldyssian! Snap out of—" Her voice was cut off.

He turned—and suddenly was snagged around the legs and one arm by what he at first thought were slim tentacles. They were nothing of the sort, though. Instead, the very grass sought to bring him down. Worse, he quickly saw that edyrem everywhere were in stages of being strangled or dragged into the dirt. Some were even sinking.

And the worst-struck place was where the children and others who could not truly defend themselves stood. Despite the bravery of their protectors, they were being torn from one another and pulled in every direction. Their screams were horrific to hear.

Uldyssian put a hand to some of the grass binding him. Fire burned away those blades, but almost immediately, twice their number sprouted from the cindered ends. The same disaster was repeated all over, with even Rathma struggling in vain to free himself.

This was no coincidence. Uldyssian had done exactly as Inarius had desired of him. He had purposely set about a situation that would distract the edyrem leader—a situation that demanded Uldyssian's attention—even if for only a moment. The son of Diomedes had obliged him yet again by walking right into the trap. All the angel had needed was that moment.

Grass strained for his throat. Uldyssian tugged as best he could on what was already wrapped around him. With some effort, he summoned the power to slice clean all the nearby grass.

But once again, the field not only regenerated itself faster than he could destroy it but became more fierce. The screams that constantly bombarded Uldyssian's hearing were not merely of fright . . . they were of agony.

His people were dying. Once more, Uldyssian was failing them.

His mind raged at the Prophet's uncaring nature. To the angel, humans were less than nothing. That their kind still existed was likely only because Inarius could not stand having no one to honor his greatness. That, and the fact that such utter isolation would have been too much even for him.

That Inarius could call himself a warrior of the Light, a champion of Good, was a jest that Uldyssian found too cruel. He envisioned Inarius as the Prophet, the handsome, eternal youth laughing at his helplessness.

As that vision magnified in his head, Uldyssian burned inside with an anger he never experienced before. The son of Diomedes felt as if he were about to explode, yet he had no outlet. He needed something at which to strike, and there was only the grass.

The grass . . .

The *grass* . . .

As had happened before, fire burst into manic life all around him. It was not merely fire as might have been seen in the camp last night, but gargantuan emerald and yellow flames that devoured the nearest blades so quickly and thoroughly that there was nothing left from which to sprout new grass.

And that fire then shot through the region, racing with calculated madness among the edyrem. It left of the grass only black dust, but not one of Uldyssian's people was so much as singed. For them, the flames felt instead like a brief moment of cool air caressing them.

But it was not enough simply to save the edrem from the trap into which he had led them. Uldyssian's anger knew no bounds. Suddenly, everything around him he perceived as a threat to his followers and, especially, to himself. Every blade of grass for as far as the eye could see was a monster, a servant of the Prophet. Glaring at them, Uldyssian only wished them gone.

The fire bowed to his will. It shot forth from the vicinity of the edrem, devouring plant life in all other directions. In its wake, it left a blackened landscape that, thanks to the son of Diomedes, was not in the least bit hot.

And as the edrem watched in awe, the rest of the grasslands surrendered to Uldyssian's fury. From where he stood, the burnt area spread farther and farther. The flames rushed on unchecked, growing more distant but also more voracious.

Uldyssian watched it all without hardly drawing a breath. He watched it all without any care for the destruction he caused. Why, in fact, should he stop with merely the grasslands? If Inarius enjoyed these little plots, then even the jungles were suspect. Was it not for the best to let the fire go as far as it could, even into the capital, where there was nothing but deceit and evil almost on par with what the angels and demons offered? Why—

Someone slapped him hard across the face. Uldyssian let out a roar and focused a good part of his power on the miscreant.

The raw blast of energy struck Mendeln square before Uldyssian realized just who his target was.

"Nooo!" Horrified, he fought to quell his work. Mendeln fell out of sight, adding to his shock. Despite all that, it was still a struggle for Uldyssian to bring himself under control.

There was not a living blade of grass in sight. In fact, the only living things left were the edrem . . . and not all of them. There were bodies here, there, and too many other places.

Many of them were children.

However, Uldyssian had no time for Inarius's innocent victims, so concerned was he about the one belonging to him. He shoved Rathma aside and ran toward where he had last seen his brother. With such force as he had leveled against Mendeln, it was certain that the younger sibling was not only dead but mangled unrecognizably.

But Mendeln's face and form were in perfect condition, although lying at an angle that sent chills through Uldyssian. Letting out a sob, the older brother bent by the black-robed figure's side. He had healed others very close to death. If there was a chance to do it once more, he prayed this would be that moment.

The sky crackled with lightning.

Despite the tragedy of his own situation, Uldyssian could not help but glance up at what should not have been. He had created only thick clouds to shield his followers from Inarius's damnable sun. No storm had been part of that spell.

But now it came nonetheless.

The rain fell with terrible strength, as if a huge bucket had been turned over, a bucket that never finished emptying. The savage torrent mercilessly battered people into the ground. Even Uldyssian found himself hard pressed to stand, but stand he did.

And as the son of Diomedes straightened, he saw the movement from the north. At first, it appeared to flow toward him and his followers much as the terrible rain did. However, as it drew relentlessly nearer, it divided into hundreds and hundreds of robed, helmeted figures on horseback. They wielded curved swords and maces, and their wild shouts were like thunder.

Inquisitor warriors—the militant arm of the Cathedral of Light.

But there was more to them than what at first was obvious. Uldyssian sensed that difference more than he saw it. Wary, he stared at the oncoming legions, reaching out to see them as if he stood just before the pounding hooves.

And then Uldyssian made out just what it was about them that bothered him. It was best revealed in their eyes— their eyes that were now without pupils. Instead, a radiant gold fire blazed forth from beneath the lids, an inhuman force that he saw filled each and every warrior he searched.

It took only a glance at their rabid expressions to see that there was little left of the original minds that had inhabited these bodies. Of all those in the ranks, only the helmeted woman in the lead and a handful of high-ranking priests mixed among the fighters still had eyes that indicated that they were themselves. The rest had all been utterly subjugated by Inarius's will.

At that moment, Rathma stepped up next to him, the Ancient's hood and cloak untouched by the incessant rain. He somehow still looked no more pleasant than a drenched Uldyssian.

His words had nothing to do with the ferocious onslaught racing toward them. "Be not concerned about your brother, for I was able to shield him just as you struck out."

Uldyssian glanced down at his sibling again. Mendeln moaned, and his eyes fluttered open. As Rathma had indicated, he seemed entirely well . . . no thanks to Uldyssian. The older brother had been too distraught to notice.

But as guilty as Uldyssian felt about Mendeln and as concerned he was about his unthinking outburst, the events now unfolding before them demanded his attention. He stared anew at the charging Inquisitors, hoping that, as with Mendeln, his initial beliefs had been incorrect.

Unfortunately, in the case of the Prophet's warriors, Uldyssian immediately sensed that he was not. The dread spectacle was exactly as he feared it.

"He has fallen even more than I could imagine," Inarius's son shouted, "and may have shown us at last why he is not concerned that a heavenly host is nigh upon Sanctuary!"

"What do you mean?"

"You sense his power within those misguided fools, do you not? Then you can also sense where my father has been able to draw so much from, for this is surely more than he himself could bear alone!"

Uldyssian eyed the oncoming horde closer. He looked within one random warrior and finally recognized what he should have known all along. Rathma was right. The angel was not this strong by himself.

Inarius was drawing all the power he could from the Worldstone, power against which the efforts of Uldyssian and all the edyrem combined could very well prove futile.

ΠΙΠΕΤΕΕΠ

Uldyssian shook his head, wanting the truth to be nothing more than a bad dream. Yet the Inquisitors continued to ride toward the edyrem, and the power of the angel filled them to overflowing. These would not be simple fighters easy to defeat, as would have been the case with the Kehjani. Uldyssian was not sure how powerful the individual Inquisitors would be, but he and his people were certain to face a terrible foe.

He reached out to the others, preparing them for the imminent battle. Even when warned that these would not be mere mortal men that they faced, his edyrem remained stalwart. Their courage both stirred and concerned Uldyssian, who knew that many would die.

And still Inarius did not deign to enter the conflict.

"Where is he?" the son of Diomedes demanded of Rathma.

"Everywhere. Be not impatient to face Inarius," the Ancient replied. "You will do that soon enough."

The edyrem formed a great circle. They had no choice. Uldyssian would have liked to have created a vast line with reserves in the rear but was hampered by Serenthia's discovery. Surely the demons intended to attack him from behind once his people were occupied by those before them. It was the strategy he would have used and that Rathma agreed made sense. That forced him to rely on the circle.

Most of the edyrem were to focus on the Inquisitors, but enough kept sentinel on every other direction so that warning could go out and some of those facing the front could immediately shift their attention wherever needed. Despite the complexity already inherent in the situation because of such planning, Uldyssian had also kept the edyrem constantly on the move . . . until now.

Serenthia readied her spear. "They're almost upon us!" She seemed more eager than most to throw herself into the fight. "Give the word, Uldyssian!"

But he held back, trying to decipher what else the Prophet might have in mind. Unfortunately, nothing was apparent, and the massive charge was closing fast.

He saw no other choice. He let the edyrem strike.

A wave of blackened earth shot up, rising well above the oncoming riders. Guided by Uldyssian, the edyrem sent it crashing down on the first ranks.

Men and horses screamed as tons of stone and dirt buried them. Only a few managed to escape the crashing wall, one of them the female priest leading the charge. Her mount was not so fortunate, though, all but its forelegs crushed under the magical onslaught.

However, those behind did not even pause but drove their animals *over* the carnage. There clearly existed no desire for them but for the edyrem's blood.

And worse, from the vast burial site Uldyssian's followers had just created, several robed forms burrowed to the surface. Death should have claimed those the spell had struck, but the power Inarius funneled through his minions had saved many. Bereft of their horses, they grabbed whatever weapons they could locate and simply ran behind their mounted brethren, shrieking for the enemy's death.

Only a few paces now separated the two sides. Uldyssian had time for only one more attack, which he set into motion. Despite the rain, the edyrem readily created a veritable storm of their own, fireballs that bombarded the Inquisitors with the ferocity of lightning.

This time, the attack had more effect. Several riders were blasted from their mounts. Many became fireballs in their own right, transforming into blazing corpses that dropped among their unsuspecting comrades. There was no doubting the fates of those struck; little enough remained of them that could even be identified as human.

But although the first wave of the edyrem's attack proved quite effective, subsequent ones garnered little success. Suddenly, the Inquisitors were better able to shield themselves. Fireballs dissipated harmlessly against their breastplates. The Cathedral's minions were no longer even slowed.

And moments later, the first of them collided with Uldyssian's band.

He had already prepared his followers for combat, but the edyrem were at first hard pressed. The lack of outright success against the Inquisitors had dampened their confidence enough to allow the warriors to push in the right side of the circle. It might have collapsed entirely if not for Serenthia and Jonas guiding the others in immediately rebuilding the ranks.

The curved swords and spiked maces of the Inquisitors clashed with the edyrem's varied assortment of salvaged weapons and farm implements, yet the struggle was anything but ordinary.

Both sides fueled their fight with the gifts they had. The Prophet's warriors—often acting in inhuman unison—drove hard into their foes. Inquisitors and edyrem alike struck with weapons that flashed with raw energy when meeting each other. But the latter had other tools at their disposal as well. More than one robed warrior would suddenly rise into the air and go flying across the field of combat. Others fell as hovering edyrem tossed more potent missiles than previously used among the Inquisitors' ranks. The sky as much as the ground became the site of what Uldyssian already thought of as the Battle of the Golden Path.

The place where the edyrem might be making their last stand.

Horses shrieked as silver bolts peppered the Inquisitor ranks. However, despite mounting losses, the robed riders continued their relentless assault, battering away with their glittering maces against the mighty, invisible shields of the edyrem. Although those shields mostly held well, the sheer fanaticism of the Inquisitors' attacks was daunting even to the most hardened.

It became, at least for the time being, a frustrating stalemate. However, Uldyssian knew that a stalemate only meant eventual victory for Inarius. The longer the edyrem struggled uselessly, the more strength they expended. Unlike the Inquisitors, who drew from their powerful master, the edyrem only had what was within themselves.

All the while that Uldyssian struggled with that knowledge, he nevertheless fought hard. A robed warrior who attempted to batter in his skull instead lost his weapon to the son of Diomedes, who then sent the mace barreling through the man's chest. Breastplate, flesh, and bone did nothing even to slow the missile—which then burst out the back. Uldyssian found that he had no compassion whatsoever for those he fought; they had already killed too many innocents in their zealous adoration of the Prophet.

A massive whirlwind clearly of no natural origin suddenly cut through the edyrem, seeking to pluck them selectively from the ground. Uldyssian spotted the priests responsible for the oncoming catastrophe, but before he himself could do anything, Serenthia suddenly appeared among them. She drove her spear through one, then kicked another hard in the chest. That priest went flying far into the sea of Inquisitors still rushing forward.

Swearing more at Serenthia for risking herself than anything else, Uldyssian clapped his hands together in the direction in which the merchant's daughter fought.

The booming sound he created plowed a path through the enemy, bowling them over as if they were nothing. He then raced toward her, his leaping gait nearly flying.

He bounded among the Inquisitors closing on her and seized two by their necks. His rage caused both men literally to explode. He then raised his left hand and summoned into it a black broadsword formed from the ash that had once been the deadly grass. With that blade, the son of Diomedes cut through one opponent after another, until at last he reached Serenthia.

She, meanwhile, finished off a third priest entirely unaware of how near she had been to being slain. Serenthia looked up at Uldyssian, her strained countenance almost as unnerving as those of the magically enhanced fanatics with whom they were struggling.

He knew why immediately. "Serry! Get back among the others!"

"I'm all right! Don't worry about me!"

"Serry! Achilios might not be gone! Do you want to die not knowing?"

Before she could answer, a terrible thud shook the ground. Men toppled everywhere.

Another thud followed the first. Uldyssian also felt the air grow very cold.

It was also, he realized, no longer raining . . . or, at least, no water was dropping from the sky.

There were, however, huge fragments of *ice* plummeting from the clouds, some of them as large as wagons. Uldyssian looked up and saw that there was still rain, but midway down, it was all coalescing together and freezing into the mammoth blocks now threatening all.

Once again, Inarius had taken Uldyssian's work—the cloud cover—and twisted it into a fiendish assault. That it also slew his own followers meant nothing, just as long as the rebels perished.

The monstrous ice chunks did what the Inquisitors could not, shattering the cohesiveness of the edyrem circle. Too many were not powerful enough to deal with such a fearsome threat. Men and women ran wherever they could, hoping to avoid being crushed like insects.

The Cathedral's warriors made good use of their disorganization, heedless or uncaring of the threat the ice caused them as well. More than one of Uldyssian's followers perished with a blazing sword through the back or a gleaming mace spilling open their skulls. That some Inquisitors were caught unable to escape Inarius's magic did nothing to counter the horror that they reaped.

Furious, Uldyssian dismissed the black sword, grabbed Serenthia by the wrist, and returned both of them to among the edyrem. He immediately reached out to those nearest, reassuring them as best he could and *demanding* their help. Most listened. He hoped they were enough for what he intended.

"Focus with me, Serry!" he all but shouted in her face. With great reluctance, the raven-tressed woman nodded. Immediately, her mind and his were almost one, with the others he had reached adding to their will.

A vast shadow loomed over the pair. Uldyssian did not need to look up to know what it was and how little time he had.

Be with me, he told the others again.

The shadow darkened. Uldyssian sensed the massive block of ice just above.

Gritting his teeth, he thrust both hands skyward.

The explosion utterly shattered the gargantuan block. Yet the pieces did not come raining down but rather flew with purpose through the air. They struck other huge chunks of ice even as the latter formed, shattering those, too.

Eyes shut from strain, heart beating faster, Uldyssian imagined the dramatic scene above him. He saw with far more accuracy than his mortal eyes could where each fragment had to strike to avert more slaughter.

And when at last it seemed Inarius could not keep pace with his efforts, Uldyssian took the thousands and thousands of sharp pieces and threw them down upon the bulk of the Inquisitor legions. He threw them with as much force as he could, defying the power that the Prophet fed his servants to save them from this peril.

The needlelike shards dove toward the ground with a swiftness that left in their wakes a high, hissing sound. The Inquisitors gazed up to see their deaths coming. They used their power to try to prevent the oncoming missiles from reaching them . . . used that power and still failed utterly to stop even one.

The shards drove through metal, flesh, and bone without pause. Eyes and mouths were punctured with ease. In mere seconds, men became nothing more than quivering pincushions, so many were the icy missiles that dropped upon them.

The screams rose to a crescendo, then quickly died down. So swift was the slaughter that for the space of a single heartbeat, more than half of the Inquisitors still stood. Their bodies were drenched with blood, and their ruined countenances were slack, but they stood.

Then, as one, the might of the Cathedral crumpled like rag dolls to the unforgiving ground. The bodies lay sprawled at all angles.

Of the many Inarius had sent, only those mixed among the edyrem yet survived. Their numbers, though, dropped quickly as Uldyssian's people vented their fury for the deaths of their own on the Cathedral's survivors.

Momentarily sickened by events, Uldyssian fought to stop the executions. He succeeded, but only after far too many more were slain. The rest of the Inquisitors were slowly rounded up, although what to do with them was a question for which he had no answer.

As he stumbled among the dead, his eyes watching for whatever next the Prophet would send at them, the son of Diomedes ran across a figure he had not seen since early on. It was the gray-haired priestess who had been leading the riders. Unlike the rest, she had no discernible mark on her, yet she was definitely dead. Her open eyes stared up at him almost accusingly.

"Master Uldyssian?"

His inspection of the body was interrupted by wiry Jonas. The bald former brigand moved toward him with tentative steps.

There were red, liquid lines across the right side of his face, but otherwise he was unharmed.

"Jonas! Did you see what happened to this one?"

The edyrem glanced at the priestess. "Nay. Was she of some import?"

Giving it some thought, Uldyssian shook his head. "Not anymore."

The other man peered sharply at him. "Master Uldyssian! You look all done in! Let me give you a hand. . . ."

The son of Diomedes was tempted, but he could show no weakness now. Whatever reprieve that they had been given was certain to be a short one. He waved off the hand. "It's not necessary. . . ."

"As you wish, Master Uldyssian," the Parthan returned abruptly. With an equally curt bow, Jonas quickly retreated. "I will go see to the others."

Even as he rushed off, Uldyssian became aware of someone coming from the opposite direction. He turned to find Mendeln. "Well?"

Uldyssian's brother knew exactly what he asked. "There are many dead. Many. If I had to guess, I would say nearly a quarter of our number since this first began."

"Nearly a quarter . . ." So many lives lost. It was made worse by the fact that although the Cathedral had suffered far, far greater, those lives meant nothing to the true enemy. Inarius considered his dead servants less than nothing.

The thought stirred Uldyssian's rage anew.

Mendeln quickly took hold of his shoulder. "Uldyssian, do not let this happen to you again! Each time you permit your base emotions to rise to the forefront, you risk losing mastery of your powers. Think about it! Would that not play into Inarius's hands?"

His brother had a point, but Uldyssian kept seeing all those who had perished here. Even the woman at his feet, who had obviously served as one of the Prophet's chief acolytes, was a victim of the angel's madness.

"Uldyssian . . . listen to me. . . ."

But he no longer paid any mind to Mendeln, for at that moment, Uldyssian spotted something on the corpse that made every muscle tense. He quickly bent down and examined the face. With trepidation, Uldyssian turned the priestess's head to the side in order to get a better look.

"Mendeln, look at this."

His black-robed sibling bent near, and a gasp escaped Mendeln. "By the dragon!"

There were two dark lesions near the ear, lesions whose origins were unmistakable.

"Malic!" Mendeln whispered. "He was among us!"

"You didn't notice him?"

The younger brother shook his head. "I must be near, and even then it would take a moment. Malic . . ."

"Inarius never runs out of tricks." Uldyssian surveyed the body, seeking again the cause of death. He needed badly to find a cause. A single wound. A cracked gap at the back of the skull. Anything.

But there was no mark.

Uldyssian looked around, but the nearest edyrem were far away. "We can't have this now, Mendeln! I can't concentrate on both him and Inarius—"

"Malic is my mistake," Mendeln hissed, his eyes narrowed in self-loathing. "My curse to bear. I was reckless, and because of that, I let a fiend as terrible as any demon back into the world." He straightened. "I will deal with him. You must focus on Inarius only."

They both knew that there was far more of an impending threat than just the renegade angel, but Inarius was indeed the imminent problem. Nothing else would matter if they failed to defeat him.

Still, Uldyssian could not help considering their new problem—and a possible answer finally came to him. "He was here. He was the only one nearby."

"Who?"

"*Jonas*." Now that he thought more about it, Uldyssian recalled also what he felt had been the Parthan's odd behavior. "Yes . . . it's Jonas, damn it!"

That was all Mendeln evidently needed. He held the ivory dagger ready. It glowed with a deathly light. "I will find him. He will not escape this time."

Neither suggested telling the others of the monster in their midst. That would be the final panic as edyrem turned on one another believing Malic was about to take over their bodies. The high priest was invisible to Uldyssian's senses, and that no doubt had to do with Inarius. That meant that none of the others—save perhaps Mendeln—could sense Malic, either.

Worse, who was to say the specter even looked like Jonas anymore?

He could not think about it. Uldyssian had to trust Mendeln. Mendeln would not let him down.

Rathma suddenly stood next to him. It said something for Uldyssian's current mood that he found no surprise in the Ancient's abrupt arrival. Such things were becoming much too commonplace for the former farmer.

"I have a thought," Rathma declared.

"Those are never good. What is it?"

The Ancient cocked his head, then granted Uldyssian his point. "This one has the hopes of being something better . . . at least, I think so."

"Does it have the same chance of success that your visit to your father had?" the mortal asked with open sarcasm in his tone.

"More than that." Rathma pursed his lips. "But possibly not much more."

Uldyssian was more concerned with what Inarius was currently plotting. He glanced to the north but only saw the

Cathedral of Light. Something was brewing, though. Inarius would not remain idle. . . .

"We can't do anything to help you this time."

The cowled figure wrapped his cloak tight about him. His inhumanly handsome face held no emotion. "I expect none. But this must be attempted."

There was obviously no talking Rathma out of whatever it was that he thought he needed to do, but Uldyssian wanted at least to know what the Ancient thought so important that he would leave the edyrem at such a juncture. "Just tell me what you think you can accomplish. Where are you going this time?"

His face as still as death, Inarius's son casually replied, "I'm going for what help I might be able to find. I'm calling a family gathering. . . ."

Mendeln rushed among the edyrem, no doubt looking to them like death itself come to gather more victims. For all their might, even the most skilled of his brother's followers looked away as he passed. Only one of his handful of "students" acknowledged him, but he immediately indicated to her that he was on a task demanding the utmost privacy.

Of necessity, Uldyssian's brother paused now and then to ask some unsettled edyrem if they had seen the Parthan. Most had not, but finally two directed him toward where they had last noticed him. Not at all confident that he would still find the false Jonas there, Mendeln nonetheless vigorously pursued his only lead.

He continued to hold the dagger in front of him, but thus far, it had given no sign that he was near the ghoulish shade. Mendeln eyed everyone he passed, seeking whether one of them might be Malic's latest host.

Inarius's attacks and the edyrem's defenses had left much of the area churned up. The massive chunks of ice had raised entire hills when they had come crashing down, and although they were now rapidly melting, they, too, created more barriers, more places around which to hide.

But as Mendeln neared one particularly jagged hill, his sharp eyes caught sight of something pale peeking out from the unstable rubble. At the same time, he sensed the wrongness that was Malic in the nearby vicinity.

A spell ready on his lips, Uldyssian's brother approached whatever it was the upturned stone and dirt all but covered. With caution, he used his free hand to brush some of the rubble away.

A scarred, bone-white elbow revealed itself. It was a body, just as he had assumed, but it did not wear the garments of Jonas. That it was very likely Parthan—for there was none of the light-skinned Kehjani among the edyrem—was all Mendeln could tell of it. He dismissed the corpse quickly, still aware that Malic had to be close by.

He would have asked the ghosts, but since the moment Uldyssian and the rest had entered the grasslands, all the ghosts had vanished. Even those of the recent dead had not remained in the vicinity, as was usual. It was as if they dared not stay near the confrontation. Mendeln was frustrated by the lack of such company. Now, more than ever, he could have used their eyes, their knowledge.

From the north, there suddenly came what sounded—impossibly—like a glorious chorus. Light glistened above him, a fantastic light reflected by the huge chunk of ice. That light also illuminated everything save the area shadowed by the churned ground.

Mendeln froze. He knew what the light and the chorus presaged.

Inarius had finally entered the fray.

For the moment, all thought of Malic vanished as Mendeln concerned himself with Uldyssian and the angel. He wanted to rush to his brother's side, even though he knew that Serenthia and Rathma would already be there. He had sworn to himself that when the Prophet appeared, he, too, would face him.

But Malic could not be ignored.

The dagger flared.

Mendeln started to turn.

He could only imagine that it was because of his swift reaction that his skull was not cracked open. Even still, the rock in Malic's fist sent shock waves through Mendeln's head. Uldyssian's brother collapsed against the hill.

Through blurry eyes, he beheld Jonas's leering face. The smile was exactly as he recalled Malic's.

"A crude method, but effective," remarked the specter, holding forth the rock. "I dared not use a spell other than to add to the masking shield. We wanted you to notice me just enough and no more. . . ."

We. That could only mean Inarius had planned this with the shade. "You—" Mendeln's head ached. "This moment was to—"

"This moment was all arranged, if that is what you mean!" Throwing away the rock, the bald figure retrieved Mendeln's dagger. "This should help." Malic reached into a pouch on Jonas's belt, removing from it a red stone. "Between the two, I should have no trouble taking your body this time."

Mendeln could not fathom why Malic would want a body so badly injured, but then he realized that his head wound was not life-threatening. He was merely stunned, something that would not affect the ghost.

As for why Malic would want him at all, the answer was obvious. Mendeln ul-Diomed *would* stand by his brother's side—and then with a touch steal Uldyssian's body while simultaneously killing the older sibling.

And hardly lifting a finger, the Prophet would defeat his adversary.

Mendeln sought to focus his thoughts enough to cast a spell, but too late he realized that the high priest had struck with calculation. He had never meant to hit his victim anywhere but where he had and Mendeln had foolishly obliged him by turning as planned. Better if Uldyssian's brother had simply stood with his back to the creature, for then perhaps Malic would have killed him.

In actuality, that was doubtful. Malic was not so careless. He wanted Uldyssian's body, and the only way to achieve that was through Mendeln.

"You—you are being used!" the son of Diomedes managed. "Inarius—the angels—"

Malic grinned. "Will find that the fate of Sanctuary is beyond their control."

And suddenly, Mendeln recalled what Serenthia had found, that demonic hordes waited to attack. But they were not in league with Inarius anymore. Instead, they prepared to battle over Sanctuary and its humans, especially the edyrem, with Tyrael's host.

And the high priest intended to profit by that, assuming—perhaps wrongly—that the Burning Hells would triumph. Uldyssian's brother considered pointing out the risk the double-dealing ghost was taking but chose not to. More important than Malic's plot was the fact that Mendeln at last felt his head clearing. The words he had sought came back to him. He blurted out the first—

Malic held the red stone before his eyes. Immediately, Mendeln could not help but stare at it. His spell died on his lips.

"Your gaze cannot escape," mocked the specter, leaning close. "Your mind cannot think save to hear me."

His victim sought to protest but could not. Mendeln's last coherent thought was that he could expect no aid from anyone else, for they were all focused upon Inarius's coming.

Beyond the crystal, Malic raised the dagger. It was not his intention to stab Mendeln but to use the ethereal weapon's magic against its owner.

"So very close now . . ." The shade's words echoed in Mendeln's numbed mind. "Soon—"

Without warning, the mesmerizing stone vanished from sight. Mendeln blinked. His brain and body seemed disconnected from each other, but his ears apparently worked, for they registered the sounds of struggle. Uldyssian's brother tried to clear his vision—

And as he did, he beheld Jonas—no, Malic—battling with someone who held the high priest's wrists from behind. The hand wielding the dagger thrust straight up as the two fought over it. Of the crystal, there was no sign.

But all that mattered to Mendeln was just who had come to his rescue, the person he would have least expected.

Achilios.

TWENTY

The invisible chorus was the first hint of his coming. The perfect voices sang their wordless praises from seemingly every direction. They were both beautiful and awful to hear, for although they touched even Uldyssian's heart, they also reminded him that they presaged the coming of the Prophet.

Indeed, even as the edyrem came to grips with the unseen singers, a blaze of wondrous light erupted from the Cathedral. It burned away the clouds in that direction. It was blinding, yet no one who gazed at it could look away.

And in its midst, the golden figure of the Prophet—riding in a glittering diamond chariot pulled by two winged horses—materialized several yards above the startled rebels. The glorious youth was clad for battle, his armor gleaming, the shining, bejeweled sword at his side sharp enough to cut the very air.

He reined the chariot to a halt while it was still several feet above the ground. The Prophet looked over the edyrem. "My wayward children," he began, smiling sadly. "Led astray as surely as if by demons . . ."

Somewhere behind Uldyssian, a man sobbed. The son of Diomedes quickly sent a reassuring touch to the minds of all his followers.

Inarius stepped away from the chariot—which then faded away. He slowly descended to the ground as if walking down a flight of nonexistent steps. As he did, behind him, the brilliant glow magnified.

"Let those who would seek my forgiveness fall to their knees," commanded Inarius.

Aware that even the slightest of words spoken by the angel had the strength to demand absolute obedience, Uldyssian silently roared, *Keep standing!*

Uldyssian could not entirely be certain if his own order had succeeded, but Inarius's expression did grow more disappointed. That was enough to encourage the mortal.

"So many determined unbelievers as that . . . too many unbelievers." The Prophet steepled his hands, then shook his head. "Too many unbelievers. The world must be cleansed."

And as he opened his hands again, a searing white force swept over Uldyssian and the rest.

"Mendeln!" called Achilios. "You . . . must . . . stop him!"

Uldyssian's brother sought to rise, but his body would not obey his commands properly. There had been magic in the head blow, he now understood. His continually scattered thoughts and weakness were not merely by chance.

Letting out a growl, Malic tore the hand bearing the crystal from Achilios's grip. He immediately thrust his palm against the archer's side.

Aware of just what that would do, Mendeln let out a gasp. He teetered to his feet, but far too late to stop the high priest's foul work.

But Malic and Achilios merely stood there for a moment, their eyes locked upon each other's. From Jonas's mouth erupted furious and somewhat confused words. "Not possible! I cannot possess you! I cannot make your life mine!"

"Your lord . . . Lucion . . . did that already," muttered Achilios. "There's no more . . . no more life to take, you . . . you bastard!"

"Then there are other ways to be rid of you!"

Somehow, Mendeln managed to throw himself toward the pair. He collided with Malic's back just as the latter uttered something that made the crimson stone flare bright.

Achilios fell back as if hit by a bolt of lightning. However, in doing so, he wrenched Mendeln's dagger free. Uldyssian's brother and Malic went crashing into the side of the makeshift hill.

A strong hand gripped Mendeln's throat tightly. Malic squeezed.

Mendeln did the only thing of which he could think. He grabbed some of the dirt and threw it in Malic's face.

The high priest coughed as much of the dirt filled his mouth and nose. Unfortunately, his grip did not weaken much.

But it was still enough to enable Mendeln to recover his wits somewhat. With his voice cut off by the specter's hand, he concentrated on the one thing that might serve him. He had done it before. If it would only work now—

The ivory dagger materialized in his left hand.

Mendeln drove it into the body once belonging to Jonas, praying that he would hit some spot vital to Malic. Unfortunately, Malic tried to block his arm, and the blade sank lower, cutting into an area that Uldyssian's brother knew might hurt the high priest a bit but certainly would not destroy him.

Yet the specter howled wildly as soon as the blade even touched, so wildly, in fact, that Mendeln had to release the dagger and cover his ears. From what had been Jonas's mouth, there erupted a wind that buffeted the black-robed figure as if it were a tornado.

Despite the dagger still deep in his lower torso, Malic managed to rise. All the while, though, he continued to howl in agony. Jonas's face became a parody of itself, the eyes growing too wide, the mouth a gaping hole large enough to swallow a small child and growing larger yet.

The bulging eyes gazed furiously at the blade. Congealing blood dripped from the wound, but to Mendeln's gaze, the cut should not have been a deadly one. He finally understood what was actually happening. The dagger itself was anathema to the dread shadow, its magic slowly but surely consuming him.

Malic evidently realized that, too, for, clutching at the hilt with one hand, he desperately sought to remove it. Fearing what would happen if he succeeded, Mendeln again flung himself at the high priest. He caught Malic just below the lungs. Uldyssian's brother planted both hands over Malic's, trying to force the dagger to remain embedded.

Still howling, the ghost used his other hand to grasp for Mendeln's eyes. Mendeln forced himself to endure Malic's attack. The howling grew more incessant; he felt certain that if he could just keep the dagger in a little longer—

Malic's head bent back beyond living limits. The bone cracked, the sound sickening Mendeln. Still, the ghoulish figure shrieked.

Then a thick black substance like tar flew up out of Malic's mouth. It shot into the air above Uldyssian's brother, pouring out of what had once been Jonas like a geyser. It was accompanied by a stench that reminded Mendeln of rotting flesh and vegetation mixed together.

The last of it issued forth. The figure before Mendeln teetered, and then the corpse collapsed like parchment in his arms.

Above there was one last, long shriek. It finally ended when the floating black tar melted into nothing.

But the effort had been too much for Mendeln. His head wound pounded more than ever. Vertigo overtook Rathma's student. Even the weight of the emaciated body was more than he could handle. Uldyssian's brother fell back, the corpse draping across him.

Mendeln blacked out before he hit the ground.

The edyrem were scattered like leaves in the wind as the Prophet's hands spread apart. Even Uldyssian was nearly swept away. At the last, he dug his feet into the scorched land, pushing forward despite the angel's fearsome spell.

And as he battled Inarius's work, he strained to keep his tie to each and every one of his people, reassuring them and guiding them. Through Uldyssian, the edyrem began to regain their ground, and they, in turn, helped to strengthen him.

Gritting his teeth, Uldyssian thrust his hands forward. He focused on the Prophet.

The wind instantly vanished, but not because the angel had ceased his assault. Rather, it was now because the son of Diomedes had summoned a wall of solid air that spread all the way across the charred grasslands, protecting everyone behind it. The power of the Prophet buffeted his creation with such force that Uldyssian's every muscle strained, but the wall held.

Then Uldyssian sensed some slight shift from Inarius. The gale-force wind faltered, finally ceasing entirely. It was almost as if something had happened not to Inarius's liking, something significant enough to distract him.

Although he had no idea just what that might have been, Uldyssian immediately used the hesitation to his advantage. He sent the invisible wall barreling into the Prophet with all the strength that he and the added wills of the edyrem could muster.

The landscape around the golden-haired youth exploded. Vast chunks of dirt and stone flew back. The sky above the Prophet was briefly darkened with ash that had once been the malevolent grass.

Inarius, the grand helmet blown from his head, took one step back . . . and that was it. As dirt rained down behind him, he eyed Uldyssian. The Prophet looked untouched, but his expression had changed. There was a terrible coldness in it that almost made Uldyssian flinch.

"Such impudence!" Inarius roared in a voice magnified by his magic. "And such foolishness! You would raise yourself up so high, you who are less than the worms that burrow through the ground? I offered you absolution, Uldyssian ul-Diomed, time and time again, but you remain the darkest of unbelievers, the most arrogant of heretics." His eyes flashed, no longer human even as pretense. Now they were the blazing orbs of the angel. "There is nothing left for you but death."

The grasslands burst into white flame. Uldyssian screamed as the holy fire burned at his flesh. He felt the additional consternation of the edyrem, who were likewise assailed.

"I will cleanse my world!" Inarius continued. "I will make it perfect again!"

Now the screams of the others filled Uldyssian's ears. They were all about to be burned alive because he had sorely underestimated the fury of the Prophet.

No—the vision of so many slaughtered because they had simply believed in him and his words tore once more at Uldyssian. He could not let them suffer for his sins. Better he take from the others the punishment Inarus meted out and turn it on himself, who deserved it.

Imagining the white flames, Uldyssian drew them with his will to engulf only him. He took the sum of the Prophet's monstrous retribution and let it fall on his own person. The pain was savage, and it felt as if his skin sloughed off, yet still Uldyssian embraced the flames.

But as he did, a strange thing happened. The edyrem knew what he planned, that he sought to save them at cost to him. Serenthia was among the first. Rather than merely allow fate to take its course, she sought with her lesser skills to douse the celestial fire. She was joined by a few others, then more and more, until nearly all the edyrem battled to rescue their leader.

And although it strained them beyond their known limits, they finally eradicated the Prophet's fire. Even more surprising, their power instantly healed Uldyssian's savage burns and soothed his ruined nerves.

In managing this miracle, the edyrem also presented a revelation to Uldyssian. He stared at Inarius and, while it might have been a trick of his eye, thought that the angel *flinched* ever so slightly.

"This is no longer your world," the son of Diomedes

informed the Prophet in a voice now also magnified. "And if it should perish this day, at least all will know that it did so free of you. We are our own now, Inarius, and in our power, our belief, we are united against you, the angels, or demons!"

With that, Uldyssian leapt at the Prophet.

Whether it was his audacity, hesitation on the part of Inarius, or that the angel wished him to come, the human reached his adversary without any interference. The gleaming youth met Uldyssian's outstretched hands with his own, and the two grappled. The ground shook as their feet planted firmly, and raw energy crackled between them.

"You compound your crimes over and over," Inarius quietly declared into his face. The Prophet's eyes were blinding, and his perfect smile no longer revealed uncertainty.

But Uldyssian dared not let the imposing sight eat away at his own confidence. Matching Inarius's tone, he retorted, "Then if there's no hope of me seeing *your* light, you should stop prattling and do something."

The angel's eyes seemed to flash a little angrier. He said nothing more, but suddenly the ground beneath Uldyssian began to liquefy. The human's feet sank in up to the ankle, then the legs began to follow.

Inarius pressed down on him. The Prophet's strength was tremendous, and although Uldyssian could match it, his sinking set him more and more at a deadly disadvantage.

He realized that he was still thinking in mortal terms, whereas Inarius did not. Uldyssian did not have to let his descent continue; he had the power to counter it.

With only that thought, he made it happen. Uldyssian rose, once again facing the Prophet eye-to-eye. He felt the ground solidify.

Grinning darkly, Uldyssian then twisted his hands around and threw the Prophet up into the air. Inarius spun over and over, and for a moment, Uldyssian looked victorious.

But as he tumbled, the Prophet transformed. The image of the perfect youth burned away. Tendrils of brightly colored energy blossomed from his back, and he grew in size. His face melted into what was part shadow, part visor.

Midway through the air, Inarius righted himself. He hovered above Uldyssian, radiant in his celestial glory. From what he could sense, Uldyssian knew that everyone else also saw the Prophet in his true form.

I HAVE BEEN PATIENT WITH YOU, MORTAL. . . . I HAVE TRIED TO TEMPER MY FURY AND GRANT YOU A DEATH INVOLVING SOME SWIFTNESS AND LESS PAIN! YOU HAVE NOT BEEN GRATEFUL, THOUGH.

The angel's voice shook both Uldyssian's mind and soul. It truly felt as if Inarius spoke from within him as well as without.

YOU RETAIN THIS FALSE BELIEF, the winged warrior continued. *THAT YOU HAVE ANY CHOICE BUT TO DIE! YOU WILL UNDERSTAND THAT THERE IS NO OTHER WAY. . . . I AM SANCTUARY, AND SANCTUARY IS I! YOU SEEK TO FIGHT THE VERY WORLD ITSELF WHEN YOU SEEK TO STAND AGAINST ME.*

The wind picked up again. The clouds—no longer Uldyssian's to control—spun and churned with wild abandon. The ground heaved, settled, then heaved again.

Uldyssian felt Inarius drawing upon the Worldstone and understood just how little of it the angel had thus far utilized. He was astounded and dismayed by what he now faced and at last also saw why the renegade had so little concern over facing a host of his own kind. How could even a thousand angelic warriors—or a hundred times that number—face such might?

YOU PERCEIVE YOUR ERROR, Inarius mocked. *ALBEIT MUCH TOO LATE!* The Prophet spread wide his arms, as if he sought to embrace the world and all in it. *BUT YOU HAVE PERFORMED ME ONE SERVICE, ULDYSSIAN UL-DIOMED! YOU HAVE SHOWN ME THAT FOR MY WORLD TO BE AS IT SHOULD BE, I*

MUST NOT WEAR TRAPPINGS UNWORTHY OF MY GLORY! ALL SANCTUARY WILL FROM HERE ON KNOW OF MY GREATNESS, MY PERFECTION, AS I REMAKE IT INTO MY IMAGE.

The charade would be over. Assuming that Inarius defeated all his enemies—a feat not impossible, it now was apparent—Inarius would rule as himself, demanding utter mastery, utter obedience, over all that he would allow to live. The Prophet had removed his veil; all would know him and fear his celestial wrath.

And all would curse the son of Diomedes for his failure, for his sins against their *god*.

HERE SHALL IT BE MARKED, FOR ALL ETERNITY, THE PLACE WHERE THIS WORLD WAS SET RIGHT! HERE SHALL BE CONSTRUCTED A NEW EDIFICE HONORING THE BEGINNING OF MY TRANSFORMATION OF THIS WRETCHED MISTAKE TO PERFECTION INCARNATE.

Inarius gestured at the ground before Uldyssian. The tremor that shook the area this time was of a magnitude far greater than any previous. The ground burst up with such ferocity that Uldyssian was tossed high into the air.

With a second gesture, the angel paused the human's flight. *BEHOLD . . .*

A tower of dirt and rock taller than any building Uldyssian had ever seen—even the grand Cathedral— formed under the angel's direction. As it continued to swell in size, it also molded itself. Sharp angles came into being. Arched windows lined the sides. Magnificent reliefs and statues—all of Inarius—formed fully on the walls and at the entrance of what was clearly more of a shrine rather than a new, glorious cathedral.

HERE AT THIS SITE, WHICH I SHALL CALL GETTERAC—THE GATE OF PARADISE—SHALL BE HONORED THIS DAY. . . . Inarius looked to his captive. *AND YOU, HERETIC, SHALL HAVE ONE HONOR . . . YOU SHALL FOREVER BE A PART OF THIS SITE, YOUR*

BONES AT THE CENTER OF IT AS TESTAMENT TO THIS
LAST, FEEBLE STAND AGAINST WHAT IS MY RIGHT. . . .

Against such a staggering display, Uldyssian's will weakened. Perhaps it was better to let this all come to pass. At least, if Inarius was indeed so formidable, then Sanctuary and some of its people would survive. With the son of Diomedes dead, even the edyrem might be forgiven for their transgressions.

But even as Uldyssian began to give in, Inarius's gargantuan monument to his victory shook as if a new tremor had begun. Yet only the structure shook, nothing else.

The entire edifice ripped free and flew directly at the angel, crashing into him with a wrath that shocked Uldyssian. He suddenly began falling again, but his drop ended only a moment later as the air underneath him grew thick enough to hold his weight.

Only when that happened did Uldyssian's wits return enough for him to understand that yet again, his people had come to his salvation. They had not cared what Inarius might do to them because of it; they would live and die with their leader, whatever the overall fate of their world.

It was very likely that such a wish would soon be granted, too, for barely had the edyrem's amazing missile collided with Inarius than it exploded into thousands and thousands of tiny fragments that fell upon Uldyssian and the others as if shot by a sling. Several among the edyrem crumpled, slain by rocks or chunks of hard dirt that cracked their skulls or crushed in their ribs.

Uldyssian began dropping again, but now his mind was clear enough to enable him to slow his descent. His mind was clear in many other ways as well, for only then did the son of Diomedes recognize that his surrender to his fate had been as much an intricate use of the angel's influence on his thoughts as it had his own beliefs. Inarius had subtly taken his fears and twisted them to his desire. If not for the desperate efforts of his followers, Uldyssian would have willingly surrendered to his own execution.

But now surrender was the furthest thing from his desires. Instead, disgust with himself and with the hubris of the angel overwhelmed Uldyssian. It mattered not whether he perished, as long as no more of those who believed in him suffered.

He felt the power surge within him, and whether or not it was enough to bring down Inarius, Uldyssian did not care. He would do everything within his ability to end it here and now.

If that were possible at all.

The renegade angel saw him approach. Inarius merely opened his arms as he had earlier, this time seemingly to invite the mortal to him. Uldyssian obliged his foe.

He was nearly upon the angel when Inarius abruptly flicked his armored hand toward the upstart human. The very air about Uldyssian crackled. He felt as if a thousand hooks ripped away at his flesh, his eyes . . . all of him.

But where this might have previously caused him to falter, it now did not slow Uldyssian in the least. He hurtled forward regardless of the torture through which his body went, desiring only that he reach the winged figure.

When they collided this time, the crash split open the clouds above and sent a quake through the ground beneath. Uldyssian feared for the edyrem but could not risk any distraction. He and Inarius spun through the air, each feeding into the other such forces as could have brought the city of Kehjan to rubble. Yet somehow the son of Diomedes staved off the fury flung at him by his adversary just as well as Inarius dispelled his own attack.

They crashed onto Sanctuary, their impact causing a new upheaval of dirt and stone. The two titans opened up a small valley in the wake of their collision, a valley they widened as they pushed against each other over and over.

Even in the harrowing midst of the epic struggle, there arose hope within Uldyssian. Inarius did not hold back, yet somehow the human continually matched him. Uldyssian did not ask by what miracle this could happen but used the very fact to fuel his will further. He now pressed Inarius back, all the while battering the angel with the raw forces within him.

Raw forces that suddenly made the winged warrior bend down before him.

"The world is no longer yours!" Uldyssian repeated to Inarius. "The fates of men are theirs to decide, not yours! This day'll be marked, yes, but as the day of freedom for all Sanctuary from you!"

THERE IS NO SANCTUARY WITHOUT ME, the Prophet said defiantly. *WHETHER IN VICTORY OR DEFEAT.*

It was the first time Uldyssian had heard Inarius speak of anything other than the absolute certainty of his success. Encouraged, Uldyssian battered at the angel, sending both of them hurtling toward the Cathedral of Light. They struck the ground just before the gleaming citadel, a great fissure opening up as they hit. The Cathedral trembled, and cracks shot through its magnificent walls.

Screams arose, but they had nothing to do with the now-distant edyrem. Many were the Prophet's acolytes, those that had had no place in the battle. To Uldyssian's surprise, there were also scores and scores of pilgrims, many of them obviously from Kehjan.

As he and Inarius dragged each other up, Uldyssian once again faced the golden youth. The transformation distracted the son of Diomedes—apparently exactly what Inarius sought. From the angel's mouth came not words but a shining silver sphere. It swelled, wrapping over Uldyssian until it had swallowed him whole, then tore him away from his adversary.

"To the end of all for you," declared the Prophet, one hand raised toward the human. "There to suffer an emptiness far worse than death could ever be."

The sphere began shrinking.

Uldyssian planted his hands on the smooth, inner surface of his prison. He had come too far to let this be his finish. His hands flared black and melted away the barrier.

"There can be nothing worse than what I've already suffered because of you and Lilith," Uldyssian grated. "You two belong in damnation together!"

He brought up the ground around both Inarius and the Cathedral. Those of the faithful who had not already fled in panic now did so as the spire cracked off and plummeted point down into the marble entrance. Tons of soil and rock flowed up and over the angel as great fragments of the shattered spire bounded toward him from behind.

But all of this was merely used by Uldyssian to create his own distraction. Inarius did not fear such devastation, not with his abilities. He reacted as the human intended, contemptuously waving his hand to dismiss what had been cast against him . . . and gaining Uldyssian the opportunity he needed once again to reach the mad celestial.

They crashed into the ruined entrance of the crumbling building. Each time they struck each other, the magic unleashed wreaked more chaos upon the land. At last, the roof of the Cathedral, no longer sufficiently supported by the ruined walls, caved in.

But even then, the pair saw only each other. The Prophet no longer spoke, and his shape twisted into some nightmarish form between his mortal guise and his true appearance. He flung such power at Uldyssian that the human expected to die a thousand times over, but the son of Diomedes continued to outduel the angel miraculously.

And it began to tell. Inarius's attacks grew ever so slightly weaker. It was not any trick this time; Uldyssian could sense that. The angel was faltering. He very likely was not tired, but now uncertainty was eating at him as it had done to Uldyssian in the past.

Then Uldyssian struck Inarius a blow that sent the winged figure tumbling into the wreckage of his once-imposing sanctum. Uldyssian quickly fell upon the Prophet and began pounding away at him with all the forces he could summon from within. His strikes were such that lightning flashed each time he hit, and the ground was torn asunder.

He raised a fist surrounded by a black aura, a fist with which he intended the final blow—and suddenly his attention was snared by something other than Inarius. Uldyssian fought to ignore whatever it was, certain that the angel was simply seeking to create another distraction.

But then a faint voice penetrated the heat burning through his head.

Serenthia's voice . . . pleading with him to look to the sky.

He did—and at that moment, Inarius became less than nothing to him. Their entire struggle, all the destruction and death that had taken place because of their feud, none of it meant anything.

For now the sky looked as if it were not real, as if it were instead a vast drawing on a gargantuan piece of parchment. More impossible, that parchment had a vast rip running across it, a literal tear in the sky.

And through that tear flowed an astounding, breathtaking swarm of magnificent beings whose armor gleamed brighter than the sun and whose many wings created a dazzling display of colors unmatched upon the mortal plane.

The armed hosts of the High Heavens spilled out over the world.

TWENTY-ONE

There seemed no end to their ranks. They flew through the unnatural tear by the hundreds, in the process making the gap widen so as to let those behind them enter in even greater numbers. Already, they filled a good portion of the heavens, and the clouds seemed to react to their presence by churning worse.

Uldyssian knew this had always been inevitable, but to watch the incredible spectacle unfold shook him to his very core. Inside, there had always been that minute hope that something would somehow prevent the angels from reaching Sanctuary, be it the work of Trag'Oul, some last-minute change of heart . . . or sheer prayer.

But none of that was to be. The end of the world was upon them.

Uldyssian screamed as his body was wracked with new, horrific agony. He was tossed backward into the air, and he faintly understood that Inarius had used the moment to save himself.

Uldyssian crashed to the ground a moment later, bouncing several times before coming to a stop. Astoundingly, he did not even come close to dying. His gifts had done what he had failed to do; they had protected him from both the Prophet's fury and the awful collision.

He had still hit hard enough to leave him stunned. Eyes tearing, he watched as vague visions of winged warriors continued to spread across everything. At that moment, Uldyssian wished that he had been slain. At least then he would not have had to endure the annihilation of all that he held dear.

A blinding light obscured all else. To Uldyssian's horror, Inarius, his true form once again revealed, hovered over him.

YOUR PUNISHMENT IS LONG OVERDUE, HERETIC! With a gesture, he dragged Uldyssian from the ground.

It was impossible to believe that Inarius could ignore what was happening above, but Uldyssian quickly saw that this was the truth. All that mattered in the renegade angel's eyes was retribution against Uldyssian.

It was so ludicrous that despite his pain, Uldyssian unleashed a laugh that bordered on madness. Sanctuary was about to fall, and he was the Prophet's only focus.

But then Inarius fluttered back from him, almost as if startled. Uldyssian did not understand why the angel should react so, any more than he understood the reason for him falling now that his foe's magic no longer held him aloft.

WHAT . . . ARE YOU . . . DOING? demanded Inarius. *WHAT?*

The son of Diomedes frowned, wondering with whom the winged figure spoke. Inarius appeared to be looking at the human, but Uldyssian knew that *he* was not doing a single thing to defend himself.

Or was he? Uldyssian finally noticed that a warmth was spreading through his body, a warmth that ate away at the pain and healed any and all wounds he had suffered. As it reached his head, his mind, he felt a lifting of his spirit that he had not experienced since first awakening his abilities. His confidence soared, and suddenly he had utter command of his body again. A golden glow emanated from him, a glow so brilliant that it made the fiery wings of Inarius drab and sickly by comparison.

A glow that *blinded* his adversary.

Fully in command—no, *better* in command of himself than he had ever been before, Uldyssian gazed upon

Inarius almost contemptuously. The renegade had done nothing with all the power that he had at his hand save conquer, condemn, or kill those he felt were imperfect or defiant. To him, there had been nothing worthy of life save himself.

The irony was, Inarius was far from worthy of the very humans he so despised. They had grown into something he could not comprehend, and Uldyssian represented the epitome of that.

Inarius abruptly slapped his gauntleted hands together, and a silver shard of energy sliced at the human. Uldyssian assumed that it was intended to cut him in twain. He dismissed it with a sneer, leaving the angel frozen in the air.

And while Inarius hovered there—to Uldyssian, obviously stunned by the mortal's refusal to accept his fate—the son of Diomedes stretched forth his open hand in the Prophet's direction. Yet it was not Inarius himself upon which Uldyssian focused. Instead, through eyes that saw so much more at the moment, he gazed upon the link between the angel and the Worldstone.

There was far more to the Worldstone than anyone else understood. That much was at least clear to Uldyssian. He also sensed that there were reasons he should not pursue that notion any further. What he had to do now, though, was finish what he had instinctively begun in the cavern where he had seen the great artifact.

Distance had no meaning where the Worldstone was concerned. Though it physically appeared to be hundreds of miles away, it was, in truth, *everywhere*, and so Uldyssian had no difficulty reaching out to it with his mind. He saw into its vast structure and located the anomaly he had created when standing before it with Rathma. Uldyssian had been so close to making the bloody events of the past months something that need not have occurred. Then he had been blind.

But now he saw. It was only a matter of one more alteration in the impossible, six-sided facet he had formed.

Uldyssian made that adjustment. . . .

And Inarius howled. He shimmered, and it seemed as if a part of him burned away. Physically, the angel appeared unchanged, yet as Uldyssian concentrated on him again, Inarius looked . . . much less. He was still what he was, a celestial warrior of tremendous might, but that might was nothing compared to what the Worldstone had enabled him to do.

Uldyssian had severed the renegade's link. Inarius no longer could call upon the Worldstone.

The angel continued to howl, but now that cry was tinged by rage. Inarius summoned his full power—and Uldyssian easily quashed his attempt.

He was about to do the same to the Prophet himself, but then once more, Uldyssian heard in his mind the calls of Serenthia and the others. This last confrontation between himself and Inarius had lasted but seconds as Sanctuary measured time, but even seconds were vital now.

"The fate of this world is no longer yours to dictate," he reminded the fallen angel for the last time. With that, he created a sphere much like the silver one into which Inarius had sought to cast him, then imprisoned his vanquished opponent within.

Inarius raged inside, but the sphere had been made to keep all sound locked with him. His silent tirade would have been almost humorous to watch if the son of Diomedes had not seen so many people suffer because of him.

Leaving the sphere to rest among the ruins of the Cathedral of Light, Uldyssian turned—

And a terrible jolt ran through him that sent him to his knees.

YOU WILL NOT INTERFERE WITH WHAT WILL BE, stated a voice that was very much like Inarius's yet was not.

Tyrael.

Uldyssian could not see the other angel, but he felt his power. Tyrael was naturally far stronger than Inarius. Uldyssian might have still defeated him easily, but the second angel had wisely used the Prophet's fury to hide his own efforts until it was too late for the human to notice.

Tyrael kept him down on his knees. *THE ABOMINATION THAT INARIUS CREATED SHALL BE CLEANSED FROM THE MEMORY OF THE UNIVERSE. . . . THE TAINT OF DEMON AND ANGEL TOGETHER SHALL BE RIGHTLY FORGOTTEN . . . AND JUSTICE SHALL BE SERVED. . . .*

"Who—whose justice?" Uldyssian snarled, seeking to fight both the pain and his invisible bonds.

But the angel ignored his question, instead declaring, *BEHOLD! THE PURIFICATION PROGRESSES.*

Despite himself, Uldyssian could not help but look, and he saw that it now literally rained angels. The celestial host dove in perfect order, row upon row spreading out in every direction over Sanctuary. All held ready fiery weapons— from swords to lances to scythes and more—which somehow Uldyssian understood were actually manifestations of their individual powers. With them, they prepared to sweep over the people and places and leave nothing but flame.

However, something happened next that surely Tyrael did not desire. From the ruined ground erupted huge, steaming craters. They blossomed without warning, sending the edyrem scattering. Uldyssian knew what they were, and his hopes for his home did not improve in the least, especially when the first scaled fiend leapt out to meet the angels.

The Burning Hells had come to have their say in the fate of Sanctuary.

The demons were not like the angels. They had no uniformity save their savageness. They did not come in rank upon rank but spilled out like water, quickly covering vast ground, then rising up into the sky.

Those among the host that had been heading to more distant parts of the world immediately veered around to join their brethren against the demons. They moved with a smoothness that made Uldyssian suspect they had awaited just this moment. Now, events did not focus on Sanctuary itself; instead, the end of his world and his people were becoming just part of the endless conflict between the two sides. Everyone would perish and then be forgotten as the angels and demons went on to their next conflict.

Forgotten as if they had never existed.

Achilios bent over Mendeln, fearful that his aid had come too late. Providence had taken a hand in his being here just when Uldyssian's brother and Malic had been struggling. Providence and, ironically, Inarius.

It was the angel's fault that the hunter had been nearby, for here was the area where the Prophet's sinister plants had been set to attack the unsuspecting edyrem in a first wave intended to demoralize them completely. Here Achilios had been buried all night, his face turned to the depths of the world. He had truly believed himself trapped forever, even when he had heard through the packed soil the movements of Uldyssian's followers above.

The archer had also sensed when the grass had started to attack them, and though his mouth had been full of dirt and grass, the magic inherent in him had still enabled the undead to somewhat scream his frustration—although no one above had been able to hear.

But then a miracle that Achilios felt certain could be laid at the feet of Uldyssian had happened. First, there had been an incredible heat which had coursed over him without harm but had burned to ash even the roots of the strangling blades. After that, as Achilios had battled to dig himself out, the ground itself had heaved upward as if struck by some great force.

It might have slain a living man, but what it did for the archer was finally lift him above the surface. He had ended up still buried, but cracks of light had hinted that now he was part of some mound or hill—a far more promising situation than at first.

But someone had approached, and, fearing that it might be one of the Prophet's servants, Achilios had done what he could do so well: play dead. The figure had investigated him very briefly, not even bothering to uncover more than part of his arm, and then had moved on.

Yet just when Achilios had deemed it safe to begin digging out, he had heard the struggle between the pair. The voices had helped him identify just who that pair was, and, had it been beating, his heart would have leapt. Achilios knew that Mendeln was skilled at what Rathma had taught him but also that Malic was inhumanly cunning. There had been no doubt in the hunter's mind that Uldyssian's brother would need his aid.

As it turned out, they had ended up needing each other's. Malic could not steal Achilios's dead body, it seemed, but neither could Achilios gain an upper hand against the high priest. He was grateful when Mendeln put an end to their demonic foe but anxious when the black-robed figure had collapsed afterward. Now, as he knelt over him, Achilios prayed that Mendeln had not sacrificed himself in the effort.

There was no sign of mortal injury, but Mendeln refused to stir. In fact, Achilios had to look close just to see that his friend breathed.

The ground shook, and the sounds of desperate battle came at him from every direction. Achilios wanted desperately to rush to Serenthia, but she would never have expected him to abandon Mendeln. He would have been shamed in her eyes, the final blow to his already horrific existence.

But what could he do? Searching around, Achilios spotted the ivory dagger. While the archer had shown no sign in the past, its presence disturbed him greatly. Not only was it in part responsible for him being here, but it also hinted of that place of which he was now a part—what Mendeln and Rathma called the *afterdeath*. Achilios feared that if he touched it, it would somehow cast him into a darkness that would forever cut him off from the woman he loved.

But he also felt that the blade was perhaps the only manner by which he might be able to do *something* for Uldyssian's brother.

Holding a breath he no longer had, Achilios seized the handle. He expected to feel a cold like the grave, but the weapon radiated only a comfortable coolness. Less fearful now, the blond archer brought the weapon to Mendeln and, for lack of any other notion, finally placed the dagger directly on the center of the latter's chest.

The blade flared brightly, startling Achilios so much that he stumbled back. The light spread around Mendeln . . . and in its illumination, Achilios saw *ghosts*.

These were not merely the specters of dead edyrem or servants of the Prophet, though. Their beauty, their perfection, was extraordinary. Human they looked for the most part—but human in the very same way that Rathma was.

They could only be the children of those who had founded Sanctuary . . . the first nephalem.

It was only where the light of the dagger shone that he could see them, yet there was just enough to hint that their numbers were greater yet. Achilios understood why they were present. These were those who had perished long ago fighting for the world upon which they had been born, the ones who had first sacrificed themselves for the survival of all their kind and later for the humans descended from them.

The nephalem stared down at Mendeln, and then the pale illumination drew them into the dagger.

Mendeln let out a gasp and sat up. His eyes widened, and he looked to both sides as if expecting to find something. Finally, his gaze fixed on the hunter.

"Achilios! Malic! Is he—"

"Gone to the Burning Hells . . . I hope."

The ground rocked again. Mendeln struggled to his feet, the dagger now firmly in his grip. "Uldyssian!"

Achilios nodded, although his thoughts were not entirely on Mendeln's older sibling. "Can you . . . walk?"

"I can run."

"All . . . the better." He did not wait for Mendeln, certain that the other would follow right behind him. The hunter had done his part; he had saved his friend. Now he hoped to do the same for the woman he loved, even if it only meant that they would stand together when the world ended.

The landscape was covered in gore, much of it from demons but also too much from the edyrem. Serenthia discovered that she was particularly frustrated with the angels, for they left no sign of their passing and made it look as if only their enemies perished. There should have been *some* remains to mark their dead, something to enable the edyrem to feel that they were standing well against *both* invaders, not just one.

It did not even help that the demons were far more interested in their winged foes than they were in her people, that they only attacked the edyrem because their bloodlust was so strong. She knew that the Triune had sought to make Mankind slave soldiers of the Burning Hells, and thus the bestial warriors should be doing their best to avoid the edyrem, but that simple fact was beyond most of the fiends. She and the rest would be slaughtered just for being in the way.

Of Uldyssian there was no hint. He was invisible to her gifts, and that made her worry that he was dead. Mendeln was also again among the missing, and she could not ask Rathma if he knew anything, for he was also gone. All Serenthia could keep doing was fighting, fighting until some angel or demon chopped her into tiny pieces.

The angels began to press. It was not so much that they suddenly saw the edyrem as a danger but that a fresh horde of demons had arisen behind the humans and the Heavenly Hosts intended to meet them head-on . . . after they cut through the refuse between the two sides. Serenthia dueled with a female angel wielding a mace. The angel differed little from her male counterparts, save that her general outline was more feminine and what appeared to be hair hung longer. Not certain what was real and what was illusion, Serenthia fought her just as she had all the rest and did not mourn when her lance bore through the angel's breastplate.

Fueled by her powers, the fearsome lance literally shook apart her foe. The armored female finally exploded in a flash of astounding colors and a sharp, keening noise. The angels seemed as much sound and light as substance, and it was only because—like the demons—the edyrem utilized their magic through their weapons that they had any chance against the winged furies.

The host closed, filling her view with their towering, sanctimonious forms. Serenthia found herself battling two, and although it amazed her that she briefly kept both at bay, her aching arms told her that soon she would fall.

Indeed, as she tried to deflect a sword strike, her right arm faltered. She saw the fiery blade drive toward her—

And, with a scream, Achilios dove in front of her, some massive, shimmering sword likely plucked up from a dead demon gripped in both his hands. He not only deflected the angel's attack but thrust immediately after. With the strange, high-pitched sound that ever marked their doom, the angel exploded in what to Serenthia had previously seemed a breathtaking and colorful display of energy but now just sickened her.

"Get back!" Achilios roared to her. "Get away . . . from here, Serenthia!"

But now that she suddenly had him with her again, Serenthia had no desire to depart. Instead, she stepped beside him and took on the next foe. "I won't leave you again! I won't!"

"Mendeln! Take her . . . take her . . . away!"

Daring to glance back, Serenthia saw Uldyssian's brother far from them. He was trying to join Rathma in forging some spell. From Achilios's call, the two had clearly arrived together but had become separated without the hunter realizing it.

That suited her fine. She was with the man she loved. It was the way Serenthia wanted her life to end.

Achilios was not so pleased, however. "Damn . . . it, Serenthia! You must . . . must listen . . . to me! I'm . . . begging you! Run!"

"I won't leave you!" she insisted. "I won't—"

Fending off his opponent, Achilios turned to argue with her. At the same time, another angel swooped down unnoticed.

"Nooo!" Visions of the archer dying again urging her on, Serenthia lunged forward. Her spear caught the winged warrior dead-on, the earsplitting sound of the angel's demise almost deafening her.

But in vanquishing Achilios's attacker, Serenthia paid no mind to her own safety. A female angel to her right suddenly veered toward her.

The blazing sword cut across her midsection, opening Serenthia up.

The world fell out of focus. She heard Achilios scream out her name. Serenthia wanted to tell him not to worry about her, to protect himself instead, but the words would not come.

His face appeared before hers, the only thing distinct in her murky view. Smiling, Serenthia put a hand to his cheek . . . and died.

The level of fury that had enabled Uldyssian to confront Inarius once more overtook him, yet Tyrael's spell still held. He did not understand why the angel had not simply destroyed him; what was the point of making the son of Diomedes watch his realm be ravaged?

And why had Tyrael left it to the human to bring Inarius down? It could not have been merely to humble the renegade. Uldyssian doubted that such would concern this angel. The way he had spoken of justice precluded that.

Thoughts began to swirl through Uldyssian's head, thoughts that were fueled by his raw emotions as he watched the battle commence—with the edyrem caught between.

The angels and their monstrous adversaries paid no heed to anything between them. The fiends trampled over several humans who did not move quickly enough, while the winged warriors simply cut a swath before them that not only severed heads and limbs of demons but slaughtered innocents in the process. The edyrem did their best against both sides, funneling all their power into their swords, pitchforks, and the like, and then into their opponents, but they were sorely outnumbered.

This is justice? Uldyssian strained to be free. At the very least, he knew that he should be with the others, dying with them.

A demon with three reptilian heads and thick, ursine arms ripped apart an angel who flew too near. The angel did not scatter in bloody pieces but rather exploded in a burst of light that left no trace. That explosion was accompanied by an odd, keening sound that caused shivers through Uldyssian. The demon's victory was short-lived, however, as another angel wielding a lance thrust it through the center head. The creature let out a pair of pained roars from the heads, then turned to ash.

The entire region was dotted by astounding flashes of pure magical energies as both sides utilized their powers in myriad fashions. Uldyssian expected the edyrem to perish quickly, but a strange thing happened. They did not. In fact, those who could gathered together in what was roughly the center of the struggle and did what they could to shield themselves and the rest from the cataclysm taking place.

And there were others with them, others who were not exactly edyrem but who were in some ways much, much more.

Rathma had returned . . . and not alone.

With him had come several other tall figures either handsome, beautiful, or even grotesque in nature. He recognized only one: Bul-Kathos. The giant warrior stood at the forefront of those protecting the less powerful, the earthen guardian using a huge club to batter away at a horned demon who dared cross his path. The might of the fiend was nothing compared to the Ancient. Bul-Kathos crushed in its chest with one blow, then battered the thick skull to jelly with another.

Of the rest of Rathma's counterparts, Uldyssian could make out only a sleek warrior woman who fought with more abandon than even Serenthia had ever exhibited. Her hair flying about as if alive, she met the blade of an angel with a black axe. The adversaries exchanged two blows, then the Ancient lunged and cut across the winged figure's breastplate. The armor—if it was such in truth—did nothing to slow her strike.

Like those before him, the angel vanished in a burst of fantastic light and an unsettling—and slightly different— sound.

He could not sense his friends or his brother, and that added to Uldyssian's fears. His body trembled with pent-up emotions and energies.

ACCEPT WHAT MUST BE, Tyrael told him, the angel not sounding sanctimonious like Inarius but rather simply stating a fact. *IT IS INEVITABLE. SURRENDER TO IT. . . .*

But his words had the opposite effect on the son of Diomedes. It was almost as if his captor *needed* to persuade him to surrender.

Uldyssian considered the ways of the Prophet and his constant twisting of facts or his choice evasion of facts. The truth was not entirely the truth where these beings were concerned. They were, in their own way, as manipulative as any demon.

And that, in the end, was the last factor. Uldyssian wondered just how much control Tyrael had over his captivity and how much of it was the human's doubts.

Suddenly, all Uldyssian desired was to be free.

His body shimmered. Out of the corner of his eye, he saw Tyrael react—but, unlike Inarius, all this angel did was step back and watch. The winged being cocked his head and seemed ready to speak, although as he had no mouth, that might have simply been the human's imagination.

Then Tyrael no longer mattered. Uldyssian demanded that the angel's spell be no more . . . and it vanished. He stood straight, somehow feeling as if he now loomed above Tyrael.

He expected the angel to attack, but Tyrael only stood there watching, almost as if expecting the human's startling escape.

Feeling the winged warrior of no concern to him anymore, Uldyssian turned upon the savage scene and was revolted beyond all possible belief. He saw the dead piling up in great numbers and the futility of the angels' and demons' eternal struggle. He saw that his world would become merely one more battle among thousands, its reason forgotten almost as soon as it ended. No one would mourn Sanctuary. No one . . .

Uldyssian could not let it end thus. He could not. With every fiber of his being, the son of Diomedes took into himself all the deaths that had happened thus far because of the endless conflict—including all those his crusade had caused—and let them override any hesitation that might make him hold back.

Raising his fists toward the winged host and the fiendish horde, watching as his people continued to be massacred, Uldyssian ul-Diomed quietly spoke.

"Stop it."

And everyone . . . everything . . . froze.

†WEN†Y-†WO

There was not a sound, not even the slightest hint of wind. Uldyssian could not even hear his own breathing, nor did he care about that fact. He only knew that he had stopped the bloodshed. He had stopped the devastation.

But that was just the beginning. Angels hung as still as death in the sky. Demons hovered in mid-leap. The edyrem stood steadfast.

Nothing moved . . . save him, naturally.

His head pounded with the knowledge that he had the power to do what even the Burning Hells or the High Heavens could not. He was more than merely Sanctuary's savior; he was the *god* that Inarius had believed himself.

Uldyssian eyed the combatants. Raising his hands again, this time with the palms open, he willed the angels and demons to be pushed back.

They were, but the effort took more than he expected. Stubborn and certain that the power was within him, Uldyssian fought to gain what he desired. The ground trembled, and even the sky shook as if it were about to crack in two, but the angels and demons were at last separated from his edyrem.

"No more," he thundered to the still figures. "No more."

Uldyssian glanced at the demons. He made a slicing motion with his hand and sent the hordes tumbling back. Demons ten times his height bounced helplessly along the ruined land, bounced until they and all their brethren reached the portals through which they had come.

The son of Diomedes willed them back through those

portals, forcing them to return to the Burning Hells. The demons had no choice. Although released from the spell that had frozen them, they now scrambled uselessly for some handhold. Within seconds, the only signs of the horde's presence were the tattered bits of the slaughtered.

And then Uldyssian turned his attention to the angels. However, as he did, he thought he felt a faint voice call out to him from beyond. There was no creature, though, to whom he cared to listen. This was his domain; the interests of any other were nothing to him.

So far from where he stood, the Heavenly Host appeared like nothing more than gnats. Uldyssian could scarcely believe that he had ever been frightened of them. He inhaled, then blew the winged warriors back through the rip in the sky. A childlike glee filled the onetime farmer as he watched the pristine battle lines jumble together and the angels pass through the tear in tangled heaps.

Uldyssian.

There came the voice again, and this time he recognized it. The dragon, Trag'Oul. Yet, although the being was no enemy of his, the son of Diomedes saw no reason to acknowledge the creature's call. Trag'Oul had failed to protect Sanctuary; he had no more say than anyone else about what Uldyssian would do with his world.

The ground shook once more. Annoyed, Uldyssian demanded that it stop. It did . . . and then shook anew.

He threw his power into insisting that the tremor cease. This time, all was as it should be.

At that point, Uldyssian turned to face the two remaining angels, but Tyrael was gone. Only Inarius remained.

Ignoring the other angel's abrupt departure, Uldyssian confronted the trapped Prophet. "Your kind called us abominations," the human said. "What do you say now?"

Inarius, though, remained silent—and that left the son of Diomedes more unsettled. Although the renegade angel wore his true form and thus had no discernible expression, at that moment, Uldyssian could have sworn that Inarius was quietly *laughing* at the mortal.

The certainty of this drove Uldyssian to greater fury. The sphere crackled, blue lightning striking inside. Clearly in agony, Inarius fell to his knees . . . but the sense that he laughed continued.

Uldyssian would have punished him again for his impudence, but a new and more powerful tremor rattled the land for as far as he could sense, reaching even to distant Kehjan and far beyond. He glanced at Inarius but could detect no manner by which the Prophet could have caused it.

Deciding that origin did not matter, Uldyssian focused his power on the new quake and willed it to be gone.

Instead, though, it more than doubled in strength. As that happened, the sky turned a dark crimson, the constantly shifting clouds looking like stirred blood.

He glanced back at Inarius. "What've you done? Tell me!"

The angel finally spoke. *I HAVE DONE NOTHING.*

A huge fissure opened up just to the south. It ran a ragged but steady course toward the capital. Another ripped open to Uldyssian's right.

A third erupted near the edyrem.

Reacting instinctively, Uldyssian used his gifts to force the last fissure to seal. The effort nearly caused him to pass out, and worse, while he sought to recover, the tremor turned more and more violent. He could feel his followers' growing fear, and although he tried to quiet the land around them, it instead began heaving up and down and ripping apart.

Pulse pounding, Uldyssian threw his will into bringing order, but the opposite again happened. The ground beneath began to collapse. He leapt aside just in time.

As the son of Diomedes watched, what was left of the Cathedral of Light vanished into the depths. Inarius's sphere was swallowed along with it, the captive angel passively staring at Uldyssian as he dropped into the carnage.

Uldyssian stood stunned, unsure of what to do anymore. Sanctuary was coming apart around him—and there was nothing he could do about it. He could not understand *why*, either. With his astounding power, he had routed both the High Heavens and the Burning Hells so easily, yet now some dread force was doing what he had feared would come of their struggle. If not Inarius, though, what was the cause? There was no great magical force that Uldyssian could sense that was capable of all this new calamity.

Battling his own rising fear at the same time as he did the swelling cataclysm, Uldyssian cast a sweeping spell over *all* that existed on Sanctuary. He would have order. He would have the world restored.

Instead, he watched in horror as the grasslands to the south rose high. A shifting mound formed, swelled into a huge, earthen bubble, and then exploded with volcanic fury. In the sky above, the clouds began to spin in an ever-tightening maelstrom that set into motion the first hints of what looked to be a colossal whirlwind. Bolts of blue lightning darted down over the city and the jungle.

And only then did Uldyssian understand that *he* was the reason for all this. Not Inarius. Not the hosts of the High Heavens or the bestial horde of the Burning Hells.

He, Uldyssian ul-Diomed, was responsible for Sanctuary's imminent annihilation.

It was so clear to him now. Uldyssian could feel his heart pounding, his blood racing. It was as if he were two men in one. There was that part of him that still tried to think coherently, that tried to find focus and solutions.

But there was the more primal Uldyssian, the one who had watched loved ones slaughtered and entire lands razed. The one who had been seduced by a demoness, then stripped of his trust in everything because of her. The one who had watched betrayal after betrayal take place when all he had ever wanted was peace for all.

How often in the recent past had he lashed out unthinkingly? How often had his *power*, not Uldyssian himself, controlled events? Driven by his basest emotions, it had finally grown beyond his conscious control. It now lashed out at Sanctuary, at the world that would not become as he so badly wanted it. It was an unthinking, unfocused eruption of magic, and as such, it could only cause more chaos, more destruction.

And each time he had sought to create order, he had also unwittingly fed into that part of him that was fear, anxiety, anger . . . every dark emotion. He had been fighting himself—and losing more and more with each attempt.

Uldyssian stood there, unable to react. He wanted to save the world, but already his attempt to do so had unleashed such forces throughout it that he feared to try once more would finally destroy it utterly. Yet if the son of Diomedes did nothing, the same tragic results would take place, regardless.

He felt the edyrem awaiting their terrible end. Kehjan, too, radiated a terrible hopelessness as the city at last took notice of the disaster swiftly approaching it. Uldyssian felt the terror of the jungle dwellers, of the Ascenians, as his own kind were called, and of people in lands far, far away. He sensed both men and beasts preparing for what they were certain was their doom.

If only I'd known sooner! he desperately thought. *If only I'd listened to Mendeln and others, I could have fought it down, buried it deep inside! But now—*

Uldyssian hesitated. Eyes wide, he considered one wild thought. This was *his* power that wrought such devastation. His power. Perhaps there was a way that he *could* control it. He would . . .

Spurred by the imminency of the situation, Uldyssian tried to draw back into him what he had unleashed. Yet he quickly discovered that once loose, those forces had amplified a thousandfold and more. They were as much a part of the natural forces of Sanctuary now as they were *his*. Even if he drew into himself all that he had sent forth, that would no longer be sufficient to save anything.

But Uldyssian could not turn back. There existed nothing for him but reversing what he had caused. He would take in whatever he had to. He had no choice. He would.

There had been a point when the son of Diomedes had wondered if, ultimately, there was no end to the potential of his edyrem gifts. Now he prayed that, if there was an end, it would be just enough to accomplish this epic feat.

Bracing himself and taking a deep breath, Uldyssian began willing the wild forces to return.

He cried out as the first wave coursed into him, for it burned hotter than fire. Yet Uldyssian imagined his brother, imagined Serenthia and Achilios and all those who had faithfully followed him. With their faces in his head, he demanded that his will be done. Nothing else mattered, either consciously or subconsciously.

His body already blazed a brilliant gold and grew yet more blinding as Uldyssian absorbed into himself all that fueled Sanctuary's end. The area surrounding him radiated powerful amounts of magical energy, all of it heading toward the human. Caught up in the flow of such staggering forces, huge rocks, fragments of wood, and much, much more spun in the air surrounding him.

Uldyssian paid them no mind. Nothing existed for him but to complete what he had started. He saw only the continual rush of magic into not only his body but his very soul. Each moment, the former farmer was certain that he could take no more, and yet he continued to stand, suffering a thousand punishments a thousand times over, each worse than any ever inflicted on a single being.

Faintly, he heard voices, but certain that they were the screams of the dying, Uldyssian fought to ignore them. He could not be distracted. Everything he had needed to be concentrated purely on fulfilling his last hope.

It kept coming. Uldyssian screamed but still managed to hold on. He prayed that when at last he finally faltered, at least he would have somehow saved a few people.

It continued to flow into him like a raging river of molten

earth. He went down to his knees but still held on. Yet the flow was also relentless. It kept coming and coming and coming . . .

Then—

It ceased.

Certain that something had gone awry, Uldyssian continued to try to draw more into him, but nothing else came.

He all but sobbed at this miracle—not for himself, though, but because it meant hope for the others. However, it was far from over. Uldyssian felt everything he had taken in straining to be rereleased. It was all he could do to keep it trapped, and how long that would last, the son of Diomedes could not say.

There came a point of clarity then, an acknowledgment of what it would take to end the threat. Uldyssian found that he had no difficulty with what had to be, for it was not just the only choice but the right choice.

He stood. Shining brighter than the sun and looking far more than human, the son of Diomedes gazed around at all that was his world. Uldyssian admired the rivers, forests, mountains, and seas. He surveyed the many peoples of Sanctuary and marveled at the diversity. More astonishing, like him, they all had the same potential, the same possible greatness.

But the trouble, in Uldyssian's case, in the case of all his followers, was that it had come too soon. Humanity—and he, in particular—had been thrust too fast into their destiny. That had been Lilith's doing, the demoness too impatient to let the centuries lead men in the same direction. Uldyssian had not been given the opportunity to mature properly into his gifts.

It was too soon for a being such as Uldyssian had nearly become. Too soon . . .

You understand. . . .

Uldyssian knew who spoke. *Trag'Oul?*

I have been trying to touch your mind . . . but it has been over-whelming, the dragon admitted. The celestial sounded weak but pleased. *I knew you would succeed.*

No . . . not until it—I—no longer threaten Sanctuary!

He sensed the dragon's concurrence. *I can show you where it can be unleashed, but it is you who must pay.*

I don't care! Show me!

Trag'Oul did, and Uldyssian gazed in wonder at what the creature revealed. *Then . . . that . . .*

Yes was all Trag'Oul needed to reply.

Uldyssian smiled, his concerns all fading away. He raised his hands to the sky. *Is that all I have to do? Just will it to happen?*

The choice is yours. It always has been.

Uldyssian felt the dragon recede. He was no longer needed for what the human had to do.

The son of Diomedes used his powers to gaze one last time at those dearest to him—Mendeln, Achilios, and Serenthia. There were two things that he had to do before he continued. With what he could safely command, Uldyssian set about making things right for his brother and friends.

That finished, Uldyssian looked up, but he stared not at the sky. Instead, he gazed far beyond, to that place and time the dragon had revealed to him.

Within, the fury that he kept imprisoned struggled to be free.

It was time. Uldyssian smiled once more—and began to send it forth. The light that erupted shone across the grasslands, across the jungles, across all of Sanctuary. Yet it did not harm, but rather soothed. It touched all living things and made certain they were healed of whatever ill the coming of the edyrem and the near destruction of the world might have caused them.

Uldyssian then drew it together again and let it pour out into the beyond, where it spilled in all directions. He felt the pressure building up again—this time for the final moment—and readied himself and his world for it.

And when it came, it did so with an explosion of pure energy that ever so briefly shook Sanctuary to its foundations. Uldyssian roared, not because of pain but rather the sheer ecstasy of his transformation. He was no longer a mere human but something of which even the angels and demons could not conceive. He *was* Sanctuary for one moment, and all that surrounded it. His presence dwarfed that of Trag'Oul . . . of any being near. His consciousness spread out above his treasured world, where he looked at it one last time.

Then, finishing what had to be done, what he desired to be done, Uldyssian ul-Diomed let himself scatter throughout *all*, his passing from the mortal plane marked for those below by a fiery yet arresting flash of light that did not frighten but rather gladdened.

And forever, whether any knew it or not, would change the world of Sanctuary.

Mendeln was the first to realize that something was amiss. In fact, it was so obvious to him that he was surprised people were not screaming.

The grasslands had been completely restored. Brown and green blades waved gently in a slight breeze. Mendeln cautiously surveyed the area with his dagger and found no malice in the plants.

But he did find something else, the reason for the edyrem's quiet. They were all as still as statues.

No, not all of them. There were two figures moving toward him, two welcome—and startling—figures.

Achilios and Serenthia—and both looking very much among the living.

They stared at him with equal wonder, clearly as mystified not only about what had happened to their surroundings but also themselves. Mendeln was certain of the cause of the latter, at least.

"Uldyssian," he told them, his voice shaking. "Uldyssian did it."

"But how can that be possible?" the archer asked, unable to cease smiling. He was the Achilios they had all known so well, even the torn gap in his throat gone. "How?"

"That is a question that even they are debating heavily," answered the voice of Rathma.

They turned to find the Ancient looking more haggard, more his centuries-old age. His hair had gray in it, and lines coursed his once-youthful visage. In contrast to the trio, Rathma did not look at all cheerful.

And when they followed his outthrust finger, they saw why.

Five there were of the towering, winged figures, five who radiated such might as to make the host that had flown down into Sanctuary look like children.

"The Angiris Council," Inarius's son breathed. "They can be no other. My father spoke of them. The Council has come to our world."

Mendeln shivered at such a sight. "But why?"

The Ancient glared at the newcomers. "As we are the only ones unfrozen, it behooves us to find out."

He led them toward the angels, who stood in a half-circle. As the four approached, Mendeln began to hear—and feel—their voices.

And even more astounding, the landscape abruptly shifted. It became a grand chamber of gleaming crystal and diamond carved with a perfection that no human artisan could reproduce. Gigantic statues of other winged champions loomed over the interior. The floor was composed of the most intricate of marble mosaics, with patterns that made no sense to Mendeln but were utterly beautiful and very difficult from which to tear his eyes.

But no less beautiful—and terrifying—were the five themselves.

THERE IS NO NEED FOR THIS DEBATE TO CONTINUE. . . . OR TO HAVE EVEN BEGUN, declared a majestic angel with robes of royal red and a shining breastplate upon which the image of an upturned sword blazed. *THE PATH IS OBVIOUS. . . . WHAT HAS BEEN WROUGHT BY THE TRAITOR MUST BE UNDONE! LET THE HOST FINISH WHAT IT BEGAN, EVEN IF WE MUST CUT*

THROUGH A HUNDRED RANKS OF DEMONS TO ACCOMPLISH IT!

SHOULD WE NOT DEAL WITH THE RENEGADE FIRST, IMPERIUS? asked one whose robes were a softer blue and who seemed, as angels appeared, a female. *AND LEAVE THIS MATTER FOR ITS OWN TIME?*

THE MATTERS ARE ONE AND THE SAME, the first retorted. One gloved hand thrust to the area between them, and suddenly Inarius—shackled by black streaks of energy—knelt in the midst of the Angiris Council. *FROM HIS CRIMES WAS THIS ABOMINATION CALLED SANCTUARY CREATED! JUDGE ONE, AND YOU RIGHTLY JUDGE BOTH, AURIEL!*

The female angel refused this argument. She was the most animated of the five, turning her head to each of the other four as she spoke. *YOU HAVE ALL SEEN MORE THAN ENOUGH EVIDENCE THAT THESE CHILDREN OF THAT ORIGINAL CRIME ARE NOT THEIR PARENTS . . . AND NOT THE ABOMINATIONS THAT WE FIRST BELIEVED THEM.*

"Where are we?" Serenthia suddenly whispered.

Rathma signaled her to be silent but then quietly replied, "We are both in the grasslands where we stood and in what, from the stories I know, must be the central meeting chamber of the Council in the legendary Silver City itself! The Council is judging our world, and I fear the verdict may yet go against us."

Mendeln was shocked. "After all that Uldyssian did, the outcome is still in doubt?" Before he realized just what he was doing, he marched among the angels. "What right have you? What audacity! We are not vermin to be slaughtered!"

Imperius gazed down at him. *AND YOU ARE NOT ANGELS, WITH THE RIGHT TO STAND BEFORE THE COUNCIL.*

Mendeln was thrust back by an unseen force. He might have crashed into the others, but Auriel glanced at him, and he settled softly to the ground.

AND IS SUCH ARROGANCE NOW VIRTUE? she asked of her counterpart. *THESE ARE HERE AT MY BEHEST AND BECAUSE THEY HAVE EARNED, THANKS TO THEIR COMPANION, THE RIGHT TO LISTEN TO WHAT-EVER THE FATE OF THEIR HOME.*

Imperius did not reply, but if he had had a face, Mendeln felt certain that it would have glowered.

Rathma next stepped to the forefront. "You must give humanity a chance. They are capable of many wondrous things, if you will but let them survive! They have the possibility of truly becoming an integral part of the Balance—"

I SAY IT IS TIME TO VOTE, Imperius rumbled, utterly ignoring him.

LET IT BE SO, interjected a gray-clad angel who seemed neither male nor female in aspect. *LET THIS BE DONE.*

IT IS SECONDED! the first angel boomed triumphantly. *WE BEGIN, THEN! I SAY THAT THE RENEGADE MUST BE FOREVER IMPRISONED AND HIS NEST OF DEMON-SPAWN ERADICATED!* Imperius stretched out a fist and turned it downward.

Mendeln started to speak again, then saw the futility of it. The angels would pay no mind.

Auriel was quick to react to Imperius's vote. She turned her fist upward, then added, *LET THEIR POTENTIAL BE DEVELOPED . . . FOR IN THEM I THINK THERE IS A CHANCE THAT WE MAY SEE THE END OF OUR STRUG-GLE AT LAST!* The female angel looked to a fourth member of their council, a very gaunt figure whose robes were black and whose breastplate was likewise colored. *WHAT SAY YOU, MALTHAEL? WILL YOU STAND WITH ME ON THIS?*

A visible shiver ran through not only Mendeln but also the rest when the angel Malthael spoke. His voice brought nightmares of death to Mendeln—a permanent, empty death.

WHATEVER THE CHOICE, IN THE END IT DOES NOT MATTER FOR ME. . . . I ABSTAIN.

Auriel leaned back in clear disappointment. Imperius, on the other hand, appeared satisfied. It was he who spoke to the next, the gray-clad one who had previously spoken. *ITHERAEL, WHAT VERDICT DO YOU GIVE?*

There was a pause, as if the fourth angel considered hard this question. *THEY ARE THE GET OF ANGELS AND DEMONS, WITH THE TAINT AND PROMISE INHERENT. . . . LEFT TO GROW, THEY MIGHT BECOME MORE MONSTROUS THAN ANYTHING RISING FROM THE BURNING HELLS.*

AND SO THEY MUST BE DESTROYED! Imperius insisted.

Itherael raised a finger. *BUT THEY ALSO HAVE THE GREATEST POTENTIAL TO SERVE THE LIGHT . . . A POTENTIAL THAT COULD SURPASS OUR OWN ROLES . . . AND SO I VOTE THAT THEY BE GIVEN THEIR CHANCE.*

Mendeln's hopes rose. The angels were at a stalemate. Even if Tyrael—certainly no friend of the humans—did as was likely and voted against them, it would end up a tie. Sanctuary would survive.

The four angels looked at the last. Tyrael had been staring at Inarius's bound form as if in constant thought.

WELL, OLD FRIEND? asked Imperius. *HOW WILL YOU CHOOSE, YOU WHO HAVE SEEN THEM AT THEIR MOST FOUL? WILL YOU VOTE WITH ME AND PUT AN END TO THIS MOST HEINOUS OF SPAWNING GROUNDS?*

"What does he mean by that?" Uldyssian's brother blurted. "The vote would be tied!"

Rathma wore a sorrowful expression. "An equal vote, it seems, means no decision in our favor and, thus, no reason to let us live."

Mendeln could not stand for it. Once more, he dared step forward. "How can you so casually condemn us? You claim to be servants of the Light, yet you callously execute what you deem not worthy! My brother could have destroyed you all, but he did not. All he wanted to do was save his home and his people, even though it cost him his life."

Imperius looked prepared again to remove what he obviously considered an annoyance from his sight, but Tyrael spoke, his tone demanding the attention of all.

THIS WAR HAS GONE ON SINCE TIME IMMEMORIAL, AND THERE IS NOT ONE OF US WHO HAS NOT GROWN WEARY . . . YET EVER DO WE ANSWER THE CALL TO BATTLE.

The other winged guardians nodded.

Pointing at Inarius, Tyrael continued, *THIS RENEGADE DID LEAD OTHERS INTO THE CREATION OF WHAT SHOULD NOT HAVE BEEN, WHAT NEVER SHOULD HAVE BEEN! HE CAUSED THE UNTHINKABLE, AND IF I HAD BEEN THERE, I WOULD HAVE FOUGHT ALL TO PREVENT IT . . .*

They were doomed. Mendeln saw that. His only hope now was Trag'Oul. Surely the dragon could do something. Mendeln tried to reach out to the creature but could find no trace.

BUT I WAS NOT THERE . . . AS WERE NONE OF YOU, Tyrael reminded his counterparts. *AND SO THIS THING GREW . . . AND GREW . . . UNTIL IT BECAME WHAT NONE COULD FATHOM, WHAT NONE COULD HAVE EXPECTED! THIS PLACE CALLED SANCTUARY HAS BROUGHT FORTH SUCH AS WE HAVE NEVER WITNESSED, THINGS I MYSELF CALLED ABOMINATIONS!* Before Imperius could interrupt, Tyrael pressed, *BUT ABOMINATIONS DO NOT FEEL SUFFERING, THEY DO NOT STRUGGLE FOR ONE ANOTHER AGAINST GREAT ODDS AND THEY DO NOT . . . THEY DO NOT . . . OF THEIR OWN FREE WILL . . . CHOOSE . . . YES . . . CHOOSE TO COMMIT SUCH GREAT SACRIFICE FOR THE SAKE OF OTHERS.*

Mendeln felt the hope rising among his companions, even the generally dour Rathma. Was it possible of *Tyrael,* of all the angels?

WE SACRIFICE, responded Imperius. *OF WHAT DIF-FERENCE WAS HIS?*

WE SACRIFICE BECAUSE WE MUST ... BECAUSE IT IS PART OF OUR CALLING! WE DO IT BECAUSE IT IS OUR DUTY AND NO MORE! THE MORTAL, ULDYSSIAN UL-DIOMED ... HE CHOSE TO SELFLESSLY GIVE HIMSELF BECAUSE HE CARED FOR HIS COMPANIONS! IT WAS NOT HIS DUTY ... BUT HIS DESIRE. Tyrael looked at each of the other judges, ending with Imperius. *I DID CALL THEM ABOMINATIONS ... AND I WAS WRONG! MY VOTE IS FOR THEM ... FOR I WOULD SEE WHAT THEY MIGHT BECOME ... AND MARVEL IN IT.*

It was only by the strongest of efforts that the humans held their relief inside. Mendeln's cheer was tempered by the fact that the five still acted as if the matter was not at an end.

SO IT IS DECIDED, Imperius declared with a slight hint of bitterness unbecoming an angel. *BUT WHAT DO ANY OF YOU NOW SUGGEST BE DONE TO PREVENT THE BURNING HELLS FROM SPREADING THEIR TAINT ACROSS THIS WORLD YOU HAVE SAVED? ARE WE TO HAVE A HOST STAND GUARD OVER THIS ... THIS SANCTUARY?*

He no sooner asked this than a deep, bloodcurdling chuckle caused all to look around. Imperius summoned a sword of fire.

"This is a *peaceful* visit, oh, councilors," rasped a voice like a nest of angry vipers. "Peaceful—if you would have it so."

A shadow crossed them then, a shadow of such darkness as Mendeln had never witnessed. With it came a sense of evil that reminded Uldyssian's brother of another ... *Lilith.*

YOU OFFER PARLEY ... LORD MEPHISTO? Auriel asked the shadow. *YOU ... NOT YOUR BROTHER?*

The shadow coalesced somewhat into a tall, macabre shape that instantly brought to Mendeln's mind the monstrous morlu or, worse yet, their heinous master, Lucion, who, like Lilith, was also offspring of this sudden and dread visitor.

"My dear brother is beside himself. Therefore, I, who am also supreme, do indeed offer parley—and more! I offer . . . a truce." Although Mephisto remained mostly hidden in shadow as Uldyssian had said his brother Diablo had done, what was evident was still more than enough to set Mendeln's nerves on edge. "A pact that shall relieve the situation *this one* brought upon us."

A green, scaly hand thrust forth from the shadow to condemn Inarius. The renegade flared bright in defiance.

Imperius took over the situation from Auriel. WHAT PACT IS THIS THAT YOU PROPOSE?

A hint of great, sharp teeth momentarily flashed into sight where the demon's head should have been. "We, like you, made false assumptions about this place, false assumptions about the creatures spawned by both our kind."

A blazing red eye materialized, then winked in the direction of Auriel, who utterly ignored it.

With a chuckle, Mephisto added, "But Sanctuary is much more than we envisioned! All you said is true, and we would let it grow and see where it leads, good or ill, untouched by either side."

AND WE SHOULD TRUST THE WORD OF YOU, mocked Imperius.

"This world cost me my children, both who sought its survival. I would also have it grow for their sakes."

To Mendeln, at least, the unsettling thing about the demon lord's answer was that he *believed* Mephisto. Believed him in part, that is. Certainly, the only reason Lucion and Lilith had tried to preserve Sanctuary and humanity was so that it could serve the Burning Hells.

But even believing the demon a little was unnerving. It showed the subtle influence of Mephisto's tremendous power.

The angels were clearly not very trusting of the intruder, but Tyrael suddenly stepped beside Imperius.

IF YOU WOULD WISH A TRUCE, LORD DEMON . . .

WOULD YOU CAST YOUR MARK ON A PLACE CHOSEN BY ME?

Mephisto seemed to hesitate. "Show me, and it shall be done—but only if something is in turn given to me by right of the aspect of justice you champion."

The angels glanced at one another. Imperius nodded to Tyrael.

SPEAK WHAT IT IS, the latter said to the shadowed form.

Again, the taloned hand thrust forth—at the prisoner. "Him . . . let he whose crimes are already legion among you now be cast to me to pay for my loss—and the sealing of the truce, as it happens."

Inarius did an odd thing upon hearing this. He laughed. He laughed loudly until Imperius, with a contemptuous wave of his hand, caused all sound from the captive to cease.

IF IT IS AGREED, YOU WILL CAST YOUR MARK? asked the haughty angel.

"Before the eyes of all—and even these," Lord Mephisto concluded, his red orb shifting around to survey Mendeln's group.

Even as the demon proclaimed this, the chamber faded, and once more they stood on Sanctuary, but in a slightly different location. The rubble of the Cathedral of Light surrounded them.

"The humor of angels," Mephisto mocked.

Imperius pointed at the center of what Mendeln realized was the great chamber where the Prophet had likely preached to the masses. *THERE RESTS A POINT OF FLUX! A POINT WHERE THIS WORLD WAS SEALED TOGETHER . . . YOUR MARK.*

Uldyssian's brother expected to watch the demon lord draw some symbol in fire, but instead, Mephisto raised his hand to where the teeth glinted, then bit deep into his own limb.

A black substance oozed from the bite, and this the demon let drip onto the spot the angels had chosen. As it touched, there was a searing sound, and several red runes suddenly materialized above the stain. They turned twice in a circle, then sank into what passed for Mephisto's blood. The black substance melted into the floor, vanishing.

Of the wound, there was also no more trace. Mephisto withdrew the hand into the shadow. "And now . . . him, yes?"

The Angiris Council looked down as one at Inarius, who refused to cease laughing madly.

YOU HAVE BROUGHT THIS UPON YOURSELF, BROTHER . . . declared Tyrael.

From out of the shadow burst a score of inky tendrils. They wrapped eagerly around the renegade angel. Without effort, they dragged him back into the darkness with them.

His voice seeping with satisfaction, Mephisto murmured, "And the cavern and the find within?"

Imperius shifted as if angry. Tyrael replied, *FOR WHAT SHALL BE NEEDED TO BE DONE THERE, ANOTHER PACT MUST BE MADE.*

"Agreed." The orb shifted yet again to the humans and Rathma. "And now?"

Achilios reached for his knife. Serenthia gripped her spear, and even Mendeln sought his dagger. Rathma did nothing.

It was Auriel who interjected. *FOR HIS SACRIFICE, THEY SHOULD ALL BE ALLOWED TO REMEMBER.*

THAT WILL NOT DO, Imperius declared.

"No," agreed Mephisto, who seemed to take relish in watching Imperius's reaction when the angel realized that the pair agreed with each other. "That firstborn," he added, meaning Rathma, "and his kind . . . they may remember, for they are few, and their day is already over. The rest, though . . . if they are to grow, they must begin at the beginning."

From the background, Itherael responded, *HE IS COR-RECT.*

Auriel wished to argue, but her comrades were clearly as one on this.

THEY SHALL BEGIN ANEW, agreed Tyrael.

"They plan to make us forget everything!" Serenthia gasped. "They plan to wipe our powers and Uldyssian's memory from us!"

"You can't do this!" Achilios added.

Mendeln only clutched the dagger, awaiting what he knew he and his friends could not stop. Yet in his head, he pictured his brother, all the while repeating Uldyssian's name.

BACK TO THE BEGINNING, Tyrael reiterated. *AND FROM THERE, WE SHALL LEAVE THEM TO THEIR OWN DESTINY, WHETHER GOOD OR ILL, FOR AS LONG AS THE TRUCE HOLDS.*

"For as long as it holds," Mephisto repeated.

Mendeln jerked, his desire to preserve Uldyssian's memory distracted by the demon lord. Mephisto already plotted to abuse the pact. If he did that—

Before Mendeln could react any further, Tyrael raised his palm toward the three humans.

HE WILL BE REMEMBERED, the Angel of Justice told them . . . but Mendeln in particular. *HE WILL BE REMEMBERED.*

A breathtaking white light enveloped them.

TWENTY-THREE

The plague had been a terrible one, taking as it had
Serenthia's father and several others, including missionaries from some nameless sect. Rumors brought by travelers who had passed through a larger town called Partha
indicated that the inhabitants there had been particularly
struck hard, with at least half the population dead and
burned. Other regions appeared more fortunate, and
from what the village elders gathered, the crisis appeared
to be over.

Mendeln approached the trading station just in time to
catch Achilios arriving with a batch of hares his expert
markmanship had caught for him. The hunter started to
smile, but the smile faltered when he saw both the horse his
friend rode and the packed mule behind it.

"You said you were going to do it . . . and you meant it,
evidently."

"Yes. The farm is sold, and all I have is with me."
Mendeln glanced past him to where a tall, burly young man
was being castigated by Serenthia. As capable as her brothers were, it still fell to Cyrus's daughter to keep them in line.

She turned from reprimanding her sibling and saw the
two men. As she ran toward them, the raven-haired
woman's countenance took on an expression much akin to
that on her new husband's.

"You're leaving! Oh, Mendeln, you can't!"

He steeled himself. "With Uldyssian dead from plague, I
have no more desire for the farm . . . and the memories are
too strong for me to stay anywhere in Seram."

Serenthia shed a tear but nodded. Achilios lowered his catch and put an arm around her shoulder.

"Send us word when you can," Achilios muttered, well aware that they likely would never hear from him again. The world was vast and, beyond a few days' travel, contact between Seram and the outside was nearly impossible.

"I will do my best," Mendeln responded with a nod. He did not bother dismounting, wanting to be away before his nerves broke.

Serenthia came to his side and took his hand, Achilios following her.

"May your lives be simple and happy ones," Uldyssian's brother added.

Achilios chuckled. "Here in Seram, the simple part is guaranteed!" Again he hugged his new wife. "And, in my case, so will be the happy!"

She kissed the archer lightly, then the two of them shook hands one last time with Mendeln. The son of Diomedes turned his horse toward the woods.

"Going through the old hunter's path?" asked Achilios.

"Yes . . . with Partha so terribly hit, I would prefer to stay clear no matter what they say about the plague no longer a threat."

"Wise. Fare you well, then!"

"I shall try."

The couple waved as he started off. Mendeln kept his eye on them for as long as he could . . . and when that was no more possible, he urged the horse and mule to the best pace of which they were capable.

The hunter's path was an old trail that faded to thick woods about half a mile from Seram. Achilios assumed that Mendeln would do the logical and veer south when that happened, for east and north were too complicated for his animals to navigate. However, the moment he reached the trail's end, Mendeln instead reined the horse to a halt and paused to stare at the trees ahead.

After a moment's reflection, he reached into his travel cloak and pulled out the ivory dagger.

"I am already here."

Looking over his shoulder, Uldyssian's brother found Rathma standing atop a fallen tree trunk. The cowled figure still had the graying hair and age lines earned during the battle, but his demeanor was more as Mendeln knew it.

"Thank you for leaving me my memory," he told the Ancient.

"That was beyond my ability. Trag did that."

Mendeln nodded. "He is well?"

"It still galls him that he had to shield his presence while the angels and demons discussed Sanctuary's end, but that is all. He is recovered from initially trying to steer the host away from the world, yes. He also regrets your loss but honors Uldyssian's choice . . . as do I."

Clutching the dagger tight, Mendeln muttered, "I saw it, Rathma. He let me. I saw him give all that he held and all that he was into that beyond Sanctuary! I saw that he was happy in the end, because he knew that he had become part of something—something wonderful. I'm sorry that I cannot explain better, but I understand no more of it than that!"

Rathma stepped down from the trunk. "Do not worry. I know what it is as little as you do. Trag understands far more, but apparently even I am not ready to be told. We shall both learn together, eh?"

And that you shall, came the dragon's voice. *That you shall, Mendeln ul-Diomed.*

Mendeln shook his head. "I am tired of myself. I died when the last of my family died. I died when Uldyssian did. Call me anything else, but no longer call me that."

Rathma looked perturbed. "Mendeln—"

It is his wish . . . in fact, if he so desires another name, I have one I hope is worthy of him.

Despite himself, Mendeln was intrigued. After all, the

dragon had renamed Inarius's and Lilith's son from Linarian to Rathma. "What?"

I would call you Kalan. In the tongue of that of which I am, it means teacher, for you have risen far too high to be called by me a mere student . . . and we have need of you to show others the truth of the Balance.

Mendeln did not know what to say. In many ways, he felt it a path by which to give honor to Uldyssian and also protect his world from the treachery of demons . . . and angels.

"There must be more who will fight to maintain the Balance," Rathma said to him. "The Balance is Sanctuary's best hope. When that day comes that the edyrem return, they must not fall into either camp, for then humanity will merely be an appendage of one side or another, dying for their causes and nothing else. Keep humanity balanced between the two, and it becomes the master of its own destiny."

As is the intention . . .

Both men glanced up at the sky.

"What do you mean by that, Trag?" Rathma asked, looking as confused as Mendeln.

But the dragon did not answer. At last, Rathma turned again to Uldyssian's brother. "There is a bit more to show you. The jungles of Kehjan are rich in the magical forces that will best encourage both your learning and the learning of your students. Trag will bring us there."

"And then?"

"And then I prepare you for when I am gone. The day of the nephalem is, as *they* said, long over. One by one, I and my kind will cease to be. There are fewer now than during the battle even." He waved off any question concerning the others like him. "The future is what is important. You will need to teach as many as will listen. The three among the edyrem whom you began with shall be gathered first, though they will not recall the time before. That is your burden alone."

We can speak more of this when he is settled and ready, Trag'Oul suddenly said.

Rathma grimaced slightly. "Then, if you are so impatient, eternal one, it would be best if you brought us there as soon as possible." To the son of Diomedes, the Ancient added, "What you need shall come also. The animals will be back among your friends' mounts, the change unnoticed by any."

"Just like so much."

The cowled figure grunted. "There was nothing that could be done at the time . . . but the future will be different. We shall see to that."

But the past could *not* be forgotten. Mendeln—no, *Kalan*—was determined to see to that. Already he had plans to mark down on both parchment and stone all that he could recall, if only for the sake of those who followed in his path. The world could not forget the lesson of Uldyssian and the hope that his sacrifice had gained for all.

"Let's be off," he suddenly demanded of the dragon. "The sooner I start, the better."

From Rathma, he earned a rare grin. From Trag'Oul, there was a sense of hope.

Prepare yourself, the dragon warned.

Kalan tightened his grip on the dagger more, but his mind was not on the spell with which Trag'Oul would magically cast him hundreds of miles distant. It was instead on Uldyssian.

You have given us a chance for a future, brother . . . and come the High Heavens or the Burning Hells, we shall work to make certain that we are its makers and no others.

And as he thought that, as the woods around him faded, Kalan believed he glimpsed a figure built much like a farmer but who was obviously so much more. The figure was not even there for the blink of an eye and was likely only Kalan's imagination, but even so, it raised the brother's hopes.

The edyrem would rise again—and with the sacrifice of Uldyssian to guide them, next time as their *own* masters.

About the Author

Richard A. Knaak is the *New York Times* bestselling author of some three dozen novels, including the *War of the Ancients* trilogy for *Warcraft* and the *Legend of Huma* for *Dragonlance*. No stranger to the *Diablo* world, in addition to this, the third in his *Sin War* saga, he has penned three stand-alone novels, including *Moon of the Spider*. His other works include his own *Dragonrealm* series, the *Minotaur Wars* for *Dragonlance*, the *Aquilonia* trilogy of the *Age of Conan*, and the *Sunwell Trilogy*—the first *Warcraft* manga. In addition, his novels and short stories have been published worldwide in such diverse places as China, Iceland, the Czech Republic, and Brazil.

Currently, the author is at work on several projects, including a sequel to *Day of the Dragon* for *Warcraft*, a second manga set, the *Ogre Titans* trilogy for *Dragonlance*, and more. Besides *The Veiled Prophet*, his most recent releases include background storywork for a recent game release by D3P and *The Black Talon*, first of the *Ogre Titans* novels. He looks forward to continuing to return to Sanctuary and Azeroth in future stories.

LOOK FOR THESE

BOOKS BY *NEW YORK TIMES*
BESTSELLING AUTHOR

RICHARD KNAAK!

WARCRAFT: WAR OF THE ANCIENTS TRILOGY
BOOK ONE: THE WELL OF ETERNITY
BOOK TWO: THE DEMON SOUL
BOOK THREE: THE SUNDERING

WARCRAFT: DAY OF THE DRAGON

DIABLO: LEGACY OF BLOOD

DIABLO: THE KINGDOM OF SHADOW

DIABLO: MOON OF THE SPIDER

DIABLO: THE SIN WAR TRILOGY
BOOK ONE: BIRTHRIGHT
BOOK TWO: SCALES OF THE SERPENT

**AVAILABLE WHEREVER BOOKS ARE SOLD
OR AT WWW.SIMONSAYS.COM.**

POCKET
STAR BOOKS
A Division of Simon & Schuster
A CBS COMPANY

BDRK.02

OTHER NOVELS IN THE WORLD OF

DIABLO

LEGACY OF BLOOD
BY RICHARD KNAAK

THE BLACK ROAD
BY MEL ODOM

KINGDOM OF SHADOW
BY RICHARD KNAAK

MOON OF THE SPIDER
BY RICHARD KNAAK

THE SIN WAR TRILOGY
BOOK ONE: BIRTHRIGHT
BY RICHARD KNAAK

BOOK TWO:
SCALES OF THE SERPENT
BY RICHARD KNAAK

POCKET
STAR BOOKS
A Division of Simon & Schuster
A CBS COMPANY

ODN.01